CHICAGO LIGHTNING

The Collected Nathan Heller Short Stories

CHICAGO LIGHTNING

The Collected Nathan Heller Short Stories

MAX ALLAN COLLINS

THOMAS & MERCER

Text copyright ©2011 Max Allan Collins
Printed in the United States of America

Published by Thomas & Mercer
P.O. Box 400818
Las Vegas, NV 89140

ISBN-13: 9781612180915
ISBN-10: 1612180914

For Bob Randisi—
who, in 1984,
asked me to write a
Nate Heller short story

Table of Contents

Although the historical incidents in these stories are portrayed more or less accurately (as much as the passage of time and contradictory source material will allow), fact, speculation and fiction are freely mixed here; historical personages exist side by side with composite characters and wholly fictional ones—all of whom act and speak at the author's whim.

"Chicago lightning" –

1930s Underworld slang for gunfire.

BLACKSMITH IN AN AUTOMOTIVE WORLD
AN INTRODUCTION
BY MAX ALLAN COLLINS

Back in 1981, when I began work on my first Nathan Heller novel, *True Detective*, the historical mystery was no hot trend I was latching onto. I was just looking for a way to write my favorite kind of mystery—the private eye story—in a manner that didn't seem anachronistic.

A lot of smart people—my then-agent, Knox Burger; my mentor, Donald E. Westlake—begged me to rewrite the novel in the third-person, and to make Nate Heller a cop or a reporter or anything but a private eye. That genre was dead, or at least an embarrassing niche, and I had hold of a great Chicago yarn that could be the breakthrough of my career...*if* I would just abandon my embarrassing insistence on writing it as a private eye story.

I remember Don saying, "Do you really think *anybody* wants to read a first-person private eye novel that's as long as *Moby Dick*?"

It was sobering.

I eventually broke with Burger, who was willing to "show the book around" but was painfully unenthusiastic. Once editor of the legendary Gold Medal line of paperbacks, Knox had always made for me a downbeat advocate. When my Writers Workshop instructor, Richard Yates, first approached Burger about looking at my stuff, Burger did so, only to say: "I'm afraid young Collins is a blacksmith in an automotive world." He wasn't wrong, but finally he wasn't right for me.

Don was another matter. He was a god. My first published novel, *Bait Money* (1973), was an homage to his work. Fortunately, I had also shown the book to another mentor (and god) of mine—Mickey Spillane—and Mickey had loved it.

"I think this is the best private novel I ever read!" Mickey said over the phone.

A good thing I was a tough guy writer, or my eyes might have welled up.

See, I got hooked on private eyes when I was still in grade school—a spate of P.I. series (*Peter Gunn*, *77 Sunset Strip*, *Perry Mason*, *The Thin Man*, *Mike Hammer*, etc.) made up the latest TV craze, driving the adult westerns of *Gunsmoke*, *Have Gun Will Travel* and *Maverick* if not into submission, then into second position among adolescents of all ages.

As part of the first television generation, I was always a kid who wanted to read the book a movie or TV show was based on—I was probably the only seven year-old who ever tried to read Thorne Smith's sexy ghost story, *Topper* (inspired by the ancient sitcom that was partially written by a young Stephen Sondheim!). At age eight, Tarzan movies had led me to Tarzan comics and, of course, the novels of Edgar Rice Burroughs. Sherlock Holmes flicks on TV meant I simply had to get to know Sir Arthur Conan Doyle.

So it was no surprise that during the TV private-eye craze, I immersed myself in Dashiell Hammett, Raymond Chandler, Erle Stanley Gardner and Mickey Spillane. The key figure there is probably Spillane, because the paperback racks (and used bookstores) were swimming in Mike Hammer imitations. I read every private eye paperback I could lay my hands on, and my first sex education lessons came courtesy of Richard Prather's leering Shell Scott novels.

Starting in the ninth grade, I began trying to write my own private eye novels, and while I never found a publisher for any of the half dozen or so (thank God), I learned a lot. By the time I got out of high school, I had professional skills few young writers possessed. And maybe some talent.

Along the way, however, a couple of things happened—for one, spies and their high-tech world had taken the place of private eyes in popular culture. In fact, my last high school novel was about a spy named (are you ready for this?) Erik Flayr. There's a little noted irony here—Mickey Spillane was on his famous decade-long hiatus between Hammer novels—from *Kiss Me, Deadly* in 1952 to *The Girl Hunters* in '62—and his paperback publisher, NAL, sought to fill the gap with a writer named Ian Fleming who had been branded the British Mickey Spillane. Signet even used the same cover artist.

Just when the Vietnam war becoming a major campus issue, I was entering college, and antiheroes were taking over the screens (and paperback racks). After seeing the Lee Marvin/John Boorman film *Point Blank*, I got hooked on the source material, the hard-bitten series about one-named thief Parker (Don Westlake writing as Richard Stark). Jim Thompson, Lawrence Block and Dan Marlowe were also writing "crook books," and I was already a fan of James M. Cain (*The Postman Always Rings Twice, Double Indemnity*) and W. R. Burnett (*Asphalt Jungle, High Sierra*). The notion of writing about a criminal protagonist seemed a simple step to one side from tough detectives.

Among my other enthusiasms growing up were police procedurals. The obsession of my childhood was the DICK TRACY comic strip (never dreaming I would take the strip over from Chester Gould himself one day), and I loved Jack Webb's 1950s *Dragnet* TV series as well as a paperback series commissioned to take advantage of Webb's tube success—Ed McBain's great, dialogue-driven 87th Precinct crime novels.

So in addition to training to write private eye novels, I felt ready to take on police procedurals as a form. But there was a problem. In the late '60s and early '70s, cops were guys with nightsticks clubbing my friends at Chicago's 1968 Democratic Convention.

So crook books it was.

My early career consisted of novels about a Parker-like thief known as Nolan and a Vietnam-traumatized hitman called Quarry. Yet I still dreamed of finding a meaningful way to write about private eyes—my mystery-writing amateur sleuth Mallory was essentially an unlicensed private eye, and appeared in five novels during this same period. But the traditional private eye himself seemed to have no place in contemporary pop culture. Sam Spade, Phillip Marlowe and Mike Hammer were fondly remembered, but frozen in the amber of their times.

Well, I was wrong.

Plenty of writers came along in the later '70s and beyond to find interesting ways to tell private eye stories in modern dress (eventually so would I, in the graphic-novel series *Ms. Tree*). But back around 1974, I was longing to write the pure P.I., the tough/ tender guy in the trenchcoat and fedora with a bottom-drawer bottle of wry. I didn't want to update him, nor did I wish to plop him down in contemporary times like a drunk who tumbled off a time machine.

This classic character—as devised by Hammett, refined by Chandler, and redefined by Spillane—is a prototypical American hero, a child of the Old West by way of the Great Depression and a world war (or two), whose voice is as wonderfully, distinctively American as Huckleberry Finn's. I remained enthralled by Chandler's first-person poetry, and fascinated by Spillane's war-traumatized knight in a surrealistic world.

But it was Hammett who showed the way. Back in '74, I was re-reading for the umpteenth time the greatest of all detective novels, *The Maltese Falcon*, when I noticed the copyright, which stopped me long enough to muse, "1929...year of the St. Valentine's Day massacre—Al Capone and Sam Spade were contemporaries."

In the comics business (like Spillane and Hammett, I'm a veteran of that field), a light bulb would've popped on above me: *the private eye had been around long enough to exist in an historical context!*

In other words, rather than have Phillip Marlowe meet an *Al Capone* type, Al Capone could meet a *Phillip Marlowe* type.

My first attempt at this concept was a comic strip called "Heaven and Heller" about a Chicago private eye, one Nate Heller, whose opening case had to do with Houdini's widow and a seance designed to bring back her dead husband. Drawn by the great sports cartoonist Ray Gotto ("Ozark Ike"), the strip sold to Field Syndicate (Chicago again); but before it really got into the pipeline, the editor who bought it was fired, and all his projects dropped. It was shown elsewhere but not bought—story strips were even deader than the private eye novel.

In the meantime, the film *Chinatown,* a one-season TV show called *Banyon*, and a few novels by a handful of top-notch mystery writers (Andrew Bergman, Joe Gores, Stu Kaminsky) were demonstrating that the "period" private eye story was becoming a niche within the genre. The late great Stephen Cannell created a short-lived TV series called *City of Angels*, with Wayne Rogers spot on as a Bogart-ish private eye, that convinced me I was on the right track.

But I didn't just want to do a period piece: I wanted to do an historical novel. Next to mysteries, historical fiction had been my favorite genre growing up, and in particular I adored the (now unfortunately forgotten) Samuel Shellabarger, who wrote such vividly told tales as *Captain from Castille* and *Prince of Foxes*, in which swashbuckling fictional heroes mingled with historical figures. My idea was to create a private eye who could enter history in the same fashion, and "solve" famous unsolved cases.

As a Midwesterner (and old *Untouchables* fan), I figured Chicago made the ideal setting, and—gathering a team of Windy City research experts (led by literacy advocate George Hagenauer and comics editor Mike Gold)—I prepared the first novel as if I were writing the definitive nonfiction treatment of the assassination of Mayor Anton Cermak.

Then I wrote a mystery novel instead: *True Detective* (1983) was indeed the longest first-person private eye novel ever written, if not really rivaling Melville's long *Dick*, and eventually being out-word-counted by my later *Stolen Away* (1993). Both novels won the "Shamus" Best Novel award from the Private Eye Writers of America in their respective years.

Nathan Heller was given an elaborate background—father, mother, grandparents, unusual trappings for a P.I. Like Mike Hammer, Heller is a battle-scarred veteran of World War Two; unlike Hammer, Nate takes us along with him to Guadalcanal (*The Million Dollar Wound*, 1986) to see how he got that way. He would marry, and would be a father—not typical private eye, well...fodder.

In the course of thirteen novels, Heller has solved the Lindbergh kidnapping, Huey Long's assassination, Bugsy Siegel's gangland hit, Sir Harry Oakes' locked-room murder, the Roswell incident, the Black Dahlia case, and most recently (in *Bye Bye, Baby*) the murder of Marilyn Monroe. He has played Paul Drake to Clarence Darrow's Perry Mason in *Damned in Paradise* (1996) and found Amelia Earhart in *Flying Blind* (1998). He does a lot more than just *find* Amelia, actually—let's just say Heller has a unique way of learning whether or not said client's wife is staying faithful. Unlike Chandler's Marlowe, Chicagoan Heller does not always play by the private-eye rules. In *True Detective*, I made a point of him violating every tenant of Chandler's famous "mean streets" code, including taking a bribe and despoiling a virgin.

Heller's "bad boy" qualities seem to endear him to women readers, which to his creator is very gratifying (and a relief). In the post WWII war novels, Nate is frequently as psychotic as Mike Hammer and has often served up rough justice that goes beyond just about anything I can think of in private eye fiction. I find it interesting that readers accept Heller's homicidal tendencies so casually. Sign of the times, perhaps, or maybe Nate is good enough company that we forgive him the occasional righteous slaying.

I do think that part of what separates Heller from the pack is the combination of influences. Many devotees of Hammett and Chandler dislike and/or dismiss Spillane. Heller, who has also been compared to Archie Goodwin (which I hope is apt, because Rex Stout is another favorite of mine), combines aspects of Spade, Marlowe and Hammer. I don't think many mystery writers have shaken up that particular cocktail.

It's been my hope that Nate could enjoy the conventions— even the cliches—of the classic private eye and yet be a fully dimensional character, growing and changing over the years. That the mysteries themselves are real—history mysteries— makes for challenging research, and a rewarding experience for a writer...for readers, too, I hope. The most unusual accolade Heller and I have received is the inclusion of the novels in the bibliographies of a number of non-fiction works. Not bad for a mystery writer and a fictional P.I.

Gathered in this collection is every Heller short story to date, spanning the length of Heller's career as recorded thus far. Omitted only are three short novels that will be gathered in their own collection. I have arranged the stories not in their order as written, but chronologically by the years in which they are set.

One challenge of writing Heller's memoirs is that they jump around in his life, which means I have to keep track of the arc of his characterization as well as the continuity of where he is and where he has been. And I hope you will note differences in Nate, as a man and as a detective, according to his age and the time period in which he's operating.

When I was asked by AmazonEncore to gather all of the Heller short stories into one collection, I admit to being a little surprised by how many of them there are. Initially we included the three novellas as well, but the book would have been massive, even for a Heller. We *would* have given *Moby Dick* a run for it.

While I take pride in my ability to work as a storyteller in various forms, I admit I consider myself first and foremost a novelist. My wife Barb—with whom I write the "Trash 'n' Treasures" mystery series (most recently *Antiques Knock-Off*)—considers herself primarily a short story writer, and enjoys working in miniature. She's been much lauded for that. I am instinctively a novelist, and I suppose that most of these tales play as little novels.

Even at the University of Iowa, under Dick Yates, Gina Berriault, Walter Tevis and other gifted authors, I always worked on novels, submitting to the Writers Workshop not the expected short stories, but chapters. It wasn't that I didn't like short stories, but in the late '60s and early '70s, the market for them was already shrinking. Getting a story published in *Ellery Queen Mystery Magazine* seemed like the longest of long shots. The novel field, particularly paperback originals, appeared an easier place to break in. And it was.

I believe my first short story sale was "The Strawberry Teardrop," also the first Heller short story (written after *True Detective*). I only wrote it because my writer pal Bob Randisi invited me to contribute to a Private Eye Writers of America anthology. Most of the stories here were written by invitation for various editors of anthologies.

For me, the real pleasure of writing a Heller short story is that I can get away from the signature "famous crime" approach of the novels and allow Nate to explore the dirtier, dingier, lesser known corners of Chicago crime (though we get to California, Ohio, and Florida, as well).

My chief research associate and prized collaborator on the Nathan Heller memoirs remains George Hagenauer, who literally wrote the book on true-crime pulps (*True Crime Detective Magazines*, 2008, with Dian Hanson and Eric Godtland). George and I both have poured through old magazines, newspapers, and true-crime anthologies, searching out gems of Chicago crime that might have the makings for a Heller short story. Like the novels, the stories are firmly rooted in fact. Very often Heller fills in the role a cop, insurance investigator or even private eye played in real life.

The idea of Heller was to set a private eye and his stories in the context of the era during which Hammett, Chandler and Spillane first spun their yarns. So I take great pleasure and a certain pride in turning these little-known crimes into the kind of story that might have been published in the great pulp, *Black Mask*, where Hammett and Chandler appeared, and where Mickey Spillane read the work of *his* childhood idol, Carroll John Daly, father of the fictional private eye.

And, as you might imagine, I find it gratifying that the Shamus-nominated "The Blonde Tigress" was one of the first stories purchased by *Ellery Queen Mystery Magazine* to launch their new *Black Mask* category.

My thanks to the editors of the anthologies and magazines where these stories originally ran, and to editor Alan Turkus, for having the vision to bring all of the Heller memoirs back into print.

—Max Allan Collins
February 19, 2011

KADDISH
FOR THE KID

The first operative I ever took on, in the A-1 Detective Agency, was Stanley Gross. I hadn't been in business for even a year—it was summer of '33—and was in no shape to be adding help. But the thing was—Stanley had a car.

Stanley had a '28 Ford coupe, to be exact, and a yen to be a detective. I had a paying assignment, requiring wheels, and a yen to make a living.

So it was that at three o'clock in the morning, on that un-seasonably cool summer evening, I was sitting in the front seat of Stanley's Ford, in front of Goldblatt's department store on West Chicago Avenue, sipping coffee out of a paper cup, waiting to see if anybody came along with a brick or a gun.

I'd been hired two weeks before by the manager of the down-town Goldblatt's on State, just two blocks from my office at Van Buren and Plymouth. Goldblatt's was sort of a working-class Marshall Field's, with six department stores scattered around the Chicago area in various white ethnic neighborhoods.

The stores were good-size—two floors taking up as much as half a block—and the display windows were impressive enough; but once you got inside, it was like the push carts of Maxwell Street had been emptied and organized.

I bought my socks and underwear at the downtown Goldblatt's, but that wasn't how Nathan Heller—me—got hired.

I knew Katie Mulhaney, the manager's secretary; I'd bumped into her, on one of my socks and underwear buying expeditions, and it blossomed into a friendship. A warm friendship.

Anyway, the manager—Herman Cohen—had summoned me to his office where he filled me in. His desk was cluttered, but he was neat—moon-faced, mustached, bow- (and fit-to-be-) tied.

"Maybe you've seen the stories in the papers," he said, in a machine-gun burst of words, "about this reign of terror we've been suffering."

"Sure," I said.

Goldblatt's wasn't alone; every leading department store was getting hit—stench bombs set off, acid sprayed over merchandise, bricks tossed from cars to shatter plate glass windows.

He thumbed his mustache; frowned. "Have you heard of 'Boss' Rooney? John Rooney?"

"No."

"Well, he's secretary of the Circular Distributors Union. Over the past two years, Mr. Goldblatt has provided Rooney's union with over three-thousand dollars of business—primarily to discourage trouble at our stores."

"This union—these are guys that hand out ad fliers?"

"Yes. Yes, and now Rooney has demanded that Mr. Goldblatt order three hundred of our own sales and ad people to join his union—at a rate of twenty-five cents a day."

My late father had been a diehard union guy, so I knew a little bit about this sort of thing. "Mr. Cohen, none of the unions in town collect daily dues."

"This one does. They've even been outlawed by the AFL, Mr. Heller. Mr. Goldblatt feels Rooney is nothing short of a racketeer."

"It's an extortion scam, all right. What do you want me to do?"

2

"Our own security staff is stretched to the limit. We're getting *some* support from State's Attorney Courtney and his people. But they can only do so much. So we've taken on a small army of nightwatchman, and are fleshing out the team with private detectives. Miss Mulhaney recommended you."

Katie knew a good dick when she saw one.

"Swell. When do I start?"

"Immediately. Of course, you do have a car?"

Of course, I lied and said I did. I also said I'd like to put one of my "top" operatives on the assignment with me, and that was fine with Cohen, who was in a more-the-merrier mood, where beefing up security was concerned. Stanley Gross was from Douglas Park, my old neighborhood. His parents were bakers two doors down from my father's bookstore on South Homan. Stanley was a good eight years younger than me, so I remembered him mostly as a pestering kid.

But he'd grown into a tall, good-looking young man—a brown-haired, brown-eyed six-footer who'd been a star football and basketball player in high school. Like me, he went to Crane Junior College; unlike me, he finished.

I guess I'd always been sort of a hero to him. About six months before, he'd started dropping by my office to chew the fat. Business was so lousy, a little company—even from a fresh-faced college boy—was welcome.

We'd sit in the deli restaurant below my office and sip coffee and gnaw on bagels and he'd tell me this embarrassing shit about my being somebody he'd always looked up to.

"Gosh, Nate, when you made the police force, I thought that was just about the keenest thing."

He really did talk that way—gosh, keen. I told you I was desperate for company.

3

He brushed a thick comma of brown hair away and grinned in a goofy boyish way; it was endearing, and nauseating. "When I was a kid, coming into your pop's bookstore, you pointed me toward those Nick Carters, and Sherlock Holmes books. Gave me the bug. I *had* to be a detective!"

But the kid was too young to get on the force, and his family didn't have the kind of money or connections it took to get a slot on the PD.

"When you quit," he said, "I admired you so. Standing up to corruption—and in *this* town! Imagine."

Imagine. My leaving the force had little to do with my "standing up to corruption"—after all, graft was high on my list of reasons for joining in the first place—but I said nothing, not wanting to shatter the child's dreams.

"If you ever need an op, I'm your man!"

He said this thousands of times in those six months or so. And he actually did get some security work, through a couple of other, larger agencies. But his dream was to be my partner.

Owning that Ford made his dream come temporarily true.

For two weeks, we'd been living the exciting life of the private eye: sitting in the coupe in front of the Goldblatt's store at Ashland and Chicago, waiting for window smashers to show. Or not.

The massive graystone department store was like the courthouse of commerce on this endless street of storefronts; the other businesses were smaller—re-sale shops, hardware stores, pawn shops, your occasional Polish deli. During the day things were popping here. Now, there was just us—me draped across the front seat, Stanley draped across the back—and the glow of neons and a few pools of light on the sidewalks from streetlamps. "You know," Stanley said, "this isn't as exciting as I pictured."

"Just a week ago you were all excited about 'packing a rod.'"

"You're making fun of me."

"That's right." I finished my coffee, crumpled the cup, tossed it on the floor.

"I guess a gun is nothing to feel good about."

"Right again."

I was stretched out with my shoulders against the rider's door; in back, he was stretched out just the opposite. This enabled us to maintain eye contact. Not that I wanted to, particularly.

"Nate...if you hear me snoring, wake me up."

"You tired, kid?"

"Yeah. Ate too much. Today...well, today was my birthday."

"No kidding! Well, happy birthday, kid."

"My pa made the keenest cake. Say, I...I'm sorry I didn't you invite you or anything."

"That's okay."

"It was a surprise party. Just my family—a few friends I went to high school and college with."

"It's okay."

"But there's cake left. You want to stop by pa's store tomorrow and have a slice with me?"

"We'll see, kid."

"You remember my pa's pastries. Can't beat 'em."

I grinned. "Best on the West Side. You talked me into it. Go ahead and catch a few winks. Nothing's happening."

And nothing was. The street was an empty ribbon of concrete. But about five minutes later, a car came barreling down that concrete ribbon, right down the middle; I sat up.

"What is it, Nate?"

"A drunk, I think. He's weaving a little...."

It was a maroon Plymouth coupe; and it was headed right our way.

"Christ!" I said, and dug under my arm for the nine millimeter.

The driver was leaning out the window of the coupe, but whether man or woman I couldn't tell—the headlights of the car, still a good thirty feet away, were blinding.

The night exploded and so did our windshield.

Glass rained on me, as I hit the floor; I could hear the roar of the Plymouth's engine, and came back up, gun in hand, saw the maroon coupe bearing down on us, saw a silver swan on the radiator cap, and cream colored wheels, but people in the car going by were a blur, and as I tried to get a better look, orange fire burst from a gun and I ducked down, hitting the glass-littered floor, and another four shots riddled the car and the night, the side windows cracking, and behind us the plate glass of display windows was fragmenting, falling to the pavement like sheets of ice.

Then the Plymouth was gone.

So was Stanley.

The first bullet must have got him. He must have sat up to get a look at the oncoming car and took the slug head on; it threw him back, and now he still seemed to be lounging there, against the now-spiderwebbed window, precious "rod" tucked under his arm; his brown eyes were open, his mouth too, and his expression was almost—not quite—surprised.

I don't think he had time to be truly surprised, before he died.

There'd been only time enough for him to take the bullet in the head, the dime-size entry wound parting the comma of brown hair, streaking the birthday boy's boyish face with blood.

Within an hour I was being questioned by Sgt. Charles Pribyl, who was attached to the State's Attorney's office. Pribyl was a decent enough guy, even if he did work under Captain Daniel "Tubbo" Gilbert, who was probably the crookedest cop in town. Which in this town was saying something.

Pribyl had a good reputation, however; and I'd encountered him, from time to time, back when I was working the pickpocket detail. He had soft, gentle features and dark alert eyes. Normally, he was an almost dapper dresser, but his tie seemed hastily knotted, his suit and hat looked as if he'd thrown them on—which he probably had; he was responding to a call at four in the morning, after all.

He was looking in at Stanley, who hadn't been moved; we were waiting for a coroner's physician to show. Several other plainclothes officers and half a dozen uniformed cops were milling around, footsteps crunching on the glass-strewn sidewalk.

"Just a kid," Pribyl said, stepping away from the Ford. "Just a damn kid." He shook his head. He nodded to me and I followed him over by a shattered display window.

He cocked his head. "How'd you happen to have such a young operative working with you?"

I explained about the car being Stanley's.

He had an expression you only see on cops: sad and yet detached. His eyes tightened.

"How—and why—did stink bombs and window smashing escalate into bloody murder?"

"You expect me to answer that, Sergeant?"

"No. I expect you to tell me what happened. And, Heller—I don't go into this with any preconceived notions about you. Some people on the force—even some good ones, like John Stege—hold it against you, the Lang and Miller business."

They were two crooked cops I'd recently testified against.

"Not me," he said firmly. "Apples don't come rotter than those two bastards. I just want you to know what kind of footing we're on."

"I appreciate that."

I filled him in, including a description of the murder vehicle, but couldn't describe the people within at all. I wasn't even sure how many of them there were.

"You get the license number?"

"No, damnit."

"Why not? You saw the car well enough."

"Them shooting at me interfered."

He nodded. "Fair enough. Shit. Too bad you didn't get a look at 'em."

"Too bad. But you know who to go calling on."

"How's that?"

I thrust a finger toward the car. "That's Boss Rooney's work—maybe not personally, but he had it done. You know about the Circular Union and the hassles they been giving Goldblatt's, right?"

Pribyl nodded, somewhat reluctantly; he liked me well enough, but I was a private detective. He didn't like having me in the middle of police business.

"Heller, we've been keeping the union headquarters under surveillance for six weeks now. I saw Rooney there today, myself, from the apartment across the way we rented."

"So did anyone leave the union hall tonight? Before the shooting, say around three?"

He shook his head glumly. "We've only been maintaining our watch during department-store business hours. The problem of night attacks is where hired hands like you come in."

"Okay." I sighed. "I won't blame you if you don't blame me."

"Deal."

"So what's next?"

"You can go on home." He glanced toward the Ford. "We'll take care of this."

"You want me to tell the family?"

"Were you close to them?"

"Not really. They're from my old neighborhood, is all."

"I'll handle it."

"You sure?"

"I'm sure." He patted my shoulder. "Go home."

I started to go, then turned back. "When are you going to pick up Rooney?"

"I'll have to talk to the State's Attorney, first. But my guess? Tomorrow. We'll raid the union hall tomorrow."

"Mind if I come along?"

"Wouldn't be appropriate, Heller."

"The kid worked for me. He got killed working for me."

"No. We'll handle it. Go home! Get some sleep."

"I'll go home," I said.

A chill breeze was whispering.

"But the sleep part," I said, "that I can't promise you."

The next afternoon I was having a beer in a booth in the bar next to the deli below my office. Formerly a blind pig—a speakeasy that looked shuttered from the street (even now, you entered through the deli)—it was a business investment of fighter Barney Ross, as was reflected by the framed boxing photos decorating the dark, smoky little joint.

I grew up with Barney on the West Side. Since my family hadn't practiced Judaism in several generations, I was shabbes goy for Barney's very Orthodox folks, a kid doing chores and errands for them from Friday sundown through Saturday.

But we didn't become really good friends, Barney and me, till we worked Maxwell Street as pullers—teenage street barkers who literally pulled customers into stores for bargains they had no interest in.

Barney, a roughneck made good, was a real Chicago success story. He owned this entire building, and my office—which, with its Murphy bed, was also my residence—was space he traded me for keeping an eye on the place. I was his nightwatchman, unless a paying job like Goldblatt's came along to take precedence. The lightweight champion of the world was having a beer, too, in that back booth; he wore a cheerful blue and white sportshirt and a dour expression.

"I'm sorry about your young pal," Barney said.

"He wasn't a 'pal,' really. Just an acquaintance."

"I don't know that Douglas Park crowd myself. But to think of a kid, on his twenty-first birthday..." His mildly battered bulldog countenance looked woeful. "He have a girl?"

"Yeah."

"What's her name?"

"I don't remember."

"Poor little bastard. When's the funeral?"

"I don't know."

"You're going, aren't you?"

"No. I don't really know the family that well. I'm sending flowers."

He looked at me with as long a face as a round-faced guy could muster. "You oughta go. He was working for you when he got it."

"I'd be intruding. I'd be out of place."

"You should do kaddish for the kid, Nate."

A mourner's prayer.

"Jesus Christ, Barney, I'm no Jew. I haven't been in a synagogue more than half a dozen times in my life, and then it was social occasions."

"Maybe you don't consider yourself a Jew, with that Irish mug of yours your ma bequeathed you...but you're gonna have a rude awakening one of these days, boyo."

"What do you mean?"

"There's plenty of people you're just another 'kike' to, believe you me."

I sipped the beer. "Nudge me when you get to the point."

"You owe this kid kaddish, Nate."

"Hell, doesn't that go on for months? I don't know the lingo. And if you think I'm putting on some fuckin' beanie and..."

There was a tap on my shoulder. Buddy Gold, the bartender, an ex-pug, leaned in to say, "You got a call."

I went behind the bar to use the phone. It was Sergeant Lou Sapperstein at Central HQ in the Loop; Lou had been my boss on the pickpocket detail. I'd called him this morning with a request.

"Tubbo's coppers made their raid this morning, around nine," Lou said. Sapperstein was a hardnosed, balding cop of about forty-five and one of the few friends I had left on the PD.

"And?"

"And the union hall was empty, 'cept for a bartender. Pribyl and his partner Bert Gray took a whole squad up there, but Rooney and his boys had flew the coop."

"Fuck. Somebody tipped them."

"Are you surprised?"

"Yeah. Surprised I expected the cops to play it straight for a change. You wouldn't have the address of that union, by any chance?"

"No, but I can get it. Hold a second."

A sweet union scam like the Circular Distributors had Outfit written all over it—and Captain Tubbo Gilbert, head of the State Prosecutor's police, was known as the richest cop in Chicago. Tubbo was a bagman and police fixer so deep in Frank Nitti's pocket he had Nitti's lint up his nose.

Lou was back: "It's at 7 North Racine. That's Madison and Racine."

"Well, hell—that's spitting distance from Skid Row."

"Yeah. So?"

"So that explains the scam—that 'union' takes hobos and makes day laborers out of them. No wonder they charge daily dues. It's just bums handing out ad circulars...."

"I'd say that's a good guess, Nate."

I thanked Lou and went back to the booth where Barney was brooding about what a louse his friend Heller was.

"I got something to do," I told him.

"What?"

"My kind of kaddish."

Less than two miles from the prominent department stores of the Loop they'd been fleecing, the Circular Distributors Union had their headquarters on the doorstep of Skid Row and various Hoovervilles. This Madison Street area, just north of Greek Town, was a seedy mix of flophouses, marginal apartment buildings and storefront businesses, mostly bars. Union HQ was on the second floor of a two-story brick building whose bottom floor was a plumbing supply outlet.

I went up the squeaking stairs and into the union hall, a big high-ceilinged open room with a few glassed-in offices toward the front, to the left and right. Ceiling fans whirred lazily, stirring stale smoky air; folding chairs and cardtables were scattered everywhere on the scuffed wooden floor, and seated at some were unshaven, tattered "members" of the union. Across the far end stretched a bar, behind which a burly blond guy in rolled-up white-shirt sleeves was polishing a glass. More hobos leaned against the bar, having beers.

I ordered a mug from the bartender, who had a massive skull and tiny dark eyes and a sullen kiss of a mouth.

I salted the brew as I tossed him a nickel. "Hear you had a raid here this morning."

He ignored the question. "This hall's for union members only."

"Jeez, it looks like a saloon."

"Well, it's a union hall. Drink up and move along."

"There's a fin in it for you, if you answer a few questions."

He thought that over; leaned in. "Are you a cop?"

"No. Private."

"Who hired you?"

"Goldblatt's."

He thought some more. The tiny eyes narrowed. "Let's hear the questions."

"What do you know about the Gross kid's murder?"

"Not a damn thing."

"Was Rooney here last night?"

"Far as I know, he was home in bed asleep."

"Know where he lives?"

"No."

"You don't know where your boss lives."

"No. All I know is he's a swell guy. He don't have nothin' to do with these department store shakedowns the cops are tryin' to pin on him. It's union-busting, is what it is."

"Union busting." I had a look around at the bleary-eyed clientele in their patched clothes. "You have to be a union, first, 'fore you can get busted up."

"What's *that* supposed to mean?"

"It means this is a scam. Rooney pulls in winos, gets 'em day-labor jobs for $3.25 a day, then they come up here to pay their daily dues of a quarter, and blow the rest on beer or booze. In other words, first the bums pass out ad fliers, then they come here and just plain pass out."

"I think you better scram. Otherwise I'm gonna have to throw you down the stairs."

I finished the beer. "I'm leaving. But you know what? I'm not gonna give you that fin. I'm afraid you'd just drink it up."

I could feel his eyes on my back as I left, but I'd have heard him if he came out from around the bar. I was starting down the stairs when the door below opened and Sgt. Pribyl, looking irritated, came up to meet me on the landing, half-way. He looked more his usual dapper self, but his eyes were black-bagged.

"What's the idea, Heller?"

"I just wanted to come bask in the reflected glory of your triumphant raid this morning."

"What's that supposed to mean?"

"It means when Tubbo's boys are on the case, the Outfit gets advance notice."

He winced. "That's not the way it was. I don't know why Rooney and Berry and the others blew. But nobody in our office warned 'em off."

"Are you sure?"

He clearly wasn't. "Look, I can't have you messing in this. We're on the damn case, okay? We're maintaining surveillance from across the way...that's how we spotted you."

"Peachy. Twenty-four surveillance, now?"

"No." He seemed embarrassed. "Just day shift."

"You want some help?"

"What do you mean?"

"Loan me the key to your stakeout crib. I'll keep nightwatch. Got a phone in there?"

"Yeah."

"I'll call you if Rooney shows. You got pictures of him and the others you can give me?"

"Well...."

"What's the harm? Or would Tubbo lower the boom on you, if you really did your job?"

He sighed. Scratched his head and came to a decision. "This is unofficial, okay? But there's a possibility the door to that apartment's gonna be left unlocked tonight."

"Do tell."

"Third-floor—301." He raised a cautionary finger. "We'll try this for one night...no showboating, okay? Call me if one of 'em shows."

"Sure. You tried their homes?"

He nodded. "Nothing. Rooney lives on North Ridgeland in Oak Park. Four kids. Wife's a pleasant, matronly type."

"Fat, you mean."

"She hasn't seen Rooney for several weeks. She says he's away from home a lot."

"Keeping a guard posted there?"

"Yeah. And that *is* twenty-four hour." He sighed, shook his head. "Heller, there's a lot about this case that doesn't make sense."

"Such as?"

"That maroon Plymouth. We never saw a car like that in the entire six weeks we had the union hall under surveillance. Rooney drives a blue LaSalle coupe."

"Any maroon Plymouths reported stolen?"

He shook his head. "And it hasn't turned up abandoned, either. They must still have the car."

"Is Rooney *that* stupid?"

"We can always hope," Pribyl said.

I sat in an easy chair with sprung springs by the window in room 301 of the residential hotel across the way. It wasn't a flophouse cage, but it wasn't a suite at the Drake, either. Anyway, in the dark it looked fine. I had a flask of rum to keep me company, and the breeze fluttering the sheer, frayed curtains remained unseasonably cool.

Thanks to some photos Pribyl left me, I now knew what Rooney looked like: a good-looking, oval-faced smoothie, in his mid-forties, just starting to lose his dark, slicked-back hair; his eyes were hooded, his mouth soft, sensual, sullen. There were also photos of bespectacled, balding Berry and pockmarked, cold-eyed Herbert Arnold, V.P. of the union.

But none of them stopped by the union hall—only a steady stream of winos and bums went in and out.

Then, around seven, I spotted somebody who didn't fit the profile.

It was a guy I knew—a fellow private op, Eddie McGowan, a Pinkerton man, in uniform, meaning he was on nightwatch-man duty. A number of the merchants along Madison must have pitched in for his services.

I left the stakeout and waited down on the street, in front of the plumbing supply store, for Eddie to come back out. It didn't take long—maybe ten minutes.

"Heller!" he said. He was a skinny, tow-haired guy in his late twenties with a bad complexion and a good outlook. "What no good are you up to?"

"The Goldblatt's shooting. That kid they killed was work-ing with me."

"Oh! I didn't know! Heard about the shooting, of course, but didn't read the papers or anything. So you were involved in that? No kidding."

"No kidding. You on watchman duty?"

"Yeah. Up and down the street, here, all night."

"Including the union hall?"

"Sure." He grinned. "I usually stop up for a free drink, 'bout this time of night."

"Can you knock off for a couple of minutes? For another free drink?"

"Sure!"

Soon we were in a smoky booth in back of a bar and Eddie was having a boilermaker on me.

"See anything unusual last night," I asked, "around the union hall?"

"Well...I had a drink there, around two o'clock in the morning. *That* was a first."

"A drink? Don't they close earlier than that?"

"Yeah. Around eleven. That's all the longer it takes for their 'members' to lap up their daily dough."

"So what were you doing up there at two?"

He shrugged. "Well, I noticed the lights was on upstairs, so I unlocked the street level door and went up. Figured Alex... that's the bartender, Alex Davidson...might have forgot to turn out the lights, 'fore he left. The door up there was locked, but then Mr. Rooney opened it up and told me to come on in."

"Why would he do that?"

"He was feelin' pretty good. Looked like he was workin' on a bender. Anyway, he insists I have a drink with him. I says, sure. Turns out Davidson is still there."

"No kidding?"

"No kidding. So Alex serves me a beer. Henry Berry—he's the union's so-called business agent, mousy little guy with glasses—he was there, too. He was in his cups, also. So was Rooney's wife—she was there, and also feeling giddy."

I thought about Pribyl's description of Mrs. Rooney as a matronly woman with four kids. "His *wife* was there?"

"Yeah, the lucky stiff."

"Lucky?"

"You should see the dame! Good-lookin' tomato with big dark eyes and a nice shape on her."

"About how old?"

"Young. Twenties. It'd take the sting out of a ball and chain, I can tell you that."

"Eddie...here's a fin."

"Heller, the beer's enough!"

"The fin is for telling this same story to Sgt. Pribyl of the State's Attorney's coppers."

"Oh. Okay."

"But do it tomorrow."

He smirked. "Okay. I got rounds to make, anyway."

So did I.

At around eleven fifteen, bartender Alex Davidson was leaving the union hall; his back was turned, as he was locking the street-level door, and I put my nine-millimeter in it.

"Hi, Alex," I said. "Don't turn around, unless you prefer being gut-shot."

"If it's a stick-up, all I got's a couple bucks. Take 'em and bug off!"

"No such luck. Leave that door unlocked. We're gonna step back inside."

He grunted and opened the door and we stepped inside.

"Now we're going up the stairs," I said, and we did, in the dark, the wooden steps whining under our weight. He was a big man; I'd have had my work cut out for me—if I hadn't had the gun.

We stopped at the landing where earlier I had spoken to Sgt. Pribyl. "Here's fine," I said.

I allowed him to face me in the near-dark.

He sneered. "You're that private dick."

"I'm sure you mean that in the nicest way. Let me tell you a little more about me. See, we're going to get to know each other, Alex."

"Fuck you."

I slapped him with the nine millimeter.

He wiped blood off his mouth and looked at me with hate, but also with fear. And he made no more smart-ass remarks.

"I'm the private dick whose twenty-one-year-old partner got shot in the head last night."

Now the fear was edging out the hate; he knew he might die in this dark stairwell.

"I know you were here with Rooney and Berry and the broad, last night, serving up drinks as late as two in the morning," I said. "Now you're going to tell me the whole story—or you're the one who's getting tossed down the fucking stairs."

He was trembling, now; a big hulk of a man trembling with fear. "I didn't have anything to do with the murder. Not a damn thing!"

"Then why cover for Rooney and the rest?"

"You saw what they're capable of!"

"Take it easy, Alex. Just tell the story."

Rooney had come into the office about noon the day of the shooting; he had started drinking and never stopped. Berry and several other union "officers" arrived and angry discussions about being under surveillance by the State's Attorney's cops were accompanied by a lot more drinking.

"The other guys left around five, but Rooney and Berry, they just hung around drinking all evening. Around midnight, Rooney handed me a phone number he jotted on a matchbook, and gave it to me to call for him. It was a Berwyn number. A woman answered. I handed him the phone and he said to her, 'Bring one.'"

"One what?" I asked.

"I'm gettin' to that. She showed up around one o'clock—good-looking dame with black hair and eyes so dark they coulda been black, too."

"Who was she?"

"I don't know. Never saw her before. She took a gun out of her purse and gave it to Rooney."

"That was what he asked her to bring."

"I guess. It was a .38 revolver, a Colt I think. Anyway, Rooney and Berry were both pretty drunk; I don't know what *her* excuse was. So Rooney takes the gun and says, 'We got a job to pull at Goldblatt's. We're gonna throw some slugs at the windows and watchmen.'"

"How did the girl react?"

He swallowed. "She laughed. She said, 'I'll go along and watch the fun.' Then they all went out."

Jesus.

Finally I said, "What do you did do?"

"They told me to wait for 'em. Keep the bar open. They came back in, laughing like hyenas. Rooney says to me, 'You want to see the way he keeled over?' And I says, 'Who?' And he says, 'The guard at Goldblatt's.' Berry laughs and says, 'We really let him have it.'"

"That kid was twenty-one, Alex. It was his goddamn birthday."

The bartender was looking down. "They laughed and joked about it till Berry passed out. About six in the morning, Rooney has me pile Berry in a cab. Rooney and the twist slept in his office for maybe an hour. Then they came out, looking sober and kind of...scared. He warned me not to tell anybody what I seen, unless I wanted to trade my job for a morgue slab."

"Colorful. Tell me, Alex. You got that girl's phone number in Berwyn?"

"I think it's upstairs. You can put that gun away. I'll help you."

It was dark, but I could see his face well enough; the big man's eyes looked damp. The fear was gone. Something else was in its place. Shame? Something.

We went upstairs, he unlocked the union hall and, under the bar, found the matchbook with the number written inside: Berwyn 2981.

"You want a drink before you go?" he asked.

"You know," I said, "I think I'll pass."

I went back to my office to use the reverse-listing phone book that told me Berwyn 2981 was Rosalie Rizzo's number; and that Rosalie Rizzo lived at 6348 West 13th Street in Berwyn.

First thing the next morning, I borrowed Barney's Hupmobile and drove out to Berwyn, the clean, tidy Hunky suburb populated in part by the late Mayor Cermak's patronage people. But finding a Rosalie Rizzo in this largely Czech and Bohemian area came as no surprise: Capone's Cicero was a stone's throw away.

The woman's address was a three-story brick apartment building, but none of the mailboxes in the vestibule bore her name. I found the janitor and gave him Rosalie Rizzo's description. It sounded like Mrs. Riggs to him.

"She's a doll," the janitor said. He was heavy-set and needed a shave; he licked his thick lips as he thought about her. "Ain't seen her since yesterday noon."

That was about nine hours after Stanley was killed.

He continued: "Her and her husband was going to the country, she said. Didn't expect to be back for a couple of weeks, she said."

Her husband.

"What'll a look around their apartment cost me?"

He licked his lips again. "Two bucks?"

Two bucks it was; the janitor used his passkey and left me to it. The well-appointed little apartment included a canary that sang in its gilded cage, a framed photo of slick Boss Rooney on an end table, and a closet containing two sawed-off shotguns and a repeating rifle.

I had barely started to poke around when I had company: a slender, gray-haired woman in a flowered print dress.

"Oh!" she said, coming in the door she'd unlocked.

"Can I help you?" I asked.

"Who are you?" Her voice had the lilt of an Italian accent.

Under the circumstances, the truth seemed prudent. "A private detective."

"My daughter is not here! She and her-a husband, they go to vacation. Up north some-a-where. I just-a come to feed the canary!"

"Please don't be frightened. Do you know where she's gone, exactly?"

"No. But...maybe my husband do. He is-a downstairs...."

She went to a window, threw it open and yelled something frantically down in Italian.

I eased her aside in time to see a heavy-set man jump into a maroon Plymouth with a silver swan on the radiator cap, and cream colored wheels, and squeal away.

And when I turned, the slight gray-haired woman was just as gone. Only she hadn't squealed.

The difference, this time, was a license number for the maroon coupe; I'd seen it: 519-836. In a diner I made a call to Lou Sapperstein, who made a call to the motor vehicle bureau, and phoned back with the scoop: the Plymouth was licensed to Rosalie Rizzo, but the address was different—2848 South Cuyler Avenue, in Berwyn.

The bungalow was typical for Berwyn—a tidy little frame house on a small perfect lawn. My guess was this was her folks' place. In back was a small matching, but unattached garage, on the alley. Peeking in the garage windows, I saw the maroon coupe and smiled.

"Is Rosalie in trouble again?"

The voice was female, sweet, young.

I turned and saw a slender, almost beautiful teenage girl with dark eyes and bouncy, dark shoulder-length hair. She wore a navy-blue sailor-ish playsuit. Her pretty white legs were bare.

"Are you Rosalie's sister?"

"Yes. Is she in trouble?"

"What makes you say that?"

"I just know Rosalie, that's all. That man isn't really her husband, is he? That Mr. Riggs."

"No."

"Are you here about her accident?"

"No. Where is she?"

"Are you a police officer?"

"I'm a detective. Where did she go?"

"Papa's inside. He's afraid he's going to be in trouble."

"Why's that?"

"Rosalie put her car in our garage yesterday. She said she was in an accident and it was damaged and not to use it. She's going to have it repaired when she gets back from vacation."

"What does that have to do with your papa being scared?"

"Rosalie's going to be mad as H at him, that he used her car." She shrugged. "He said he looked at it and it didn't look damaged to him, and if mama was going to have to look after Rosalie's g.d. canary, well he'd sure as H use *her* gas not his."

"I can see his point. Where did your sister go on vacation?"

"She didn't say. Up north someplace Someplace she and Mr. Riggs like to go to, to...you know. To get away?"

I called Sgt. Pribyl from a gas station where I was getting Barney's Hupmobile tank re-filled. I suggested he have another talk with bartender Alex Davidson, gave him the address of "Mr. and Mrs. Riggs," and told him where he could find the maroon Plymouth.

He was grateful but a little miffed about all I had done on my own.

"So much for not showboating," he said, almost huffily. "You've found everything but the damn suspects."

"They've gone up north somewhere," I said.

"Where up north?"

"They don't seem to've told anybody. Look, I have a piece of evidence you may need."

"What?"

"When you talk to Davidson, he'll tell you about a matchbook Rooney wrote the girl's number on. I got the matchbook."

It was still in my pocket. I took it out, idly, and shut the girl's number away, revealing the picture on the matchbook cover: a blue moon hovered surrealistically over a white lake on which two blue lovers paddled in a blue canoe—Eagle River Lodge, Wisconsin.

"I suppose we'll need that," Pribyl's voice over the phone said, "when the time comes."

"I suppose," I said, and hung up.

Eagle River was a town of 1,386 (so said the sign) just inside the Vilas County line at the junction of US 45 and Wisconsin State Highway 70. The country was beyond beautiful—green pines towering higher than Chicago skyscrapers, glittering blue lakes nestling in woodland pockets.

The lodge I was looking for was on Silver Lake, a gas station attendant told me. A beautiful dusk was settling on the woods as I drew into the parking of the large resort sporting a red city-style neon saying, DINING AND DANCE. Log-cabin cottages were flung here and there around the periphery like Paul Bunyan's tinker-toys. Each one was just secluded enough—ideal for couples, married or un-.

Even if Rooney and his dark-haired honey weren't staying here, it was time to find a room: I'd been driving all day. When Barney loaned me his Hupmobile, he'd had no idea the kind of miles I'd put on it. Dead tired, I went to the desk and paid for a cabin.

The guy behind the counter had a plaid shirt on, but he was small and squinty and Hitler-mustached, smoking a stogie, and looked more like a bookie than a lumberjack.

I told him some friends of mine were supposed to be staying here.

"We don't have anybody named Riggs registered."

"How 'bout Mr. and Mrs. Rooney?"

"Them either. How many friends you got, anyway?"

"Why, did I already catch the limit?"

Before I headed to my cabin, I grabbed some supper in the rustic restaurant. I placed my order with a friendly brunette girl of about nineteen with plenty of personality, and make-up. A road-company Paul Whiteman outfit was playing "Sophisticated Lady" in the adjacent dance hall, and I went over and peeked in, to look for familiar faces. A number of couples were cutting a rug, but not Rooney and Rosalie. Or Henry Berry or Herbert Arnold, either. I went back and had my green salad and fried trout and well-buttered baked potato; I was full and sleepy when I stumbled toward my guest cottage under the light of a moon that bathed the woods ivory.

Walking along the path, I spotted something: snuggled next to one of the secluded cabins was a blue LaSalle coupe with Cook County plates.

Suddenly I wasn't sleepy. I walked briskly back to the lodge check-in desk and batted the bell to summon the stogie-chewing clerk.

"Cabin seven," I said. "I think that blue LaSalle is my friends' car."

His smirk turned his Hitler mustache Chaplinesque. "You want I should break out the champagne?"

"I just want to make sure it's them. Dark-haired doll and an older guy, good-looking, kinda sleepy-eyed, just starting to go bald?"

"That's them." He checked his register. "That's the Ridges." He frowned. "Are they usin' a phony name?"

"Does a bear shit in the woods?"

He squinted. "You sure they're friends of yours?"

"Positive. Don't call their room and tell 'em I'm here, though—I want to surprise them...."

I knocked with my left hand; my right was filled with the nine millimeter. Nothing. I knocked again.

"Who is it?" a male voice said gruffly. "*What* is it?"

"Complimentary fruit basket from the management."

"Go away!"

I kicked the door open.

The lights were off in the little cabin, but enough moonlight came in with me through the doorway to reveal the pair in bed, naked. She was sitting up, her mouth and eyes open in a silent scream, gathering the sheets up protectively over white skin, her dark hair blending with the darkness of the room, making a cameo of her face. He was diving off the bed for the sawed-off shotgun, but I was there to kick it away, wishing I hadn't, wishing I'd let him grab it so I could have had an excuse to put one in his forehead, right where he'd put one in Stanley's.

Boss Rooney wasn't boss of anything, now: he was just a naked, balding, forty-four year-old scam artist, sprawled on the floor. Kicking him would have been easy.

So I did; in the stomach.

He clutched himself and puked. Apparently he'd had the trout, too.

I went over and slammed the door shut, or as shut as it could be, half-off its hinges. Pointing the gun at her retching naked boy friend, I said to the girl, "Turn on the light and put on your clothes."

She nodded dutifully and did as she was told. In the glow of a nightstand lamp, I caught glimpses of her white, well-formed body as she stepped into her step-ins; but you know what? She didn't do a thing for me.

"Is Berry here?" I asked Rooney. "Or Arnold?"

"N...no," he managed.

"If you're lying," I said, "I'll kill you."

The girl said shrilly, "They aren't here!"

"You can put your clothes on, too," I told Rooney. "If you have another gun hidden somewhere, do me a favor. Make a play for it."

His hooded eyes flared. "Who the hell are you?"

"The private cop you *didn't* kill the other night."

He lowered his gaze. "Oh."

The girl was sitting on the bed, weeping; body heaving.

"Take it easy on her, will you?" he said, zipping his fly. "She's just a kid."

I was opening a window to ease the stench of his vomit. "Sure," I said. "I'll say kaddish for her."

I handcuffed the lovebirds to the bed and called the local law; they in turn called the State Prosecutor's office in Chicago, and Sergeants Pribyl and Gray made the long drive up the next day to pick up the pair.

It seemed the two cops had already caught Henry Berry—a tipster gave them the West Chicago Avenue address of a second-floor room he was holed up in.

I admitted to Pribyl that I'd been wrong about Tubbo tipping off Rooney and the rest about the raid.

"I figure Rooney lammed out of sheer panic," I said, "the morning after the murder."

Pribyl saw it the same way.

The following March, Pribyl arrested Herbert Arnold running a northside handbill distributing agency.

Rooney, Berry and Rosalie Rizzo were all convicted of murder; the two men got life, and the girl twenty years. Arnold hadn't been part of the kill-happy joyride that took Stanley

Gross' young life, and got only one to five for conspiracy and extortion.

None of it brought Stanley Gross back, nor did my putting on a beanie and sitting with the Gross family, suffering through a couple of stints at a storefront synagogue on Roosevelt Road.

But it did get Barney off my ass.

AUTHOR'S NOTE

Research materials for this fact-based story include "The Wynekoop Case" in *The Chicago Crime Book* (1947) by Craig Rice; "Who Killed Rheta Wynekoop?" by Harry Read in *Real Detective* magazine, April 1934; and "The Justice Story," a 1987 New York *Daily News* column by Joseph McNamara.

THE BLONDE
TIGRESS

August 1933 in Chicago was surprisingly cool, unless you were a crook, in which case it was hotter than usual. We were suffering through one of those periodic anti-crime drives the city subjected itself to now and then, and since the Capone/Nitti Outfit got a free pass on its fun and games, small fry like the Blonde Tigress and her "mob" (two male accomplices) got the brunt.

Did the Blonde Tigress have a damn thing to do with the policeman who got himself shot in a Cook County courtroom? No. She and her gang of two merely got caught up in the over-reaction when the Honorable John Prystalski, the county's chief judge, ordered all the other judges back from summer vacation to work through the jammed-up docket. Two-hundred-thirty-five defendants got the book thrown at them that August, including three death sentences.

And that was *before* the Blonde Tigress had appeared in the dock....

In my big under-furnished one-room office on Van Buren, I sat at my desk, working on a pile of retail-credit checks, with the window open behind me to let in a cool morning breeze and the occasional rumble of the El.

I tried to let the phone ring five times before answering, but was short enough on clients to settle for three. "A-1 Detective Agency," I said. "Nathan Heller speaking."

"Nate, Sam Backus."

My hopes sank. Backus—small, nervous, with ferret features—was with the Public Defender's Office, which made him the kind of criminal attorney who couldn't afford my help.

"Hiya, Sam. Any of your clients get a ticket for the hot squat today?"

"No, but the day's young. Listen, I got the Tigress."

I sat up. "What?"

"You heard me. Eleanor Jarman is my client."

All summer, the Blonde Tigress case had been plastered across the front pages, and the radio was all over it, too. The so-called Blonde Tigress—a good-looking lady bandit with "tawny hair" and a "voluptuous figure"—had led her two-man mob on a series of stickups all around the West and Northwest sides. The Tigress was said to carry a big revolver in her purse and a blackjack, too, one of her male accomplices using the gun, the Tigress adept with the jack. The usual target was the small merchant, grocery stores and other shops, the robbery victims often roughed up for intimidation or maybe just the hell of it.

After the August 4 hold-up of a clothing shop near Oak Park—and the murder of its seventy-year-old proprietor—sometime waitress Eleanor Jarman, her live-in guy George Dale, and Dale's ex-fighter buddy Leo Minneci had been identified as the perpetrators and brought in by two top Detective Bureau dicks.

"Well, she's guilty as sin, isn't she?" I asked him cheerfully. "Maybe you can arrange for her to sit on her boyfriend's lap when they fry him, and save the state on its electricity bill."

"Nate, I think she's being railroaded. These characters Dale and Minneci are stick-up guys, sure, and there's no doubt Dale pulled the trigger on the old boy. But Eleanor's just the girl friend. Wrong place at the wrong time."

"Are they being tried separately?"

"No, but each has separate representation from the Public Defender's office."

I was shaking my head. "If she's innocent in this, why was she charged? Didn't Tuohy and Glass make the arrest? They're as close to real detectives as the police department gets."

"Nate, you know about this clean-up and crackdown campaign that's going on. When did you ever hear of somebody getting arrested for murder in this town and then have the trial go on the same damn month?"

"Okay, you stumped me. But I—"

"Think it through, Nate. This is about the papers looking for a hot story, and what's better than a sexy baby leading her 'gang' on a bunch of robberies?"

I shifted in my chair. "Listen, I don't care if she's guilty or not guilty. I'd be glad to work for you, Sam, if you were a real criminal lawyer with some scratch to spend."

"That's the good part about all this press nonsense, Nate. Think about the publicity! There's no bigger story right now."

"Then I'm right—there *isn't* any money in this."

"Actually, pal, there is."

That got my attention, but I said, "Don't call me 'pal.' Makes me nervous. When do I ever see you, Sam, when we aren't in a courtroom?"

"Nate, if you take this case, you can peddle your story to one of the papers afterwards, with my blessing. And I've got a true detective magazine that'll pay even better. That'll beat any of your five-dollar-a-day action, any time."

"That's ten and expenses, and what do you have in mind?"

"Just meet with my client. See if she doesn't deserve the benefit of the doubt."

"So then you have no case?"

"...I have no case. I need you to go get me one."

If I was the private eye who cleared the Blonde Tigress, I'd be in demand with every criminal lawyer in town.

"I can meet with her," I said, "any time today."

Now a guy can get some pretty funny thoughts sometimes. And by funny, I mean stupid. But while I'd been around, I was only twenty-eight, and I couldn't keep from wondering if some exotic, erotic encounter might not occur between the Blonde Tigress and me, behind the closed door of that First District Station interrogation room. The matron standing guard would hear the muffled sounds and wonder what might be happening in there, between the curvaceous blonde gun moll and that handsome six-footer with the reddish brown hair, and dare she interrupt?

I was expecting the combination Jean Harlow and Mata Hari that the papers had been pumping, and in my defense I must say that they'd taken some fairly fetching photos of Eleanor Jarman. And the woman seated at the scarred table in a brick-walled enclosure whose windows were barred and throwing appropriately moody shadows—was certainly attractive, albeit in a quiet, modest, even mousy way.

Her hair was not tawny, at least not by my standards—more a dishwater blonde, curling-ironed locks framing her heart-shaped face. I'd call her pretty, or anyway pretty enough, with big gray eyes that dominated her face and a nice mouth, full lips lightly rouged. Prisoners awaiting trial were allowed street clothes—in this case, a simple white dress with angular blue stripes and a white collar with a bow, the stripes giving the faintest unintentional prison-uniform touch. She had a nice shape, but "voluptuous" was torturing a point.

She gave me a big smile and stood and held her hand out for me to shake. The smile was disarming—I might have been a brother she hadn't seen for some time.

"Thank you for this, Mr. Heller," she said warmly, as I took a chair at the table, her at the end, me alongside.

"I haven't agreed to take the job, Mrs. Jarman," I said, and took my hat off and tossed it on the table. "I said I'd have a talk with you and see."

Her smile remained but she put the teeth away and nodded. "It's because Mr. Backus can't afford to hire you. But what if *I* could?"

"Could what?"

"Afford to hire to you."

I squinted at her. "How could you afford to hire a private detective if you can't afford your own lawyer?"

She shrugged and half a smile lingered. "That was strategy, Mr. Heller. I could've hired a lawyer, not an expensive one, but I do have some money salted away. It's just, well..."

And I got it.

"If you could hire a criminal attorney," I said, "it would make you look more like a criminal. Somebody pulling off heists all summer could afford counsel. Smart."

"I'm not rich. But I could offer you one hundred dollars."

"I charge ten a day and expenses. That'll take you a fair way."

"Fine. I'll have it sent over to your office."

"You're not what I expected."

She grinned. "Not a Tigress?"

"Not the femme fatale the papers paint, and not the victim Sam Backus would make you, either."

"What, then?"

"A smart, resourceful cookie."

"Thanks. Could I call you something besides 'Mr. Heller'?"

"Sure. Nate'll do. And I'll call you Eleanor."

They had provided a pitcher of ice water and I served us up some. The breezy afternoon was making its way through windows that were open onto their bars.

"Do you need to hear my story, Nate, before you say yes?"

"I want to hear your story, but I already said yes to your hundred dollars."

She had a whole repertoire of smiles, and she gave me another one, a chin-crinkler. But the gray eyes had a sadness that fit neither her happy kisser nor her business-like brain.

She started with the story of her life, which didn't take long, because it wasn't much of one. She was from Sioux City, Iowa, daughter of immigrant German parents who died in a flu epidemic when she was fourteen, just the right age to start working as a waitress in a joint near the stockyards. She married Leroy Jarman, who told her she deserved better, and gave her two sons and put her to work as a laundress. Earlier this year, after Jarman took a powder, she moved to Chicago, where she continued to do laundry in her little apartment while taking care of her two boys. A neighbor introduced her to George Dale, and her life changed.

"George never said what he did for a living," she told me. "I always figured it was something a little shady, but hell, I ran a beer flat in Sioux City, so who was I to talk? Anyway, he always had plenty of dough and we lived in nice apartments."

Then she got to the meat of the matter: the crime.

She and her boy friend George and George's friend Leo were on their way to a Cubs game at Wrigley Field. They were running early and decided to stop and do a little shopping; George had spotted the clothing store sign and pulled in, saying he needed some shirts. They had all three gone inside.

"George was talking to Mr. Hoeh up in front," she said. Her eyes were not on me; they seemed to be staring into her memory. "The old man was getting shirts from behind the counter and laying boxes out for George to see. Leo wasn't interested, and just hanging by the door. I was in the back of the store, looking at ties and other boys clothing—my sons are nine and eleven—and was caught up in making some selections." Now she looked at me, gray eyes wide and earnest. "Then I heard the sound of a scuffle."

"Was the old boy still behind the counter?"

"No, he was coming around after George, who was heading out."

"Leaving you in back of the store?"

"No, that's the other thing that alerted me that something was wrong—George was calling, 'Eleanor! Hurry!'"

"What did you think was happening?"

"Honestly, I had no idea. I guess I thought the old man had gone off his rocker or something. Leo was there at the door, holding it open, but Mr. Hoeh was attacking George. Then all of sudden George had this gun...."

"You didn't know George had a gun?"

She shook her head. "And the old man wrestled with George, had a hold of his wrist and twisted the thing around, and it went off!"

"And the old boy got hit?"

"No! *Leo* did—in his hand, his left hand I think. Leo yelled something like, 'Jesus, George, you shot me!' Then George shoved Mr. Hoeh away, and I was coming up from the back of the shop now, and I followed them out onto the sidewalk—I was the last one out, kind of trailing the old man, who was all over George. Why did he do that? He *knew* George had a gun!"

I shrugged. "It was his store. A guy his age, builds a business, he might do anything to defend it. Go on."

"I know Mr. Hoeh was old, but he was big and tough, slugging and swinging, and I almost jumped on his back, trying to pull him off George, trying to stop this."

"You must've have known it was a hold-up by now."

She shook her head firmly. "No. I wasn't thinking, not rationally, anyway. It was all so fast. I just knew George was in trouble and this crazy old man was attacking him."

"All right. What happened then?"

She swallowed; no smiles now. "The old man shoved me away. That's when George shot him. Twice."

I drew in a breath; I let it out. "And Mr. Hoeh died before he made it to the hospital."

"I know." She was shaking her head, eyes glued to the scarred table top. "I'm so sorry. I had no idea George was some kind of... stick-up man. But I can't believe he did that, with *me* along."

"You'd never been along before?"

"No. Never."

"They say something like sixty witnesses have identified you and George and Leo in a whole slough of other robberies. Thirty-some?"

"I don't care what they say. These witnesses are only saying what the police tell them to. Do you think they had us stand in the show-up line? No. Hell, no. They'd haul their witnesses into the women's cell block and point at me and say, 'That's her, isn't it? The Tigress?' And I'll bet they've done the same kind of thing with George and Leo."

"That's not a point I'd care to argue. You're not saying that this was a spur of the moment thing for George, that he suddenly decided to become a stick-up artist on his way to a Cubs game? He didn't grow that gun."

She got out another smile: a bitter one. "No. I understand that now. I believe George and Leo have been at this a long time. George had been throwing a lot of money around and that's where it came from, obviously. They saw an opportunity with that old man alone in that shop, and they took it—putting me in this fix."

"You're not saying there's another 'Tigress' working with George and Leo?"

"Why not? And, anyway, I'm no 'Tigress,' and if there *is* a real female accomplice, she probably isn't, either."

I frowned at her. "You think George has another girl friend who goes out on robberies with him?"

"No. But Leo might."

"Is Leo married?"

"Yeah. Does that mean he can't have a girl friend?"

"If it did," I said, and grinned at her, "I'd be out of business."

"It's also possible," she said, "that George and Leo pulled some robberies, but on their own. *Without* a female accomplice, and we're taking the blame for some other bunch."

"You each have your own lawyers."

"Yeah. Our stories don't exactly jibe. Leo says he had no idea George was going to pull a robbery at that haberdashery. George says there wasn't any robbery."

"Then why did George have the gun?"

She held her hands up in surrender. "I think it was the old man's. Look, they don't exactly let me talk to George and Leo. You'll have to ask them, if you can....Well, Nate? Do you think you can help?"

"I'll give it a hundred bucks worth of college try," I said.

"Do you believe my version of what happened?"

"I don't exactly believe you. But I don't exactly disbelieve you, either. I'll keep an open mind. How's that?"

"That's the best I could hope for," she said, and offered me her hand to shake.

The handshake lingered and her gray eyes sent me the tiniest signal that her gratitude might be shown in ways beyond that hundred bucks.

Which is as close as my Tigress daydream came to playing out.

In the hallway of the First District Station, a new modern facility, I encountered an old-fashioned cop—Captain John Stege, who greeted me much as I'd expect: "What the hell are you doing here, Heller?"

Stege was a fiftyish fireplug with a round white face and round black-rimmed glasses. He was in shirtsleeves and a blue bow tie, which was about as casual as he ever got, a revolver on his hip.

"Fine, Captain," I said. "How are you?"

The owlish cop frowned at me. "Get your ass in my office."

I was an irritant to Stege because I confused him: when I'd been on the Detective Bureau, not so long ago, I'd ratted out some corrupt coppers, which he considered disloyal of me, and yet he was one of the most honest flatfeet on the force.

I sat across his desk from him. The office was as small and clean and compact as he was. He just looked at me, asking no question but clearly expecting an answer.

"I'm doing a job for Sam Backus," I said.

"Since when does the Public Defender's office have money to hire investigators?"

"Since never." I shrugged. "Maybe I'm doing it out of a sense of public duty."

His tiny eyes tightened behind the lenses. "Hell—not the *Tigress?* That's it, isn't it? You figure you can peddle your story to the papers!"

"I don't care what anybody says. You're a detective."

The door to the office was open. I was sitting there with my hat on. He told me to close the door and take off my hat. I did so. What was this about?

"I'm glad you're on it," Stege said.

"What?"

"Something smells about that case."

"Oh, you mean like taking witnesses down to the cell block and pointing to the suspect, in lieu of a line-up?"

He tasted his mouth and it obviously wasn't a pleasant flavor. "Something like that. This clean-up campaign, I never saw so many corners cut. If I can help you, let me know. I mean, keep it on the q.t.—but let me know."

"This is so sudden, Captain."

"Don't get cute. It's just that lately I feel like we're working for these yellow damn journalists—trying to make ourselves look good instead trying to do our jobs."

I sat forward. "They're taking this to trial right away. I could use some help."

"All right." Stege squinted at me meaningfully. "But don't ask to see the files—I won't go sneaking around on honest cops. Anyway, the papers told the story accurately enough, if you take out the 'Tigress' hooey."

"Do you think Dale and Minneci were part of this stick-up gang hitting small merchants on the West and Northwest Sides?"

"They could be. And so could that woman, for that matter. There's definitely been a rash of robberies where two men and a woman go in to a store, once they've established no other customers are around. They'd make a lot of noise, one of the men and the woman, too, yelling and threatening and even shoving, waving a gun and a blackjack around."

"That's not a stupid approach."

"You don't think sticking up innocent merchants is stupid, Heller?"

"Sure. My old man ran a bookshop on the West Side, remember? Anybody kills a shop owner for what's in his till, I'd like to take their tonsils out with a penknife. But by making a big commotion, intimidating their victim? It can make turn the whole thing into a big blur. Hard to get a good identification out of somebody who's been put through that. What was the woman's role?"

Stege shrugged. "Like I said, she was part of the show. Apparently she'd come in with a big handbag and the man would dip into it and that's where the gun came from. She was the one waving the blackjack around, and some victims claimed they'd been struck by it."

"They'd clean out the cash drawer?"

"Yeah, and sometimes help themselves to some merchandise. This woman, in clothing shops with female apparel, she'd pick herself out some pretty things and take 'em along."

"Women do love to shop."

Stege grimaced; helping me was hard on him. "I don't want you bothering the dicks on this case. They're good boys. I'm afraid all this pressure for arrests and publicity may have got the better of 'em, is all."

"I won't even talk to them," I said. "Who I want to talk to are the Tigress's little cubs—George Dale and Leo Minneci."

The little round-faced copper nodded and reached out his pudgy little fingers for the phone.

Within an hour I was sitting in another interrogation room, smaller but also with brick walls, barred windows and a scarred table. I might have still been at the First District Station, but I wasn't: this was the Cook County Jail on Dearborn, and a cell block guard was ushering in the first name on my dance card: George Dale.

Dale was tall, maybe six two, a good-looking guy with an athletic build; he had a certain Lothario look undercut by thinning brown hair. Dale was in a white shirt, open at the collar, and brown suit pants with dark shoes and white socks.

The guard deposited him across the table from me. Dale wasn't in handcuffs or leg irons or anything—just a big guy with a friendly face, unless you knew how to read the coldness of his dark eyes. And I did. I was glad I wasn't packing my nine millimeter, because this character could have made a reasonable go of taking it off me.

"What's the idea?" Dale asked. "Where's my lawyer? If I'm talking to another copper, I want my lawyer."

"My name's Heller, private operative. Working for your sweetheart's attorney."

He sat forward, some life coming into the hard eyes. "How is Eleanor? Is she doing all right?"

"She's sweating the hot seat like you are. I think I can help get her out of this, if you can confirm she wasn't an accomplice."

"She's innocent as a newborn baby!"

"Well, let's not get carried away, George...."

"Look, Heller, I'm no stick-up man. I'm a gambler. I make my money on dice and poker, you ask around. This is all just a terrible misunderstanding. An accident."

"An accident."

"Yeah. That old man was crazy! I wanted to buy some shirts, and I wanted 'em in quantity—said I'd buy half a dozen if he'd give me a decent discount. He said his price was firm and I tried to haggle and he just shook his head and gave me a nasty look. I had this box of shirts in my hands, and he yanked it away, and I yanked back, and he shoved me, and I shoved him back."

"Across the counter, this is?"

"Yeah!"

"He was seventy, wasn't he?"

"So they say, but he was a wild man! After I shoved him, he pulled the gun out from under the counter and came around and chased me, waving the thing. It was, you know, close quarters, and I tried to grab it away from him, and it went off and shot Leo through the hand. Then we ran out on the street—Eleanor was in back of the store and came running up behind us. The old fellow and me, we were struggling over the gun, and Eleanor was pounding him on the back, and he kind of tossed her off, like you'd toss off a kid that jumped you. Then the gun just... went off."

"Just went off. Twice."

"Well...yeah. I was scared. He was vicious."

"Okay, George. Maybe we should start over."

He shook his head. "Look, I didn't pull any stick-up. They found fourteen bucks in the cash drawer, you know."

"Right. But you had a roll of bills in your pocket adding up to three hundred bucks."

"That was *my* money! I don't deny I shot the old man. But it was an accidental type thing."

"George. Don't kid a kidder—you're a seasoned stick-up artist, and you stopped at that clothing store for a smash and grab."

He just sat there, the eyes going hard again. "I don't say I'm a saint. But Eleanor was never in on anything illegal I ever done, and these witnesses that say we were some kind of gang, the three of us, it's a goddamn lie. The cops are just looking to clear a bunch of robberies off their books, in one fell swoop."

"The three of us, you said. Where does Minneci figure in?"

"He was just along for the ride. I'm sorry he got his hand shot up."

"Going to the Cubs game."

"Right."

I didn't press. The story held water like a paper sack, but it was close enough to Eleanor's to make them both look credible. Of course, they'd known for several days that the cops were after them and had had time to get their stories straight before getting hauled in.

Leo Minneci was a dark, handsome guy, or anyway handsome if you didn't mind the cauliflower ears and the flattened nose. I never met him before, but I remembered him from his pug days—he'd been a pretty fair heavyweight, going up against Tuffy Griffiths and other headliners.

He wore a blue workshirt, sleeves rolled up, and blue jeans with his left hand bandaged. He had a confused expression, like a stranger had called to him from across the street.

Seated opposite me, he asked, "What's this about? You another cop?"

"I'm a private dick working for Eleanor Jarman's attorney. I'd like to get your version of what happened at that clothing shop."

He shrugged. "Listen, I'm one of them victims of circumstance you hear about."

"Really. I always wanted to meet one of those."

"This has nothing to do with me. It's Dale and that dame of his. I was just riding with them to a ball game. We was running a little early, and I said I could use a shirt and we stopped at that place. We were only in there a coupla minutes before Dale pulled a gun and stuck up the old guy. I tried to keep George from shooting the geezer and I, you know, wrestled with him, and the thing went off and..." He raised his bandaged mitt. "... got a bullet through the hand."

"Did Eleanor know anything about the stick-up?"

He shook his head. "I think it was, what you call it, spur of the moment on George's part. Look, I got a wife and two kids. I do all right with day labor, and I wouldn't risk putting them in a bad spot."

"What's your wife's name?"

"Why?"

"I'm just gathering information, Leo. Don't get jumpy."

"It's Tina. You want the address?"

I wrote that down.

I left the jail feeling better about my client. George Dale might or might not be a stick-up artist, and Leo Minneci might or might not be his accomplice; but their stories both put Eleanor Jarman on the sidelines.

I talked to half a dozen of the merchants on the witness list. Advertising that I was working for the Tigress would have turned them into clams, so I would just tell them I was a detective, and flash my little private investigator's badge, and that'd do the trick.

Mrs. Swan G. Swanson (no joke) was typical. She was the proprietor of a little gift shop across from the clothing store on West Division Street. This was a busy shopping area, the tree-tops of fashionable, sleepy Oak Park visible above the bustle of commerce and traffic on this late afternoon.

She was about sixty-five, five foot five in heels and maybe one-hundred-and-sixty pounds that still had some shape to them, well-served by a cotton dress with white polka dots on dark blue; with that pretty face highlighted by nice light blue eyes behind round wire-framed glasses, she was who you hoped your wife would turn out to be at that age.

"Detective Heller," she said, in a whispery soprano, "it was one of the most vicious things I ever saw."

"I know you've been over this several times, but I'm new on the case. Don't spare the details."

She nodded. "Two men came running out of the store. The first man was dark and he was holding onto his hand, which was bleeding, dripping all over the sidewalk. The other man was struggling with Mr. Hoeh, who ran after them. Mr. Hoeh was very brave, fighting hand to hand with a man holding a gun."

Very brave or very dumb.

"Then this wildcat of a woman, a blonde, came out and was swinging this blackjack around and was hitting Mr. Hoeh with it. Mr. Hoeh sort of stumbled and stopped fighting and the woman stepped to one side and the man with the gun shot Mr. Hoeh—twice! And then when Mr. Hoeh was on the side-walk, bleeding, dying, that vixen kicked him! Kicked him right in the face!"

"That is vicious. Tell me, when did you notice the blackjack?"

"Oh, uh...well, right away, I guess. When she started swinging it."

"I was just wondering if the detectives you spoke to earlier had mentioned that the Tigress sometimes used a blackjack. Did you notice the blackjack at the time? Or when they mentioned this to you, did you *remember* you'd seen it?"

She frowned. "Actually...I guess I just thought she was pounding on him. But on reflection, I was sure, pretty sure, she had a blackjack."

"What does a blackjack look like, anyway?"

The light blue eyes froze behind the lenses. "Uh...well, it's black, obviously. It's a sort of wrench, isn't it?"

When I grew tired of talking to these witnesses who'd been played like a kazoo by the Detective Bureau, I had a Coke and a grilled cheese at the drug store on the corner of Austin Boulevard and Division. Then I called the First District Station to see if that dedicated little public servant Captain Stege was still in his office.

He was, and I asked, "Was there anything in the reports about Hoeh having any facial injuries?"

"Just minor stuff, from the scuffle with Dale, I understand."

"Then nobody kicked him in the face?"

He grunted a laugh. "I saw that in the papers, some of the witnesses saying that. But, no, Heller, nobody kicked the old man. The two bullets were enough."

"Usually are. I read something about a cache of weapons being collected at the apartment where the dicks caught up with Dale and Eleanor. Was there a blackjack among the stuff?"

"No. Pretty good arsenal, though—four revolvers and a shotgun."

Dale had said he was no saint.

I went back to the office, not because I was as dedicated as Captain Stege, but owing to the fact that I lived there, with the Murphy bed to prove it. There was a Depression going on, as you may have heard, and I had an arrangement with the building's owner to keep an eye on things at night in exchange for rent.

That evening I needed to get over to the Century of Progress, where I was doing some security work—without the World's Fair, my summer would have been a bust—and I was just getting ready to go when a knock rattled the pebbled glass of my door.

"Come in," I said, wondering what I'd done to deserve two clients in one day, but it wasn't that at all.

For a moment I thought Leo Minneci had escaped and come around, because this was a dark young man who resembled Minneci strongly. On a closer inspection, he was smaller and younger than Leo, without the flattened nose, and better dressed—white short-sleeved shirt, red tie, white summer slacks and white bluchers—also a boater-style straw hat, which was in his right hand.

"I'm Tony Minneci," he said. "Leo's brother. I have something for you, Mr. Heller."

I gestured to the client's chair and he came over and filled it.

"This may seem a little strange," he said. "I'm not here because of my brother."

"Oh?"

"I'm kind of mad at Leo. He got me in trouble."

Then I remembered—the car used in the robbery, whose license number had been reported by three or four witnesses, turned out to belong to Tony here, a University of Illinois student working as a grocery clerk for a summer job.

"Leo asked to borrow my car that day," his young doppelganger said, "but I said no. Then he took it, anyway."

"Did you know Leo was doing stick-ups? Is that why you didn't want him using your wheels?"

He shook his head. "I didn't know anything about that. It's just my car, is all. Let him get his own car." He got into his pocket and fished out some bills—twenties. He put five of them on my desk. That was a lot of cabbage for a college-kid grocery clerk to haul around. A well-dressed college-kid grocery clerk.

He smiled shyly. "That's to cover what you're doing for Eleanor."

"You're Leo's brother, but you're running an errand for Eleanor? Why?"

"She's a nice girl. She's innocent in all this. We were friendly."

"You and Eleanor?"

"No, all of us, Eleanor and George and Leo."

"This is the same Leo? Let-him-get-his-own-car Leo?"

He shrugged. "I get along fine with my brother. We don't agree on everything under the sun, but—"

"What don't you agree with? Him sticking up stores?"

"Look, Mr. Heller, my brother may not be perfect, but he does his best to keep that wife of his happy. If he did do something he shouldn't have, you can blame her for it."

"Why?"

"Because she's a nag, that's why. You should go talk to her. See for yourself. If you ask me...nothing."

"Make your point, Tony."

"They got two kids now, Mr. Heller, but she was a wild one, Tina. She got my brother in all kinds of scrapes, and then she trapped him, far as I'm concerned."

"How?"

"Back when he was boxing and making good money, she got pregnant on purpose to bag him. If I was on this case? I'd see what her alibi was, the day of that robbery, and all those other robberies."

"Does your sister-in-law know you feel this way?"

"No." He shrugged again. "I'm nice to her. Leo asked me to keep an eye on her, and the two kiddies, make sure they're okay. I'm on my way there now, as it happens."

"Really?"

"Yeah, she's broke. I'm gonna give her some grocery money."

"You are a nice guy, Tony. Why don't we go over there together?"

He frowned. "Why would you want to do that?"

"She's on my list to talk to. Maybe you could pave the way for me, a little."

"Well...okay. I don't see why not. You'll see, I don't let it show, how I feel—my only interest is in those two little kids. My nephews."

"Sure. You have a car?"

"Yeah." He got to his feet and put the straw hat on. "You want a ride, Mr. Heller?"

"No, I have the address. I'll meet you over there."

The Minneci apartment was four handsomely furnished rooms over a florist shop on the corner of Madison and Homan. These were fairly nice digs, suggesting hubby Leo had been doing all right for his little family before the cops took him away.

Tony Minneci introduced me as a private detective trying to help clear Leo. Tina Minneci—tall, dark-haired, dark-eyed, slender—immediately warmed to me, and seemed genuinely bewildered that anyone could ever think her gentle, loving husband could have robbed or hurt anybody. (It would have been impolite to point out that gentle, loving Leo used to bash other guys' brains out for a living.) She wore about a buck's worth of cotton house dress, blue plaid with a ruffled collar, nicely feminine, and her narrow face would have been pretty with a little make-up and a good night's sleep.

She sat us down at a round wooden table in the kitchen; a highchair was shoved to one side. She had a pot of coffee going as well as a bottle of milk in a saucepan on the stove.

We all had coffee while we sat and talked—quietly, because she had just put baby Jimmy down for the night.

"He's a good boy," she said, almost whispering, "unless something wakes him—then look out!"

I said, "You have another child, don't you?"

"Yes—Leo, Jr. He's six. He's been with his grandparents since...since Leo, Sr., went away. They have a nice flat on the West Side—Daddy has a little restaurant over there, and does pretty well."

"I see."

"Little Jimmy and I may be joining Leo, Jr. I may have to move back in with my folks—my rent here is due in a week and I'm flat broke."

I nodded toward the living room. "You have a pretty nice place here. This isn't exactly a Hooverville."

"I know, but we didn't have any money stashed away in the bank or under a pillow, either. Leo's always been a good provider. He made a really decent living as a fighter, and when that dwindled, he always brought enough in to keep us comfortable."

"Where did he work?"

"No one place, but he always had something going. He did day labor, sometimes he helped out at the gym where he used to train."

I kept my tone easy. "You don't think that money could've come from...somewhere else?"

Her eyes flared. "Mr. Heller, my husband is an honest man. He got in with a bad crowd, is all. I always thought George Dale was a slickster."

"What about Eleanor Jarman?"

Mrs. Minneci gave up a benefit-of-the-doubt shrug. "She always seemed all right. She has two little ones of her own to look after, you know."

Tony sat forward; his straw boater was on the table next to his coffee cup like an upturned soup bowl. "Listen, I got some grocery money for you, Tina. Five bucks I squeezed out of my clerk job. If I go over there with you, I can get the employee discount."

Mrs. Minneci turned her dark eyes on me and explained: "The little grocery store where Tony works part-time is just a block from here....You're a sweetheart, Tony, but I can't leave Jimmy here alone, and I'm not about to wake him."

"I can babysit," I said, "if you're not gone too long."

She beamed at me, then frowned with parental concern. "What would a nice young man like you know about taking care of a baby?"

"This nice young man used to go out with a nice divorcee with three kids, two in diapers. I know all about changing 'em, and I wield a mean milk bottle, too."

Mrs. Minneci glanced at her brother-in-law, who shrugged and said, "Mr. Heller's reliable. No worries. We can be over there and back in fifteen, twenty minutes."

A small discussion ("Do you mind? Are you sure?") followed, but finally dutiful Tony took the sister-in-law he claimed to despise—although I'd seen no sign of that—out the door and into the hall and down the stairs.

The tricky part was that slumbering kid. Jimmy was in a crib in the bedroom where I needed to poke around. So I did my quietest, most careful work, and I'd like to say I was able to pull off the find because I was a real professional, but a blind man could have pawed around and come up with the stuff.

Under the bed, in a trio of clothing boxes, were lovely fashions, long-sleeved wool and rabbit's hair numbers, stylish with Ascot ties and metal buttons and all the most fashionable current touches. Stege had said the Blonde Tigress had helped herself to pretty things on the robberies, and these brand-new, never worn dresses certainly qualified.

Most damning were two items dropped on top of the final box I opened, nestled on a long-sleeved rayon satin two-color frock with a bow at the neck: a blonde wig and a blackjack.

Some things never go out of style.

I thought about laying all this stuff out on the kitchen table, like a meal; but instead I just put the caboodle away and went out and helped myself to another cup of coffee. Something about the set-up made me think maybe I should have taken that bottle of warm milk out of that pan instead.

They returned in just over twenty minutes, with their arms full of grocery sacks and Tina Minneci all smiles. She was saying, "I think I'll have the folks send Leo, Jr., home for a few days. We can eat like a proper family again. How can I thank you, Tony?"

Tony was all smiles, too, but his eyes kept flicking toward me expectantly. I pitched in with my hostess and her brother-in-law and helped unload the groceries sacks and turned the cupboard shelves from empty to full.

Leaning back against the kitchen counter, looking happy and with a hint of how lovely she really could be, Tina Minneci said, "Any trouble with Jimmy?"

"No," I said. "Slept like a baby."

That made her laugh. "Shall we sit down, and I'll try to answer the rest of your questions?"

"I don't have any more questions, thanks. You've been very gracious, Mrs. Minneci. Tony, isn't it time we were going?"

Tony nodded and we made our goodbyes and we started down the steps and I waited until we were two-thirds of the way before I tripped him and sent him rattling down those stairs in a pile of arms and legs until he knocked up against the closed door.

I stood over him in the little entryway and he gazed up at me, astounded. "What the hell did you do that for?"

"That's the clumsiest frame I ever saw."

He got to his feet, brushing off his white pants. He picked up his boater, which had cracked. "You busted my hat!"

"I should bust more."

His chin stuck out at me. "Listen, my brother is a boxer. He's taught me a thing or two. I can take a punch."

"Can you take a slap?" I asked, and slapped him four times, twice per cheek, ringing like gunshots in the stairwell.

Then I grabbed him by the shirt front and slammed him into some little wall-mounted mailboxes, which probably hurt. He was crying.

"I've seen low," I said. "But framing your own sister-in-law.... Did Eleanor put you up to it?"

"I'm not talking to you!"

"Question is, am I talking to the cops?"

"You work for us!"

"Shut-up." I shook my head. "Get the hell out of here. You make me sick."

He and his busted boater scooted out. Under normal circumstances, he might have been able to give me worse than I'd just dished out to him. But I had righteous indignation on my side, which I admit was something new.

The next morning, Eleanor Jarman and I sat in the same interrogation room as before. Her arms were folded, her eyes cold, her mouth a wide tight line, straight as a ruler's edge.

My arms were folded, too, but I was smiling. "Here's the deal. I keep the hundred. I intend to send thirty bucks of it to Minneci's wife, to help out on her rent. But I keep the rest— you're getting off cheap, because if I sold what I know to the papers, you'd really be sunk."

I had just filled her in on a bunch of stuff, including that I knew Leo's brother was part of their little gang, possibly fencing boodle, certainly providing the car.

She gave me a gray-eyed glare. "I ask my lawyer for the shiftiest private eye around, and *you're* what he comes up with? A goody two-shoes?"

"This isn't about right or wrong. This is about me not being stupid. Scratch that—it's about me not liking being taken for stupid. You and George and Leo have been knocking over little shops since, when? April, May?"

She just shrugged.

"The clothes I found under Mrs. Minneci's bed were strictly fall and winter items."

Her eyebrows went up. "If I wanted to frame her, and had a bunch of stolen summer frocks of my own, why didn't I just have that dope Tony stick some of *those* under that bitch's bed?"

"Because you girls don't wear the same size. She's tall and skinny, you're short and curvy. You had to frame her with clothing that would fit her—and that dope Tony, as you accurately put it, went out and bought new things...fall and winter items that just hit the stores."

"You said you found a blonde wig and a blackjack."

"Yeah. The wig was new, but the blackjack wasn't. You really did go around terrorizing small merchants with that thing, didn't you?"

She sighed and her face softened. She unfolded her arms and put her hands on the scarred table and leaned forward. "Listen, Heller—dumbbell Tina wouldn't've served any time. That was just to muddy the waters and help get me off—when the cops looked into it, she'd probably have alibis for some of those robberies, maybe including the Hoeh thing."

"Probably. Maybe."

"And as for waving around that blackjack? That was just theater. I never slugged anybody, I never kicked anybody. These are hard times, as you may have noticed, and these hands..." She held them up; they were cracked and almost arthritic-looking, fifty-year-old hands on a woman not thirty. "...these hands had done all the laundry they could take."

"But the cops wanted to make themselves look good, and the papers went along, turning you into a Tigress."

She smiled. "Hey, fella, I *was* a tigress, but that was part of the show. Scare 'em, rattle 'em, and get them to give up their money. And we lived pretty darn good these last few months."

"Until Gustav Hoeh didn't cooperate."

Her smile faded. "I hate that. You can believe me or not believe me, I don't give a damn. But the truth is, I never wanted anybody hurt. This was just about some fast, easy cash."

"That gun you hauled around in your bag for George—you never thought he'd use it?"

"No. He's a coward at heart."

"Hell, Eleanor. Don't you know? That's who *uses* guns."

Some of the details I never got. I was only on the case for two days, so I never found out exactly what hold Eleanor Jarman had over Tony Minneci, and I have no idea what became of Tina and her two boys after I sent the thirty-bucks rent money.

On the witness stand, Eleanor wore a pretty blue frock (where had she picked that up, I wondered?) and told her sad tale of being an orphan and waiting tables and doing laundry. She denied knowing that Hoeh's store was going to be robbed, while Dale had changed his story to put the blame on Minneci, who told a similar story with Dale cast as the heavy. Assistant State's Attorney Crowley went after the death sentence for all three, but only George Dale got the chair; his last act, in April of 1934, was to write Eleanor a love letter.

As for Eleanor, she and Leo each got 199 years, a sentence designed to beat any reasonable chance of parole—and the longest stretch ever assigned a woman in Illinois.

That should be the end of the story, but the Blonde Tigress had other ideas. For seven years Eleanor served her time at Joliet as (to quote the warden) "an industrious, obedient, and model prisoner in every respect." Then, on the morning of August 8, 1940, she wore a guard's dress stolen from a locker and used a rope fashioned from sheets to go over the ten-foot wall.

Supposedly she had heard her youngest son had threatened to run away from home. The story goes that Eleanor Jarman returned to Sioux City, spent some time with her two boys, and then disappeared, not turning up till she met with family members briefly in 1975 before vanishing again.

No one, except perhaps her blood relatives, knows how Eleanor spent the rest of her life or where. My take on it was that she was neither the Tigress of the press nor the victim she pretended to be. And maybe seven years was enough time for her to serve, though numerous attempts by her family to get her pardoned went nowhere.

Anyway, the part I liked best was how she got out of prison. By stealing a dress.

AUTHOR'S NOTE

While Nathan Heller is a fictional character, this story is based on a real case—names have not been changed, and the events are fundamentally true; source material included an article by John J. McPhaul and information provided by my research associate, George Hagenauer, who I thank for his insights and suggestions on this story and all the others in this collection.

PRIVATE CONSULTATION

I grabbed the Lake Street El and got off at Garfield Park; it was a short walk from there to the "Death Clinic" at 3406 West Monroe Street. That's what the papers, some of them anyway, were calling the Wynekoop mansion. To me it was just another big old stone building on the West Side, one of many, though of a burnt-reddish stone rather than typical Chicago gray. And, I'll grant you, the three-story structure was planted on a wealthier residential stretch than the one I'd grown up on, twelve blocks south.

Still, this was the West Side, and more or less my old stamping grounds, and that was no doubt part of why I'd been asked to drop by the Wynekoop place this sunny Saturday afternoon. The family had most likely asked around, heard about the ex-cop from nearby Douglas Park who now had a little private agency in the Loop.

And my reputation on the West Side—and in the Loop—was of being just honest enough, and just crooked enough, to get most jobs done.

But part of why I'd been called, I would guess, was Earle Wynekoop himself. I knew Earle a little, from a distance. We'd both worked at the World's Fair down on the lakefront last summer and fall. I was working pickpocket duty, and Earle was in the front office, doing whatever front-office people do. We were both about the same age—I was twenty-seven—but he seemed like a kid to me.

Earle mostly chased skirts, except at the Streets of Paris exhibition, where the girls didn't wear skirts. Tall, handsome, wavy-haired Earle, with his white teeth and pencil-line mustache, had pursued the fan dancers with the eagerness of a plucked bird trying to get its feathers back. Funny thing was, nobody—including me—knew Earle was a married man, till November, when the papers were full of his wife. His wife's murder, that is.

Now it was a sunny, almost-warm afternoon in December, and I had been in business just under a year. And like most small businessmen, I'd had less than a prosperous 1933. A retainer from a family with the Wynekoop's dough would be a nice way to ring out the old and ring in the new.

Right now, I was ringing the doorbell. I was up at the top of the first-floor landing; Dr. Alice Wynekoop's office was in an English basement below. I was expecting a maid or butler to answer, considering the size of this place. But Earle is what I got.

His white smile flickered nervously. He adjusted his bowtie with one hand and offered the other for me to shake, which I did. His grip was weak and moist, like his dark eyes.

"Mr. Heller," he said. "Thank you for stopping by."

"My pleasure," I said, stepping into the vestibule, hat in hand.

Earle, snappily dressed in a pinstripe worsted, took my topcoat and hung it on a hall tree.

"Perhaps you don't remember me," he said. "I worked in the front office at the fair this summer."

"Sure I remember you, Mr. Wynekoop."

"Why don't you call me 'Earle.'"

"Fine, Earle," I said. "And my friends call me 'Nate.'"

He grinned nervously and said, "Step into the library, Nate, if you would."

"Is your mother here?"

"No. She's in jail."

"Why haven't you sprung her?" Surely these folks could afford to make bail. On the phone, Earle had quickly agreed to my rate of fifteen bucks a day and one-hundred-dollar non-refundable retainer. And that was the top of my sliding scale.

An eyebrow arched in disgust on a high, unwrinkled brow. "Mother is ill, thanks to these barbarians. We've decided to let the state pay for her illness, considering they've provoked it."

He tried to sound indignant through all that, but petulance was the result.

The interior of the house was on the gloomy side: a lot of dark, expensive, well-wrought woodwork, and heavy, plush furnishings that dated back to the turn of the century, when the house was built. There were hints that the Wynekoops might not be as well fixed as the rest of us thought: ornate antiquated light fixtures, worn Oriental carpets and a layer of dust indicated yesterday's wealth, not today's.

I sat on a dark horsehair couch; two of the walls were bookcases, filled with leather-bound volumes, and the others were hung with somber landscapes. The first thing Earle did was give me an envelope with one hundred dollars in tens in it. Now Earle was getting himself some sherry off a liquor cart.

"Can I get you something?" Earle asked. His hands were shaking as he poured himself the sherry.

"This will do nicely," I said, counting the money.

"Don't be a wet blanket, Nate."

I put the money-clipped bills away. "Rum, then. No ice."

He gave me a glass and sat beside me. I'd have rather he sat across from me; it was awkward, looking sideways at him. But he seemed to crave the intimacy.

"Mother's not guilty, you know."

"Really."

"I confessed, but they didn't believe me. I confessed five times."

"Cops figured you were trying to clear your mama."

"Yes. I'm afraid so. I rather botched it, as a liar."

It was good rum. "Then you didn't kill your wife?"

"Kill Rheta! Don't be silly. I loved her, once. Just because our marriage had gone...well, anyway, I didn't do it, and Mother didn't do it, either."

"Who did, then?"

He smirked humorlessly. "I think some moron did it. Some fool looking for narcotics and money. That's why I called you, Nate. The police aren't looking for the killer. They think they have their man in Mother."

"What does your mother's attorney think?"

"He thinks hiring an investigator is a splendid idea."

"Doesn't he have his own man?"

"Yes, but I wanted you. I remembered you from the fair... and, I asked around."

What did I tell you? Am I detective?

"I can't promise I can clear her," I said. "She confessed, after all—and the cops took her one confession more seriously than your five."

"They gave her the third-degree. A sixty-three-year-old woman! Respected in the community! Can you imagine?"

"Who was the cop in charge?"

Earle pursed his lips in disgust. "Captain Stege himself, the bastard."

"Is this *his* case? Damn."

"Yes, it's Stege's case. Didn't you read about all this in the papers?"

"Sure I did. But I didn't read it like I thought I was going to be involved. I probably did read Stege was in charge, but when you called this morning, I didn't recall..."

"Why, Nate? Is this a problem?"

"No," I lied.

I let it go at that, as I needed the work, but the truth was, Stege hated my guts. I'd testified against a couple of cops, which Stege—even though he was honest and those two cops were bent even by Chicago standards—took as a betrayal of the police brotherhood.

Earle was up pouring himself another sherry. Already. "Mother is a sensitive, frail woman, with a heart condition, and she was ruthlessly, mercilessly questioned for a period of over twenty-four hours."

"I see."

"I'm afraid..." And Earle sipped his sherry greedily. Swallowed. Continued: "I'm afraid I may have made the situation even worse."

"How?"

He sat again, sighed, shrugged. "As you probably know, I was out of town when Rheta was...slain."

That was an odd choice of words; "slain" was something nobody said, a word in the newspapers, not real life.

"I went straight to the Fillmore police station, when I returned from Kansas City. I had a moment with Mother. I said..." He slumped, shook his head.

"Go on, Earle."

"I said...God help me, I said, 'For God's sake mother, if you did this on account of me, go ahead and confess.'" He touched his fingertips to his eyes.

"What did she say to you?"

"She...she said, 'Earle, I did not kill Rheta.' But then she went in for another round with Captain Stege, and..."

"And made that cockamamie confession she later retracted."

"Yes."

"Why did you think your mother might have killed your wife for you, Earle?"

"Because...because Mother loves me very much."

Dr. Alice Lindsay Wynekoop had been one of Chicago's most esteemed female physicians for almost four decades. She had met her late husband Frank in medical college, and with him continued the Wynekoop tradition of care for the ill and disabled. Her charity work in hospitals and clinics was well-known; a prominent clubwoman, humanitarian, a leader in the woman's suffrage movement, Dr. Wynekoop was an unlikely candidate for a murder charge.

But she had indeed been charged: with the murder of her daughter-in-law, in the basement consultation office in this very house.

Earle led me there, down a narrow stairway off the dining room. In the central basement hallway were two facing doors: Dr. Wynekoop's office, at left; and at right, an examination room. The door was open. Earle motioned for me to go in, which I did, but he stayed in the doorway.

The room was narrow and wide and cold; the steam heat was off. The dominant fixture was an old-fashioned, brown-leather-covered examination table. A chair under a large stained-glass window, whose ledge was lined with medical books, sat next to a weigh-and-measure scale. In one corner was a medicine and instrument cabinet.

"The police wouldn't let us clean up properly," Earle said.

The leather exam table was blood-stained.

"They said they might take the whole damn table in," Earle said. "And use it in court, for evidence."

I nodded. "What about your mother's office? She claimed burglary."

"Well, yes...some drugs were taken from the cabinet, in here. And six dollars from a drawer..."

He led me across the hall to an orderly office area with a big rolltop desk, which he pointed to.

"And," Earle said, pulling open a middle drawer, "there was the gun, of course. Taken from here."

"The cops found it across the hall, though. By the body."

"Yes," Earle said, quietly.

"Tell me about her, Earle."

"Mother?"

"Rheta."

"She...she was a lovely girl. A beautiful redhead. Gifted musician...violinist. But she was...sick."

"Sick how?"

He tapped his head. "She was a hypochondriac. Imagining she had this disease, and that one. Her mother died of tuberculosis...in an insane asylum, no less. Rheta came to imagine she had t.b., like her mother. What they did have in common, I'm afraid, was being mentally deranged."

"You said you loved her, Earle."

"I did. Once. The marriage was a failure. I...I had to seek affection elsewhere." A wicked smile flickered under the pencil mustache. "I've never had trouble finding women, Nate. I have a little black book with fifty girl friends in it."

It occurred to me that a real man could get by on a considerably shorter list; but I keep opinions like that to myself, when given a hundred-buck retainer.

"What did the little woman think about all these girl friends? A crowd like that is hard to hide."

He shrugged. "We never talked about it."

"No talk of a divorce?"

He licked his lips, avoided my eyes. "I wanted one, Nate. She wouldn't give it to me. A good Catholic girl." Four of the most frightening words in the English language, to any healthy male anyway.

"The two of you lived here, with your mother?"

"Yes...I can't really afford to live elsewhere. Times are hard, you know."

"So I hear. Who else lives here? Isn't there a roomer?"

"Yes. Miss Shaunesey. She's a high school teacher."

"Is she here now?"

"Yes. I asked if she'd talk to you, and she is more than willing. Anything to help Mother."

Back in the library, I sat and spoke with Miss Enid Shaunesey, a prim, slim woman of about fifty. Earle lurked in the background, helping himself to more sherry.

"What happened that day, Miss Shaunesey?"

November 21, 1933.

"I probably arose at about a quarter to seven," she said, with a little shrug, adjusting her wire-frame glasses. "I had breakfast in the house with Dr. Alice. I don't remember whether Rheta had breakfast with us or not...I don't really remember speaking to Rheta at all that morning."

"Then you went on to school?"

"Yes," I said. "I teach at Marshall High. I completed my teaching duties and signed out about three fifteen. I went to the Loop and shopped until a little after five and went home."

"What, at about six?"

"Or a little after. When I came home, Dr. Alice was in the kitchen, preparing dinner. She fried up some pork chops. Made a nice salad, cabbage, potatoes, peaches. It was just the two of us. We're good friends."

"Earle was out of town, of course, but what about Rheta?"

"She was supposed to dine with us, but she was late. We went ahead without her. I didn't think much of it. The girl had a mind of her own; she frequently went here and there—music lessons, shopping." There was a faint note of disapproval, though the conduct she was describing mirrored her own after-school activities of that same day.

"Did Dr. Wynekoop seem to get along with Rheta?"

"They had their tiffs, but Dr. Alice loved the girl. She was family. That evening, during dinner, she spoke of Rheta, in fact."

"What did she say?"

"She was worried about the girl."

"Because she hadn't shown up for supper?"

"Yes, and after the meal she telephoned a neighbor or two, to see if they'd seen Rheta. But she also expressed a more general concern—Rheta was fretting about her health, you see. As I said, Rheta frequently stayed out. We knew she'd probably gone into the Loop to shop and, as she often did, she probably went to a motion picture. That was what we thought."

"I see."

Miss Shaunesey sat up, her expression suddenly thoughtful. "Of course, I'd noticed Rheta's coat and hat on the table

70

here in the library, but Dr. Alice said that she'd probably worn her good coat and hat to the Loop. Anyway, after dinner we talked, and then I went to the drug store for Dr. Alice, to have a prescription refilled."

"When did you get back?"

"Well, you see, the drug store is situated at Madison and Kedzie. That store did not have as many tablets as Dr. Alice wanted, so I walked to the drug store at Homan and Madison and got a full bottle."

"So it took a while," I said, trying not to get irritated with her fussy old-maid-school-teacher thoroughness. It beat the hell out of an uncooperative, unobservant witness, though. I guessed.

"I was home by half past seven, I should judge. Then we sat down in the library and talked for about an hour. We discussed two books—*Strange Interlude* was one and the other was *The Forsyte Saga.*"

"Did Dr. Wynekoop seem relaxed, or was she in any way preoccupied?"

"The former," Miss Shaunesey said with certainty. "Any concern about Rheta's absence was strictly routine."

"At what point did Dr. Wynekoop go downstairs to her consultation room?"

"Well, I was complaining of my hyperacidity. Dr. Alice said she had something in her office that she thought I could use for that. It was in a glass case in her consulting room. Of course, she never got that medicine for me."

Dr. Wynekoop had been interrupted in her errand by the discovery of the body of her daughter-in-law Rheta. The corpse was face down on the examination table, head on a white pillow. Naked, the body was wrapped in a sheet and a blanket, snugged in around the feet and pulled up over the shoulders, like a child lovingly tucked into bed. Rheta had been shot, once, in the back. Her lips were scorched as if by acid. A wet towel was under her mouth, indicating perhaps that chloroform had been administered. A half-empty bottle of chloroform was found on the washstand. And a gauze-wrapped .32 Smith and Wesson rested on the pillow above the girl's head.

"Dr. Wynekoop did not call the police?" I asked, knowing the answer. This much I remembered from the papers.

"No."

"Or an undertaker, or the coroner's office?"

"No. She called her daughter, Catherine."

Earle looked up from his sherry long enough to interject: "Catherine is a doctor, too. She's a resident at the Children's Department at Cook County Hospital."

And that was my logical first stop. I took the El over to the hospital, a block-square graystone at Harrison and Ogden; this job was strictly a West Side affair.

Dr. Catherine Wynekoop was a beautiful woman. Her dark hair was pulled back from her pale, pretty face; in her doctor's whites, she sat in the hospital cafeteria stirring her coffee as we spoke.

"I was on duty here when Mother called," she said. "She said, 'Something terrible has happened at home...it's Rheta... she's dead...she has been shot.'"

"How did she sound? Hysterical? Calm?"

"Calm, but a shocked sort of calm." She sighed. "I went home immediately. Mother seemed all right, but I noticed her gait was a little unsteady. Her hands were trembling, her face was flushed. I helped her to a chair in the dining room and rushed out in the kitchen for stimuli. I put a teaspoonful of aromatic spirits of ammonia in water and had her drink it."

"She hadn't called anyone but you, as yet?"

"No. She said she'd just groped her way up the stairs, that on the way everything went black, she felt dizzy, that the next thing she knew she was at the telephone calling me."

"Did you take charge, then?"

A half-smile twitched at her cheek. "I guess I did. I called Mr. Ahearn."

"Mr. Ahearn?"

"The undertaker. And I called Dr. Berger, our family physician."

"You really should have called the coroner."

"Mother later said that she'd asked me to, on the phone, but I didn't hear that or understand her or something. We were upset. Once Dr. Berger and Mr. Ahearn arrived, the coroner's office was called."

She kept stirring her coffee, staring into it.

"How did you and Rheta get along?"

She lifted her eyebrows in a shrug. "We weren't close. We had little in common. But there was no animosity."

She seemed goddamn guarded to me; I decided to try and knock her wall down, or at least jar some stones loose.

I said: "Do you think your mother killed Rheta?"

Her dark eyes rose to mine and flashed. "Of course not. I never heard my mother speak an unkind word to or about Rheta." She searched her mind for an example, and came up with one: "Why—whenever Mother bought me a dress, she bought one for Rheta, also."

She returned her gaze to the coffee, which she stirred methodically.

Then she continued: "She was worried about Rheta, actually. Worried about the way Earle was treating her. Worried about all

73

the...well, about the crowd he started to run around with down at the World's Fair. Mother asked me to talk to him about it."

"About what, exactly?"

"His conduct."

"You mean, his girl friends."

She looked at me sharply. "Mr. Heller, my understanding is that you are in our family's employ. Some of these questions of yours seem uncalled for."

I gave her my most charming smile. "Miss Wynekoop... doctor...I'm like you. Sometimes I have to ask unpleasant questions, if I'm going to make the proper diagnosis."

She considered that a moment, then smiled. It was a honey of a smile, making mine look like the shabby sham it was.

"I understand, Mr. Heller." She rose. She'd never touched the coffee once. "I'm afraid I have afternoon rounds to make."

She extended her hand; it was delicate, but her grasp had strength, and she had dignity. Hard to believe she was Earle's sister.

I had my own rounds to make, and at a different hospital; it took a couple of streetcars to do the job. The County Jail was a grim, low-slung graystone lurking behind the Criminal Courts Building. This complex of city buildings was just south of a West Side residential area, just eight blocks south of Douglas Park. Old home week for me.

Alice Wynekoop was sitting up in bed, reading a medical journal, when I was led to her by a matron. She was in the corner and had much of the ward to herself; the beds on either side were empty.

She was of average size, but frail-looking; she appeared much older than her sixty-three years, her flesh freckled with liver spots, her neck creped. The skin of her face had a wilted look, dark patches under the eyes, saggy jowls.

But her eyes were dark and sharp. And her mouth was a stern line.

"Are you a policeman?" she asked. Her tone was neutral.

I had my hat in hand. "I'm Nathan Heller," I said. "I'm the private investigator your son hired."

She smiled in a business-like way, extended her hand for me to shake, which I did. Surprisingly strong for such a weak-looking woman.

"Pull up a chair, Mr. Heller," she said. Her voice was clear and crisp. Someone very different than the woman she outwardly appeared to be lived inside that worn-out body.

I sat. "I'm going to be asking around about some things... inquire about burglaries in your neighborhood and such."

She nodded, twice, very business-like. "I'm certain the thief was after narcotics. In fact, some narcotics were taken, but I keep precious few in my surgery."

"Yes. I see. What about the gun?"

"It was my husband's. We've had it for years. I've never fired it in my life."

I took out my small spiral notebook. "I know you're weary of telling it, but I need to hear your story. Before I go poking around the edges of this case, I need to understand the center of it."

She nodded and smiled. "What would you like to know, exactly?"

"When did you last see your daughter-in-law?"

"About three p.m. that Tuesday. She said she was going for a walk with Mrs. Donovan..."

"Who?"

"A neighbor of ours who was a good friend to the child. Verna Donovan. She's a divorcee; they were quite close."

I wrote the name down. "Go on."

"Anyway, Rheta said something about going for a walk with Mrs. Donovan. She also said she might go downtown and get some sheet music. I urged her to go out in the air, as it was a fine day, and gave her money for the music. After she left, I went for a walk myself, through the neighborhood. It was an usually beautiful day for November, pleasantly warm."

"How long were you gone?"

"I returned at about four forty-five p.m. I came in the front door. Miss Shaunesey arrived from school about six o'clock. I wasn't worried then about Rheta's absence, because I expected her along at any minute. I prepared dinner for the three of us— Miss Shaunesey, Rheta and myself—and set the table. Finally, Miss Shaunesey and I sat down to eat...both wondering where Rheta was, but again, not terribly worried."

"It wasn't unusual for her to stay out without calling to say she'd miss supper?"

"Not in the least. She was quiet, but rather...self-absorbed. If she walked by a motion-picture marquee that caught her eye, she might just wander on in, without a thought about anyone who might be waiting for her."

"She sounds inconsiderate."

Alice Wynekoop smiled tightly, revealing a strained patience. "She was a strange, quiet girl. Rather moody, I'm afraid. She had definite feelings of inferiority, particularly in regards to my daughter, Catherine, who is after all a physician. But I digress. At about a quarter to seven, I telephoned Mrs. Donovan and asked her if she had been with Rheta. She said she hadn't seen her since three o'clock, but urged me not to worry."

"Were you worried?"

"Not terribly. At any rate, at about seven o'clock I asked Miss Shaunesey to go and get a prescription filled for me. She left the house and I remained there. She returned about an hour later and was surprised that Rheta had not yet returned. At this point, I admit I was getting worried about the girl."

"Tell me about finding the body."

She nodded, her eyes fixed. "Miss Shaunesey and I sat and talked in the library. Then about eight thirty she asked me to get her some medicine for an upset stomach. I went downstairs to the examination room to get the medicine from the cabinet." She placed a finger against one cheek, thoughtfully. "I recall now that I thought it odd to find the door of the examination room closed, as it was usually kept open. I turned the knob and slipped my hand inside to find the electric switch."

"And you found her."

She shuddered, but it seemed a gesture, not an involuntary response. "It is impossible for me to describe my feelings when I saw Rheta lying there under that flood of light! I felt as if I were somewhere else. I cannot find words to express my feelings."

"What did you do?"

"Well, I knew something had to be done at once, and I called my daughter, Catherine, at the county hospital. I told her Rheta was dead. She was terribly shocked, of course. I...I thought I had asked Catherine to notify the coroner and to hurry right over. It seemed ages till she got there. When she did arrive, I had her call Dr. Berger and Mr. Ahearn. It wasn't until some time after they arrived that I realized Catherine had not called the coroner as I thought I'd instructed her. Mr. Ahearn then called the authorities."

I nodded. "All right. You're doing fine, doctor. Now tell me about your son and his wife."

"What do you mean?"

"It wasn't a happy union, was it."

Her smile was a sad crease in her wrinkled face. "At one time it was. Earle went with me to a medical convention in Indianapolis in...must have been '29. Rheta played the violin as part of the entertainment, there. They began to correspond. A year later they were wed."

"And came to live with you."

"Earle didn't have a job—you know, he's taken up photography of late, and has had several assignments, I'm really very proud—and, well...anyway. The girl was barely nineteen, when they married. I redecorated and refurnished a suite of rooms on the second floor for my newlyweds. She was a lovely child, beautiful red hair, and of course, Earle...he's as handsome a boy as ever walked this earth."

"But Rheta was moody...?"

"Very much so. And obsessed with her health. Perhaps that's why she married into the Wynekoop family. She was fearful of tuberculosis, but there were no indications of it at all. In the last month of her life, she was rather melancholy, of a somewhat morbid disposition. I discussed with her about going out into the open and taking exercise. We discussed that often."

"You did not kill your daughter-in-law."

"No! Mr. Heller, I'm a doctor. My profession, my life, is devoted to healing."

I rose. Slipped the notebook in my pocket. "Well, thank you, Dr. Wynekoop. I may have a few more questions at a later date."

She smiled again, a warm, friendly smile, coming from so controlled a woman. "I'd be pleased to have your company. And

I appreciate your help. I'm very worried about the effect this is having on Earle."

"Dr. Wynekoop, with all due respect...my major concern is the effect this going to have on you, if I can't find the real killer."

Her smile disappeared and she nodded sagely. She extended her hand for a final handshake, and I left her there.

I used a pay phone in the visitor's area to call Sergeant Lou Sapperstein at Central Headquarters in the Loop. Lou had been my boss on the pickpocket detail. I asked him to check for me to see what officer in the Fillmore district had caught the call the night of the Wynekoop homicide.

"That's Stege's case," Lou said. Sapperstein was a hardnosed, fair-minded balding cop of about forty-five seasoned years. "You shouldn't mess in Stege's business. He doesn't like you."

"God you're a great detective, picking up on a detail like that. Can you get me the name?"

"Five minutes. Stay where you are."

I gave him the pay phone number and he called back in a little over three minutes.

"Officer Raymond March, detailed with squad fifteen," he said.

I checked my watch; it was after four.

"He's on duty now," I said. "Do me another favor."

"Why don't you get a goddamn secretary?"

"You're a public servant, aren't you? So serve, already."

"So tell me what you want, already."

"Get somebody you trust at Fillmore to tell Officer March to meet me at the drug store on the corner of Madison and Kedzie. Between six and seven."

"What's in it for Officer March?"

"Supper and a fin."

"Why not," Lou said, a shrug in his voice.

He called me back in five or six minutes and said the message would be passed.

I hit the streetcars again and was back on Monroe Street by a quarter to five. It was getting dark already, and colder.

Mrs. Verna Donovan lived in the second-floor two-flat of a graystone three doors down from the Wynekoop mansion. The smell of corned beef and cabbage cooking seeped from under the door.

I knocked.

It took a while, but a slender, attractive woman of perhaps thirty in a floral dress and a white apron opened the door wide.

"Oh!" she said. Her face was oblong, her eyes a luminous brown, her hair another agreeable shade of brown, cut in a bob that was perhaps too young for her.

"Didn't mean to startle you, ma'am. Are you Mrs. Donovan?"

"Yes, I am." She smiled shyly. "Sorry for my reaction—I was expecting my son. We'll be eating in about half an hour..."

"I know this is a bad time to come calling. Perhaps I could arrange another time..."

"What is your business here?"

I gave her one of my A-1 Detective Agency cards. "I'm working for the Wynekoops. Nathan Heller, president of the A-1 agency. I'm hoping to find Rheta's killer."

Her eyes sparkled. "Well, come in! If you don't mind sitting in the kitchen while I get dinner ready..."

"Not at all," I said, following her through a nicely but not lavishly furnished living room, overseen by an elaborate print of the Virgin Mary, and back to a good-size blue and white kitchen.

She stood at the counter making cole slaw while I sat at the kitchen table nearby.

"We were very good friends, Rheta and I. She was a lovely girl, talented, very funny."

"Funny? I get the impression she was a somber girl."

"Around the Wynekoops she was. They're about as much fun as falling down the stairs. Do you think the old girl killed her?"

"What do you think?"

"I could believe it of Earle. Dr. Alice herself, well...I mean, she's a doctor. She's aloof, and she and Rheta were anything but close, of course. But kill her?"

"I'm hearing that the doctor gave Rheta gifts, treated her like a family member."

Verna Duncan shrugged, putting some muscle into her slaw-making efforts. "There was no love lost between them. You're aware that Earle ran around on her?"

"Yes."

"Well, that sort of thing is hard on a girl's self-esteem. I helped her get over it as much as I could."

"How?"

She smiled slyly over her shoulder. "I'm a divorcee, Mr. Heller. And divorcees know how to have a good time. Care for a taste?"

She was offering me a forkful of slaw.

"That's nice," I said, savoring it. "Nice bite to it. So, you and Rheta went out together? Was she seeing other men, then?"

"Of course she was. Why shouldn't she?"

"Anyone in particular?"

"Her music teacher. Violin instructor. Older man, very charming. But he died of a heart attack four months ago. It hit her hard."

"How did she handle it?"

"Well, she didn't shoot herself in the back over it, if that's what you're thinking! She was morose for about a month...then she just started to date all of a sudden. I encouraged her, and she came back to life again."

"Why didn't she just divorce Earle?"

"Why, Mr. Heller...she was a good Catholic girl."

She asked me to stay for supper, but I declined, despite the tempting aroma of her corned beef and cabbage, and the tang of her slaw. I had another engagement, at a drugstore at Madison and Kedzie.

While I waited for Officer March to show up, I questioned the pharmacist behind the back counter.

"Sure I remember Miss Shaunesey stopping by that night," he said. "But I don't understand why she did."

"Why is that?"

"Well, Dr. Wynekoop herself stopped in a week before, to fill a similar prescription, and I told her our stock was low."

"She probably figured you'd've got some in by then," I said.

"The doctor knows we only get a shipment in once a month."

I was mulling that over at the lunch counter when Officer March arrived. He was in his late twenties and blond and much too fresh-faced for a Chicago cop.

"Nate Heller," he said, with a grin. "I've heard about you."

We shook hands.

"Don't believe everything Captain Stege tells you," I said.

He took the stool next to me, took off his cap. "I know Stege thinks you're poison. But that's 'cause he's an old-timer. Me, I'm glad you helped expose those two crooked bastards."

"Let's not get carried away, Officer March. What's the point of being a cop in this town if you can't take home a little graft now and then?"

"Sure," March said. "But those guys were killers. West Side bootleggers."

"I'm a West Side boy myself," I said.

"So I understand. So what's your interest in the Wynekoop case?"

"The family hired me to help clear the old gal. Do you think she did it?"

He made a clicking sound in his cheek. "Hard one to call. She seemed pretty shook up, at the scene."

"Shook up like a grieved family member, or a murderer?"

"I couldn't read it."

"Order yourself a sandwich and then tell me about it."

He did. The call had come in at nine-fifty-nine over the police radio, about five blocks away from where he and his partner were patrolling.

"The girl's body was lying on that table," March said. "She was resting on her left front side with her left arm under her, with the right forearm extending upward so that her hand was about on a level with her chin, with her head on a white pillow. Her face was almost out of sight, but I could see that her mouth and nose were resting on a wet, crumpled towel. She'd been bleeding from the mouth."

"She was covered up, I understand," I said.

"Yes. I drew the covers down carefully, and saw that she'd been shot through the left side of the back. Body was cold. Dead about six hours, I'd guess."

"But that's just a guess."

"Yeah. The coroner can't nail it all that exact. It can be a few hours either direction, you know."

"No signs of a struggle."

"None. That girl laid down on that table herself—maybe at gun point, but whatever the case, she did it herself. Her clothes were lying about the floor at the foot of the examination table, dropped, not thrown, just as though she'd undressed in a leisurely fashion."

"What about the acid burns on the girl's face?"

"She was apparently chloroformed before she was shot. You know, that confession Stege got out of Dr. Wynekoop, that's how she said she did it."

The counterman brought us coffee.

"I'll be frank, officer," I said, sipping the steaming java. "I just came on this job. I haven't had a chance to go down to a newspaper morgue and read the text of that confession."

He shrugged. "Well, it's easily enough summed up. She said her daughter-in-law was always wanting physical examinations. That afternoon, she went downstairs with the doctor for an exam, and first off, stripped, to weigh herself. She had a sudden pain in her side and Dr. Wynekoop suggested a whiff of chloroform as an anesthetic. The doc said she massaged the girl's side for about fifteen minutes, and..."

"I'm remembering this from the papers," I said, nodding. "She claimed the girl 'passed away' on the examining table, and she panicked. Figured her career would be ruined, if it came out she'd accidentally killed her own daughter-in-law with an overdose of chloroform."

"Right. And then she remembered the old revolver in the desk, and fired a shot into the girl and tried to make it look like a robbery."

The counterman came and refilled our coffee cups.

"So," I said, "what do you make of the confession?"

"I think it's bullshit any way you look at it. Hell, she was grilled for almost three days, Heller—you know how valid *that* kind of confession is."

I sipped my coffee. "She may have thought her son was guilty, and was covering up for him."

"Well, her confession was certainly a self-serving one. After all, if she was telling the truth—or even if her confession was made up outa whole cloth, but got taken at face value—it'd make her guilty of nothing more than involuntary manslaughter."

I nodded. "Shooting a corpse isn't a felony."

"But she *had* to know her son didn't do it."

"Why?"

March smirked. "He sent her a telegram; he was in Peoria, a hundred and ninety miles away."

"Telegram? When did she receive this telegram?"

"Late afternoon. Funny thing, though."

"Oh?"

"Initially, Dr. Wynekoop said she'd seen Earle last on November twelfth, when he left on a trip to the Grand Canyon, to take some photographs. But Earle came back to Chicago on the nineteenth, two days before the murder."

I damn near spilled my coffee. *"What?"*

March nodded emphatically. "He and his mother met at a restaurant, miles from home. They were seen sitting in a back booth, having an intense, animated, but hushed, conversation."

"But you said Earle was in Peoria when his wife was killed..."

"He was. He left Chicago, quietly, the next day—drove to Peoria. And from Peoria he went to Kansas City."

"Do his alibis hold up? Peoria isn't Mars; he could've established an alibi and made a round trip..."

"I thought you were working for the family?"

"I am. But if I proved Earle did it, they'd spring his mother."

March laughed hollowly. "She'd be pissed off at you, partner."

"I know. But I already got their retainer. So. Tell me. What did you hold back from the papers?"

It was standard practice to keep back a few details in a murder case; that helped clear up confessions from crazy people.

"I shouldn't," he said.

I handed him a folded fin.

He slipped it in the breast pocket of his uniform blouse.

"Hope for you yet," I said.

"Two items of interest," March said softly. "There were three bullets fired from that gun."

"Three? But Rheta was shot only once..."

"Right."

"Were the other bullets found?"

"No. We took that examining room apart. Then we took the house apart. Nothing."

"What do you make of that?"

"I don't know. You'd have to ask Stege...if you got nerve enough."

"You said two things."

March swallowed slowly. "This may not even come out at the trial. It's not necessarily good for the prosecution."

"Spill."

"The coroner's physician picked up on something of interest, even before the autopsy."

"What?"

"Rheta had syphilis."

"Jesus. You're kidding!"

"A very bad dose."

I sat and pondered that.

"We asked Earle to submit to a physical," March said, "and he consented."

"And?"

"And he's in perfect health."

I took the El back to the Loop and got off at Van Buren and Plymouth, where I had an office on the second floor of the corner building. I lived there, since I kept an eye on the building in lieu of paying rent. Before I went up, I drank in the bar downstairs for half an hour so, chatting with bartender Buddy Gold, who was a friend. I asked him if he was following the Wynekoop case in the papers.

"That old broad is innocent," the lumpy-faced ex-boxer said. "It's a crime what they're doin' to her."

"What are they doing to her?"

"I saw her picture in the paper, in that jailhouse hospital bed. Damn shame, nice woman like that, with her charities and all."

"What about the dead girl? Maybe she was 'nice.'"

"Yeah, but some dope fiend did it. Why don't they find him and put him in jail?"

I said that was a good idea and had another beer. Then I went up to my office and pulled down the Murphy bed and flopped. It had been a long, weird day. I'd earned my fifteen bucks.

The phone woke me. When I opened my eyes, it was morning but the light filtering in around the drawn shades was gray. It would be a cold one. I picked up the receiver on the fifth ring.

"A-1 Detective Agency," I said.

"Nathan Heller?" a gravelly male voice demanded.

I sat on the edge of the desk, rubbing my eyes. "Speaking."

"This is Captain John Stege."

I slid off the desk. "What can I do for you?"

"Steer clear of my case, you son of a bitch."

"What case is that, Captain?"

Stege was a white-haired fireplug with dark-rimmed glasses, a meek-looking individual who could scare the hell out of you when he felt like it. He felt like it.

"You stay out of the goddamn Wynekoop case. I won't have you mucking it up."

How did he even know I was on the case? Had Officer March told him?

"I was hired by the family to try to help clear Dr. Wynekoop. It's hardly uncommon for a defendant in a murder case to hire an investigator."

"Dr. Alice Lindsay Wynekoop murdered her daughter-in-law! It couldn't be any other way."

"Captain, it could be a lot of other ways. It could be one of her boy friends; it could be one of her husband's girl friends. It could be a break-in artist looking for drugs. It could be..."

"Are you telling me how to do my job?"

"Well, you're telling me how not to do mine."

There was a long pause.

Then Stege said: "I don't like you, Heller. You stay out of my way. You go manufacturing evidence, and I'll introduce you to every rubber hose in this town...and I know plenty of 'em."

"You have the wrong idea about me, Captain," I said. "And you may have the wrong idea about Alice Wynekoop."

"Bull! She insured young Rheta for five grand, fewer than thirty days before the girl's death. With double indemnity, the policy pays ten thousand smackers."

I hadn't heard about this.

"The Wynekoops *have* money," I said. "A murder-for-insurance-money scheme makes no sense for a well-to-do family like that..."

"Dr. Wynekoop owes almost five thousand dollars back taxes and has over twenty thousand dollars in overdue bank notes. She's prominent, but she's not wealthy. She got hit in the crash."

"Well..."

"She killed her daughter-in-law to make her son happy, and to collect the insurance money. If you were worth two cents as a detective, you'd know that."

"Speaking of detective work, Captain, how did you know I was on this case?"

"Don't you read the papers?"

The papers had me in them, all right. A small story, but well placed, on several front pages in fact; under a picture of Earle seated at his mother's side in the jail hospital, the *News* told how the Wynekoops had hired a local private investigator, one Nathan Heller, to help prove Dr. Alice's innocence.

I called Earle Wynekoop and asked him to meet me at the County Jail hospital wing. I wanted to talk to both of my clients.

On the El, I thought about how I had intended to pursue this case. Having done the basic groundwork with the family and witnesses, I would begin searching for the faceless break-in artist whose burglary had got out of hand, leading to the death of Rheta Wynekoop. Never mind that it made no sense for a thief to take a gun from a rolltop desk, make his victim un-dress, shoot her in the back, tuck her in like a child at bedtime, and leave the gun behind. Criminals did crazy things, after all. I would spend three or four days sniffing around the West Side pawn shops and re-sale shops, and the Maxwell Street market, looking for a lead on any petty crook whose drug addiction might lead to violence. I would comb the flophouses and bars hopheads were known to frequent, and....

But I had changed my mind, at least for the moment.

Earle was at his mother's bedside when the matron left me there. Dr. Alice smiled in her tight, business-like manner and offered me a hand to shake; I took it. Earle stood and nodded and smiled nervously at me. I nodded to him, and he sat again.

But I stayed on my feet.

"I'm off this case," I said.

"What?" Earle said, eyes wide.

Dr. Alice remained calm. Her appraising eyes were as cold as the weather.

"Captain Stege suggested it," I said.

"That isn't legal!" Earle said.

"Quiet, Earle," his mother said, sternly but with gentleness.

"That's not why I'm quitting," I said. "And I'm keeping the retainer, too, by the way."

"Now that *isn't* legal!" Earle said, standing.

"Shut-up," I said to him. To her, I said: "You two used me. I'm strictly a publicity gimmick. To help you make you look sincere, to help you keep up a good front...just like staying in the jail's hospital ward, so you can pose for pitiful newspaper pics."

Dr. Alice blinked and smiled thinly. "You're revealing an obnoxious side, Mr. Heller, that is unbecoming."

"You killed your daughter-in-law, Dr. Wynekoop. For Sonny Boy, here."

Earle's face clenched like a fist, and he clenched his fists, too, while he was at it. "I ought to..."

I looked at him hard. "I wish to hell you would."

His eyes flickered at me, then he glanced at his mother. She nodded and motioned for him to sit again, and he did.

"Mr. Heller," she said, "I assure you, I am innocent. I don't know what you've been told that gave you this very false impression, but..."

"Save it. I know what happened, and why. You discovered, in one of your frequent on-the-house examinations of your hypochondriac daughter-in-law, that she really *was* ill. Specifically, she had a social disease."

Anger flared in the doctor's eyes.

"You could forgive Earle all his philandering...even though you didn't approve. You did ask your daughter to talk to him about his excesses of drink and dames. But those were just misdemeanors. For your husband's wife to run around, to get a nasty disease that she might just pass along to your beloved boy, should their marriage ever heat up again, well, that was a crime. And it deserved punishment."

"Mr. Heller, why don't you go. You may keep your retainer, if you keep your silence."

"Oh, hitting a little close to home, am I? Well, let me finish. You paid for this. I don't think it was your idea to kill Rheta, despite the dose of syph she was carrying. I think it was Earle's idea. She wouldn't give him a divorce, good Catholic girl that she was, and Earle's a good Catholic, too, after all. It'd be hell to get excommunicated, right, Earle? Right, Mom?"

Earle was shaking; his hands clasped, prayerfully. Dr. Wynekoop's wrinkled face was a stern mask.

"Here's what happened," I said, cheerfully. "Earle came to you and asked you to put the little woman to sleep...she was a tortured girl, after all, if it were done painlessly, why, it would be a merciful act. But you refused—you're a doctor, a healer. It wouldn't be right."

Earle's eyes were shifting from side to side in confirmation of my theory.

I forged ahead: "But Earle came to you again, and said, Mother dear, if you don't do it, I will. I've found father's old .32, and I've tried it...fired two test rounds. It works, and I know how to work it. I'm going to kill Rheta myself."

Earle's eyes were wide as was his mouth. I must have come very, very close, even perhaps to his very language. Dr. Alice continued to maintain a poker face.

"So, Mom, you decided to take matters in hand. When Earle came back early from his Grand Canyon photo trip, the two of you rendezvoused away from home—though you were seen, unfortunately—and came up with a plan. Earle would resume his trip, only go no farther than Peoria, where he would establish an alibi."

Earle's face was contorted as he took in every damning word.

"On the day of the murder," I told her, "you had a final private consultation with your daughter-in-law...you overdosed her with chloroform, or smothered her."

"Mr. Heller," Dr. Alice said icily, looking away from me, "this fantasy of yours holds no interest whatsoever for me."

"Well, maybe so—but Earle's all perked up. Anyway, you left the body downstairs, closing the examining room door, locking it probably, and went on about the business of business as usual... cooking supper for your roomer, spending a quiet evening with her...knowing that Earle would be back after dark, to quietly slip in and, what? Dispose of the body somehow. That was the plan, wasn't it? The unhappy bride would just disappear. Or perhaps turn up dead in ditch, or...whatever. Only it didn't happen that way. Because Sonny Boy chickened out."

And now Dr. Alice broke form, momentarily, her eyes turning on Earle for just a moment, giving him one nasty glance, the only time I ever saw her look at the louse with anything but devotion.

"He sent you a telegram in the afternoon, letting you know that he was still in Peoria. And that he was going to stay in Peoria. And you, with a corpse in the basement. Imagine."

"You have a strange sense of humor, Mr. Heller."

"You have a strange way of practicing medicine, Dr. Wynekoop. You sent your roomer, Miss Shaunesey, on a fool's errand—sending her to a drug store where you knew the prescription couldn't be filled. And you knew conscientious Miss Shaunesey would try another drug store, buying you time."

"Really," Dr. Alice said, dryly.

"Really. That's when you concocted the burglary story. You're too frail, physically, to go hauling a corpse anywhere. But you remembered that gun, across the hall. So you shot your dead daughter-in-law, adding insult to injury, and faked the robbery—badly, but it was impromptu, after all."

"I don't have to listen to this!" Earle said.

"Then don't," I said. "What you didn't remember, Dr. Wynekoop, is that two bullets had already been fired from that weapon, when Earle tested it. And that little anomaly bothered me."

"Did it," she said, flatly.

"It did. Your daughter-in-law's syphilis; the two missing bullets; and the hour you spent alone in the house, while the roomer was away and Rheta was dead in your examining room.

Those three factors added up to one thing: your guilt, and your son's complicity."

"Are you going to tell your story to anyone?" she asked, blandly.

"No," I said. "You're my client."

"How much?" Earle said, with a nasty, nervous little sneer.

I held my hands up, palms out. "No more. I'm keeping my retainer. I earned it."

I turned my back on them and began to walk away.

From behind me, I heard her say, with no irony whatsoever, "Thank you, Mr. Heller."

I turned and looked at her and laughed. "Hey, you're going to jail, lady. The cops and the D.A. won't need me to get it done, and all the good publicity you cook up won't change a thing. I have only one regret."

I made them ask.

Earle took the honors.

"What's that?" Earle asked, as he stood there trembling; his mother reached her hand out and patted his nearest hand, soothing him.

I smiled at him—the nastiest smile I could muster. "That you won't be going to jail with her, you son of a bitch."

And go to jail she did.

But it took a while. A most frail-looking Dr. Alice was carried into the courtroom on the opening day of the trial; still playing for sympathy in the press, I figured.

Then, after eight days of evidence, Dr. Alice had an apparent heart seizure, when the prosecution hauled the blood-stained examination table into court. A mistrial was declared. When she recovered, though, she got a brand-new one. The press milked the case for all its worth; public opinion polls in the papers indicated half of Chicago considered Dr. Alice guilty, and the other half thought her innocent. The jury, however, was unanimous—it took them only fifteen minutes to find her guilty and two hours to set the sentence at twenty-five years.

Earle didn't attend the trial. They say that just as Dr. Alice was being ushered in the front gate at the Woman's Reformatory at Dwight, Illinois, an unshaven, disheveled figure darted from the nearby bushes. Earle kissed his mother goodbye and she brushed away his tears. As usual.

She served thirteen years, denying her guilt all the way; she was released with time off for good behavior. She died on July 4, 1955, in a nursing home, under an assumed name.

Earle changed his name, too. What became of him, I can't say. There were rumors, of course. One was that he had found work as a garage mechanic.

Another was that he had finally re-married—a beautiful redhead.

Dr. Catherine Wynekoop did not change her name, and went on to a distinguished medical career.

And the house at 3406 West Monroe, the Death Clinic, was torn down in 1947. The year Dr. Alice was released.

AUTHOR'S NOTE

This is a work of fiction based on an actual murder, and many real names are used. "Tony Minneci" is a composite of Leo Minneci's real brother and several other peripheral figures in the case, none of whom were shown to have anything to do with the robberies or murder. My longtime research associate George Hagenauer wrote about the Blonde Tigress in *The Big Book of Little Criminals* (1996). Newspaper accounts, including retrospective ones, were consulted as well as several articles in vintage "true detective" magazines, notably "Smashing the Terror Reign of Chicago's Blonde Gun Girl" by Robert Faherty in *Detective Tabloid*, February 1935. Mark Gribben's internet article, "Eleanor Jarman Please Phone Home," was also useful.

THE PERFECT CRIME

She was the first movie star I ever worked for, but I wasn't much impressed. If I were that easily impressed, I'd have been impressed by Hollywood itself. And having seen the way Hollywood portrayed my profession on the so-called silver screen, I wasn't much impressed with Hollywood.

On the other hand, Thelma Todd was the most beautiful woman who ever wanted to hire my services, and that did impress me. Enough so that when she called me, that October, and asked me to drive out to her "sidewalk café" nestled under the Palisades in Montemar Vista, I went, wondering if she would be as pretty in the flesh as she was on celluloid.

I'd driven out Pacific Coast Highway that same morning, a clear cool morning with a blue sky lording it over a vast sparkling sea. Pelicans were playing tag with the breaking surf, flying just under the curl of the white-lipped waves. Yachts, like a child's toy boats, floated out there just between me and the horizon. I felt like I could reach out for one, pluck and examine it, sniff it maybe, like King Kong checking out Fay Wray's lingerie.

"Thelma Todd's Sidewalk Café," as a billboard on the hillside behind it so labeled the place, was a sprawling two-story hacienda affair, as big as a beached luxury liner. Over its central, largest-of-many archways, a third-story tower rose like a stubby lighthouse. There weren't many cars here—it was approaching ten a.m., too early for the luncheon crowd and even I didn't drink cocktails this early in the day. Not and tell, anyway.

She was waiting in the otherwise unpopulated cocktail lounge, where massive wooden beams in a traditional Spanish mode fought the chromium-and-leather furnishings and the chrome-and-glass-brick bar and came out a draw. She was a big blonde woman with more curves than the highway out front and just the right number of hills and valleys. Wearing a clingy summery white dress, she was seated on one of the bar stools, with her bare legs crossed; they weren't the best-looking legs on the planet, necessarily. I just couldn't prove otherwise. That good a detective I'm not.

"Nathan Heller?" she asked, and her smile dimpled her cheeks in a manner that made her whole heart-shaped face smile, and the world smile as well, including me. She didn't move off the stool, just extended her hand in a manner that was at once casual and regal.

I took the hand, not knowing whether to kiss it, shake it, or press it into a book like a corsage I wanted to keep. I looked at her feeling vaguely embarrassed; she was so pretty you didn't know where to look next, and felt like there was maybe something wrong with looking anywhere. But I couldn't help myself.

She had pale, creamy skin and her hair was almost white blonde. They called her the ice-cream blonde, in the press. I could see why.

Then I got around to her eyes. They were blue of course, cornflower blue; and big and sporting long lashes, the real McCoy, not your dimestore variety. But they were also the saddest eyes I'd ever looked into. The smile froze on my face like

I was looking at Medusa, not a twenty-nine year-old former six-grade teacher from Massachusetts who won a talent search.

"Is something wrong?" she asked. Then she patted the stool next to her.

I sat and said, "Nothing's wrong. I never had a movie star for a client before."

"I see. Thanks for considering this job—for extending your stay, I mean."

I was visiting L.A. from Chicago because a friend—a fellow former pickpocket detail dick—had recently opened an office out here in sunny Southern Cal. Fred Rubinski needed an out-of-towner to pose as a visiting banker, to expose an embezzler; the firm had wanted to keep the affair in-house.

"Mr. Rubinski recommended you highly." Her voice had a low, throaty quality that wasn't forced or affected; she was what Mae West would've been if Mae West wasn't a parody.

"That's just because Fred hasn't been in town long enough to make any connections. But if Thelma Todd wants me to consider extending my stay, I'm willing to listen."

She smiled at that, very broadly, showing off teeth whiter than cameras can record. "Might I get you a drink, Mr. Heller?"

"It's a little early."

"I know it is. Might I get you a drink?"

"Sure."

"Anything special?"

"Anything that doesn't have a little paper umbrella in it is fine by me....Make it rum and Coke."

"Rum and Coke." She fixed me up with that, and had the same herself. Either we had similar tastes or she just wasn't fussy about what she drank.

"Have you heard of Lucky Luciano?" she asked, returning to her bar stool.

"Heard of him," I said. "Haven't met him."

"What do you know about him?"

I shrugged. "Big-time gangster from back east. Runs casinos all over southern California. More every day."

She flicked the air with a long red fingernail, like she was shooing away a bug. "Well, perhaps you've noticed the tower above my restaurant."

"Sure."

"I live on the second floor, but the tower above is fairly spacious."

"Big enough for a casino, you mean."

"That's right," she said, nodding. "I was approached by Luciano, more than once. I turned him away, more than once. After all, with my location, and my clientele, a casino could make a killing."

"You're doing well enough legally. Why bother with ill?"

"I agree. And if I were to get into any legal problems, that would mean a scandal, and Hollywood doesn't need another scandal. Busby Berkley's trial is coming up soon, you know."

The noted director and choreographer, creator of so many frothy fantasies, was up on the drunk-driving homicide of three pedestrians, not far from this café.

"But now," she said, her bee-lips drawn nervously tight, "I've begun to receive threatening notes."

"From Luciano, specifically?"

"No. They're extortion notes, actually. Asking me to pay off Artie Lewis. You know, the bandleader?"

"Why him?"

"He's in Luciano's pocket. Gambling markers. And I used to go with Artie. He lives in San Francisco, now."

"I see. Well, have you talked to the cops?"

"No."

"Why not?"

"I don't want to get Artie in trouble."

"Have you talked to Artie?"

"Yes—he claims he knows nothing about this. He doesn't want my money. He doesn't even want me back—he's got a new girl."

I'd like to see the girl that could make you forget Thelma Todd.

"So," I said, "you want me to investigate. Can I see the extortion notes?"

"No," she said, shaking her white blonde curls like the mop of the gods, "that's not it. I burned those notes. For Artie's sake."

"Well, for Nate's sake," I said, "where *do* I come in?"

"I think I'm being followed. I'd like a bodyguard."

I resisted looking her over wolfishly and making a wisecrack. She was a nice woman, and the fact that hers was the sort of a body a private eye would pay to guard didn't seem worth mentioning. My fee did.

"Twenty-five a day and expenses," I said.

"Fine," she said. "And you can have any meals you like right here at the Café. Drinks, too. Run a tab and I'll pick it up."

"Swell," I grinned. "I was wondering if I'd ever run into a fringe benefit in this racket."

"You can be my chauffeur."

"Well..."

"You have a problem with that, Mr. Heller?"

"I have a private investigator's license, and a license to carry a gun...in Illinois, anyway. But I don't have a chauffeur's license."

"I think a driver's license will suffice." Her bee-stung lips were poised in a kiss of amusement. "What's the real problem, Heller?"

"I'm not wearing a uniform. I'm strictly plainclothes."

She smiled tightly, wryly amused, saying, "All right, hang onto your dignity...but you have to let me pay the freight on a couple of new suits for you. I'll throw 'em in on the deal."

"Swell," I said. I liked it when women bought me clothes.

So for the next two months, I stayed on in southern Cal, and Thelma Todd was my only client. I worked six days a week for her—Monday through Saturday. Sundays God, Heller and Todd rested. I drove her in her candy-apple red Packard convertible, a car designed for blondes with wind-blown hair and pearls. She sat in back, of course. Most days I took her to the Hal Roach Studio where she was making a musical with Laurel and Hardy. I'd wait in some dark pocket of the sound studio and watch her every move out in the brightness. In a black wig, lacy bodice, and clinging, gypsy skirt, Thelma was the kind of girl you took home to Mother, and if Mother didn't like her, to hell with Mother.

Evenings she hit the club circuit, the Trocadero and the El Mocambo chiefly. I'd sit in the cocktail lounges and quietly drink and wait for her and her various dates to head home. Some of these guys were swishy types that she was doing the studio a favor appearing in public with; a couple others spent the night.

I don't mean to tell tales out of school, but this tale can't be told at all unless I'm frank about that one thing: Thelma slept around. Later, when the gossip rags were spreading rumors about alcohol and drugs, that was all the bunk. But Thelma was a friendly girl. She had generous charms and she was generous with them.

"Heller," she said, one night in early December when I was dropping her off, walking her up to the front door of the Café like always, "I think I have a crush on you."

She was alone tonight, having played girl friend to one of those Hollywood funny boys for the benefit of Louella Parsons and company. Alone but for me.

She slipped an arm around my waist. She had booze on her breath, but then so did I, and neither one of us was drunk. She was bathed gently in moonlight and Chanel Number Five.

She kissed me with those bee-stung lips, stinging so softly, so deeply.

I moved away. "No. I'm sorry."

She winced. "What's wrong?"

"I'm the hired help. You're just lonely tonight."

Her eyes, which I seldom looked into because of the depth of the sadness there, hardened. "Don't you ever get lonely, you bastard?"

"Never," I said.

She drew her hand back to slap me, but then she just touched my face, instead. Gentle as the ocean breeze, and it was gentle tonight, the breeze, so gentle.

"Goodnight, Heller," she said.

And she slipped inside, but left the door slightly ajar.

"What the hell," I said, and I slipped inside, too.

An hour later, I drove her Packard to the garage that was attached to the bungalow above the restaurant complex; to do that I had to take Montemar Vista Road to Seretto Way, turning right. The Mediterranean-style stucco bungalow, on Cabrillo, like so many houses in Montemar Vista, climbed the side of the hill like a clinging vine. It was owned by Thelma Todd's partner in the Café, movie director/producer Warren Eastman. Eastman had an apartment next to Thelma's above the restaurant, as well as the bungalow, and seemed to live back and forth between the two.

I wondered what the deal was, with Eastman and my client, but I never asked, not directly. Eastman was a thin, dapper man in his late forties, with a pointed chin and a small mustache and a window's peak that his slick black hair was receding around, making his face look diamond shaped. He often sat in the cocktail lounge with a bloody Mary in one hand and a cigarette in a holder in the other. He was always talking deals with movie people.

"Heller," he said, one night, motioning me over to the bar. He was seated on the very stool that Thelma had been, that first morning. "This is Nick DeCiro, the talent agent. Nick, this is the gumshoe Thelma hired to protect her from the big bad gambling syndicate."

DeCiro was another darkly handsome man, a bit older than Eastman, though he lacked both the mustache and receding hairline of the director. DeCiro wore a white suit with a dark sportshirt, open at the neck to reveal a wealth of black chest hair.

I shook DeCiro's hand. His grip was firm, moist, like a fistful of topsoil.

"Nicky here is your client's ex-husband," Eastman said, with a wag of his cigarette-in-holder, trying for an air of that effortless decadence that Hollywood works so hard at.

"Thelma and me are still pals," DeCiro said, lighting up a foreign cig with a shiny silver lighter that he then clicked shut with a meaningless flourish. "We broke up amicably."

"I heard it was over extreme cruelty," I said.

DeCiro frowned, and Eastman cut in glibly, "Don't believe everything you read in the papers, Heller. Besides, you have to get a divorce over something."

"But then you'd *know* that in your line of work," DeCiro said, an edge in his thin voice.

"Don't knock it," I said with my own edge. "Where would your crowd be without divorce dicks? Now, if you gents will excuse me..."

"Heller, Heller," Eastman said, touching my arm, "don't be so touchy."

I waited for him to remove his hand from my arm, then said, "Did you want something, Mr. Eastman? I'm not much for this Hollywood shit-chat."

"I don't like your manner," DeCiro said.

"Nobody does," I said. "But I don't get paid well enough for it to matter."

"Heller," Eastman said, "I was just trying to convince Nicky here that my new film is perfect for a certain client of his. I'm doing a mystery. About the perfect crime. The perfect murder."

"No such animal," I said.

"Oh, really?" DeCiro said, lifting an eyebrow.

"Murder and crime are inexact sciences. All the planning in the world doesn't account for the human element."

"Then how do you explain," Eastman said archly, "the hundreds of murders that go unsolved in this country?"

"Policework is a more exact science than crime or murder," I admitted, "but we have a lot of bent cops in this world—and a lot of dumb ones."

"Then there *are* perfect crimes."

"No. Just unsolved ones. And imperfect detectives. Good evening, gentlemen."

That was the most extensive conversation I had with either Eastman or DeCiro during the time I was employed by Miss Todd, though I said hello and they did the same, now and then, at the Café.

But Eastman was married to an actress named Miranda Diamond, a fiery Latin whose parents were from Mexico City, even if she'd been raised in the Bronx. She fancied herself as the next Lupe Velez, and she was a similarly voluptuous dame, though her handsome features were as hard as a gravestone.

She cornered me at the Café one night, in the cocktail lounge, where I was drinking on the job.

"You're a dick," she said.

We'd never spoken before.

"I hope you mean that in the nicest way," I said.

"You're bodyguarding that bitch," she said, sitting next to me on a leather and chrome couch. Her nostrils flared; if I'd been holding a red cape, I'd have dropped it and run for the stands.

"Miss Todd is my client, yes, Miss Diamond."

She smiled. "You recognize me."

"Oh yes. And I also know enough to call you Mrs. Eastman, in certain company."

"My husband and I are separated."

"Ah."

"But I could use a little help in the divorce court."

"What kind of help?"

"Photographs of him and that bitch in the sack." She said "the" like "thee."

"That would help you."

"Yes. You see...my husband has similar pictures of me, with a gentleman, in a compromising position."

"Even missionaries get caught in that position, I understand." I offered her a cigarette, she took it, and I lit hers and mine. "And if you had similar photos, you could negotiate yourself a better settlement."

"Exactly. Interested?"

"I do divorce work—that's no problem. But I try not to sell clients out. Bad for business."

She smiled; she put her hand on my leg. "I could make it worth your while. Financially and...otherwise."

It wasn't even Christmas and already here was a second screen goddess who wanted to hop in the sack with me. I must have really been something.

"Listen, if you like me, just say so. But we're not making a business arrangement—I got a client, already."

Then she suggested I do to myself what she'd just offered to do for me. She was full of ideas.

So was I. I was pretty sure Thelma and Eastman were indeed having an affair, but it was of the on-again-off-again variety. One night they'd be affectionate, in that sickening Hollywood sweetie-baby way; the next night he would be cool to her; the next she would be cool to him. It was love, I recognized it, but the kind that sooner or later blows up like an overheated engine.

Ten days before Christmas, Thelma was honored by Lupino Lane—the famous British comedian, so famous I'd never the hell heard of him—with a dinner at the Troc. At a table for twelve upstairs, in the swanky cream-and-gold dining room, Thelma was being feted by her show-biz friends, while I sat downstairs in the oak-paneled Cellar Lounge with other people not famous enough to sit upstairs, nursing a rum and Coke at the polished copper bar. I didn't feel like a polished copper, that was for sure.

I was just a chauffeur with a gun, and a beautiful client who didn't need me.

That much was clear to me: in the two months I'd worked for Thelma, I hadn't spotted anybody following her except a few fans, and I couldn't blame them. I think I was just a little bit in love with the ice-cream blonde myself. We'd only had that one slightly inebriated night together—and neither of us had mentioned it since, or even referred to it. Maybe we were both embarrassed; I didn't figure either of us were exactly the type to be ashamed.

Anyway, she was a client, and she slept around, and neither of those things appealed to me in a girl—though everything else about her, including her money, did.

About half an hour into the evening, I heard a scream upstairs. A woman's scream, a scream that might have belonged to Thelma.

I took the stairs four at a time and had my gun in my hand when I entered the fancy dining room. Normally when I enter fancy dining rooms with a gun in my hand, all eyes are on me. Not this time.

Thelma was clawing at her ex-husband, who was laughing at her. She was being held back by Patsy Kelly, the dark-haired rubber-faced comedienne who was Thelma's partner in the two-reelers. DeCiro, in a white tux, had a starlet on his arm, a blonde about twenty with a neckline down to her shoes. The starlet looked frightened, but DeCiro was having a big laugh.

I put my gun away and took over for Patsy Kelly.

"Miss Todd," I said, gently, whispering into her ear, holding onto her two arms from behind, "don't do this."

She went limp for a moment, then straightened and said, with stiff dignity, "I'm all right, Nathan."

It was the only time she ever called me that.

I let go of her.

"What's the problem?" I asked. I was asking both Thelma Todd and her ex-husband.

"He embarrassed me," she said, without any further explanation.

And without any further anything, I said to DeCiro, "Go."

DeCiro twitched a smile. "I was invited."

"I'm uninviting you. Go."

His face tightened and he thought about saying or doing something. But my eyes were on him like magnets on metal and instead he gathered his date and her decolletage and took a powder.

"Are you ready to go home?" I asked Thelma.

"No," she said, with a shy smile, and she squeezed my arm, and went back to the table of twelve where her party of Hollywood types awaited. She was the guest of honor, after all.

Two hours, and two drinks later, I was escorting her home. She sat in the back of the candy-apple red Packard in her mink coat and sheer mauve-and-silver evening gown and diamond necklace and told me what had happened, the wind whipping her ice-blonde hair.

"Nicky got himself invited," she said, almost shouting over the wind. "Without my knowledge. Asked the host to reserve a seat next to me at the table. Then he wandered in late, with a date, that little *starlet*, which you may have noticed rhymes with harlot, and sat at another table, leaving me sitting next to an empty seat at a party in *my* honor. He sat there necking with that little tramp and I got up and went over and gave him a piece of my mind. It...got a little out of hand. Thanks for stepping in, Heller."

MAX ALLAN COLLINS

"It's what you pay me for."

She sat in silence for a while; only the wind spoke. It was a cold Saturday night, as cold as a chilled martini. I had asked her if she wanted the top up on the convertible, but she said no. She began to look behind us as we moved slowly down Sunset.

"Heller," she said, "someone's following us."

"I don't think so."

"Somebody's following us, I tell you!"

"I'm keeping an eye on the rear-view mirror. We're fine."

She leaned forward and clutched my shoulder. "Get moving! Do you want me to be kidnapped, or killed? It could be Luciano's gangsters, for God's sake!"

She was the boss. I hit the pedal. At speeds up to seventy miles per, we sailed west around the curves of Sunset; there was a service station at the junction of the boulevard and the coast highway, and I pulled in.

"What are you doing?" she demanded.

I turned and looked into the frightened blue eyes. "I'm going to get some gas, and keep watch. And see if anybody comes up on us, or suspicious goes by. Don't you worry. I'm armed."

I looked close at every car that passed by the station. I saw no one and nothing suspicious. Then I paid the attendant and we headed north on the coast highway. Going nice and slow.

"I ought to fire you," she said, pouting back there.

"This is my last night, Miss Todd," I said. "I'm getting homesick for Chicago. They got a better breed of dishonest people back there. Anyway, I like to work for my money. I feel I'm taking yours."

She leaned forward, clutched my shoulder again. "No, no, I tell you, I'm frightened."

"Why?"

"I...I just feel I still need you around. You give me a sense of security."

"Have you had any more threatening notes?"

"No." Her voice sounded very small, now.

"If you do, call me, or the cops. Or both."

It was two a.m. when I slid the big car in in front of the sprawling Sidewalk Café. I was shivering with cold; a sea breeze was blowing, Old Man Winter taking his revenge on California. I turned and looked at her again. I smiled.

"I'll walk you to the door, Miss Todd."

She smiled at me, too, but this time the smile didn't light up her face, or the world, or me. This time the smile was as sad as her eyes. Sadder.

"That won't be necessary, Heller."

I was looking for an invitation, either in her eyes or her voice; I couldn't quite find one. "Are you sure?"

"Yes. Do me one favor. Work for me next week. Be my chauffeur one more week, while I decide whether or not to replace you with another bodyguard, or...what."

"Okay."

"Go home, Heller. See you Monday."

"See you Monday," I said, and I watched her go in the front door of the Café. Then I drove the Packard up to the garage above, on the Palisades, and got in my dusty inelegant 1925 Marmon and headed back to the Roosevelt Hotel in Hollywood. I had a hunch Thelma Todd, for all her apprehensions, would sleep sounder than I would, tonight.

My hunch was right, but for the wrong reason.

Monday morning, sunny but cool if no longer cold, I pulled into one of the parking places alongside the Sidewalk Café; it was around ten thirty and mine was the only car. The big front door was locked. I knocked until the Spanish cleaning woman let me in. She said she hadn't seen Miss Todd yet this morning. I went up the private stairway off the kitchen that led up to the two apartments. The door at the top of the stairs was unlocked; beyond it were the two facing apartment doors. I knocked on hers.

"Miss Todd?"

No answer.

I tried for a while, then went and found the cleaning woman again. "Maria, do you have any idea where Miss Todd might be? She doesn't seem to be in her room."

"She might be stay up at Meester Eastmon's."

I nodded, started to walk away, then looked back and added as an afterthought, "Did you see her yesterday?"

"I no work Sunday."

I guess Maria, like God, Heller and Thelma Todd, rested on Sunday. Couldn't blame her.

I thought about taking the car up and around, then said to hell with it and began climbing the concrete steps beyond the pedestrian bridge that arched over the highway just past the Café. These steps, all two-hundred and eighty of them, straight up the steep hill, were the only direct access from the coast road to the bungalow on Cabrillo Street. Windblown sand had drifted over the steps and the galvanized handrail was as cold and wet as a liar's handshake.

I grunted my way to the top. I'd started out as a young man, had reached middle age by step one hundred and was now ready for the retirement home. I sat on the cold damp top step and poured sand out of my scuffed-up Florsheims, glad I hadn't bothered with a shine in the last few weeks. Then I stood and looked past the claustrophobic drop of the steps, to where the sun was reflecting off the sand and sea. The beach was blinding, the ocean dazzling. It was beautiful, but it hurt to look at. A seagull was flailing with awkward grace against the breeze like a fighter losing the last round. Suddenly Lake Michigan seemed like a pond.

Soon I was knocking on Eastman's front door. No answer. Went to check to see if my client's car was there, swinging up the black-studded blue garage door. The car was there, all right, the red Packard convertible, next to Eastman's Lincoln sedan.

My client was there, too.

She was slumped in front, sprawled across the steering wheel. She was still in the mink, the mauve-and-silver gown, and the diamond necklace she'd worn to the Troc Saturday night. But her clothes were rumpled, in disarray, like an unmade bed; and there was blood on the front of the gown, coagulated rubies beneath the diamonds. There was blood on her face, on her white, white face.

She'd always had pale creamy skin, but now it was as white as a wedding dress. There was no pulse in her throat. She was cold. She'd been dead a while.

I stood and looked at her and maybe I cried. That's my business, isn't it? Then I went out and up the side steps to the loft above the garage and roused the elderly fellow named Jones who lived there; he was the bookkeeper for the Sidewalk Café. I asked him if he had a phone, and he did, and I used it.

I had told my story to the uniformed men four times before the men from Central Homicide showed. The detective in charge was Lieutenant Rondell, a thin, somber, detached man in his mid-forties with smooth creamy gray hair and icy eyes. His brown gabardine suit wasn't expensive but it was well-pressed.

His green pork-pie lightweight felt hat was in his hand, in deference to the deceased. Out of deference to me, he listened to my story as I told it for the fifth time. He didn't seem to think much of it.

"You're telling me this woman was murdered," he said.

"I'm telling you the gambling syndicate boys were pressuring her, and she wasn't caving in."

"And you were her bodyguard," Rondell said.

"Some bodyguard," said the other man from homicide, Rondell's brutish shadow, and cracked his knuckles and laughed. We were in the garage and the laughter made hollow echoes off the cement, like a basketball bouncing in an empty stadium.

"I was her bodyguard," I told Rondell tightly. "But I didn't work Sundays."

"And she had to go to Chicago to hire a bodyguard?"

I explained my association with Fred Rubinski, and Rondell nodded several times, seemingly accepting it.

Then Rondell walked over and looked at the corpse in the convertible. A photographer from Homicide was snapping photos; pops and flashes of light accompanied the detective's trip around the car as if he were a star at a Hollywood opening.

I went outside. The smell of death is bad enough when it's impersonal; when somebody you know has died, it's like having asthma in a steam room.

Rondell found me leaning against the side of the stucco garage.

"It looks like suicide," he said.

"Sure. It's supposed to."

He lifted an eyebrow and a shoulder. "The ignition switch is turned on. Carbon monoxide."

"Car wasn't running when I got here."

"Long since ran out of gas, most likely. If what you say is true, she's been there since Saturday night...that is, early Sunday morning."

I shrugged. "She's wearing the same clothes, at least."

"When we fix time of death, it'll all come clear."

"Oh, yeah? See what the coroner has to say about that."

Rondell's icy eyes froze further. "Why?"

"This cold snap we've had, last three days. It's warmer this morning, but Sunday night, Jesus. That sea breeze was murder—if you'll pardon the expression."

Rondell nodded. "Perhaps cold enough to retard decomposition, you mean."

"Perhaps."

He pushed the pork pie back on his head. "We need to talk to this bird Eastman."

"I'll say. He's probably at his studio. Paramount. When he's on a picture, they pick him up by limo every morning before dawn."

Rondell went to use the phone in old man Jones' loft flat. Rondell's brutish sidekick exited the garage and slid his arm around the shoulder of a young uniformed cop, who seemed uneasy about the attention.

"Ice cream blonde, huh?" the big flatfoot said. "I woulda liked a coupla of scoops of that myself."

I tapped the brute on the shoulder and he turned to me and said, "Huh?", stupidly, and I cold-cocked him. He went down like a building.

But not out, though. "You're gonna pay for that, you bastard," he said, sounding like the school-yard bully he was. He touched the blood in the corner of his mouth, hauled himself up off the cement. "In this, town, you go to goddamn jail when you hit a goddamn cop!"

"You'd need a witness, first," I said.

"I got one," he said, but when he turned to look, the young uniformed cop was gone.

I walked up to him and stood damn near belt buckle to belt buckle and smiled a smile that had nothing to do with smiling. "Want to go another round, see if a witness shows?"

He tasted blood and fluttered his eyes like a girl and said something unintelligible and disappeared back inside the garage.

Rondell came clopping down the wooden steps and stood before me and smiled firmly. "I just spoke with Eastman. We'll interview him more formally, of course, but the preliminary interrogation indicates a possible explanation." "Oh?"

He was nodding. "Yeah. Apparently Saturday night he bolted the stairwell door around midnight. It's a door that leads to both apartments up top the Sidewalk Café. Said he thought Miss Todd had mentioned she was going to sleep over at her mother's that night."

"You mean, she couldn't get in?"

"Right."

"Well, hell, man, she would've knocked."

"Eastman says if she did, he didn't hear her. He says there was high wind and pounding surf all night; he figures that drowned out all other sounds."

I smirked. "Does he, really? So what's your scenario?"

"Well, when Miss Todd found she couldn't get into her apartment, she must've decided to climb the steps to the street above, walked to the garage and spent the rest of the night in her car. She must've have gotten cold, and switched on the ignition to keep warm, and the fumes got her."

I sighed. "A minute ago you were talking suicide."

"That's still a possibility."

"What about the blood on her face and dress?"

He shrugged. "She may have fallen across the wheel and cut her mouth, when she fell unconscious."

"Look, if she wanted to get warm, why would she sit in her open convertible? That Lincoln sedan next to her is unlocked and has the keys in it."

"I can't answer that—yet."

I was shaking my head. Then I pointed at him. "Ask the elderly gent upstairs if he heard her opening the garage door, starting up the Packard's cold engine sometime between two a.m. and dawn. Ask him!"

"I did. He didn't. But it was a windy night, and..."

"Yeah, and the surf was crashing something fierce. Right. Let's take a look at her shoes."

"Huh?"

I pointed down to my scuffed-up Florsheims. "I just scaled those two-hundred-and-eighty steps. This shoeshine boy's nightmare is the result. Let's *see* if she walked up those steps."

Rondell nodded and led me into the garage. The print boys hadn't been over the vehicle yet, so the Lieutenant didn't open the door on the rider's side, he just leaned carefully in.

Then he stood and contemplated what he'd seen. For a moment he seemed to have forgotten me, then he said, "Have a look yourself."

I had one last look at the beautiful woman who'd driven to nowhere in this immobile car.

She wore delicate silver dress heels; they were as pristine as Cinderella's glass slippers.

The Coroner at the inquest agreed with me on one point: "The high winds and very low cold prevailing that week-end would have preserved the body beyond the usual time required for decomposition to set in."

The inquest was, otherwise, a bundle of contradictions, and about as inconclusive as the virgin birth. A few new, sinister facts emerged. She had bruises *inside* her throat. Had someone shoved a bottle down her throat? Her alcohol level was high—.13 percent—much higher than the three or four drinks she was seen to have had at the Troc. And there *was* gas left in the car, it turned out—several gallons; yet the ignition switch was turned on....

But the coroner's final verdict was that Thelma died by carbon monoxide poisoning, "breathed accidentally." Nonetheless, the papers talked suicide, and the word on the streets of Hollywood was "hush-up." Nobody wanted another scandal. Not after Mary Astor's diaries and Busby Berkley's drunk-driving fatalities.

I wasn't buying the coroner's verdict, either.

I knew that three people, on the Monday I'd found Thelma, had come forward to the authorities and reported having seen her on *Sunday*, long after she had "officially" died.

Miranda Diamond, Eastman's now ex-wife (their divorce had gone through, finally, apparently fairly amicably), claimed to have seen Thelma, still dressed in her Trocadero fineries, behind the wheel of her distinctive Packard convertible at the corner of Sunset and Vine Sunday, mid-morning. She was, Miranda told the cops, in the company of a tall, swarthy, nattily dressed young man whom Miranda had never seen before.

Mrs. Wallace Ford, wife of the famed director, had received a brief phone call from Thelma around four Sunday afternoon.

Thelma had called to say she would be attending the Fords' cocktail party, and was it all right if she brought along "a new, handsome friend?"

Finally, and best of all, there was Warren Eastman himself. Neighbors had reported to the police that they heard Eastman and Thelma quarreling bitterly, violently, at the bungalow above the restaurant, Sunday morning, around breakfast time. Eastman said he had thrown her out, and that she had screamed obscenities and beaten on the door for ten minutes (and police did find kick marks on the shrub-secluded, hacienda-style door).

"It was a lover's quarrel," Eastman told a reporter. "I heard she had a new boy friend—some Latin fellow from San Francisco—and she denied it. But I knew she was lying."

Eastman also revealed, in the press, that Thelma didn't own any real interest in her Sidewalk Café; she had made no investment other than lending her name, for which she got 50 percent of the profits.

I called Rondell after the inquest and he told me the case was closed.

"We both know something smells," I said. "Aren't you going to do something?"

"Yes," he said.

"What?"

"I'm going to hang up."

And he did.

Rondell was a good cop in a bad town, an honest man in a system so corrupt the Borgias would've felt moral outrage; even a Chicago boy like me found it disgusting. But he couldn't do much about movie-mogul pressure by way of City Hall; Los Angeles had one big business and the film industry was it. And I was just an out-of-town private detective with a local dead client.

On the other hand, she'd paid me to protect her, and ultimately I hadn't. I had accepted her money, and it seemed to me she ought to get something for it, even if it was posthumous.

I went out the next Monday morning—one week to the day since I'd found the ice-cream blonde melting in that garage—and at the Café, sitting alone in the cocktail lounge, reading *Variety* and drinking a bloody Mary, was Warren Eastman. He was between pictures and just two stools down from where she had sat when she first hired me. He was wearing a blue blazer, a cream silk cravat, and white pants. He lowered the paper and looked at me; he was surprised to see me, but it was not a pleasant surprise, even though he affected a toothy smile under the twitchy little mustache.

"What brings you around, Heller? I don't need a bodyguard."

"Don't be so sure," I said genially, sitting next to him.

He looked down his nose at me through slitted eyes; his diamond-shaped face seemed handsome to some, I supposed, but to me it was a harshly angular thing, a hunting knife with hair.

"What exactly," he said, "do you mean by that?"

"I mean I know you murdered Thelma," I said.

He laughed and returned to his newspaper. "Go away, Heller. Find some schoolgirl who frightens easily if you want to scare somebody."

"I want to scare somebody all right. I just have one question...did your ex-wife help you with the murder itself, or was she just a supporting player?"

He put the paper down. He sipped the bloody Mary. His face was wooden but his eyes were animated.

I laughed gutturally. "You and your convoluted murder mysteries. You were so clever you almost schemed your way into the gas chamber, didn't you? With your masquerades and charades."

"What in the hell are you talking about?"

"You were smart enough to figure out that the cold weather would confuse the time of death. But you thought you could make the coroner think Thelma met her fate the *next* day—Sunday evening, perhaps. You didn't have an alibi for the early a.m. hours of Sunday. And that's when you killed her."

"Is it, really? Heller, I saw her Sunday morning, breakfast. I argued with her, the neighbors heard..."

"Exactly. They *heard*—but they didn't *see* a thing. That was something you staged, either with your ex-wife's help, or whoever your current starlet is. Some actress, the same actress who later called Mrs. Ford up to accept the cocktail party invite and further spread the rumor of the new lover from San Francisco. Nice touch, that. Pulls in the rumors of gangsters from San Francisco who threatened her; was the 'swarthy man' Miranda saw a torpedo posing as a lover? A gigolo with a gun? A member of Artie Lewis' dance band, maybe? Let the cops and the papers wonder. Well, it won't wash with me; I was with her for her last month. She had no new serious love in her life, from San Francisco or elsewhere. Your 'swarthy man' is the little Latin lover who wasn't there."

"Miranda *saw* him with her, Heller..."

"No. Miranda didn't see anything. She told the story you wanted her to tell; she went along with you, and you treated her right in the divorce settlement. You can afford to. You're sole owner of Thelma Todd's Sidewalk Café, now. Lock, stock and barrel, with no messy interference from the star on the marquee. And now you're free to accept Lucky Luciano's offer, aren't you?"

That rocked him, like a physical blow. "What?"

"That's why you killed Thelma. She was standing in your way. You wanted to put a casino in upstairs; it would mean big money, very big money."

"I have money."

"Yes, and you spend it. You live very lavishly. I've been checking up on you. I know you intimately already, and I'm going to know you even better."

His eyes quivered in the diamond mask of his face. "What are you talking about?"

"You tried to scare her at first—extortion notes, having her followed; maybe you did this with Luciano's help, maybe you did it on your own. I don't know. But then she hired me, and you scurried off into the darkness to think up something new."

He sneered and gestured archly with his cigarette holder, the cigarette in which he was about to light up. "I'm breathlessly awaiting just what evil thing it was I conjured up next."

"You decided to commit the perfect crime. Just like in the movies. You would kill Thelma one cold night, knocking her out, shoving booze down her, leaving her to die in that garage with the car running. Then you would set out to make it seem that she was still alive—during a day when you were very handsomely, unquestionably alibied."

"You're not making any sense. The verdict at the inquest was accidental death..."

"Yes. But the time of death is assumed to have been the night *before* you said you saw her last. Your melodrama was too involved for the simple-minded authorities, who only wanted to hush things up. They went with the more basic, obvious, tidy solution that Thelma died an accidental death early Saturday morning." I laughed, once. "You were so cute in pursuit of the 'perfect crime' you tripped yourself, Eastman."

"Did I really," he said dryly. It wasn't a question.

"Your scenario needed one more rewrite. First you told the cops you slept at the apartment over the café Saturday night, bolting the door around midnight, accidentally locking Thelma out. But later you admitted seeing Thelma the next morning, around breakfast time—at the *bungalow*."

His smile quivered. "Perhaps I slept at the apartment, and went up for breakfast at the bungalow."

"I don't think so. I think you killed her."

"No charges have been brought against me. And none will."

I looked at him hard, like a hanging judge passing sentence. "I'm bringing a charge against you now. I'm charging you with murder in the first degree."

His smile was crinkly; he stared into the redness of his drink. Smoke from his cigarette-in-holder curled upward like a wreath. "Ha. A citizen's arrest, is it?"

"No. Heller's law. I'm going to kill you myself."

He looked at me sharply. "What? Are you mad..."

"Yes, I'm mad. In sense of being angry, that is. Sometime, within the next year, or two, I'm going to kill you. Just how, I'm not just sure. Might be me who does it, might be one of my Chicago pals. Just when, well...perhaps tomorrow. Perhaps a month from tomorrow. Maybe next Christmas. I haven't decided yet."

"You can't be serious..."

"I'm deadly serious. Right now I'm heading home to Chicago, to mull it over. But don't worry—I'll be seeing you."

And I left him there at the bar, the glass of bloody Mary mixing itself in his hand.

Here's what I did to Warren Eastman: I hired Fred Rubinski to spend two weeks shadowing him. Letting him see he was being tailed by an ugly intimidating-looking bastard, which Fred was. Letting him extrapolate from this that I was, through my surrogate, watching his every move. Making him jump at that shadow, and all the other shadows, too.

Then I pulled Fred off Eastman's case. Home in Chicago, I slept with my gun under my pillow for a while, in case the director got ambitious. But I didn't bother him any further.

The word in Hollywood was that Eastman was somehow— no one knew exactly how, but somehow—dirty in the Todd murder. And nobody in town thought it was anything but a murder. Eastman never got another picture. He went from one of the hottest directors in town, to the coldest. As cold as the weekend Thelma Todd died.

The Sidewalk Café stopped drawing a monied, celebrity crowd, but it did all right from regular-folks curiosity seekers. Eastman made some dough there, all right; but the casino never happened. A combination of the wrong kind of publicity, and the drifting away of the high-class clientele, must have changed Lucky Luciano's mind.

Within a year of Thelma Todd's death, Eastman was committed to a rest home, which is a polite way of saying insane asylum or madhouse. He was in and out of such places for the next four years, and then, one very cold, windy night, he died of a heart attack.

Did I keep my promise? Did I kill him?

I like to think I did, indirectly. I like to think that Thelma Todd got her money's worth from her chauffeur/bodyguard, who had not been there when she took that last long drive, on the night her sad blue eyes closed forever.

I like to think, in my imperfect way, that I committed the perfect crime.

AUTHOR'S NOTE

I have taken liberties in this story based on the probable murder of actress Thelma Todd, changing some names and fictionalizing extensively. A number of books dealing with the death of Thelma Todd were consulted, but I wish in particular to cite Marvin J. Wolf and Katherine Mader, authors of *Fallen Angels* (1986).

HOUSE CALL

Nineteen-thirty-six began for me with a missing persons case. It didn't stay a missing persons case long, but on that bitterly cold Chicago morning of January 3rd, all Mrs. Peacock knew was that her doctor husband had failed to come home after making a house call the night before.

It was Saturday, just a little past ten, and I was filling out an insurance adjustment form when she knocked. I said come in, and she did, an attractive woman of about thirty-five in an expensive fur coat. She didn't look high-hat, though: she'd gone out today without any make-up on, which, added to her generally haggard look, told me she was at wit's end.

"Mr. Heller? Nathan Heller?"

I said I was, standing, gesturing to a chair across from my desk. My office at the time was a large single room on the fourth floor of a less than fashionable building on the corner of Van Buren and Plymouth, in the shadow of the El. She seemed a little posh to be coming to my little one-man agency for help.

"Your name was given to me by Tom Courtney," she said. "He's a friend of the family."

State's Attorney Thomas J. Courtney and I had crossed paths several times, without any particular mishap; this explained why she'd chosen the A-1 Detective Agency, but not why she needed a detective in the first place.

"My husband is missing," she said.

"I assume you've filed a missing person's report."

"Yes I have. But I've been told until twenty-four hours elapse, my husband will not be considered missing. Tom suggested if my concern was such that I felt immediate action warranted, I might contact you. Which I have."

She was doing an admirable job of maintaining her composure; but there was a quaver in her voice and her eyes were moist.

"If you have any reason to suspect a kidnapping or foul play," I said, keeping my voice calm and soft, to lessen the impact of such menacing words, "I think you're doing the right thing. Trails can go cold in twenty-four hours."

She nodded, found a brave smile.

"My husband, Silber, is a doctor, a pediatrician. We live in the Edgewater Beach Apartments."

That meant money; no wonder she hadn't questioned me about my rates.

"Last evening Betty Lou, our eight year-old, and I returned home from visiting my parents in Bowen. Silber met us at Union Station and we dined at little restaurant on the North Side—the name escapes me, but I could probably come up with it if it proves vital—and then came home. Silber went to bed; I was sitting up reading. The phone rang. The voice was male. I asked for a name, an address, the nature of the business, doing my best to screen the call. But the caller insisted on talking to the doctor. I was reluctant, but I called Silber to the phone, and I heard him say, 'What is it?....Oh, a child is ill? Give me the address and I'll be there straight away.'"

"Did your husband write the address down?"

She nodded. "Yes, and I have the sheet right here." She dug in her purse and handed it to me.

In the standard barely readable prescription-pad scrawl of any doctor, the note said: "G. Smale. 6438 North Whipple Street."

"Didn't the police want this?"

She shook her head no. "Not until it's officially a missing persons case they don't."

"No phone number?"

"My husband asked for one and was told that the caller had no phone."

"Presumably he was calling on one."

She shrugged, with sad frustration. "I didn't hear the other end of the conversation. All I can say for certain is that my husband hung up, sighed, smiled and said, 'No rest for the wicked,' and dressed. I jotted the information from the pad onto the top of the little Chicago street guide he carries, when he's doing house calls."

"So he never took the original note with him?"

"No. What you have there is what he wrote. Then Silber kissed me, picked up his black instrument bag and left. I remember glancing at the clock in the hall. It was 10:05 p.m."

"Did you hear from him after that?"

"No I did not. I slept, but fitfully, and woke around one thirty a.m. Silber wasn't home yet. I remember being irritated with him for taking a call from someone who wasn't a regular patient; he has an excellent practice, now—there's no need for it. I called the building manager and asked if Silber's car had returned to the garage. It hadn't. I didn't sleep a wink after that. When dawn broke, so, I'm afraid, did I. I called Tom Courtney; he came around at once, phoned the police for me, then advised me to see you, should I feel the need for immediate action."

"I'm going to need some further information," I said.

"Certainly."

Questioning her, I came up with a working description and other pertinent data: Peacock was forty years old, a member of the staff of Children's Memorial. He'd been driving a 1931 black Cadillac sedan, 1936 license 25-682. Wearing a gray suit, gray top-coat, gray felt hat. Five foot seven, 150 pounds, wire frame glasses.

I walked her down to the street and helped her hail a cab. I told her I'd get right on the case, and that in future she needn't call on me; I'd come to her at her Edgewater Beach apartment. She smiled, rather bravely I thought, as she slipped into the backseat of the cab; squeezed my arm and looked at me like I was something noble.

Well, I didn't feel very noble. Because as her cab turned down Plymouth Court I was thinking that her husband the good doctor had probably simply had himself a big evening. He'd show up when his head stopped throbbing, or when something below the belt stopped throbbing, anyway. In future he'd need to warn his babe to stop calling him at home, even if she did have a brother or a knack for doing a convincing vocal imitation of a male.

Back in my office I got out the private detective's most valuable weapon—the telephone book—and looked up G. W. Smale. There was a listing with the same street number—6438—but the street was wrong, South Washtenaw. The names and house numbers tallied, yes, but the streets in question were on opposite sides of the city. The reverse directory listing street numbers followed by names and numbers told me that no "G. Smale" was listed at 6438 North Whipple.

What the hell; I called the Smale on South Washtenaw.

"I don't know any Dr. Peacock," he said. "I never saw the man in my life."

"Who do you take your kids to when they're sick?"

"Nobody."

"Nobody?"

"I don't have any kids. I'm not a father."

I talked to him for fifteen minutes, and he seemed forthright enough; my instincts, and I do a lot of phone work, told me to leave him to the cops, or at least till later that afternoon. I wanted to check out the doctor's working quarters.

So I tooled my sporty '32 Auburn over to 4753 Broadway, where Dr. Peacock shared sumptuous digs with three other doctors, highly reputable medical specialists all. His secretary was a stunning brunette in her late twenties, a Miss Kathryn Mulrooney. I like a good-looking woman in white; the illusion of virginity does something for me.

"I know what you're going to ask," she said, quickly, before I'd asked anything. All I'd done was show her my investigator's i.d. and say I was in Mrs. Peacock's employ. "Dr. Peacock had no patient named Smale; I've been digging through our files ever since Mrs. Peacock called this morning, just in case my memory is faulty."

She didn't look like she had a faulty anything.

"What's even stranger," she said, with a tragic expression, "he almost never answered night calls. Oh, he once upon a time did—he hated to turn away any sick child. His regular patients seldom asked him to do so, however, and this practice has become so large that he wasn't accepting any new cases. It's unbelievable that..."

She paused; I'd been doing my job, asking questions, listening, but a certain part of me had been undressing the attractive nurse in my mind's eye—everybody needs a hobby—and she misread my good-natured lechery toward her for something else.

"Please!" she said. "You mustn't leap to horrid conclusions. Dr. Peacock was a man of *impeccable* character. He loved his family and his home, passionately. He was no playboy; he loathed night clubs and all they stand for. He didn't even drink!"

"I see," I said.

"I hope you do," she said curtly. "That he might have been involved in an affair with a woman other than his wife is unthinkable. Please believe me."

"Perhaps I do. But could you answer one question?"

"What's that?"

"Why are you referring to the doctor in the past tense?"

She began to cry; she'd been standing behind a counter—now she leaned against it.

"I...I wish I believed him capable of running around on Ruth, his wife. Then I wouldn't be so convinced that something... something *terrible* has happened."

I felt bad; I'd been suspicious of her, been looking to find her between the doctor's sheets, and had made her cry. She was a sincere young woman, that was obvious.

"I'm very sorry," I said, meaning it, and turned to go.

But before I went out, another question occurred to me, and I asked it: "Miss Mulrooney—had the parents of any patient ever blamed Dr. Peacock for some unfortunate results of some medical treatment he administered? Any threats of reprisal?"

"Absolutely not," she said, chin trembling.

On this point I didn't believe her; her indignation rang shrill. And, anyway, most doctors make enemies. I only wished she had pointed to one of those enemies.

But I'd pushed this kid enough.

I dropped by the Edgewater Beach Apartments—not to talk to Mrs. Peacock. I went up to the attendant in the lobby, a distinguished-looking blue-uniformed man in his late fifties; like so many doormen and lobby attendants, he looked like a soldier from some foreign country in a light opera.

Unlike a good solider, he was willing to give forth with much more than his name and rank. I had hoped to get from him the name of the night man, who I hoped to call and get some information from; but it turned out *he* was the night man.

"George was sick," he said. "So I'm doing double-duty. I can use the extra cash more than the sleep."

"Speaking of cash," I said, and handed him a buck.

"Thank you, sir!"

"Now, earn it: what can you tell me about Dr. Peacock? Does he duck out at night very often?"

The attendant shook his head no. "Can't remember the last time, before the other night. Funny thing, though."

"Yeah?"

"He was rushing out of here, then all of a sudden stopped and turned and stood five minutes blabbing in the phone booth over there."

Back in the Auburn, my mind was abuzz. Why else would Dr. Peacock use the lobby phone, unless it was to make a call he didn't want his wife to hear? The "poor sick child" call had been a ruse. The baby specialist obviously had a babe.

I didn't have a missing persons case at all. I had a stray husband who had either taken off for parts unknown with his lady love or, more likely considering the high-hat practice the doc would have to leave behind, would simply show up with some cock-and-bull story for the missus after a torrid twenty-four hour shack-up with whoever-she-was.

I drove to 6438 North Whipple Street. What my reverse phone book hadn't told me was that this was an apartment building, a six-flat. Suddenly the case warmed up again; I found a place for the Auburn along the curb and walked up the steps into the brownstone.

No "G. Smale" was a resident, at least not a resident who had a name on any of the vestibule mailboxes.

I walked out into the cold air, my breath smoking, my mind smoking a little too: the "patient" hadn't had a phone, but in a nice brownstone like this most likely *everybody* had a phone. Nothing added up. Except maybe two plus two equals rendezvous.

The doc had a doll, that's all there was to it. Nonetheless, I decided to scout the neighborhood for Peacock's auto. I went two blocks in all directions and saw no sign of it. I was about to call it an afternoon, and a long one at that, when I extended the canvassing to include a third block, and on the 6000 block in North Francisco Avenue, I saw it: a black Caddy sedan with the license 25-682.

I approached the car, which was parked alongside a vacant lot, across from several brownstones. I peeked in; in the back-seat was a topcoat, but the topcoat was covering something. Looking in the window, you couldn't tell what. I tried the door. It was unlocked.

I pulled the rider's seat forward, and there he was, in a kneeling position, in the back, facing the rear, the top half of him bent over the seat, covered by the topcoat. Carefully, I lifted it off, resting it on the hood of the car. Blood was spattered on the floor and rear windows; the seat was crusty black with it, dried. His blood-flecked felt hat, wadded up like a discarded tissue, lay on the seat. His medical bag was on the seat next to him; it too had been sheltered from sight by the topcoat, and was open and had been disturbed. The little street map book, with the address on it in Mrs. Peacock's handwriting, was nearby, speckled with blood.

A large caliber bullet had gone in his right temple and come out behind the left ear. His skull was crushed; his brain was showing, but scrambled. His head and shoulders bore numerous knife slashes. His right hand was gloved, but his left was bare and had been caught, crushed, in the slamming car door.

This was one savage killing.

Captain Stege himself arrived, after I called it in; if my name hadn't been attached to it, he probably wouldn't have come. The tough little cop had once been Chief of Detectives till, ironically, a scandal had cost him—one of Chicago's few verifiably honest cops—his job. Not long ago he'd been chief of the PD's Dillinger squad. It was on the Dillinger case that Stege and I had put our feud behind us; we were uneasily trying to get along these days.

I quickly showed him two more discoveries I'd made, before he or any of his boys in blue had arrived: a .45 revolver shell that was in the snow, near the car, on the vacant lot side; and a pinkish stain in the snow, plus deep tire tracks and numerous cigarette butts, in front of the apartment building at 6438 North Whipple. The tire tracks and cigarettes seemed to indicate that whoever had lured the doctor from his bed had indeed waited at this address; the pink stain pointed toward the violence having started there.

"What's your part in this?" he said, as we walked back to the scene of the crime. He was a small gray man in a gray topcoat and gray formless hat; tiny eyes squinted behind round, black-rimmed lenses. "How'd you happen to find the body, anyway?"

I explained that Mrs. Peacock had hired me to find her husband. Which, after all, I had.

A police photographer was taking pictures, the body not yet moved.

"How do you read this, Heller?"

"Not a simple robbery."

"Oh?"

I pointed to the corpse. "He took God knows how many brutal blows; he was slashed and slashed again. It takes hate to arouse pointless violence like that."

"Crime of passion, then."

"That's how I see it, Captain."

"The wife have an alibi?"

"Don't even bother going down that road."

"You mind if I bother, Heller? You ever seen the statistics of the number of murders committed within families?"

"She was home with her daughter. Go ahead. Waste your time. But she's a nice lady."

"I'll remember that. Give your statement to Phelan, and go home. This isn't your case, anymore."

"I know it isn't. But do you mind if I, uh....if I'm the one to break the news to Mrs. Peacock?"

Stege cleared his throat; shot a wad of phlegm into the nearby snow. "Not at all. Nobody envies duty like that."

So I told her. I wanted her told by somebody who didn't suspect her and, initially, I'd be the only one who qualified.

She sat in a straightback chair at her dining room table, in the Peacock's conservative yet expensively appointed apartment high in the Edgewater Beach, and wept into a lace hanky. I sat with her for fifteen minutes. She didn't ask me to go, so I didn't.

Finally she said, "Silber was a fine man. He truly was. A perfect husband and father. His habits regular and beyond reproach. No one hated Silber. No one. He was lured to his death by thieves."

"Yes, ma'am."

"Did you know that once before he was attacked by thieves, and that he did not hesitate to fight them off? My husband was a brave man."

"I'm sure he was."

I left her there, with her sorrow, thinking that I wished she was right, but knowing she was wrong. I did enough divorce work to know how marriages, even "perfect" ones, can go awry. I also had a good fix on just how much marital cheating was going on in this Christian society.

The next morning I called Stege. He wasn't glad to hear from me, exactly, but he did admit that the wife was no longer a suspect; her alibi was flawless.

"There *was* a robbery of sorts," Stege said.

"Oh?"

"Twenty dollars was missing from Peacock's wallet. On the other hand, none of his jewelry—some of it pretty expensive stuff—was even touched."

"What was taken from the medical bag?" I asked.

"Some pills and such were taken, but apparently nothing narcotic. A baby specialist doesn't go toting dope around."

"An addict might not know that; an addict might've picked Dr. Peacock's name at random, not knowing he was a baby doc."

"And what, drew him to that vacant lot to steal a supposed supply of narcotics?"

"Yeah. It might explain the insanity, the savagery of the attack."

"Come on, Heller. You know as well as I do this is a personal killing. I expect romance to rear its lovely head any time, now.

Peacock was rich, handsome enough, by all accounts person-able. And he had, we estimate, upwards of five hundred patients. Five hundred kiddies all of whom have mothers who visited the doctor with them."

"You know something, Captain."

"What?"

"I'm glad this isn't my case anymore."

"Oh?"

"Yeah. I wish you and your boys all the best doing those five hundred interviews."

He grumbled and hung up.

I did send Mrs. Peacock a bill, for one day's services—$20 and $5 expenses—and settled back to watch, with some discomfort, the papers speculate about the late doctor's love life. Various screwball aspects to the case were chased down by the cops and the press; none of it amounted to much. This included a nutty rumor that the doctor was a secret federal narcotics agent and killed by a dope ring; and the Keystone Kops affair of the mysterious key found in the doctor's pocket, the lock to which countless police hours were spent seeking, only to have the key turn out to belong to the same deputy coroner who had produced it. The hapless coroner had accidentally mixed a key of his own among the Peacock evidence.

More standard, reliable lines of inquiry provided nothing: fingerprints found in the car were too smudged to identify; witnesses who came forth regarding two people arguing in the death car varied as to the sex of the occupants; the last-minute phone call Peacock made in the lobby turned out to have been to one of his business partners; interviews of the parents of five hundred Peacock patients brought forth not a single disgruntled person, nor a likely partner for any Peacock "love nest."

Peacock had been dead for over two weeks, when I was brought back into the case again, through no effort of my own.

The afternoon of January 16, someone knocked at my office door; in the middle of a phone credit check, I covered the receiver and called out, "Come in."

The door opened tentatively and a small, milquetoast of a man peered in.

"Mr. Heller?"

I nodded, motioned for him to be seated before me, and finished up my call; he sat patiently, a pale little man in a dark suit, his dark hat in his lap.

"What can I do for you?"

He stood, smiled in an entirely humorless, business-like manner, extending a hand to be shook; I shook it, and the grip was surprisingly firm.

"I am a Lutheran minister," he said. "My name, for the moment, is unimportant."

"Pleased to meet you, Reverend."

"I read about the Peacock case in the papers."

"Yes?"

"I saw your name. You discovered the body. You were in Mrs. Peacock's employ."

"Yes."

"I have information. I was unsure of whom to give it to."

"If you have information regarding the Peacock case, you should give it to the police. I can place a call right now..."

"Please, no! I would prefer you hear my story and judge for yourself."

"All right."

"Last New Year's Day I had a chance meeting with my great and good friend, Dr. Silber Peacock, God rest his soul. On that occasion the doctor confided that a strange man, a fellow who claimed to be a chiropodist, had come bursting into his office, making vile accusations."

"Such as?"

"He said, 'You, sir, are having an affair with my wife!'"

I sat forward. "Go on."

"Dr. Peacock said he'd never laid eyes on this man before; that he thought him a crazy man. 'Why, I never ran around on Ruth in my life,' he said."

"How did he deal with this man?"

"He threw him bodily from his office."

"When did he have this run-in? Did he mention the man's name?"

"Last October. The man's name was Thompson, and he was, as I've said, a chiropodist."

"You should go to the police with this."

The Reverend stood quickly, nervously. "I'd really rather not."

And then he was on his way out of the office. By the time I got out from behind my desk, he was out of the room, and by the time I got out into the hall, he was out of sight.

The only chiropodist named Thompson in the Chicago phone book was one Arthur St. George Thompson, whom I found at his Wilson Avenue address. He was a skinny, graying man in his early forties; he and his office were seedy. He had no patients in his rather unkempt waiting room when I arrived (or when I left, for that matter).

"I knew Silber Peacock," he said, bitterly. "I remember visiting him at his office in October, too. What of it?"

"Did you accuse him of seeing your wife?"

"Sure I did! Let me tell you how I got hep to Peacock and Arlene. One evening last June she came home stinking, her and Ann—that's the no-good who's married to Arlene's brother Carl. Arlene said she'd been at the Subway Club and her escort was Doc Peacock. So I looked in the classified directory. The only Dr. Peacock was Silber C., so I knew it was him. I stewed about it for weeks, months, and then I went to his office. The son of a bitch pretended he didn't know who I was, or Arlene, either; he just kept denying it, and shoving me out of there, shoved me clear out into the hall."

"I see."

"No you don't. I hated the louse, but I didn't kill him. Besides, I got an alibi. I can prove where I was the night he was murdered."

He claimed that because his practice was so poor of late, he'd taken on menial work at the Medinah Club. An alibi out of a reputable place like that would be hard to break. I'd leave that to Stege, when—or if—I turned this lead over to him.

First I wanted to talk to Arlene Thompson, whom I found at her brother's place, a North Side apartment.

Ann was a slender, giggly brunette, attractive. Arlene was even more attractive, a voluptuous redhead. Both were in their mid-twenties. Ann's husband wasn't home, so the two of them flirted with me and we had a gay old time.

"Were you really seeing Doc Peacock?"

The two girls exchanged glances and began giggling and the giggling turned to outright laughter. "That poor guy!" Arlene said.

"Well, yeah, I'd say so. He's dead."

"Not him! Arthur! That insane streak of jealousy's got him in hot water again, has it? Look, good-lookin'—there's nothing *to* any of this, understand? Here's how it happened."

Arlene and Ann had gone alone to the Subway Cafe one afternoon, a rowdy honky-tonk that had since lost its liquor license, and got picked up by two men. They danced till dusk. Arlene's man said he was Doc Peacock; no other first name given.

"Arthur went off his rocker when I came in, tipsy. He demanded the truth—so I told it to him! It was all innocent enough, but got him goin'. He talked days on end about Doc Peacock, about how he was going to even the score."

"Do you think he did?"

The redhead laughed again, said, "Honey, that Dr. Peacock whose puss has been in the papers ain't the guy I dated. My Peacock was much better looking—wavy hair, tall, a real dreamboat. I think my pick-up just pulled a name out of his hat."

"Your husband didn't know that. Maybe he evened the score with the wrong Peacock."

She shook her head, not believing that for a minute. "Arthur just isn't the type. He's a poor, weak sister. He never had enough pep to hurt a fly."

It was all conjecture, but I turned it over to Stege, anyway. Thompson's alibi checked out. Yet another dead-end.

The next day I was reading the morning papers over breakfast in the coffee shop at the Morrison Hotel. A very small item, buried on an inside page, caught my eye: Dr. Joseph Soldinger, 1016 North Oakley Blvd, had been robbed at gunpoint last night of $37, his car stolen.

I called Stege and pointed out the similarity to the Peacock case, half expecting him to shrug it off. He didn't. He thanked me, and hung up.

A week later I got a call from Stege; he was excited. "Listen to this: Dr. A.L. Abrams, 1600 Milwaukee Avenue, $56 lost to gunmen; Dr. L.A. Garness, 2542 Mozart Avenue, waylaid and robbed of $6. And there's two more like that."

"Details?"

"Each features a call to a doctor to rush to a bedside. Address is in a lonely neighborhood. It's an appointment with ambush. Take is always rather small. Occurrences between ten and eleven p.m."

"Damn! Sounds like Mrs. Peacock has been right all along. Her husband fought off his attackers; that's what prompted their beating him."

"The poor bastard was a hero and the papers paint him a philanderer."

"Well, we handed 'em the brush."

"Perhaps we did, Heller. Anyway, thanks."

"Any suspects?"

"No. But we got the pattern now. From eye-witness descriptions it seems to be kids. Four assailants, three tall and husky, the other shorter."

A bell was ringing, and not outside my window. "Captain, you ever hear of Rose Kasallis?"

"Can't say I have."

"I tracked a runaway girl to her place two summers ago. She's a regular female Fagin. She had a flat on North Maplewood Avenue that was a virtual 'school for crime.'"

"I have heard of that. The West North Avenue cops handled it. She was keeping a way-station for fugitive kids from the reform school at St. Charles. Sent up the river for contributing to the delinquency of minors?"

"That's the one. I had quite a run-in with her charming boy Bobby. Robert Goethe is his name."

"Oh?"

"He's eighteen years old, a strapping kid with the morals of an alley cat. And there were a couple of kids he ran with, Emil Reck, who they called Emil the Terrible, and another one whose name I can't remember..."

"Heller, Chicago has plenty of young street toughs. Why do you think these three might be suspects in the Peacock case?"

"I don't know that they are. In fact, last I knew Bobby and the other two were convicted of strong-arming a pedestrian and were sitting in the Bridewell. But that's been at least a year ago."

"And they might be out amongst us again, by now."

"Right. Could you check?"

"I'll do that very thing."

Ten minutes later Stege called and said, "They were released in December."

January 2 had been Silber Peacock's last day on earth.

"I have an address for Bobby Goethe's apartment," Stege said. "Care to keep an old copper company?"

He swung by and picked me up—hardly usual procedure, pulling in a private dick on a case, but I had earned this—and soon we were pulling up in front of the weathered brownstone in which Bobby Goethe lived. And there was no doubt he lived here.

Because despite the chilly day, he and Emil the Terrible were sitting on the stoop, in light jackets, smoking cigarettes and drinking bottles of beer. Bobby had a weak, acned chin, and reminded me of photos I'd seen of Clyde Barrow; Emil had a big lumpy nose and a high forehead, atop which was piled blond curly hair—he looked thick as a plank.

We were in an unmarked car, but a uniformed man was behind the wheel, so as soon as we pulled in, the two boys reacted, beer bottles dropping to the cement and exploding like bombs.

Bobby took off in one direction, and Emil took off in the other. Stege just watched as his plainclothes detective assistant took off after Emil, and I took off after Bobby.

It took me a block to catch up, and I hit him with a flying tackle, and we rolled into a vacant lot, not unlike the one by the Caddy in which Peacock's body had been found.

Bobby was a wiry kid, and wormed his way out of my grasp, kicking back at me as he did; I took a boot in the face, but didn't lose any teeth, and managed to reach out and grab that foot and yank him back hard. He went down on his face in the weeds and rocks. One of the larger of those rocks found its way into his hand, and he flung it at me, savage little animal that he was, only not so little. I ducked out of the rock's way, but quickly reached a hand under my topcoat and suitcoat and got my nine millimeter Browning out and pointed it down at him.

"I'm hurt," he said, looking up at me with a scraped, bloody face.

"Shall we call a doctor?" I said.

Emil and Bobby and their crony named Nash, who was arrested later that afternoon by West North Avenue Station cops, were put in a show-up for the various doctors who'd been robbed to identify. They did so, without hesitation. The trio was separated and questioned individually and sang and sang. A fourth boy was implicated, the shorter one who'd been mentioned, seventeen-year-old Mickey Livingston. He too was identified, and he too sang.

Their story was a singularly stupid one. They had been cruising in a stolen car, stopped in a candy store, picked Peacock's name at random from the phone book, picked another name and address, altered it, and called and lured the doctor to an isolated spot they'd chosen. Emil the Terrible, a heavy club in hand, crouched in the shadows across the street from 6438 North Whipple. Nash stood at the entrance, and Goethe, gun in hand, hid behind a tree nearby. Livingston was the wheel man, parked half a block north.

Peacock drove up and got out of his car, medical bag in hand. Bobby stuck the gun in the doctor's back and told him not to move. Peacock was led a block north after Emil the Terrible had smacked him "a lick for luck." At this point Peacock fought back, wrestling with Bobby, who shot the doctor in the head. Peacock dropped to the ground, and Emil the Imbecilic hit the dead man again and again with the club. A scalpel from the medical bag in one hand, the gun held butt forward in the other, Bobby added some finishing touches. Nash pulled up in the doctor's car, Livingston following. The corpse was then tossed in the backseat of the Caddy, which was abandoned three blocks away.

Total take for the daring boys: $20. Just what I'd made on the case, only they didn't get five bucks expenses.

What Bobby, Emil and Nash did get was 199 years plus consecutive terms of one year to life on four robbery counts. Little Mickey was given a thirty-year sentence, and was eventually paroled. The others, to the best of my knowledge, never were.

Ruth Peacock moved to Quincy, Illinois, where she devoted the rest of her life to social service, her church and Red Cross work, as well as to raising her two daughters, Betty Lou and Nancy. Nancy never knew her father.

Maybe that's why Ruth Peacock was so convinced of her husband's loyalty, despite the mysterious circumstances of his death.

She was pregnant with his child at the time.

AUTHOR'S NOTE

Research materials consulted for this fact-based story include "The Peacock Case" by LeRoy F. McHugh in *Chicago Murders* (1947) and various true-crime magazines of the day.

MARBLE MILDRED

In June 1936, Chicago was in the midst of the Great Depression and a sweltering summer, and I was in the midst of Chicago. Specifically, on this Tuesday afternoon, the ninth to be exact, I was sitting on a sofa in the minuscule lobby of the Van Buren Hotel. The sofa had seen better days, and so had the hotel. The Van Buren was no flophouse, merely a moderately rundown residential hotel just west of the El tracks, near the LaSalle Street Station.

Divorce work wasn't the bread and butter of the A-1 Detective Agency, but we didn't turn it away. I use the editorial "we," but actually there was only one of us, me, Nathan Heller, "president" of the firm. And despite my high-flown title, I was just a down-at-the-heels dick reading a racing form in a seedy hotel's seedy lobby, waiting to see if a certain husband showed up in the company of another woman.

Another woman, that is, than the one he was married to: the dumpy, dusky dame who'd come to my office yesterday.

"I'm not as good-looking as I was fourteen years ago," she'd said, coyly, her voice honeyed by a Southern drawl, "but I'm a darn sight younger looking than *some* women I know."

"You're a very handsome woman, Mrs. Bolton," I said, smiling, figuring she was fifty if she was a day, "and I'm sure there's nothing to your suspicions."

She had been a looker once, but she'd run to fat, and her badly hennaed hair and overdone makeup were no help; nor was the raccoon stole she wore over a faded floral print housedress. The stole looked a bit ratty and in any case was hardly called for in this weather.

"Mr. Heller, they are more than suspicions. My husband is a successful businessman, with an office in the financial district. He is easy prey to gold diggers."

The strained formality of her tone made the raccoon stole make sense, somehow.

"This isn't the first time you've suspected him of infidelity."

"Unfortunately, no."

"Are you hoping for reconciliation, or has a lawyer advised you to establish grounds for divorce?"

"At this point," she said, calmly, the Southern drawl making her words seem more casual than they were, "I wish only to know. Can you understand that, Mr. Heller?"

"Certainly. I'm afraid I'll need some details..."

She had them. Though they lived in Hyde Park, a quiet, quietly well-off residential area, Bolton was keeping a room at the Van Buren Hotel, a few blocks down the street from the very office in which we sat. Mrs. Bolton believed that he went to the hotel on assignations while pretending to leave town on business trips.

"How did you happen to find that out?" I asked her.

"His secretary told me," she said, with a crinkly little smile, proud of herself.

"Are you sure you need a detective? You seem to be doing pretty well on your own..."

The smile disappeared and she seemed quite serious now, digging into her big black purse and coming back with a folded wad of cash. She thrust it across the desk toward me, as if daring me to take it.

I don't take dares, but I do take money. And there was plenty of it: a hundred in tens and fives.

"My rate's ten dollars a day and expenses," I said, reluctantly, the notion of refusing money going against the grain. "A thirty-dollar retainer would be plenty..."

She nodded curtly. "I'd prefer you accept that. But it's all I can afford, remember; when it's gone, it's gone."

I wrote her out a receipt and told her I hoped to refund some of the money, though of course I hoped the opposite, and that I hoped to be able to dispel her fears about her husband's fidelity, though there was little hope of that, either. Hope was in short supply in Chicago, these days.

Right now, she said, Joe was supposedly on a business trip; but the secretary had called to confide in Mrs. Bolton that her husband had been in the office all day.

I had to ask the usual questions. She gave me a complete description (and a photo she'd had foresight to bring), his business address, working hours, a list of places he was known to frequent.

And, so, I had staked out the hotel yesterday, starting late afternoon. I didn't start in the lobby. The hotel was a walk-up, the lobby on the second floor; the first floor leased out to a saloon, in the window of which I sat nursing beers and watching people stroll by. One of them, finally, was Joseph Bolton, a tall, nattily attired businessman about ten years his wife's junior; he was pleasant looking, but with his wire-rimmed glasses and receding brown hair was no Robert Taylor.

Nor was he enjoying feminine company, unless said company was already up in the hotel room before I'd arrived on the scene. I followed him up the stairs to the glorified landing of a lobby, where I paused at the desk while he went on up the next flight of stairs (there were no elevators in the Van Buren) and, after buying a newspaper from the desk clerk, went up to his floor, the third of the four-story hotel, and watched from around a corner as he entered his room.

Back down in the lobby, I approached the desk clerk, an older guy with rheumy eyes and a blue bow tie. I offered him a buck for the name of the guest in Room 3C.

"Bolton," he said.

"You're kidding," I said. "Let me see the register." I hadn't bothered coming in earlier to bribe a look because I figured Bolton would be here under an assumed name.

"What it's worth to you?" he asked.

"I already paid," I said, and turned his register around and looked in it. Joseph Bolton it was. Using his own goddamn name. That was a first.

"Any women?" I asked.

"Not that I know of," he said.

"Regular customer?"

"He's been living here a couple months."

"Living here? He's here every night?"

"I dunno. He pays his six bits a day, is all I know. I don't tuck him in."

I gave the guy half a buck to let me rent his threadbare sofa. Sat for another couple of hours and followed two women upstairs. Both seemed to be hookers; neither stopped at Bolton's room.

At a little after eight, Bolton left the hotel and I followed him over to Adams Street, to the Berghoff, the best German restaurant for the money in the Loop. What the hell—I hadn't eaten yet either. We both dined alone.

That night I phoned Mrs. Bolton with my report, such as it was.

"He has a woman in his room," she insisted.

"It's possible," I allowed.

"Stay on the job," she said, and hung up.

I stayed on the job. That is, the next afternoon I returned to the Van Buren Hotel, or anyway to the saloon underneath it, and drank beers and watched the world go by. Now and then the world would go up the hotel stairs. Men I ignored; women that looked like hookers I ignored. One woman, who showed up around four thirty, I did not ignore.

She was as slender and attractive a woman as Mildred Bolton was not, though she was only a few years younger. And her wardrobe was considerably more stylish than my client's—high-collared white dress with a bright colorful figured print, white gloves, white shoes, a felt hat with a wide turned-down brim.

She did not look like the sort of woman who would be stopping in at the Van Buren Hotel, but stop in she did.

So did I. I trailed her up to the third floor, where she was met at the door of Bolton's room by a male figure. I just got a glimpse of the guy, but he didn't seem to be Bolton. She went inside.

I used a pay phone in the saloon downstairs and called Mrs. Bolton in Hyde Park.

"I can be there in forty minutes," she said.

"What are you talking about?"

"I want to catch them together. I'm going to claw that hussy's eyes out."

"Mrs. Bolton, you don't want to do that..."

"I most certainly do. You can go home, Mr. Heller. You've done your job, and nicely."

And she had hung up.

I'd mentioned to her that the man in her husband's room did not seem to be her husband, but that apparently didn't matter.

Now I had a choice: I could walk back up to my office and write Mrs. Bolton out a check refunding seventy of her hundred dollars, goddamnit (ten bucks a day, ten bucks expenses—she'd pay for my bribes and beers).

Or I could do the Christian thing and wait around and try to defuse this thing before it got even uglier.

I decided to do the latter. Not because it was the Christian thing—I wasn't a Christian, after all—but because I might be able to convince Mrs. Bolton she needed a few more days' work out of me, to figure out what was really going on here. It seemed to me she could use a little more substantial information, if a divorce was to come out of this. It also seemed to me I could use the money.

I don't know how she arrived—whether by El or streetcar or bus or auto—but as fast as she was walking, it could've been on foot. She was red in the face, eyes hard and round as marbles, fists churning as she strode, her head floating above the incongruous raccoon stole.

I hopped off my bar stool and caught her at the sidewalk.

"Don't go in there, Mrs. Bolton," I said, taking her arm gently.

She swung it away from me, held her head back and, short as she was, looked down at me, nostrils flared. I felt like a matador who dropped his cape.

"You've been discharged for the day, Mr. Heller," she said.

"You still need my help. You're not going about this the right way."

With indignation she began, "My husband..."

"Your husband isn't in there. He doesn't even get off work till six."

She swallowed. The redness of her face seemed to fade some; I was quieting her down.

Then fucking fate stepped in, in the form of that swanky dame in the felt hat, who picked that very moment to come strolling out of the Van Buren Hotel like it was the goddamn Palmer House. On her arm was a young man, perhaps eighteen, perhaps twenty, in a cream-color seersucker suit and a gold tie, with a pale complexion and sky-blue eyes and corn-silk blond hair. He and the woman on his arm shared the same sensitive mouth.

"Whore!" somebody shouted.

Who else? My client.

I put my hand over my face and shook my head and wished I was dead, or at least in my office.

"Degenerate!" Mrs. Bolton sang out. She rushed toward the slender woman, who reared back, properly horrified. The young man gripped the woman's arm tightly; whether to protect her or himself, it wasn't quite clear.

Well, the sidewalks were filled with people who'd gotten off work, heading for the El or the LaSalle Street Station, so we had an audience. Yes we did.

And Mrs. Bolton was standing nose to nose with the startled woman, saying defiantly, "I am *Mrs.* Bolton—you've been up to see my husband!"

"Why, Mrs. Bolton," the woman said, backing away as best she could. "Your husband is not in his room."

"Liar!"

"If he were in the room, I wouldn't have been in there myself, I assure you."

"Lying whore..."

"Okay," I said, wading in, taking Mrs. Bolton by the arm, less gently this time, "that's enough."

"Don't talk to my mother that way," the young man said to Mrs. Bolton.

"I'll talk to her any way I like, you little degenerate."

And the young man slapped my client. It was a loud, ringing slap, and drew blood from one corner of her wide mouth.

I pointed a finger at the kid's nose. "That wasn't nice. Back away."

My client's eyes were glittering; she was smiling, a blood-flecked smile that wasn't the sanest thing I ever saw. Despite the gleeful expression, she began to scream things at the couple: "Whore! Degenerate!"

"Oh Christ," I said, wishing I'd listened to my old man and finished college.

We were encircled by a crowd who watched all this with bemused interest, some people smiling, others frowning, others frankly amazed. In the street the clop-clop of an approaching mounted police officer, interrupted in the pursuit of parking violators, cut through the din. A tall, lanky officer, he climbed off his mount and pushed through the crowd.

"What's going on here?" he asked.

"This little degenerate hit me," my client said, wearing her bloody mouth and her righteous indignation like medals, and she grabbed the kid by the tie and yanked the poor son of a bitch by it, jerking him silly.

It made me laugh. It was amusing only in a sick way, but I was sick enough to appreciate it.

"That'll be all of that," the officer said. "Now what happened here?"

I filled him in, in a general way, while my client interrupted with occasional non sequiturs; the mother and son just stood there looking chagrined about being the center of attention for perhaps a score of onlookers.

"I want that dirty little brute arrested," Mrs. Bolton said, through an off-white picket fence of clenched teeth. "I'm a victim of assault!"

The poor shaken kid was hardly a brute, and he was cleaner than most, but he admitted having struck her, when the officer asked him.

"I'm going to have to take you in, son," the officer said.

The boy looked like he might cry. Head bowed, he shrugged and his mother, eyes brimming with tears herself, hugged him.

The officer went to a call box and summoned a squad car and soon the boy was sent away, the mother waiting pitifully at the curb as the car pulled off, the boy's pale face looking back, a sad cameo in the window.

I was at my client's side.

"Let me help you get home, Mrs. Bolton," I said, taking her arm again.

She smiled tightly, patronizingly, withdrew her arm. "I'm fine, Mr. Heller. I can take care of myself. I thank you for your assistance."

And she rolled like a tank through what remained of the crowd, toward the El station.

I stood there a while, trying to gather my wits; it would have taken a better detective than yours truly to find them, however, so, finally, I approached the shattered woman who still stood at the curb. The crowd was gone. So was the mounted officer. All that remained were a few horse apples and me.

"I'm sorry about all that," I told her.

She looked at me, her face smooth, her eyes sad; they were a darker blue than her son's. "What's your role in this?"

"I'm an investigator. Mrs. Bolton suspects her husband of infidelity."

She laughed harshly—a very harsh laugh for such a refined woman. "My understanding is that Mrs. Bolton has suspected that for some fourteen years—and without foundation. But at this point, it would seem moot, one would think."

"Moot? What are you talking about?"

"The Boltons have been separated for months. Mr. Bolton is suing her for divorce."

"What? Since when?"

"Why, since January."

"Then Bolton *does* live at the Van Buren Hotel, here?"

"Yes. My brother and I have known Mr. Bolton for years. My son Charles came up to Chicago recently, to find work, and Joe—Mr. Bolton—is helping him find a job."

"You're, uh, not from Chicago?"

"I live in Woodstock. I'm a widow. Have you any other questions?"

"Excuse me, ma'am. I'm sorry about this. Really. My client misled me about a few things." I tipped my hat to her.

She warmed up a bit; gave me a smile. Tentative, but a smile. "Your apology is accepted, mister... ?"

"Heller," I said. "Nathan. And your name?"

"Marie Winston," she said, and extended her gloved hand.

I grasped it, smiled.

"Well," I said, shrugged, smiled, tipped my hat again, and headed back for my office.

It wasn't the first time a client had lied to me, and it sure wouldn't be the last. But I'd never been lied to in quite this way. For one thing, I wasn't sure Mildred Bolton knew she *was* lying. This lady clearly did not have all her marbles.

I put the hundred bucks in the bank and the matter out of my mind, until I received a phone call, on the afternoon of June 14.

"This is Marie Winston, Mr. Heller. Do you remember me?"

At first, frankly, I didn't; but I said, "Certainly. What can I do for you, Mrs. Winston?"

"That...incident out in front of the Van Buren Hotel last Wednesday, which you witnessed..."

"Oh yes. What about it?"

"Mrs. Bolton has insisted on pressing charges. I wonder if you could appear in police court tomorrow morning, and explain what happened?"

"Well..."

"Mr. Heller, I would greatly appreciate it."

I don't like turning down attractive women, even on the telephone; but there was more to it than that: the emotion in her voice got to me.

"Well, sure," I said.

So the next morning I headed over to the south Loop police court and spoke my piece. I kept to the facts, which I felt would pretty much exonerate all concerned. The circumstances were, as they say, extenuating.

Mildred Bolton, who glared at me as if I'd betrayed her, approached the bench and spoke of the young man's "unprovoked assault." She claimed to be suffering physically and mentally from the blow she'd received. The latter, at least, was believable. Her eyes were round and wild as she answered the judge's questions.

When the judge fined young Winston one hundred dollars, Mrs. Bolton stood in her place in the gallery and began to clap. Loudly. The judge looked at her, too startled to rap his gavel and demand order; then she flounced out of the courtroom very girlishly, tossing her raccoon stole over her shoulder, exulting in her victory.

An embarrassed silence fell across the room. And it's hard to embarrass hookers, a brace of which were awaiting their turn at the docket.

Then the judge pounded his gavel and said, "The court vacates this young man's fine."

Winston, who'd been hangdog throughout the proceedings, brightened like his switch had been turned on. He pumped his lawyer's hand and turned to his mother, seated behind him just beyond the railing, and they hugged.

On the way out Marie Winston, smiling gently, touched my arm and said, "Thank you very much, Mr. Heller."

"I don't think I made much difference."

"I think you did. The judge vacated the fine, after all."

"Hell, I had nothing to do with that. Mildred was your star witness."

"In a way I guess she was."

"I notice her husband wasn't here."

Son Charles spoke up. "No, he's at work. He...well, he thought it was better he not be here. We figured *that woman* would be here, after all."

"That woman is sick."

"In the head," Charles said bitterly.

"That's right. You or I could be sick that way, too. Somebody ought to help her."

Marie Winston, straining to find some compassion for Mildred Bolton, said, "Who would you suggest?"

"Damnit," I said, "the husband. He's been with her fourteen years. She didn't get this way overnight. The way I see it, he's got a responsibility to get her some goddamn *help* before he dumps her by the side of the road."

Mrs. Winston smiled at that, some compassion coming through after all. "You have a very modern point of view, Mr. Heller."

"Not really. I'm not even used to talkies yet. Anyway, I'll see you, Mrs. Winston. Charles."

And I left the graystone building and climbed in my '32 Auburn and drove back to my office. I parked in the alley, in my space, and walked over to the Berghoff for lunch. I think I hoped to find Bolton there. But he wasn't.

I went back to the office and puttered a while; I had a pile of retail credit-risk checks to whittle away at.

Hell with it, I thought, and walked over to Bolton's office building, a narrow, fifteen-story, white granite structure just behind the Federal Reserve on West Jackson, next to the El. Bolton was doing all right—better than me, certainly—but as a broker he was in the financial district only by a hair. No doubt he was a relatively small-time insurance broker, making twenty or twenty-five grand a year. Big money by my standards, but a lot of guys over at the Board of Trade spilled more than that.

There was no lobby really, just a wide hall between facing rows of shops—newsstand, travel agency, cigar store. The uniformed elevator operator, a skinny, pockmarked guy about my age, was waiting for a passenger. I was it.

"Tenth floor," I told him, and he took me up.

He was pulling open the cage doors when we heard the air crack, three times.

"What the hell was that?" he said.

"It wasn't a car backfiring," I said. "You better stay here."

I moved cautiously out into the hall. The elevators came up a central shaft, with a squared-off "c" of offices all about. I glanced quickly at the names on the pebbled glass in the wood-partition walls, and finally lit upon BOLTON AND SCHMIDT, INSURANCE BROKERS. I swallowed and moved cautiously in that direction as the door flew open and a young woman flew out—a dark-haired dish of maybe twenty with wide eyes and a face drained of blood, her silk stockings flashing as she rushed my way.

She fell into my arms and I said, "Are you wounded?"

"No," she swallowed, "but somebody is."

The poor kid was gasping for air; I hauled her toward the bank of elevators. Even under the strain, I was enjoying the feel and smell of her.

"You wouldn't be Joseph Bolton's secretary, by any chance?" I asked, helping her onto the elevator.

She nodded, eyes still huge.

"Take her down," I told the operator.

And I headed back for that office. I was nearly there when I met Joseph Bolton, as he lurched down the hall. He had a gun in his hand. His light brown suitcoat was splotched with blood in several places; so was his right arm. He wasn't wearing his eyeglasses, which made his face seem naked somehow. His expression seemed at once frightened, pained, and sorrowful.

He staggered toward me like a child taking its first steps, and I held my arms out to him like daddy. But they were more likely his last steps: he fell to the marble floor and began to writhe, tracing abstract designs in his own blood on the smooth surface.

I moved toward him and he pointed the gun at me, a little .32 revolver. "Stay away! Stay away!"

"Okay, bud, okay," I said.

I heard someone laughing.

A woman.

I looked up and in the office doorway, feet planted like a giant surveying a puny world, was dumpy little Mildred, in her floral housedress and raccoon stole. Her mug was split in a big goofy smile.

"Don't pay any attention to him, Mr. Heller," she said, lightly. "He's just faking."

"He's shot to shit, lady!" I said.

Keeping their distance out of respect and fear were various tenth-floor tenants, standing near their various offices, as if witnessing some strange performance.

"Keep her away from me!" Bolton managed to shout. His mouth was bubbling with blood. His body moved slowly across the marble floor like a slug, leaving a slimy red trail.

I moved to Mrs. Bolton, stood between her and Bolton. "You just take it easy..."

Mrs. Bolton, giggling, peeked out from in back of me. "Look at him, fooling everybody."

"You behave," I told her. Then I called out to a businessman of about fifty near the elevators. I asked him if there were any doctors in the building, and he said yes, and I said then for Christsake go get one.

"Why don't you get up and stop faking?" she said teasingly to her fallen husband, the Southern drawl dripping off her words. She craned her neck around me to see him, like she couldn't bear to miss a moment of the show.

"Keep her away! Keep her away!"

Bolton continued to writhe like a wounded snake, but he kept clutching that gun, and wouldn't let anyone near him. He would cry out that he couldn't breathe, beating his legs against the floor, but he seemed always conscious of his wife's presence. He would move his head so as to keep my body between him and her round cold glittering eyes.

"Don't you mind Joe, Mr. Heller. He's just putting on an act."

If so, I had a hunch it was his final performance.

And now he began to scream in agony.

I approached him and he looked at me with tears in his eyes, eyes that bore the confusion of a child in pain, and he relented, allowed me to come close, handed me the gun, like he was offering a gift. I accepted it, by the nose of the thing, and dropped it in my pocket.

"Did you shoot yourself, Mr. Bolton?" I asked him.

"Keep that woman away from me," he managed, lips bloody.

"He's not really hurt," his wife said, mincingly, from the office doorway.

"Did your wife shoot you?"

"Just keep her away..."

Two people in white came rushing toward us—a doctor and a nurse—and I stepped aside, but the doctor, a middle-aged, rather heavyset man with glasses, asked if I'd give him a hand. I said sure and pitched in.

Bolton was a big man, nearly two hundred pounds I'd say, and pretty much dead weight; we staggered toward the elevator like drunks. Like Bolton himself had staggered toward me, actually. The nurse tagged along.

So did Mrs. Bolton.

The nurse, young, blond, slender, did her best to keep Mrs. Bolton out of the elevator, but Mrs. Bolton pushed her way through like a fullback. The doctor and I, bracing Bolton, couldn't help the young nurse.

Bolton, barely conscious, said, "Please...please, keep her away."

"Now, now," Mrs. Bolton said, the violence of her entry into the elevator forgotten (by her), standing almost primly, hands folded over the big black purse, "everything will be all right, dear. You'll see."

Bolton began to moan; the pain it suggested wasn't entirely physical.

On the thirteenth floor, a second doctor met us and took my place hauling Bolton, and I went ahead and opened the door onto a waiting room where patients, having witnessed the doctor and nurse race madly out of the office, were milling about expectantly. The nurse guided the doctors and their burden down a hall into an X-ray room. The nurse shut the door on them and faced Mrs. Bolton with a firm look.

"I'm sorry, Mrs. Bolton, you'll have to wait."

"Is that so?" she said.

"Mrs. Bolton," I said, touching her arm.

She glared at me. "Who invited you?"

I resisted the urge to say, *you did, you fucking cow,* and just stood back while she moved up and down the narrow corridor between the offices and examining rooms, searching for a door that would lead her to her beloved husband. She trundled up and down, grunting, talking to herself, and the nurse looked at me helplessly.

"She *is* the wife," I said, with a facial shrug.

The nurse sighed heavily and went to a door adjacent to the X-ray room and called out to Mrs. Bolton; Mrs. Bolton whirled and looked at her fiercely.

"You can view your husband's treatment from in here," the nurse said.

Mrs. Bolton smiled in tight triumph and drove her taxicab of a body into the room. I followed her. Don't ask me why.

A wide glass panel looked in on the X-ray room. Mrs. Bolton climbed onto an examination table, got up on her knees, and watched the flurry of activity beyond the glass, as her husband lay on a table being attended by the pair of frantic doctors.

"Did you shoot him, Mrs. Bolton?" I asked her.

She frowned but did not look at me. "Are *you* still here?"

"You lied to me, Mrs. Bolton."

"No, I didn't. And I didn't shoot him, either."

"What happened in there?"

"I never touched that gun." She was moving her head side to side, like somebody in the bleachers trying to see past the person sitting in front.

"Did your husband shoot himself?"

She made a childishly smug face. "Joe's just faking to get everybody's sympathy. He's not really hurt."

The door opened behind me and I turned to see a police officer step in.

The officer frowned at us, and shook his head as if to say "Oh, no." It was an understandable response: it was the same cop, the mounted officer, who'd come upon the disturbance outside the Van Buren Hotel. Not surprising, really—this part of the Loop was his beat, or anyway his horse's.

He crooked his finger for me to step out in the hall and I did.

"I heard a murder was being committed up on the tenth floor of 166," he explained, meaning 166 West Jackson. "Do you know what happened? Did you see it?"

I told him what I knew, which for somebody on the scene was damned little.

"Did she do it?" the officer asked.

"The gun was in the husband's hand," I shrugged. "Speaking of which..."

And I took the little revolver out of my pocket, holding the gun by its nose again.

"What make is this?" the officer said, taking it.

"I don't recognize it."

He read off the side: "Narizmande Eibar Spair. Thirty-two caliber."

"It got the job done."

He held the gun so that his hand avoided the grip; tried to break it open, but couldn't.

"What's wrong with this thing?" he said.

"The trigger's been snapped on empty shells, I'd say. After six slugs were gone, the shooter kept shooting. Just once around wouldn't drive the shells into the barrel like that."

"Judas," the officer said.

The X-ray room's door opened and the doctor I'd shared the elevator and Bolton's dead weight with stepped into the hall, bloody and bowed.

"He's dead," the doctor said, wearily. "Choked to death on his own blood, poor bastard."

I said nothing; just glanced at the cop, who shrugged.

"The wife's in there," I said, pointing.

But I was pointing to Mrs. Bolton, who had stepped out into the hall. She was smiling pleasantly.

She said, "You're not going to frighten me about Joe. He's a great big man and as strong as a horse. Of course, I begin to think he ought to go to the hospital this time—for a while."

"Mrs. Bolton," the doctor said, flatly, with no sympathy whatsoever, "your husband is dead."

Like a spiteful brat, she stuck out her tongue. "Liar," she said.

The doctor sighed, turned to the cop. "Shall I call the morgue, or would you like the honor?"

"You should make the call, Doctor," the officer said.

Mrs. Bolton moved slowly toward the door to the X-ray room, from which the other doctor, his smock blood-spattered, emerged. She seemed to lose her footing, then, and I took her arm yet again. This time she accepted the help. I walked her into the room and she approached the body, stroked its brow with stubby fingers.

"I can't believe he'd go," she said.

From behind me, the doctor said, "He's dead, Mrs. Bolton. Please leave the room."

Still stroking her late husband's brow, she said, "He feels cold. So cold."

She kissed his cheek.

Then she smiled down at the body and patted its head, as one might a sleeping child, and said, "He's got a beautiful head, hasn't he?"

The officer stepped into the room and said, "You'd better come along with me, Mrs. Bolton. Captain Stege wants to talk to you."

"You're making a terrible mistake. I didn't shoot him."

He took her arm; she assumed a regal posture. He asked her if she would like him to notify any relatives or friends.

"I have no relatives or friends," she said, proudly. "I never had anybody or wanted anybody except Joe."

A crowd was waiting on the street. Damn near a mob, and at the forefront were the newshounds, legmen and camera-men alike. Cameras were clicking away as Davis of the *News* and a couple of others blocked the car waiting at the curb to take Mrs. Bolton to the Homicide Bureau. The mounted cop, with her in tow, brushed them and their questions aside and soon the car, with her in it, was inching into the late afternoon traffic. The reporters and photogs began flagging cabs to take quick pursuit, but snide, boyish Davis lingered to ask me a question.

"What were you doing here, Heller?"

"Getting a hangnail looked at up at the doctor's office."

"Fuck, Heller, you got blood all over you!"

I shrugged, lifted my middle finger. "Hell of a hangnail."

He smirked and I smirked and pushed through the crowd and hoofed it back to my office.

I was sitting at my desk, about an hour later, when the phone rang.

"Get your ass over here!"

"Captain Stege?"

"No, Walter Winchell. You were an eyewitness to a homicide, Heller! Get your ass over here!"

The phone clicked in my ear and I shrugged to nobody and got my hat and went over to the First District Station, entering off Eleventh. It was a new, modern, nondescript high rise; if this was the future, who needed it.

In Stege's clean little office, from behind his desk, the clean little cop looked out his black-rimmed, round-lensed glasses at me and said, "Did you see her do it?"

"I told the officer at the scene all about it, Captain."

"You didn't make a statement."

"Get a stenographer in here and I will."

He did and I did.

That seemed to cool the stocky little cop down. He and I had been adversaries once, though were getting along better these days. But there was still a strain.

Thought gripped his doughy, owlish countenance. "How do you read it, Heller?"

"I don't know. He had the gun. Maybe it was suicide."

"Everybody in that building agrees with you. Bolton's been having a lot of trouble with his better half. They think she drove him to suicide, finally. But there's a hitch."

"Yeah?"

"Suicides don't usually shoot themselves five times, two of 'em in the back."

I had to give him that.

"You think she's nuts?" Stege asked.

"Nuttier than a fruitcake."

"Maybe. But that was murder—premeditated."

"Oh, I doubt that, Captain. Don't you know a crime of passion when you see it? Doesn't the unwritten law apply to women as well as men?"

"The answer to your question is yes to the first, and no to the second. You want to see something?"

"Sure."

From his desk he handed me a small slip of paper.

It was a receipt for a gun sold on June 11 by the Hammond Loan Company of Hammond, Indiana, to a Mrs. Sarah Weston.

"That was in her purse," Stege said, smugly. "Along with a powder puff, a hanky, and some prayer leaflets."

"And you think Sarah Weston is just a name Mrs. Bolton used to buy the .32 from the pawn shop?"

"Certainly. And that slip—found in a narrow side pocket in the lining of her purse—proves premeditation."

"Does it, Captain?" I said, smiling, standing, hat in hand. "It seems to me premeditation would have warned her to get *rid* of that receipt. But then, what do I know? I'm not a cop." From the doorway I said, "Just a detective."

And I left him there to mull that over.

In the corridor, on my way out, Sam Backus buttonholed me. "Got a minute for a pal, Nate?"

"Sam, if we were pals, I'd see you someplace besides court."

Sam was with the Public Defender's office, and I'd bumped into him from time to time, dating back to my cop days. He was a conscientious and skillful attorney who, in better times, might have had a lucrative private practice; in times like these, he was glad to have a job. Sam's sharp features and receding hairline gave the smallish man a ferretlike appearance; he was similarly intense, too.

"My client says she employed you to do some work for her," he said, in a rush. "She'd like you to continue—"

"Wait a minute, wait a minute—your client? Not Mrs. Mildred Bolton?"

"Yes."

"She's poison. You're on your own."

"She tells me you were given a hundred-dollar retainer."

"Well, that's true, but I figured I earned it."

"She figures you owe her some work, or some dough."

"Sam, she lied to me. She misrepresented herself and her intentions." I was walking out the building and he was staying right with me.

"She's a disturbed individual. And she's maintaining she didn't kill her husband."

"They got her cold." I told him about Stege's evidence.

"It could've been planted," he said, meaning the receipt. "Look, Bolton's secretary was up there, and Mrs. Bolton says he

and the girl—an Angela something, sounds like 'who-you'—
were having an affair."

"I thought the affair was supposed to be with Marie
Winston."

"Her, too. Bolton must've been a real ladies' man. And the
Winston woman was up there at that office this afternoon, too,
before the shooting."

"Was she there during the shooting, though?"

"I don't know. I need to find out. The Public Defender's office
doesn't have an investigative staff, you know that, Nate. And I
can't afford to hire anybody, and I don't have the time to do the
legwork myself. You owe her some days. Deliver."

He had a point.

I gathered some names from Sam, and the next morning I
began to interview the participants.

"An affair with Joe?" Angela Houyoux said. "Why, that's
nonsense."

We were in the outer office of Bolton and Schmidt. She'd
given me the nickel tour of the place: one outer office, and two
inner ones, the one to the south having been Bolton's. The
crime scene told me nothing. Angela, the sweet-smelling dark-
haired beauty who'd tumbled into my arms and the elevator
yesterday, did.

"I was rather shaken by Mrs. Bolton's behavior at first—and
his. But then it became rather routine to come to the office and
find the glass in the door broken, or Mr. Bolton with his hands
cut from taking a knife away from Mrs. Bolton. After a few
weeks, I grew quite accustomed to having dictation interrupted
while Mr. and Mrs. Bolton scuffled and fought and yelled. Lately
they argued about Mrs. Winston a lot."

"How was your relationship with Mrs. Bolton?"

"Spotty, I guess you'd call it. Sometimes she'd seem to think I was interested in her husband. Other times she'd confide in me like a sister. I never said much to her. I'd just shrug my shoulders or just look at her kind of sympathetic. I had the feeling she didn't have anybody else to talk to about this. She'd cry and say her husband was unfaithful—I didn't dare point out they'd been separated for months and that Mr. Bolton had filed for divorce and all. One time...well, maybe I shouldn't say it."

"Say it."

"One time she said she 'just might kill' her husband. She said they never convict a woman for murder in Cook County."

Others in the building at West Jackson told similar tales. Bolton's business partner, Schmidt, wondered why Bolton bothered to get an injunction to keep his wife out of the office, but then refused to mail her her temporary alimony, giving her a reason to come to the office all the time.

"He would dole out the money, two or three dollars at a time," Schmidt said. "He could have paid her what she had coming for a month, or at least a week—Joe made decent money. It would've got rid of her. Why parcel it out?"

The elevator operator I'd met yesterday had a particularly wild yarn.

"Yesterday, early afternoon, Mr. Bolton got on at the ninth floor. He seemed in an awful hurry and said, 'Shoot me up to eleven.' I had a signal to stop at ten, so I made the stop and Mrs. Bolton came charging aboard. Mr. Bolton was right next to me. He kind of hid behind me and said, 'For God's sake, she'll kill us both!' I sort of forced the door closed on her, and she stood there in the corridor and raised her fist and said, 'Goddamnit, I'll fix you!' I guess she meant Bolton, not me."

"Apparently."

"Anyway, I took him up to eleven and he kind of sighed and as he got off he said, 'It's just hell, isn't it?' I said it was a damn shame he couldn't do anything about it."

"This was yesterday."

"Yes, sir. Not long before he was killed."

"Did it occur to you, at the time, it might lead to that?"

"No, sir. It was pretty typical, actually. I helped him escape from her before. And I kept her from getting on the elevator downstairs, sometimes. After all, he had an injunction to keep her from 'molesting him at his place of business,' he said."

Even the heavyset doctor up on thirteen found time for me.

"I think they were *both* sick," he said, rather bitterly I thought.

"What do you mean, Doctor?"

"I mean that I've administered more first aid to that man than a battlefield physician. That woman has beaten her husband, cut him with a knife, with a razor, created commotions and scenes with such regularity that the patrol wagon coming for Mildred is a common-place occurrence on West Jackson."

"How well did you know Bolton?"

"We were friendly. God knows I spent enough time with him, patching him up. He should've been a much more successful man than he was, you know. She drove him out of one job and another. I never understood him."

"Oh?"

"Well, they live, or lived, in Hyde Park. That's a university neighborhood. Fairly refined, very intellectual, really."

"Was Bolton a scholar?"

"He had bookish interests. He liked having the University of Chicago handy. Now why would a man of his sensibilities endure a violent harridan like Mildred Bolton?"

"In my trade, Doc," I said, "we call that a mystery."

I talked to more people. I talked to a pretty blond legal secretary named Peggy O'Reilly who, in 1933, had been employed by Ocean Accident and Guarantee Company. Joseph Bolton, Jr., had been a business associate there.

"His desk was four feet from mine," she said. "But I never went out with him. There was no social contact whatsoever, but Mrs. Bolton didn't believe that. She came into the office and accused me of—well, called me a 'dirty hussy,' if you must know. I asked her to step out into the hall where we wouldn't attract so much attention, and she did—and proceeded to tear my clothes off me. She tore the clothes off my body, scratched my neck, my face, kicked me, it was horrible. The attention it attracted... oh, dear. Several hundred people witnessed the sight—two nice men pulled her off of me. I was badly bruised and out of the office a week. When I came back, Mr. Bolton had been discharged."

A pattern was forming here, one I'd seen before; but usually it was the wife who was battered and yet somehow endured and even encouraged the twisted union. Only Bolton was a battered husband, a strapping man who never turned physically on his abusing wife; his only punishment had been to withhold that money from her, dole it out a few bucks at a time. That was the only satisfaction, the only revenge, he'd been able to extract.

At the Van Buren Hotel I knocked on the door of what had been Bolton's room. 3C.

Young Charles Winston answered. He looked terrible. Pale as milk, only not near as healthy. Eyes bloodshot. He was in a T-shirt and boxer shorts. The other times I'd seen him he'd been fully and even nattily attired.

"Put some clothes on," I said. "We have to talk."

In the saloon below the hotel we did that very thing.

"Joe was a great guy," he said, eyes brimming with tears. He would have cried into his beer, only he was having a mixed drink. I was picking up the tab, so Mildred Bolton was buying it.

"Is your mother still in town?"

He looked up with sharp curiosity. "No. She's back in Woodstock. Why?"

"She was up at the office shortly before Bolton was killed."

"I know. I was there, too."

"Oh?" Now, that was news.

"We went right over, after the hearing."

"To tell him how it came out?"

"Yes, and to thank him. You see, after that incident out in front, last Wednesday, when they took me off to jail, Mother went to see Joe. They met at the Twelfth Street Bus Depot. She asked him if he would take care of my bail—she could have had her brother do it, in the morning, but I'd have had to spend the night in jail first." He smiled fondly. "Joe went right over to the police station with the money and got me out."

"That was white of him."

"Sure was. Then we met Mother over at the taproom of the Auditorium Hotel."

Very posh digs; interesting place for folks who lived at the Van Buren to be hanging out.

"Unfortunately, I'd taken time to stop back at the hotel to pick up some packages my mother had left behind. Mrs. Bolton must've been waiting here for me. She followed me to the Auditorium tap-room, where she attacked me with her fists, and told the crowd in no uncertain terms, and in a voice to wake the dead, that my mother was"—he shook his head—" 'nothing but a whore' and such. Finally the management ejected her."

"Was your mother in love with Joe?"

He looked at me sharply. "Of course not. They were friendly. That's the extent of it."

"When did you and your mother leave Bolton's office?"

"Yesterday? About one thirty. Mrs. Bolton was announced as being in the outer office, and we just got the hell out."

"Neither of you lingered."

"No. Are you going to talk to my mother?"

"Probably."

"I wish you wouldn't," he said glumly.

I drank my beer, studying the kid.

"Maybe I won't have to," I said, smiled at him, patted his shoulder, and left.

I met with public defender Backus in a small interrogation room at the First District Station.

"Your client is guilty," I said.

I was sitting. He was standing. Pacing.

"The secretary was in the outer office at all times," I said. "In view of other witnesses. The Winstons left around one thirty. They were seen leaving by the elevator operator on duty."

"One of them could have sneaked back up the stairs..."

"I don't think so. Anyway, this meeting ends my participation, other than a report I'll type up for you. I've used up the hundred."

From my notes I read off summaries of the various interviews I'd conducted. He finally sat, sweat beading his brow, eyes slitted behind the glasses.

"She says she didn't do it," he said.

"She says a lot of things. I think you can get her off, anyway."

He smirked. "Are you a lawyer now?"

"No. Just a guy who's been in the thick of this bizarre fuck-ing case since day one."

"I bow to your experience if not expertise."

"You can plead her insane, Sam."

"A very tough defense to pull off, and besides, she won't hear of it. She wants no psychiatrists, no alienists involved."

"You can still get her off."

"How in hell?"

I let some air out. "I'm going to have to talk to her before I say any more. It's going to have to be up to her."

"You can't tell me?"

"You're not my client."

Mildred Bolton was.

And she was ushered into the interrogation room by a matron who then waited outside the door. She wore the same floral print dress, but the raccoon stole was gone. She smiled faintly upon seeing me, sat across from me.

"You been having fun with the press, Mildred, haven't you?"

"I sure have. They call me 'Marble Mildred.' They think I'm cold."

"They think it's unusual for a widow to joke about her dead husband."

"They're silly people. They asked me the name of my attorney and I said, 'Horsefeathers.' " She laughed. That struck her very funny; she was proud of herself over that witty remark.

"I'm glad you can find something to smile about."

"I'm getting hundreds of letters, you know. Fan mail! They say, 'You should have killed him whether you did or not.' I'm not the only woman wronged in Chicago, you know."

"They've got you dead bang, Mildred. I've seen some of the evidence. I've talked to the witnesses."

"Did you talk to Mrs. Winston? It was her fault, you know. Her and that...that boy."

"You went to see Joe after the boy was fined in court."

"Yes! I called him and told him that the little degenerate had been convicted and fined. Then I asked Joe, did he have any money, because I didn't have anything to eat, and he said yes. So I went to the office and when I got there he tried to give me a check for ten dollars. I said, 'I guess you're going to pay that boy's fine and that's why you haven't any money for me.' He said, 'That's all you're going to get.' And I said, 'Do you mean for a whole *week*? To pay rent out of and eat on?' He said, 'Yes, that's all you get.' "

"He was punishing you."

"I suppose. We argued for about an hour and then he said he had business on another floor—that boy's lawyer is on the ninth floor, you know—and I followed him, chased him to the elevator, but he got away. I went back and said to Miss Houyoux, 'He ran away from me.' I waited in his office and in about an hour he came back. I said, 'Joe, I have been your wife for fourteen years and I think I deserve more respect and better treatment than that.' He just leaned back in his chair so cocky and said, 'You know what you are?' And then he said it."

"Said it?"

She swallowed; for the first time, those marble eyes filled with tears. "He said, 'You're just a dirty old bitch.' Then he said it again. Then I said, 'Just a dirty old bitch for fourteen years?' And I pointed the gun at him."

"Where was it?"

"It was on his desk where I put it. It was in a blue box I carried in with me."

"What did you do with it, Mildred?"

"The box?"

"The gun."

"Oh. That. I fired it at him."

I gave her a handkerchief and she dabbed her eyes with it.

"How many times did you fire the gun, Mildred?"

"I don't know. He fell over in his chair and then he got up and came toward me and he said, 'Give me that gun, give me that gun.' I said, 'No, I'm going to finish myself now. Let go of me because my hand is on the trigger!' " Her teeth were clenched. "He struggled with me, and his glasses got knocked off, but he got the gun from my hand and he went out in the hall with it. I followed him, but then I turned and went back in his office. I was going to jump out of the window, but I heard him scream in the hall and I ran to him. The gun was lying beside him and I reached for it, but he reached and got it first. I went back in the office."

"Why?"

"To jump out the window, I told you. But I just couldn't leave him. I started to go back out and when I opened the door some people were around. You were one of them, Mr. Heller."

"Where did you get that gun, Mildred?"

"At a pawn shop in Hammond, Indiana."

"To kill Joe?"

"To kill myself."

"But you didn't."

"I'm sorry I didn't. I had plenty of time to do it at home, but I wanted to do it in his office. I wanted to embarrass him."

"He was shot in the back, Mildred. Twice."

"I don't know about that. Maybe his body turned when I was firing. I don't know. I don't remember."

"You know that the prosecution will not buy your suicide claims."

"They are *not* claims!"

"I know they aren't. But they won't buy them. They'll tell the judge and the jury that all your talk of suicide is just a clever excuse to get around planning Joe's murder. In other words, that you premeditated the killing and supplied yourself with a gun—and a reason for having a gun."

"I don't know about those things."

"Would you like to walk away from this?"

"Well, of course. I'm not crazy."

Right.

"You can, I think. But it's going to be hard on you. They're going to paint you as a shrew. As a brutal woman who battered her husband. They'll suggest that Bolton was too much of a gentleman for his own good, that he should have struck back at you, physically."

She giggled. "He wasn't such a gentleman."

"Really?"

"He wasn't what you think at all. Not at all."

"What do you mean, Mildred?"

"We were married for fourteen years before he tried to get rid of me. That's a long time."

"It sure is. What is it about your husband that we're getting wrong?"

"I haven't said."

"I know that. Tell me."

"I won't tell you. I've never told a living soul. I never will."

"I think you should. I think you need to."

"I won't. I won't now. I won't ever."

"There were no other women, were there, Mildred?"

"There were countless women, countless!"

"Like Marie Winston."

"She was the worst!"

"What about her son?"

"That little..." She stopped herself.

"That little degenerate? That's what you seem to always call him."

She nodded, pursing her thin wide lips.

"Joe was living in a fleabag hotel," I said. "A guy with *his* money. Why?"

"It was close to his work."

"Relatively. I think it had to do with who he was living with. A young man."

"A lot of men room together."

"There were no other women, were there, Mildred? Your husband used you to hide behind, didn't he, for many years."

She was crying now. The marble woman was crying now. "I loved him. I loved him."

"I know you did. And I don't know when you discovered it. Maybe you never did, really. Maybe you just suspected, and couldn't bring yourself to admit it. Then, after he left you, after he moved out of the house, you finally decided to find out, really find out. You hired me, springing for a hundred precious bucks you'd scrimped and saved, knowing I might find things out you'd want kept quiet. Knowing I might confirm the suspicions that drove you bughouse for years."

"Stop it...please stop it..."

"Your refined husband who liked to be near a college campus. You knew there were affairs. And there were. But not with women."

She stood, squeezing my hanky in one fist. "I don't have to listen to this!"

"You do if you want to be a free woman. The unwritten law doesn't seem to apply to women as equally as it does to men. But if you tell the truth about your husband—about just who it was he was seeing behind your back—I guarantee you no jury will convict you."

Her mouth was trembling.

I stood. "It's up to you, Mildred."

"Are you going to tell Mr. Backus?"

"No. You're my client. I'll respect your wishes."

"I wish you would just go. Just go, Mr. Heller."

I went.

I told Backus nothing except that I would suggest he introduce expert testimony from an alienist. He didn't. His client wouldn't hear of it.

The papers continued to have a great time with Marble Mildred. She got to know the boys of the press, became bosom buddies with the sob sisters, warned cameramen not to take a profile pic or she'd break their lens, shouted greetings and wisecracks to one and all. She laughed and talked; being on trial for murder was a lark to her.

Of course, as the trial wore on, she grew less boisterous, even became sullen at times. On the stand she told her story more or less straight, but minus any hint her husband was bent. The prosecution, as I had told her they would, ridiculed her statement that she'd bought the .32 to do herself in. The prosecutor extolled "motherhood and wifehood," but expressed "the utmost comtempt for Mildred Bolton." She was described as "dirt," "filth," "vicious," and more. She was sentenced to die in the electric chair.

She didn't want an appeal, a new trial.

"As far as I am concerned," she told the stunned judge, "I am perfectly satisfied with things as they now stand."

But Cook County was squeamish about electrocuting a woman; just half an hour before the execution was to take place, hair shaved above one ear, wearing special females-only electrocution shorts, Mildred was spared by Governor Horner.

Mildred, who'd been strangely blissful in contemplation of her electrocution, was less pleased with her new sentence of 199 years. Nonetheless she was a model prisoner, until August 29, 1943, when she was found slumped in her cell, wrists slashed. She had managed to smuggle some scissors in. It took her hours to die. Sitting in the darkness, waiting for the blood to empty out of her.

She left a note, stuck to one wall:

To whom it may concern. In the event of my death do not notify anybody or try to get in touch with family or friends. I wish to die as I have lived, completely alone.

What she said was true, but I wondered if I was the only person alive who knew that it hadn't been by choice.

AUTHOR'S NOTE

I wish to acknowledge the true-crime article "Joseph Bolton, the Almost Indestructible Husband" by Nellise Child. Also helpful was the Mildred Bolton entry in *Find the Woman* by Jay Robert Nash. Most names in the preceding fact-based story have been changed or at least altered (exceptions include the Boltons and Captain Stege); fact, speculation, and fiction are freely mixed therein.

THE STRAWBERRY TEARDROP

In a garbage dump on East Ninth Street near Shore Drive, in Cleveland, Ohio, on August 17, 1938, a woman's body was discovered by a cop walking his morning beat.

I got there before anything much had been moved. Not that I was a plainclothes dick—I used to be, but not in Cleveland; I was just along for the ride. I'd been sitting in the office of Cleveland's Public Safety Director, having coffee, when the call came through. The Safety Director was in charge of both the police and fire department, and one would think that a routine murder wouldn't rate a call to such a high muckey-muck.

One would be wrong.

Because this was the latest in series of anything-but-routine, brutal murders—the unlucky thirteenth, to be exact, not that the thirteenth victim would seem any more unlucky than the preceding twelve. The so-called "Mad Butcher of Kingsbury Run" had been exercising his ghastly art sporadically since the fall of '35, in Cleveland—or so I understood. I was an out-of-towner, myself.

So was the woman.

Or she used to be, before she became so many dismembered parts flung across this rock-and-garbage strewn dump. Her nude torso was slashed and the blood, splashed here, streaked there, was turning dark, almost black, though the sun caught scarlet glints and tossed them at us. Her head was gone, but maybe it would turn up. The Butcher wasn't known for that, though. The twelve preceding victims had been found headless, and had stayed that way. Somewhere in Cleveland, perhaps, a guy had a collection in his attic. In this weather it wouldn't smell too nice.

It's not a good sign when the Medical Examiner gets sick; and the half dozen cops, and the police photographer, were looking green around the gills themselves. Only my friend, the Safety Director, seemed in no danger of losing his breakfast. He was a ruddy-cheeked six-footer in a coat and tie and vest, despite the heat; hatless, his hair brushed back and pomaded, he still seemed—years after I'd met him—boyish. And he was only in his mid-thirties, just a few years older than me.

I'd met him in Chicago, seven or eight years ago, when I wasn't yet president (and everything else) of the A-I Detective Agency, but still a cop; and he was still a Prohibition Agent. Hell, *the* Prohibition agent. He'd considered me one of the more or less honest cops in Chicago—emphasis on the less, I guess—and I made a good contact for him, as a lot of the cops didn't like him much. Honesty doesn't go over real big in Chicago, you know.

Eliot Ness said, "Despite the slashing, there's a certain skill displayed, here."

"Yeah, right," I said. "A regular ballet dancer did this."

"No, really," he said, and bent over the headless torso, pointing. He seemed to be pointing at the gathering flies, but he wasn't. "There's an unmistakable precision about this. Maybe even indicating surgical training."

"Maybe," I said. "But I think the doctor lost this patient."

He stood and glanced at me and smiled, just a little; he understood me: he knew my wise-guy remarks were just my way of holding onto my own breakfast.

"You ought to come to Cleveland more often," he said.

"You know how to show a guy a good time, I'll give you that, Eliot."

He walked over and glanced at a forearm, which seemed to reach for an empty soap box, fingers stretched toward the Gold Dust twins. He knelt and studied it.

I wasn't here on a vacation, by any means. Cleveland didn't strike me as a vacation city, even before I heard about the Butcher of Kingsbury Run (so called because a number of the bodies, including the first several, were found in that Cleveland gully). This was strictly business. I was here trying to trace the missing daughter of a guy in Evanston who owned a dozen diners around Chicago. He was one of those self-made men, who started out in the greasy kitchen of his own first diner, fifteen or so years ago; and now he had a fancy brick house in Evanston and plenty of money, considering the times. But not much else. His wife had died four or five years ago, of consumption; and his daughter—who he claimed to be a good girl and by all other accounts was pretty wild—had wandered off a few months ago, with a taxi dancer from the North Side named Tony.

Well, I'd found Tony in Toledo—he was doing a floor show in a roadhouse with a dark-haired girl named FiFi; he'd grown a little pencil mustache and they did an apache routine—he was calling himself Antoine now. And Tony/Antoine said Ginger (which was the Evanston restauranteur's daughter's nickname) had taken up with somebody named Ray, who owned (get this) a diner in Cleveland.

I'd gotten here yesterday, and had talked to Ray, and without tipping I was looking for her, asked where was the pretty waitress, the one called Ginger, I think her name is. Ray, a skinny balding guy of about thirty with a silver front tooth, leered and winked and made it obvious that not only was Ginger working as a waitress here, she was also a side dish, where Ray was concerned. Further casual conversation revealed that it was Ginger's night off—she was at the movies with some girl friends—and she'd be in tomorrow, around five.

I didn't push it further, figuring to catch up with her at the diner the next evening, after wasting a day seeing Cleveland and bothering my old friend Eliot. And now I was in a city dump with him, watching him study the severed forearm of a woman.

"Look at this," Eliot said, pointing at the outstretched fingers of the hand.

I went over to him and it—not quickly, but I went over.

"What, Eliot? Do you want to challenge my powers of deduction, or just make me sick?"

"Just a lucky break," he said. "Most of the victims have gone unidentified; too mutilated. And a lot of 'em have been prostitutes or vagrants. But we've got a break, here. Two breaks, actually."

He pointed to the hand's little finger. To the small gold filigree band with a green stone.

"A nice specific piece of jewelry to try to trace," he said, with a dry smile. "And even better..."

He pointed to a strawberry birthmark, the shape of a teardrop, just below the wrist.

I took a close look; then stood. Put a hand on my stomach.

Walked away and dropped to my knees and lost my breakfast.

I felt Eliot's hand patting my back.

"Nate," he said. "What's the matter? You've seen homicides before...even grisly ones like this...brace up, boy."

He eased me to my feet.

My tongue felt thick in my mouth, thick and restless.

"What is it?" he said.

"I think I just found my client's daughter," I said.

Both the strawberry birthmark and the filigree ring with the green stone had been part of my basic description of the girl; the photographs I had showed her to be a pretty but average-looking young woman—slim, brunette—who resembled every third girl you saw on the street. So I was counting on those two specifics to help me identify her. I hadn't counted on those specifics helping me in just this fashion.

I sat in Eliot's inner office in the Cleveland city hall; the mayor's office was next door. We were having coffee with some rum in it—Eliot kept a bottle in a bottom drawer of his rolltop desk. I promised him not to tell Capone.

"I think we should call the father," Eliot said. "Ask him to come and make the identification."

I thought about it. "I'd like to argue with you, but I don't see how I can. Maybe if we waited till...Christ. Till the head turns up..."

Eliot shrugged. "It isn't likely to. The ring and the birthmark are enough to warrant notifying the father."

"I can make the call."

"No. I'll let you talk to him when I'm done, but that's something I should do."

And he did. With quiet tact. After a few minutes he handed me the phone; if I'd thought him cold at the scene of the crime, I erased that thought when I saw the dampness in the gray eyes.

"Is it my little girl?" the deep voice said, sounding tinny out of the phone.

"I think so, Mr. Jensen. I'm afraid so."

I could hear him weeping.

Then he said: "Mr. Ness said her body was...dismembered. How can you say it's her? How...how can you know it's her?"

And I told him of the ring and the strawberry teardrop.

"I should come there," he said.

"Maybe that won't be necessary." I covered the phone. "Eliot, will my identification be enough?"

He nodded. "We'll stretch it."

I had to argue with Jensen, but finally he agreed for his daughter's remains to be shipped back via train; I said I'd contact a funeral home this afternoon, and accompany her home.

I handed the phone to Eliot to hang up.

We looked at each other and Eliot, not given to swearing, said, "I'd give ten years of my life to nail that butchering bastard."

"How long will your people need the body?"

"I'll speak to the coroner's office. I'm sure we can send her home with you in a day or two. Where are you staying?"

"The Stadium Hotel."

"Not anymore. I've got an extra room for you. I'm a bachelor again, you know."

We hadn't gotten into that yet; I'd always considered Eliot's marriage an ideal one, and was shocked a few months back to hear it had broken up.

"I'm sorry, Eliot."

"Me too. But I am seeing somebody. Someone you may remember; another Chicagoan."

"Who?"

"Evie MacMillan."

"The fashion illustrator? Nice looking woman."

Eliot smiled slyly. "You'll see her tonight, at the Country Club...but I'll arrange some female companionship for you. I don't want you cutting my time."

"How can you say such a thing? Don't you trust me?"

"I learned a long time ago," he said, turning to his desk full of paperwork, "not to trust Chicago cops—even ex-ones."

Out on the Country Club terrace, the ten-piece band was playing Cole Porter and a balmy breeze from Lake Erie was playing with the women's hair. There were plenty of good-looking women, here—low-cut dresses, bare shoulders—and lots of men in evening clothes for them to dance with. But this was no party, and since some of the golfers were still here from late afternoon rounds, there were sports clothes and a few business suits (like mine) in the mix. Even some of the women were dressed casually, like the tall, slender blonde in pink shirt and pale green pleated skirt who sat down next to me at the little white metal table and asked me if I'd have a Bacardi with her. The air smelled like a flower garden, and some of it was flowers, and some of it was her.

"I'd be glad to buy you a Bacardi cocktail," I said, clumsily.

"No," she said, touching my arm. She had eyes the color of jade. "You're a guest. I'll buy."

Eliot was dancing with his girl Evie, an attractive brunette in her mid-thirties; she'd always struck me as intelligent but sad, somehow. They smiled over at me.

The blonde in pink and pale green brought two Bacardis over, set one of them in front of me and smiled. "Yes," she said wickedly. "You've been set up. I'm the girl Eliot promised you.

But if you were hoping for somebody in an evening gown, I'm not it. I just *had* to get an extra nine holes in."

"If you were looking for a guy in a tux," I said, "I'm not it. And I've never been on a golf course in my life. What else do we have in common?"

She had a nicely wry smile, which continued as she sipped the Bacardi. "Eliot, I suppose. If I have a few more of these, I may tell you a secret."

And after a few more, she did.

And it was a whopper.

"*You're* an undercover agent?" I said. A few sheets to the wind myself.

"Shhhh," she said, finger poised uncertainly before pretty lips. "It's a secret. But I haven't been doing it much lately."

"Haven't been doing what?"

"Well, undercover work. And there's a double-entendre there that I'd rather you didn't go looking for."

"I wouldn't think of looking under the covers for it."

The band began playing a tango.

I asked her how she got involved, working for Eliot. Which I didn't believe for a second, even in my cups.

But it turned out to be true (as Eliot admitted to me when he came over to see how Vivian and I were getting along, when Vivian—which was her name, incidentally—went to the powder room with Evie).

Vivian Chalmers was the daughter of a banker (a solvent one), a divorcee of thirty with no children and a lot of social pull. An expert trapshooter, golfer, tennis player and "all 'round sportswoman," with a sense of adventure. When Eliot called on her to case various of the gambling joints he planned to raid—as a socialite she could take a fling in any joint she chose, without raising any suspicion—she immediately said yes. And she'd been an active agent in the first few years of Eliot's ongoing battle against the so-called Mayfield Road Mob—who controlled prostitution, gambling and the policy racket in the Cleveland environs.

"But things have slowed down," she said, nostalgically. "Eliot has pretty much cleaned up the place, and, besides, he doesn't want to use me anymore."

"An undercover agent can only be effective so long," I said. "Pretty soon the other side gets suspicious."

She shrugged, with resigned frustration, and let me buy the next round.

We took a walk in the dark, around the golf course, and ended up sitting on a green. The breeze felt nice. The flag on the hole—13—flapped.

"Thirteen," I said.

"Huh?"

"Victim thirteen."

"Oh. Eliot told me about that. Your 'luck' today, finding your client's missing daughter. Damn shame."

"Damn shame."

"A shame, too, they haven't found the son-of-a-bitch."

She was a little drunk, and so was I, but I was still shocked—well, amused—to hear a woman, particularly a "society" woman, speak that way.

"It must grate on Eliot, too," I said.

"Sure as hell does. It's the only mote in his eye. He's a hero around these parts, and he's kicked the Mayfield Mob in the seat of the pants, and done everything else from clean up a corrupt police department to throw labor racketeers in jail, to cut traffic deaths in half, to founding Boy's Town, to...."

"You're not in love with the guy, are you?"

She seemed taken aback for a minute, then her face wrinkled into a got-caught-with-my-pants-down grin. "Maybe a little. But he's got a girl."

"I don't."

"You might."

She leaned forward.

We kissed for a while, and she felt good in my arms; she was firm, almost muscular. But she smelled like flowers. And the sky was blue and scattered with stars above us, as we lay back on the golf-green to look up. It seemed like a nice world, at the moment.

Hard to imagine it had a Butcher in it.

I sat up talking with Eliot that night; he lived in a reconverted boathouse on the lake. The furnishings were sparse, spartan—it was obvious his wife had taken most of the furniture with her and he'd had to all but start over.

I told him I thought Vivian was a terrific girl.

Leaning back in a comfy chair, feet on an ottoman, Eliot, tie loose around his neck, smiled in a melancholy way. "I thought you'd hit it off."

"Did you have an affair with her?"

He looked at me sharply; that was about as personal as I'd ever got with him.

He shook his head, but I didn't quite buy it.

"You knew Evie MacMillan in Chicago," I said.

"Meaning what?"

"Meaning nothing."

"Meaning I knew her when I was still married."

"Meaning nothing."

"Nate, I'm sorry I'm not the Boy Scout you think I am."

"Hey, so you've slept with girls before. I'll learn to live with it."

There was a stone fireplace, in which some logs were trying to decide whether to burn any more or not; we watched them trying.

"I love Evie, Nate. I'm going to marry her."

"Congratulations."

We could hear the lake out there; could smell it some, too.

"I'd like that bastard's neck in my hands," Eliot said.

"What?"

"That Butcher. That goddamn Butcher."

"What made you think of him?"

"I don't know."

"Eliot, it's been over three years since he first struck, and you *still* don't have anything?"

"Nothing. A few months ago, last time he hit, we found some of the...body parts, bones and such...in a cardboard box in the Central Market area. There's a Hooverville over there, or what used to be a Hooverville...it's a shantytown, is more like it, genuine hobos as opposed to just good folks down on their luck. Most of the victims—before today—were either prostitutes or bums...and the bums from that shantytown were the Butcher's meat. So to speak."

The fire crackled.

Eliot continued: "I decided to make a clean sweep. I took twenty-five cops through there at one in the morning, and rousted out all the 'bo's and took 'em down and fingerprinted and questioned all of 'em."

"And it amounted to...?"

198

"It amounted to nothing. Except ridding Cleveland of that shantytown. I burned the place down that afternoon."

"Comes in handy, having all those firemen working for you. But what about those poor bastards whose 'city' you burned down?"

Sensing my disapproval, he glanced at me and gave me what tried to be a warm smile, but was just a weary one. "Nate, I turned them over to the Relief department, for relocation and, I hope, rehabilitation. But most of them were bums who just hopped a freight out. And I did 'em a favor by taking them off the potential victims list."

"And made room for Ginger Jensen."

Eliot looked away.

"That wasn't fair," I said. "I'm sorry I said that, Eliot."

"I know, Nate. I know."

But I could tell he'd been thinking the same thing.

I had lunch the next day with Vivian in a little outdoor restaurant in the shadow of Terminal Tower. We were served lemonade and little ham and cheese and lettuce and tomato sandwiches with the crusts trimmed off the toasted bread. The detective in me wondered what became of the crusts.

"Thanks for having lunch with me," Vivian said. She had on a pale orange dress; she sat crossing her brown pretty legs.

"My pleasure," I said.

"Speaking of which...about last night..."

"We were both a little drunk. Forget it. Just don't ask *me* to."

She smiled as she nibbled her sandwich.

"I called and told Eliot something this morning," she said, "and he just ignored me."

"What was that?"

"That I have a possible lead on the Butcher murders."

"I can't imagine Eliot ignoring that...and it's not like it's just *anybody* approaching him—you *did* work for him..."

"Not lately. And he thinks I'm just..."

"Looking for an excuse to be around him?"

She nibbled at a little sandwich. Nodded.

"Did you resent him asking you to be with me as a blind date last night?"

"No," she said.

"Did...last night have anything to do with wanting to 'show' Eliot?"

If she weren't so sophisticated—or trying to be—she would've looked hurt; but her expression managed to get something else across: disappointment in me.

"Last night had to do with showing *you*," she said. "And...it had a little to do with Bacardi cocktails..."

"That it did. Tell me about your lead."

"Eliot has been harping on the 'professional' way the bodies have been dismembered—he's said again and again he sees a 'surgical' look to it."

I nodded.

"So it occurred to me that a doctor—anyway, somebody who'd at least been in medical school for a time—would be a likely candidate for the Butcher."

"Yes."

"And medical school's expensive, so, it stands to reason, the Butcher just might run in the same social circles as yours truly."

"Say, you *did* work for Eliot."

She liked that.

She continued: "I checked around with my society friends, and heard about a guy whose family has money—plenty of it. Name of Watterson."

"Last name or first?"

"That's the family name. Big in these parts."

"Means nothing to me."

"Well, Lloyd Watterson used to be a medical student. He's a big man, very strong—the kind of strength it might take to do some of the things the Butcher has done. And he has a history of mental disturbances."

"What kind of mental disturbances?"

"He's been going to psychiatrist since he was a school kid."

"Do you know this guy?"

"Just barely. But I've heard things about him."

"Such as?"

"I hear he likes boys."

Lloyd Watterson lived in a two-story white house at the end of a dead-end street, a Victorian-looking miniature mansion among other such houses, where expansive lawns and towering hedges separated the world from the wealthy who lived within.

This wasn't the parental home, Vivian explained; Watterson lived here alone, apparently without servants. The grounds seemed well-tended, though, and there was nothing about this house that said anyone capable of mass murder might live here. No blood spattered on the white porch; no body parts scattered about the lawn.

It was mid-afternoon, and I was having second thoughts.

"I don't even have a goddamn gun," I said.

"I do," she said, and showed me a little .25 automatic from her purse.

"Great. If he has a dog, maybe we can use that to scare it."

"This'll do the trick. Besides, a gun won't even be necessary. You're just here to talk."

The game plan was for me to approach Watterson as a cop, flashing my private detective's badge quickly enough to fool him (and that almost always worked), and question him, simply get a feel for whether or not he was a legitimate suspect, worthy of lobbying Eliot for action against. My say-so, Vivian felt, would be enough to get Eliot off the dime.

And helping Eliot bring the Butcher in would be a nice wedding present for my old friend; with his unstated but obvious political ambitions, the capture of the Kingsbury Run maniac would offset the damage his divorce had done him, in conservative, mostly Catholic Cleveland. He'd been the subject of near hero worship, in the press here (Eliot was always good at getting press—Frank Nitti used to refer to him as "Eliot Press"); but the ongoing if sporadic slaughter of the Butcher was a major embarrassment for Cleveland's fabled Safety Director.

So, leaving Vivian behind in the roadster (Watterson might recognize her), I walked up the curved sidewalk and went up on the porch and rang the bell. In the dark hardwood door there was opaque glass behind which I could barely make out movement, coming toward me.

The door opened, and a blond man about six-three with a baby-face and ice-blue eyes and shoulders that nearly filled the doorway looked out at me and grinned. A kid's grin, on one side of his face. He wore a polo shirt and short white pants; he seemed about to say, "Tennis anyone?"

But he said nothing, as a matter of fact; he just appraised me with those ice-blue, somewhat vacant eyes. I now knew how it felt for a woman to be ogled—which is to say, not necessarily good.

I said, "I'm an officer of the court," which in Illinois wasn't exactly a lie, and I flashed him my badge, but before I could say anything else, his hand reached out and grabbed the front of my shirt, yanked me inside and slammed the door.

He tossed me like a horseshoe, and I smacked into something—the stairway to the second floor, I guess; I don't know exactly—because I blacked out. The only thing I remember is the musty smell of the place.

I woke up minutes later, and found myself tied in a chair in a dank, dark room. Support beams loomed out of a packed dirt floor. The basement.

I strained at the ropes, but they were snug; not so snug as to cut off my circulation, but snug enough. I glanced around the room. I was alone. I couldn't see much—just a shovel against one cement wall. The only light came from a window off to my right, and there were hedges in front of the widow, so the light was filtered.

Feet came tromping down the open wooden stairs. I saw his legs, first; white as pastry dough.

He was grinning. In his right hand was a cleaver. It shone, caught a glint of what little light there was.

"I'm no butcher," he said. His voice was soft, almost gentle. "Don't believe what you've heard...."

"Do you want to die?" I said.

"Of course not."

"Well then cut me loose. There's cops all over the place, and if you kill me, they'll shoot you down. You know what happens to cop killers, don't you?"

He thought that over, nodded.

Standing just to one side of me, displaying the cold polished steel of the cleaver, in which my face's frantic reflection looked back at me, he said, "I'm no butcher. This is a surgical tool. This is used for amputation, not butchery."

"Yeah. I can see that."

"I wondered when you people would come around."

"Do you want to be caught, Lloyd?"

"Of course not. I'm no different than you. I'm a public servant."

"How...how do you figure that, Lloyd?" My feet weren't tied to the chair; if he'd just step around in front of me...

"I only dispose of the flotsam. Not to mention jetsam."

"Not to mention that."

"Tramps. Whores. Weeding out the stock. Survival of the fittest. You know."

"That makes a lot of sense, Lloyd. But I'm not flotsam *or* jetsam. I'm a cop. You don't want to kill a cop. You don't want to kill a fellow public servant."

He thought about that.

"I think I have to, this time," he said.

He moved around the chair, stood in front of me, stroking his chin, the cleaver gripped tight in his right hand, held about breastbone level.

"I *do* like you," Lloyd said, thoughtfully.

"And I like you, Lloyd," I said, and kicked him in the balls.

Harder than any man tied to a chair should be able to kick; but you'd be surprised what you can do, under extreme circumstances. And things rarely get more extreme than being tied to a chair with a guy with a cleaver coming at you.

Only he wasn't coming at me, now: now, he was doubled over, and I stood, the chair strapped to my back; managed, even so, to kick him in the face.

He tumbled back, gripping his groin, tears streaming down his checks, cords in his neck taut; my shoe had caught him on the side of the face and broken the skin. Flecks of blood, like little red tears, spattered his cheeks, mingling with the real tears.

That's when the window shattered, and Vivian squeezed down in through; pretty legs first.

And she gave me the little gun to hold on him while she untied me.

He was still on the dirt floor, moaning, when we went up the stairs and out into the sunny day, into a world that wasn't dank, onto earth that was grass-covered and didn't have God knows what buried under it.

We asked Eliot to meet us at his boathouse; we told him what had happened. He was livid; I never saw him angrier. But he held Vivian for a moment, and looked at her and said, "If anything had happened to you, I'd've killed you."

He poured all of us a drink; rum as usual. He handed me my mine and said, "How could you get involved in something so harebrained?"

"I wanted to give my client something for his money," I said.

"You mean his daughter's killer."

"Why not?"

"I've been looking for the bastard three years, and you come to town and expect to find him in three days."

"Well, I did."

He smirked, shook his head. "I believe you did. But Watterson's family would bring in the highest-paid lawyers in the country and we'd be thrown out of court on our cans."

"What? The son of a bitch tried to cut me up with a cleaver!"

"Did he? Did he swing on you? Or did you enter his house under a false pretense, misrepresenting yourself as a law officer? And as far as that goes, *you* assaulted *him*. We have very little."

Vivian said, "You have the name of the Butcher."

Eliot nodded. "Probably. I'm going to make a phone call."

Eliot went into his den and came out fifteen minutes later.

"I spoke with Franklin Watterson, the father. He's agreed to submit his son for a lie detector test."

"To what end?"

"One step at a time," Eliot said.

Lloyd Watterson took the lie detector test twice—and on both instances denied committing the various Butcher slayings; his denials were, according to the machine, lies. The Watterson family attorney reminded Eliot that lie detector tests were not admissible as evidence. Eliot had a private discussion with Franklin Watterson.

Lloyd Watterson was committed, by his family, to an asylum for the insane. The Mad Butcher of Kingsbury Run—which to this day is marked "unsolved" in the Cleveland police records—did not strike again.

At least not directly.

Eliot married Evie MacMillan a few months after my Cleveland visit, and their marriage was from the start disrupted by crank letters, postmarked from the same town as the asylum where Watterson had been committed. "Retribution will catch up with you one day," said one postcard, on the front of which was a drawing of an effeminate man grinning from behind prison bars. Mrs. Ness was especially unnerved by these continuing letters and cards.

Eliot's political fortunes waned, in the wake of the "unsolved" Butcher slayings. Known for his tough stance on traffic violators, he got mired in a scandal when one pre-dawn morning in March of 1942, his car skidded into an oncoming car on the West Shoreway. Eliot and his wife, and two friends, had been drinking. The police report didn't identify Eliot by name, but his license number—EN-1, well-known to Cleveland citizens—was listed. And Eliot had left the scene of the accident.

Hit-and-run, the headlines said. Eliot's version was that his wife had been injured, and he'd raced her to a hospital—but not before stopping to check on the other driver, who confirmed this. The storm blew over, but the damage was done—Eliot's image in the Cleveland press was finally tarnished.

Two months later he resigned as Safety Director.

Lloyd Watterson kept sending the threatening mail to Eliot for many years. He died in a Dayton, Ohio, asylum in 1965.

How much pressure those cards and letters put on the marriage I couldn't say; but in 1945 Eliot and Evie divorced, and Eliot married a third time a few months later. At the time he was serving as federal director of the program against venereal disease in the military. His attempt to run for Cleveland mayor in 1947 was a near disaster: Cleveland's one-time fairhaired boy was a has-been with a hit-run scandal and two divorces and three marriages going against him.

He would not have another public success until the publication of his autobiographical book, *The Untouchables*—but that success was posthumous; he died shortly before it was published, never knowing that television and Robert Stack would give him lasting fame.

I saw Eliot, now and then, over the years; but I never saw Vivian again.

I asked him about her, once, when I was visiting him in Pennsylvania, in the early '50s. He told me she'd been killed in a boating accident in 1943.

"She's been dead for years, then," I said, the shock of it hitting me like a blow.

"That's right. But shed a tear for her, now, if you like. Tears and prayers can never come too late, Nate."

Amen, Eliot.

AUTHOR'S NOTE

Research materials included *Four Against the Mob* (1961) by Oscar Fraley, and *Cleveland—Best Kept Secret* (1967) by George E. Condon. Following extensive research at the Case Western Reserve Historical Society in Cleveland, this story was expanded into the non-Heller novel *Butcher's Dozen* (1988). The Heller novel *Angel in Black* (2001) is a sequel to both "The Strawberry Teardrop" and *Butcher's Dozen*. My play and film, *Eliot Ness: An Untouchable Life* (2007), also deals with the Mad Butcher of Kingsbury Run and "Lloyd Watterson."

SCRAP

Friday afternoon, December 8, 1939, I had a call from Jake Rubinstein to meet him at 3159 Roosevelt, which was in Lawndale, my old neighborhood. Jake was an all right guy, kind of talkative and something of a roughneck, but then on Maxwell Street, when I was growing up, developing a mouth and muscles was necessary for survival. I knew Jake had been existing out on the fringes of the rackets since then, but that was true of a lot of guys. I didn't hold it against him. I went into one of the rackets myself, after all—known in Chicago as the police department—and I figured Jake wouldn't hold that against me, either. Especially since I was private, now, and he wanted to hire me.

The afternoon was bitterly cold, snow on the ground but not snowing, as I sat parked in my sporty '32 Auburn across the street from the drug store, over which was the union hall where Jake said to meet him. The Scrap Iron and Junk Handlers Union, he said. I didn't know there was one. They had unions for everything these days. My pop, an old union man, would've been pleased. I didn't much care.

I went up the flight of stairs and into the outer office; the meeting room was adjacent, at my left. The place was modest, like most union halls—if you're running a union you don't want the rank and file to think you're living it up—but the secretary behind the desk looked like a million. She was a brunette in a trim brown suit with big brown eyes and bright red lipstick. She'd soften the blow of paying dues any day.

She smiled at me and I forgot it was winter. "Would you be Mr. Heller?"

"I would. Would you be free for dinner?"

Her smile settled in one corner of her bright red mouth. "I wouldn't. Mr. Rubinstein is waiting for you in Mr. Martin's office."

And she pointed to the only door in the wall behind her, and I gave her a can't-blame-a-guy-for-trying look and went on in.

The inner office wasn't big but it seemed bigger than it was because it was under-furnished: just a clutter-free desk and a couple of chairs and two wooden file cabinets. Jake was sitting behind the desk, feet up on in, socks with clocks showing, as he read *The Racing News.*

"How are you, Jake," I said, and held out my hand.

He put the paper down, stood and grinned and shook my hand; he was a little guy, short I mean, but he had shoulders on him and his grip was a killer. He wore a natty dark blue suit and a red hand-painted tie with a sunset on it and a hat that was a little big for him. He kept the hat on indoors—self-conscious about his thinning hair, I guess.

"You look good, Nate. Thanks for coming. Thanks for coming yourself and not sending one of your ops."

"Any excuse to get back to the old neighborhood, Jake," I said, pulling up a chair and sitting. "We're about four blocks from where my pop's bookshop was, you know."

"I know, I know," he said, sitting again. "What do you hear from Barney these days?"

"Not much. When did you get in the union racket, anyway? Last I heard you were a door-to-door salesman."

Jake shrugged. He had dark eyes and a weak chin and five o'clock shadow; make that six o'clock shadow. "A while ago," he allowed. "But it ain't really a racket. We're trying to give our guys a break."

I smirked at him. "In this town? Billy Skidmore isn't going to put up with a legit junk handler's union."

Skidmore was a portly, dapperly dressed junk dealer and politician who controlled most of the major non-Capone gambling in town. Frank Nitti, Capone's heir, put up with that because Skidmore was also a bailbondsmen, which made him a necessary evil.

"Skidmore's got troubles these days," Jake said. "He can't afford to push us around no more."

"You're talking about the income tax thing."

"Yeah. Just like Capone. He didn't pay his taxes and they got 'im for it."

"They indicted him, but that doesn't mean they got him. Anyway, where do I come in?"

Jake leaned forward, brow beetling. "You know a guy named Leon Cooke?"

"Can't say I do."

"He's a little younger than us, but he's from around here. He's a lawyer. He put this union together, two, three years ago. Well, about a year back he became head of an association of junkyard dealers, and the rank and file voted him out."

I shrugged. "Seems reasonable. In Chicago it wouldn't be *unusual* to represent both the employees *and* the employers, but kosher it ain't."

Jake was nodding. "Right. The new president is Johnny Martin. Know him?"

"Can't say I do."

"He's been with the Sanitary District for, oh, twenty or more years."

The Sanitary District controlled the sewage in the city's rivers and canals.

"He needed a hobby," I said, "so he ran for president of the junk handler's union, huh?"

"He's a good man, Nate, he really is."

"What's your job?"

"I'm treasurer of the union."

"You're the collector, then."

"Well...yeah. Does it show?"

"I just didn't figure you for the accountant type."

He smiled sheepishly. "Every union needs a little muscle. Anyways, Cooke. He's trying to stir things up, we think. He isn't even legal counsel for the union anymore, but he's been coming to meetings, hanging around. We think he's been going around talking to the members."

"Got an election coming up?"

"Yeah. We want to know who he's talking to. We want to know if anybody's backing him."

"You think Nitti's people might be using him for a front?"

"Could be. Maybe even Skidmore. Playing both ends against the middle is Cooke's style. Anyways, can you shadow him and find out?"

"For fifteen a day and expenses, I can."

"Isn't that a little steep, Nate?"

"What's the monthly take on union dues around this joint?"

"Fifteen a day's fine," Jake said, shaking his head side to side, smiling.

"And expenses."

The door opened and the secretary came in, quickly, her silk stockings flashing.

"Mr. Rubinstein," she said, visibly upset, "Mr. Cooke is in the outer office. Demanding to see Mr. Martin."

"Shit," Jake said through his teeth. He glanced at me. "Let's get you out of here."

We followed the secretary into the outer office, where Cooke, a man of medium size in an off-the-rack brown suit, was pacing. A heavy top coat was slung over his arm. In his late twenties, with thinning brown hair, Cooke was rather mild looking, with wire-rim glasses and cupid lips. Nonetheless, he was well and truly pissed off.

"Where's that bastard Martin?" he demanded of Jake. Not at all intimidated by the little strongarm man.

"He stepped out," Jake said.

"Then I'll wait. Till hell freezes over, if necessary."

Judging by the weather, that wouldn't be long.

"If you'll excuse us," Jake said, brushing by him. I followed.

"Who's this?" Cooke said, meaning me. "A new member of your goon squad? Isn't Fontana enough for you?"

Jake ignored that and I followed him down the steps to the street.

"He didn't mean Carlos Fontana, did he?" I asked.

Jake nodded. His breath was smoking, teeth chattering. He wasn't wearing a topcoat; we'd left too quick for such niceties.

"Fontana's a pretty rough boy," I said.

"A lot of people who was in bootlegging," Jake said, shrugging, "had to go straight. What are you gonna do now?"

"I'll use the phone booth in the drug store to get one of my ops out here to shadow Cooke. I'll keep watch till then. He got enough of a look at me that I don't dare shadow him myself."

Jake nodded. "I'm gonna go call Martin."

"And tell him to stay away?"

"That's up to him."

I shook my head. "Cooke seemed pretty mad."

"He's an asshole."

And Jake walked quickly down to a parked black Ford coupe, got in, and smoked off.

I called the office and told my secretary to send either Lou or Frankie out as soon as possible, whoever was available first; then I sat in the Auburn and waited.

Not five minutes later a heavy-set, dark-haired man in a camel's hair topcoat went in and up the union-hall stairs. I had a hunch it was Martin. More than a hunch: he looked well and truly pissed off, too.

I could smell trouble.

I probably should have sat it out, but I got out of the Auburn and crossed Roosevelt and went up those stairs myself. The secretary was standing behind the desk. She was scared shitless. She looked about an inch away from crying.

Neither man was in the anteroom, but from behind the closed door came the sounds of loud voices.

"What's going on?" I said.

"That awful Mr. Cooke was in using Johnny...Mr. Martin's telephone, in his office, when Mr. Martin arrived."

They were scuffling in there, now.

"Any objection if I go in there and break that up?" I asked her.

"None at all," she said.

That was when we heard the shots.

Three of them, in rapid succession.

The secretary sucked in breath, covered her mouth, said, "My God...my God."

And I didn't have a gun, goddamnit.

I was still trying to figure out whether to go in there or not when the burly, dark-haired guy who I assumed (rightly) to be Martin, still in the camel's hair topcoat, came out with a blue-steel revolver in his hand. Smoke was curling out the barrel.

"Johnny, Johnny," the secretary said, going to him, clinging to him. "Are you all right?"

"Never better," he said, but his voice was shaking. He scowled over at me; he had bushy black eyebrows that made the scowl frightening. And the gun helped. "Who the hell are you?"

"Nate Heller. I'm a dick Jake Rubinstein hired to shadow Leon Cooke."

Martin nodded his head back toward the office. "Well, if you want to get started, he's on the floor in there."

I went into the office and Cooke was on his stomach; he wasn't dead yet. He had a bullet in the side; the other two slugs went through the heavy coat that had been slung over his arm.

"I had to do it," Martin said. "He jumped me. He attacked me."

"We better call an ambulance," I said.

"So, then, we can't just dump his body somewhere," Martin said, thoughtfully.

"I was hired to shadow this guy," I said. "It starts and ends there. You want something covered up, call a cop."

"How much money you got on you?" Martin said. He wasn't talking to me.

The secretary said, "Maybe a hundred."

"That'll hold us. Come on."

He led her through the office and opened a window behind his desk. In a very gentlemanly manner, he helped her out onto the fire escape.

And they were gone.

I helped Cooke onto his feet.

"You awake, pal?"

"Y-yes," he said. "Christ, it hurts."

"Mount Sinai hospital's just a few blocks away," I said. "We're gonna get you there."

I wrapped the coat around him, to keep from getting blood on my car seat, and drove him to the hospital.

Half an hour later, I was waiting outside Cooke's room in the hospital hall when Captain Stege caught up with me.

Stege, a white-haired fireplug of a man with black-rimmed glasses and a pasty complexion—and that Chicago rarity, an honest cop—was not thrilled to see me.

"I'm getting sick of you turning up at shootings," he said.

"I do it just to irritate you. It makes your eyes twinkle."

"You left a crime scene."

"I hauled the victim to the hospital. I told the guy at the drugstore to call it in. Let's not get technical."

"Yeah," Stege grunted. "Let's not. What's your story?"

"The union secretary hired me to keep an eye on this guy Cooke. But Cooke walked in, while I was there, angry, and then Martin showed up, equally steamed."

I gave him the details.

As I was finishing up, a doctor came out of Cooke's room and Stege cornered him, flashing his badge.

"Can he talk, doc?"

"Briefly. He's in critical condition."

"Is he gonna make it?"

"He should pull through. Stay only a few minutes, gentlemen."

Stege went in and I followed; I thought he might object, but he didn't.

Cooke looked pale, but alert. He was flat on his back. Stege introduced himself and asked for Cooke's story.

Cooke gave it, with lawyer-like formality: "I went to see Martin to protest his conduct of the union. I told Martin he ought to've obtained a pay raise for the men in one junkyard. I told him our members were promised a pay increase, by a certain paper company, and instead got a wage cut—and that I understood he'd sided with the employer in the matter! He got very angry, at that, and in a little while we were scuffling. When he grabbed a gun out of his desk, I told him he was crazy, and started to leave. Then...then he shot me in the back."

Stege jotted that down, thanked Cooke and we stepped out into the hall.

"Think that was the truth?" Stege asked me.

"Maybe. But you really ought to hear Martin's side, too."

"Good idea, Heller. I didn't think of that. Of course, the fact that Martin lammed does complicate things, some."

"With all the heat on unions, lately, I can see why he lammed. There doesn't seem to be any doubt Martin pulled the trigger. But who attacked who remains in question."

Stege sighed. "You do have a point. I can understand Martin taking it on the lam, myself. He's already under indictment for another matter. He probably just panicked."

"Another matter?"

Stege nodded. "He and Terry Druggan and two others were indicted last August for conspiracy. Trying to conceal from revenue officers that Druggan was part owner of a brewery."

Druggan was a former bootlegger, a West Side hood who'd been loosely aligned with such non-Capone forces as the Bugs

Moran gang. I was starting to think maybe my old man wouldn't have been so pleased by all this union activity.

"We'll stake out Martin's place," Stege said, "for all the good it'll do. He's got a bungalow over on Wolcott Avenue."

"Nice little neighborhood," I said.

"We're in the wrong racket," Stege admitted.

It was too late in the afternoon to bother going back to the office now, so I stopped and had supper at Pete's Steaks and then headed back to my apartment at the Morrison Hotel. I was reading a Westbrook Pegler column about what a bad boy Willie Bioff was when the phone rang.

"Nate? It's Jake."

"Jake, I'm sorry I didn't call you or anything. I didn't have any number for you but the union hall. You know about what went down?"

"Do I. I'm calling from the Marquette station. They're holding me for questioning."

"Hell, you weren't even there!"

"That's okay. I'm stalling 'em a little."

"Why, for Christ's sake?"

"Listen, Nate—we gotta hold this thing together. You gotta talk to Martin."

"Why? How?"

"I'm gonna talk to Cooke. Cooke's the guy who hired me to work for the union in the first place, and..."

"What? Cooke hired you?"

"Yeah, yeah. Look, I'll go see Cooke first thing in the morning—that is, if you've seen Martin tonight, and worked a story out. Something that'll make this all sound like an accident..."

"I don't like being part of cover-ups."

"This ain't no fuckin' cover-up! It's business! Look, they got the state's attorney's office in on this already. You know who's taken over for Stege, already?"

"Tubbo Gilbert?"

"Himself," Jake said.

Captain Dan "Tubbo" Gilbert was the richest cop in Chicago. In the world. He was tied in with every mob, every fixer in town.

"The local will be finished," Jake said. "He'll find something in the books and use that and the shooting as an excuse to close the union down."

"Which'll freeze wages at current levels," I said. "Exactly what the likes of Billy Skidmore would want."

"Right. And then somebody else'll open the union back up, in six months or so. Somebody tied into the Nitti and Guzik crowd."

"As opposed to Druggan and Moran."

"Don't compare them to Nitti and Guzik. Those guys went straight, Nate."

"Please. I just ate. Moran got busted on a counterfeit railroad-bond scam just last week."

"Nobody's perfect. Nate, it's for the best. Think of your old man."

"Don't do that to me, Jake. I don't exactly think your union is what my pop had in mind when he was handing out pamphlets on Maxwell Street."

"Well, it's all that stands between the working stiffs and the Billy Skidmores."

"I take it you know where Martin is hiding out."

"Yeah. That secretary of his, her mother has a house in Hinsdale. Lemme give you the address..."

"Okay, Jake. It's against my better judgment, but okay..."

It took an hour to get there by car. Well after dark. Hinsdale was a quiet, well-fed little suburb, and the house at 409 Walnut Street was a two-story number in the midst of a healthy lawn. The kind of place the suburbs are full of, but which always seem shockingly sprawling to city boys like yours truly.

There were a few lights on, downstairs. I walked up onto the porch and knocked. I was unarmed. Probably not wise, but I was.

The secretary answered the door. Cracked it open.

She didn't recognize me at first.

"I'm here about our dinner date," I said.

Then, in relief, she smiled, opened the door wider.

"You're Mr. Heller."

"That's right. I never did get your name."

"Then how did you find me?"

"I had your address. I just didn't get your name."

"Well, it's Nancy. But what do you want, Mr. Heller?"

"Make it Nate. It's cold. Could I step in?"

She swallowed. "Sure."

I stepped inside; it was a nicely furnished home, but obviously the home of an older person: the doilies and ancient photo portraits were a dead giveaway.

"This is my mother's home," she said. "She's visiting relatives. I live here."

I doubted that; the commute would be impossible. If she didn't live with Martin, in his nifty little bungalow on South Wolcott, I'd eat every doilie in the joint.

"I know that John Martin is here," I said. "Jake Rubinstein told me. He asked me to stop by."

She didn't know what to say to that.

Martin stepped out from a darkened doorway into the living room. He was in rolled-up shirt sleeves and no tie. He looked frazzled. He had the gun in his hand.

"What do you want?" he said. His tone was not at all friendly.

"You're making too big a deal out of this," I said. "There's no reason to go on the lam. This is just another union shooting—the papers're full of 'em."

"I don't shoot a man every day," Martin said.

"I'm relieved to hear that. How about putting the heater away, then?"

Martin sneered and tossed the piece on a nearby floral couch. He was a nasty man to have a nice girl like this. But then, so often nice girls do like nasty men.

I took it upon myself to sit down. Not on the couch: on a chair, with a soft seat and curved wooden arms.

Speaking of curves, Nancy, who was wearing a blue print dress, was standing wringing her hands, looking about to cry.

"I could use something to drink," I said, wanting to give her something to do.

"Me too," Martin said. "Beer. For him, too."

"Beer would be fine," I said, magnanimously.

She went into the kitchen.

"What's Jake's idea?" Martin asked.

I explained that Jake was afraid the union would be steam-rolled by crooked cops and political fixers, should this shooting blow into something major, first in the papers, then in the courts.

"Jake wants you to mend fences with Cooke. Put together some story you can both live with. Then find some way you can run the union together, or pay him off or something."

"Fuck that shit!" Martin said. He stood up. "What's wrong with that little kike, has he lost his marbles?"

222

"A guy who works on the West Side," I said, "really ought to watch his goddamn mouth where the Jew-baiting's concerned."

"What's it to you? You're Irish."

"Does Heller sound Irish to you? Don't let the red hair fool you."

"Well fuck you, too, then. Cooke's a lying little kike, and Jake's still in bed with him. Damn! I thought I could trust that little bastard..."

"I think you can. I think he's trying to hold your union together, with spit and rubber bands. I don't know if it's worth holding together. I don't know what you're in it for—maybe you really care about your members, a little. Maybe it's the money. But if I were you, I'd do some fast thinking, put together a story you can live with and let Jake try to sell it to Cooke. Then when the dust settles you'll still have a piece of the action."

Martin walked over and pointed a thick finger at me. "I don't believe you, you slick son of a bitch. I think this is a set-up. Put together to get me to come in, give myself up and go straight to the lock-up, while Jake and Cooke tuck the union in their fuckin' belt!"

I stood. "That's up to you. I was hired to deliver a message. I delivered it. Now if you'll excuse me."

He thumped his finger in my chest. "You tell that little kike Rubinstein for me that..."

I smacked him.

He don't go down, but it backed him up. He stood there looking like a confused bear and then growled and lumbered at me with massive fists out in front, ready to do damage.

So I smacked the bastard again, and again. He went down that time. I helped him up. He swung clumsily at me, so I hit him in the side of the face and he went down again. Stayed down.

Nancy came in, a glass of beer in either hand, and said, "What...?" Her brown eyes wide.

"Thanks," I said, taking one glass, chugging it. I wiped the foam off my face with the back of a hand and said, "I needed that."

And I left them there.

The next morning, early, while I was still at the Morrison, shaving in fact, the phone rang.

It was Jake.

"How did it go last night?" he asked.

I told him.

"Shit," he said. "I'll still talk to Cooke, though. See if I can't cool this down some."

"I think it's too late for that."

"Me too," Jake said glumly.

Martin came in on Saturday; gave himself up to Tubbo Gilbert. Stege was off the case. The story Martin told was considerably different from Cooke's: he said Cooke was in the office using the phone ("Which he had no right to do!") and Martin told him to leave; Cooke started pushing Martin around, and when Martin fought back, Cooke drew a gun. Cooke (according to Martin) hit him over the head with it and knocked him down. Then Cooke supposedly hit him with the gun again and Martin got up and they struggled and the gun went off. Three times.

The gun was never recovered. If it was really Cooke's gun, of course, it would have been to Martin's advantage to produce it; but he didn't.

Martin's claim that Cooke attacked and beat him was backed up by the fact that his face was badly bruised and battered. So I guess I did him a favor, beating the shit out of him.

Martin was placed under bond on a charge of intent to kill. Captain Dan "Tubbo" Gilbert, representing the state's attorney's office, confiscated the charter of the union, announcing that it had been run "purely as a racket." Shutting it down until such time that "the actual working members of the union care to continue it, and elect their own officers."

That sounded good in the papers, but in reality it meant Skidmore and company had been served.

I talked to Stege about it, later, over coffee and bagels in the Dill Pickle deli below my office on Van Buren.

"Tubbo was telling the truth about the union being strictly a racket," Stege said. "They had a thousand members paying two bucks a head a month. Legitimate uses counted for only seven hundred bucks' worth a month. Martin's salary, for example, was only a hundred-twenty bucks."

"Well he's shit out of luck, now," I said.

"He's still got his position at the Sanitary District," Stege said. "Of course, he's got to beat the rap for the assault to kill charge, first..." Stege smiled at the thought. "And Mr. Cooke tells a more convincing story than Martin does."

The trouble was, Cooke never got to tell it, not in court. He took a sudden turn for the worse, as so many people in those days did in Chicago hospitals, when they were about to testify in a major trial. Cooke died on the first Friday of January, 1940. There was no autopsy. His last visitor, I was told, was Jake Rubinstein.

When the union was finally re-opened, however, Jake was no longer treasurer. He was still involved in the rackets, though, selling punchboards, working for Ben "Zuckie the Bookie" Zuckerman, with a short time out for a wartime stint in the Air Force. He went to Dallas, I've heard, as representative of

Chicago mob interests there, winding up running some strip joints. Rumor has it he was involved in other cover-ups, over the years.

By that time, of course, Jake was better known as Jack.

And he'd shortened his last name to Ruby.

AUTHOR'S NOTE

"Scrap" is primarily based upon newspaper research, but I should also acknowledge *Maxwell Street* (1977) by Ira Berkow; and *The Plot to Kill the President* (1981) by G. Robert Blakey and Richard N. Billings.

NATURAL DEATH, INC.

She'd been pretty, once. She was still sexy, in a slutty way, if you'd had enough beers and it was just before closing time.

Kathleen O'Meara, who ran the dingy dive that sported her last name, would have been a well-preserved fifty, if she hadn't been forty. But I knew from the background materials I'd been provided that she was born in 1899, here in the dirt-poor Irish neighborhood of Cleveland known as the Angles, a scattering of brick and frame dwellings and businesses at the north end of 25th Street in the industrial flats.

Kathleen O'Meara's husband, Frank, had been dead barely a month now, but Katie wasn't wearing black: her blouse was white with red polka dots, a low-cut peasant affair out of which spilled well-powdered, bowling ball-size breasts. Her mouth was a heavily red-rouged chasm within which gleamed white storebought choppers; her eyes were lovely, within their pouches, long-lashed and money-green.

"What's your pleasure, handsome?" she asked, her soprano voice musical in a calliope sort of way, a hint of Irish lilt in it.

I guess I was handsome, for this crowd anyway, six feet, one-hundred-eighty pounds poured into threadbare mismatched suitcoat and pants, a wilted excuse for a fedora snugged low over my reddish brown hair, chin and cheeks stubbled with two days growth, looking back at myself in the streaked smudgy mirror behind the bar. A chilly March afternoon had driven better than a dozen men inside the shabby walls of O'Meara's, where a churning exhaust fan did little to stave off the bouquet of stale smoke and beer-soaked sawdust.

"Suds is all I can afford," I said.

"There's worse ways to die," she said, eyes sparkling.

"Ain't been reduced to canned heat yet," I admitted.

At least half of the clientele around me couldn't have made that claim; while those standing at the bar, with a foot on the rail like me, wore the sweatstained workclothes that branded them employed, the men hunkered at tables and booths wore the tattered rags of the derelict. A skinny dark-haired dead-eyed sunken-cheeked barmaid in an off-white waitress uniform was collecting empty mugs and replacing them with foaming new ones.

The bosomy saloonkeeper set a sloshing mug before me. "Railroad worker?"

I sipped; it was warm and bitter. "Steel mill. Pretty lean in Gary; heard they was hiring at Republic."

"That was last month."

"Yeah. Found that out in a hurry."

She extended a pudgy hand. "Kathleen O'Meara, at your service."

"William O'Hara," I said. Nathan Heller, actually. The Jewish last name came from my father, but the Irish mug that was fooling the saloonkeeper was courtesy of my mother.

"Two O's, that's us," she grinned; that mouth must have have been something, once. "My pals call me Katie. Feel free."

"Well, thanks, Katie. And my pals call me Bill." Nate.

"Got a place to stay, Bill?"

"No. Thought I'd hop a freight tonight. See what's shakin' up at Flint."

"They ain't hiring up there, neither."

"Well, I dunno, then."

"I got rooms upstairs, Bill."

"Couldn't afford it, Katie."

"Another mug?"

"Couldn't afford that, either."

She winked. "Handsome, you got me wrapped around your little pinkie, ain't ya noticed?"

She fetched me a second beer, then attended to the rest of her customers at the bar. I watched her, feeling both attracted and repulsed; what is it about a beautiful woman run to fat, gone to seed, that can still summon the male in a man?

I was nursing the second beer, knowing that if I had enough of these I might do something I'd regret in the morning, when she trundled back over and leaned on the bar with both elbows.

"A room just opened up. Yours, if you want it."

"I told ya, Katie, I'm flat-busted."

"But I'm not," she said with a lecherous smile, and I couldn't be sure whether she meant money or her billowing powdered bosoms. "I could use a helpin' hand around here....I'm a widow lady, Bill, runnin' this big old place by her lonesome."

"You mean sweep up and do dishes and the like."

Her cute nose wrinkled as if a bad smell had caught its attention; a little late for that, in this joint. "My daughter does most of the drudgery." She nodded toward the barmaid, who was moving through the room like a zombie with a beer tray. "Wouldn't insult ya with woman's work, Bill....But there's things only a man can do."

She said "things" like "tings."

"What kind of things?"

Her eyes had a twinkle, like broken glass. "Things.... Interested?"

"Sure, Katie."

And it was just that easy.

Three days earlier, I had been seated at a conference table in the spacious dark-wood and pebbled-glass office of the Public Safety Director in Cleveland's City Hall.

"It's going to be necessary to swear you in as a part of my staff," Eliot Ness said.

I had known Eliot since we were both teenagers at the University of Chicago. I'd dropped out, finished up at a community college and gone into law enforcement; Eliot had graduated and became a private investigator, often working for insurance companies. Somewhere along the way, we'd swapped jobs.

His dark brown hair brushed with gray at the temples, Eliot's faintly freckled, boyish good looks were going puffy on him, gray eyes pouchy and marked by crow's feet. But even in his late thirties, the former Treasury agent who had been instrumental in Al Capone's fall was the youngest Public Safety Director in the nation.

When I was on the Chicago P.D., I had been one of the few cops Eliot could trust for information; and when I opened up the one-man A-1 Detective Agency, Eliot had returned the favor as my only trustworthy source within the law enforcement community. I had remained in Chicago and he had gone on to more government crimebusting in various corners of the Midwest, winding up with this high profile job as Cleveland's "top cop"; since 1935, he had made national headlines cleaning up the police department, busting crooked labor unions and curtailing the numbers racket.

Eliot was perched on the edge of the table, a casual posture at odds with his three-piece suit and tie. "Just a formality," he explained. "I caught a little heat recently from the City Council for hiring outside investigators."

I'd been brought in on several other cases, over the past five or six years.

"It's an undercover assignment?"

He nodded. "Yes, and I'd love to tackle it myself, but I'm afraid at this point, even in the Angles, this puss of mine is too well-known."

Eliot, a boyhood Sherlock Holmes fan, was not one to stay behind his desk; even as Public Safety Director, he was known to lead raids, wielding an ax, and go undercover, in disguise.

I said, "You've never been shy about staying out of the papers."

I was one of the few people who could make a crack like that and not get a rebuke; in fact, I got a little smile out of the stone face.

"Well, I don't like what's been in the papers, lately," he admitted, brushing the stray comma of hair off his forehead, for what good it did him. "You know I've made traffic safety a priority."

"Sure. Can't jaywalk in this burg without getting a ticket."

When Eliot came into office, Cleveland was ranked the second un-safest city in America, after Los Angeles. By 1938, Cleveland was ranked the safest big city, and by 1939 the safest city, period. This reflected Eliot instituting a public safety campaign through education and "warning" tickets, and reorganizing the traffic division, putting in two-way radios in patrol cars and creating a fleet of motorcycle cops.

"Well, we're in no danger of receiving any 'safest city' honors this year," he said, dryly. He settled into the wooden chair next to mine, folded his hands prayerfully. "We've already had thirty-two traffic fatalities this year. That's more than double where we stood, this time last year."

"What's the reason for it?"

"We thought it had to do with increased industrial activity."

"You mean, companies are hiring again, and more people are driving to work."

"Right. We've had employers insert 'drive carefully' cards in pay envelopes, we've made elaborate safety presentations.... There's also an increase in teenage drivers, you know, kids driving to high school."

"More parents working, more kids with cars. Follows."

"Yes. And we stepped up educational efforts, at schools, accordingly. Plus, we've cracked down on traffic violators of all stripe—four times as many speeding arrests; traffic violations arrests up twenty-five-percent, intoxication arrests almost double."

"What sort of results are you having?"

"In these specific areas—industrial drivers, teenage drivers— very positive. These are efforts that went into effect around the middle of last year—and yet this year, the statistics are far worse."

"You wouldn't be sending me undercover if you didn't have the problem pinpointed."

He nodded. "My Traffic Analysis Bureau came up with several interesting stats: seventy-two percent of our traffic fatalities this year are age forty-five or older. But only twenty percent of our population falls in that category. And thirty-six percent of those fatalities are sixty-five or up...a category that comprises only four percent of Cleveland's population."

"So more older people are getting hit by cars than younger people," I said with a shrug. "Is that a surprise? The elderly don't have the reflexes of young bucks like us."

"Forty-five isn't 'elderly,'" Eliot said, "as we'll both find out sooner than we'd like."

The intercom on Eliot's nearby rolltop desk buzzed and he rose and responded to it. His secretary's voice informed us that Dr. Jeffers was here to see him.

"Send her in," Eliot said.

The woman who entered was small and wore a white shirt and matching trousers, baggy oversize apparel that gave little hint of any shape beneath; though her heart-shaped face was attractive, she wore no make-up and her dark hair was cut mannishly short, clunky thick-lensed tortoise-shell glasses distorting dark almond-shaped eyes.

"Alice, thank you for coming," Eliot said, rising, shaking her hand. "Nate Heller, this is Dr. Alice Jeffers, assistant county coroner."

"A pleasure, Dr. Jeffers," I said, rising, shaking her cool, dry hand, as she twitched me a smile.

Eliot pulled out a chair for her opposite me at the conference table, telling her, "I've been filling Nate in. I'm just up to your part in this investigation."

With no further prompting, Dr. Jeffers said, "I was alerted by a morgue attendant, actually. It seemed we'd had an unusual number of hit-and-skip fatalities in the last six months, particularly in January, from a certain part of the city, and a certain part of community."

"Alice is referring to a part of Cleveland called the Angles," Eliot explained, "which is just across the Detroit Bridge, opposite the factory and warehouse district."

"I've been there," I said. The Angles was a classic waterfront area, where bars and whorehouses and cheap rooming houses serviced a clientele of workingmen and longshoremen. It was also an area rife with derelicts, particularly since Eliot burned out the Hoovervilles nestling in Kingsbury Run and under various bridges.

"These hit-and-skip victims were vagrants," Dr. Jeffers said, her eyes unblinking and intelligent behind the thick lenses, "and tended to be in their fifties or sixties, though they looked much older."

"Rummies," I said.

"Yes. With Director Ness's blessing, and Coroner Gerber's permission, I conducted several autopsies, and encountered individuals in advanced stages of alcoholism. Cirrhosis of the liver, kidney disease, general debilitation. Had they not been struck by cars, they would surely have died within a matter of years or possibly months or even weeks."

"Walking dead men."

"Poetic but apt. My contact at the morgue began keeping me alerted when vagrant 'customers' came through, and I soon realized that automobile fatalities were only part of the story."

"How so?" I asked.

"We had several fatal falls-down-stairs, and a surprising number of fatalities by exposure to the cold weather, death by freezing, by pneumonia. Again, I performed autopsies where normally we would not. These victims were invariably intoxicated at the times of their deaths, and in advanced stages of acute alcoholism."

I was thoroughly confused. "What's the percentage in bumping off bums? You got another psychopath at large, Eliot? Or is the Butcher back, changing his style?"

I was referring to the so-called Mad Butcher of Kingsbury Run, who had cut up a number of indigents here in Cleveland, Jack the Ripper style; but the killings had stopped, long ago.

"This isn't the Butcher," Eliot confidently. "And it isn't psychosis...it's commerce."

"There's money in killing bums?"

"If they're insured, there is."

"Okay, okay," I said, nodding, getting it, or starting to. "But if you overinsure some worthless derelict, surely it's going to attract the attention of the adjusters for the insurance company."

"This is more subtle than that," Eliot said. "When Alice informed me of this, I contacted the State Insurance Division. Their chief investigator, Gaspar Corso—who we'll meet with later this afternoon, Nate—dug through our 'drunk cards' on file at the Central Police Station, some twenty thousand of them. He came up with information that corroborated Alice's, and confirmed suspicions of mine."

Corso had an office in the Standard Building—no name on the door, no listing in the building directory. Eliot, Dr. Jeffers and I met with Corso in the latter's small, spare office, wooden chairs pulled up around a wooden desk that faced the wall, so that Corso was swung around facing us.

He was small and compactly muscular—a former high school football star, according to Eliot—bald with calm blue eyes under black beetle eyebrows. A gold watch chain crossed the vest of his three-piece tweed.

"A majority of the drunks dying either by accident or 'natural causes,'" he said in a mellow baritone, "come from the West Side—the Angles."

"And they were over-insured?" I asked.

"Yes, but not in the way you might expect. Do you know what industrial insurance is, Mr. Heller?"

"You mean, burial insurance?"

"That's right. Small policies designed to pay funeral expenses and the like."

"Is that what these bums are being bumped off for? Pennies?"

A tiny half smile formed on the impassive investigator's thin lips. "Hardly. Multiple policies have been taken out on these individuals, dozens in some cases...each small policy with a different insurance company."

"No wonder no alarms went off," I said. "Each company got hit for peanuts."

"Some of these policies are for two-hundred-and-fifty dollars, never higher than a thousand. But I have one victim here..." He turned to his desk, riffled through some papers. "...who I determined, by crosschecking with various companies, racked up a $24,000 payout."

"Christ. Who was the beneficiary?"

"A Kathleen O'Meara," Eliot said. "She runs a saloon in the Angles, with a rooming house upstairs."

"Her husband died last month," Dr. Jeffers said. "I performed the autopsy myself....He was intoxicated at the time of his death, and was in an advanced stage of cirrhosis of the liver. Hit by a car. But there was one difference."

"Yes?"

"He was fairly well-dressed, and was definitely not malnourished."

O'Meara's did not serve food, but a greasy spoon down the block did, and that's where Katie took me for supper, around seven, leaving the running of the saloon to her sullen skinny daughter, Maggie.

"Maggie doesn't say much," I said, over a plate of meat loaf and mashed potatoes and gray. Like Katie, it was surprisingly appetizing, particularly if you didn't look too closely and were half-bombed.

We were in a booth by a window that showed no evidence of ever having been cleaned; cold March wind rattled it and leached through.

"I spoiled her," Katie admitted. "But, to be fair, she's still grieving over her papa. She was the apple of his eye."

"You miss your old man?"

"I miss the help. He took care of the books. I got a head for business, but not for figures. Thing is, he got greedy."

"Really?"

"Yeah, caught him featherin' his own nest. Skimmin'. He had a bank account of his own he never told me about."

"You fight over that?"

"Naw. Forgive and forget, I always say." Katie was having the same thing as me, and she was shoveling meat loaf into her mouth like coal into a boiler.

"I'm, uh, pretty good with figures," I said.

Her licentious smile was part lip rouge, part gravy. "I'll just bet you are....Ever do time, Bill?"

"Some. I'm not no thief, though...I wouldn't steal a partner's money."

"What were you in for?"

"Manslaughter."

"Kill somebody, did you?"

"Sort of."

She giggled. "How do you 'sort of' kill somebody, Bill?"

"I beat a guy to death with my fists. I was drunk."

"Why?"

"I've always drunk too much."

"No, why'd you beat him to death? With your fists."

I shrugged, chewed meat loaf. "He insulted a woman I was with. I don't like a man that don't respect a woman."

She sighed. Shook her head. "You're a real gent, Bill. Here I thought chivalry was dead."

Three evenings before, I'd been in a yellow-leather booth by a blue-mirrored wall in the Vogue Room of the Hollenden Hotel. Clean-shaven and in my best brown suit, I was in the company of Eliot and his recent bride, the former Ev McMillan, a fashion illustrator who worked for Higbee's department store.

Ev, an almond-eyed slender attractive brunette, wore a simple cobalt blue evening dress with pearls; Eliot was in the three-piece suit he'd worn to work. We'd had prime rib and were enjoying after dinner drinks; Eliot was on his second, and he'd had two before dinner, as well. Martinis. Ev was only one drink behind him.

Personal chit-chat had lapsed back into talking business.

"It's goddamn ghoulish," Eliot said. He was quietly soused, as evidenced by his use of the word "goddamn"—for a tough cop, he usually had a Boy Scout's vocabulary.

"It's coldblooded, all right," I said.

"How does the racket work?" Ev asked.

"I shouldn't have brought it up," Eliot said. "It doesn't make for pleasant after-dinner conversation..."

"No, I'm interested," she said. She was a keenly intelligent young woman. "You compared it to a lottery...how so?"

"Well," I said, "as it's been explained to me, speculators 'invest' in dozens of small insurance policies on vagrants who were already drinking themselves to imminent graves...malnourished men crushed by dope and/or drink, sleeping in parks and in doorways in all kinds of weather."

"Men likely to meet an early death by so-called natural causes," Eliot said. "That's how we came to nickname the racket 'Natural Death, Inc.'"

"Getting hit by a car isn't exactly a 'natural' death," Ev pointed out.

Eliot sipped his martini. "At first, the speculators were just helping nature along by plying their investments with free, large quantities of drink...hastening their death by alcoholism or just making them more prone to stumble in front of a car."

"Now it looks like these insured derelicts are being shoved in front of cars," I said.

"Or the drivers of the cars are purposely running them down," Eliot said. "Dear, this really is unpleasant conversation; I apologize for getting into it..."

"Nonsense," she said. "Who *are* these speculators?"

"Women, mostly," he said. "Harridans running West Side beer parlors and roominghouses. They exchange information, but they aren't exactly an organized ring or anything, which makes our work difficult. I'm siccing Nate here on the worst offender, the closest thing there is to a ringleader—a woman we've confirmed is holding fifty policies on various 'risks.'"

Ev frowned. "How do these women get their victims to go along with them? I mean, aren't the insured's signatures required on the policies?"

"There's been some forgery going on," Eliot said. "But mostly these poor bastards are willingly trading their signatures for free booze."

Ev twitched a non-smile above the rim of her martini glass. "Life in slum areas breeds such tragedy."

The subject changed to local politics—I'd heard rumors of Eliot running for mayor, which he unconvincingly pooh-poohed—

and, a few drinks later, Eliot spotted some reporter friends of his, Clayton Fritchey and Sam Wild, and excused himself to go over and speak to them.

"If I'm not being out of line," I said to Mrs. Ness, "Eliot's hitting the sauce pretty hard himself. Hope you don't have any extra policies out on him."

She managed a wry little smile. "I do my best to keep up with him, but it's difficult. Ironic, isn't it? The nation's most famous Prohibition agent, with a drinking problem."

"*Is* it a problem?"

"Eliot doesn't think so. He says he just has to relax. It's a stressful job."

"It is at that. But, Ev—I've been around Eliot during 'stressful' times before...like when the entire Capone gang was gunning for him. And he never put it away like that, then."

She was studied the olive in her martini. "You were part of that case, weren't you?"

"What case? Capone?"

"No—the Butcher."

I nodded. I'd been part of the capture of the lunatic responsible for those brutal slayings of vagrants; and was one of the handful who knew that Eliot had been forced to make a deal with his influential political backers to allow the son of a bitch—who had a society pedigree—to avoid arrest, and instead be voluntarily committed to a madhouse.

"It bothers him, huh?" I said, and grunted a laugh. "Mr. Squeaky Clean, the 'Untouchable' Eliot Ness having to cut a deal like that."

"I think so," she admitted. "He never says. You know how quiet he can be."

"Well, I think he should grow up. For Christ sake, for somebody from Chicago, somebody who's seen every kind of crime and corruption, he can be as naive as a schoolgirl."

"An alcoholic schoolgirl," Ev said with a smirk, and a martini sip.

"...You want me to talk to him?"

"I don't know. Maybe....I think this case, these poor homeless men being victimized again, got memories stirred up."

"Of the Butcher case, you mean."

"Yes...and Nate, we've been getting postcards from that crazy man."

"What crazy man? Capone?"

"No! The Butcher...threatening postcards postmarked the town where that asylum is."

"Is there any chance Watterson can get out?"

Lloyd Watterson: the Butcher.

"Eliot says no," Ev said. "He's been assured of that."

"Well, these killings aren't the work of a madman. This is murder for profit, plain and simple. Good old-fashioned garden variety evil."

"Help him clear this up," she said, and an edge of desperation was in her voice. "I think it would...might...make a difference."

Then Eliot was back, and sat down with a fresh martini in hand.

"I hope I didn't miss anything good," he said.

My room was small but seemed larger due to the sparseness of the furnishings, metallic, institutional-gray clothes cabinet, a chair and a metal cot. A bare bulb bulged from the wall near the door, as if it had blossomed from the faded, fraying floral-print wallpaper. The wooden floor had a greasy, grimy look.

Katie was saying, "Hope it will do."

"You still haven't said what my duties are."

"I'll think of something. Now, if you need anything, I'm down the hall. Let me show you...."

I followed her to a doorway at the end of the narrow gloomy hallway. She unlocked the door with a key extracted from between her massive breasts, and ushered me into another world.

The livingroom of her apartment held a showroom-like suite of walnut furniture with carved arms, feet and base rails, the chairs and davenport sporting matching green mohair cushions, assembled on a green and blue wall-to-wall Axminster carpet. Pale yellow wallpaper with gold and pink highlights created a tapestry effect, while floral satin damask draperies dressed up the windows, venetian blinds keeping out prying eyes. Surprisingly tasteful, the room didn't look very lived in.

"Posh digs," I said, genuinely impressed.

"Came into some money recently. Spruced the joint up a little....Now, if you need me after hours, be sure to knock good and loud." She swayed over to a doorless doorway and nodded for me to come to her. "I'm a heavy sleeper."

The bedroom was similarly decked out with new furnishings—a walnut-veener double bed, dresser and nightstand and three-mirror vanity with modern lines and zebrawood design panels—against ladylike pink-and-white floral wallpaper. The vanity top was neatly arranged with perfumes and face powder and the like, their combined scents lending the room a feminine bouquet. Framed prints of airbrushed flowers hung here and there, a large one over the bed, where sheets and blankets were neatly folded back below lush overstuffed feather pillows, as if by a maid.

"I had this room re-done, too," she said. "My late husband, rest his soul, was a slob."

Indeed it was hard to imagine a man sharing this room with her. There was a daintiness that didn't match up with its inhabitant. The only sign that anybody lived here were the movie magazines on the bedstand in the glow of the only light, a creamy glazed pottery-base lamp whose gold parchment shade gave the room a glow.

The only person more out of place in this tidy, feminine suite than me, in my tattered secondhand store suit, was my blowsy hostess in her polka-dot peasant blouse and flowing dark skirt. She was excited and proud, showing off her fancy living quarters, bobbing up and down like an eager kid; it was cute and a little sickening.

Or maybe that was the cheap beer. I wasn't drunk but I'd had three glasses of it.

"You okay, Bill?" she asked.

"Demon meatloaf," I said.

"Sit, sit."

And I was sitting on the edge of the bed. She stood before me, looming over me, frightening and oddly comely, with her massive bosom spilling from the blouse, her red-rouged mouth, her half-lidded long-lashed green eyes, mother/goddess/whore.

"It's been lonely, Bill," she said, "without my man."

"Suh...sorry for your loss."

"I could use a man around here, Bill."

"Try to help."

"It could be sweet for you."

She tugged the peasant blouse down over the full, round, white-powdered melons that were her bosom, and pulled my head between them. Their suffocation was pleasant, even heady, and I was wondering whether I'd lost count of those beers when I fished in my trousers for my wallet for the lambskin.

I wasn't *that* far gone.

I had never been with a woman as overweight as Kathleen O'Meara before, and I don't believe I ever was again; many a man might dismiss her as fat. But the sheer womanliness of her was overwhelming; there was so much of her, and she smelled so good, particularly for a saloonkeeper, her skin so smooth, her breasts and behind as firm as they were large and round, that the three nights I spent in her bed remain bittersweet memories. I didn't love her, obviously, nor did she me—we were using each other, in our various nasty ways.

But it's odd, how many times, over the years, the memory of carnality in Katie's bed pops unbidden into my mind. On more than one occasion, in bed with a slender young girlish thing, the image of womanly, obscenely voluptuous Katie would taunt me, as if saying, *Now I was a* real *woman!*

Katie was also a real monster. She waited until the second night, when I lay next to her in the recently purchased bed, in her luxuriant remodeled suite of rooms in a waterfront rooming house where her pitiful clientele slept on pancake-flat piss-scented mattresses, to invite me to be her accomplice.

"Someday I'll move from here," she said in the golden glow of the parchment lamp and the volcanic sex we'd just had. She was on her back, the sheet only half-covering the globes of her bosom; she was smoking, staring at the ceiling.

I was on my back, too—I wasn't smoking, cigarettes being one filthy habit I didn't partake of. "But, Katie—this place is hunky-dory."

"These rooms are nice, love. But little Katie was meant for a better life than the Angles can provide."

"You got a good business, here."

She chuckled. "Better than you know."

"What do you mean?"

She leaned on one elbow and the sheet fell away from the large, lovely bosoms. "Don't you wonder why I'm so good to these stumblebums?"

"You give a lot of free beer away, I noticed."

"Why do you suppose Katie does that?"

"'Cause you're a good Christian woman?"

She roared with laughter, globes shimmering like Jello. "Don't be a child! Have you heard of burial insurance, love?"

And she filled me in on the scheme—the lottery portion of it, at least, taking out policies on men who were good bets for quick rides to potter's field. But she didn't mention anything about helping speed the insured to even quicker, surer deaths.

"You disappointed in Katie?" she asked. "That I'm not such a good Christian woman?"

I grinned at her. "I'm tickled pink to find out how smart you are, baby. Was your old man in on this?"

"He was. But he wasn't trustworthy."

"Lucky for you he croaked."

"Lucky."

"Hey...I didn't mean to be coldhearted, baby. I know you miss him."

Her plump pretty face was as blank as a bisque baby's. "He disappointed me."

"How'd he die?"

"Got drunk and stepped in front of a car."

"Sorry."

"Don't pay for a dipso to run a bar, too much helpin' himself....I notice you don't hit the sauce so hard. You don't drink too much, and you hold what you do drink."

"Thanks."

"You're just a good joe, down on his luck. Could use a break."

"Who couldn't?"

"And I can use a man. I can use a partner."

"What do I have to do?"

"Just be friendly to these rummies. Get 'em on your good side, get 'em to sign up. Usually all it takes is a friendly ear and a pint of rotgut."

"And when they finally drink themselves into a grave, we get a nice payday."

"Yup. And enough nice paydays, we can leave the Angles behind. Retire rich while we're still young and pretty."

His name was Harold Wilson. He looked at least sixty but when we filled out the application, he managed to remember he was forty-three.

He and I sat in a booth at O'Meara's and I plied him with cheap beers, which Katie's hollow-eyed daughter dutifully delivered, while Harold told me, in bits and pieces, the sad story that had brought him to the Angles.

Hunkered over the beer, he seemed small, but he'd been of stature once, physically and otherwise. In a face that was both withered and puffy, bloodshot powder-blue eyes peered from pouches, by turns rheumy and teary.

He had been a stock broker. When the Crash came, he chose to jump a freight rather than out a window, leaving behind a well-bred wife and two young daughters.

"I meant to go back," Harold said, in a baritone voice whose dignity had been sandpapered away, leaving scratchiness and quaver behind. "For years, I did menial jobs...seasonal work, janitorial work, chopping firewood, shoveling walks, mowing grass...and I'd save. But the money never grew. I'd either get jackrolled or spend it on..."

He finished the sentence by grabbing the latest foamy mug of warm beer from Maggie O'Meara and guzzling it.

I listened to Harold's sad story all afternoon and into the evening; he repeated himself a lot, and he signed three burial policies, one for $450, another for $750 and finally the jackpot, $1000. Death would probably be a merciful way out for the poor bastard, but even at this stage of his life, Harold Wilson deserved a better legacy than helping provide for Katie O'Meara's retirement.

Late in the evening, he said, "Did go back, once...to Elmhurst....Tha's Chicago."

"Yeah, I know, Harold."

"Thomas Wolfe said, 'Can't go home again.' Shouldn't go home again's more like it."

"Did you talk to them?"

"No! No. It was Chrissmuss. Sad story, huh? Looked in the window. Didn't expect to see 'em, my family; figured they'd lose the house."

"But they didn't? How'd they manage that?"

"Mary...that's my wife...her family had some money. Must not've got hurt as bad as me in the Crash. Figure they musta bought the house for her."

"I see."

"Sure wasn't her new husband. I recognized him; fella I went to high school with. A postman."

"A mail carrier?"

"Yeah. 'Fore the Crash, Mary, she woulda looked down on a lowly civil servant like that....But in Depression times, that's a hell of a good job."

"True enough."

The eyes were distant and runny. "My girls was grown. College age. Blond and pretty, with boy friends, holdin' hands.... The place hadn't changed. Same furniture. Chrissmuss tree where we always put it, in the front window....We'd move the couch out of the way and...anyway. Nothing different. Except in the middle of it, no me. A mailman took my place."

For a moment I thought he said "male man."

O'Meara's closed at two a.m. I helped Maggie clean up, even though Katie hadn't asked me to. Katie was upstairs, waiting for me in her bedroom. Frankly, I didn't feel like doing my duty tonight, pleasant though it admittedly was. On the one hand, I was using Katie, banging this broad I was undercover, and undercovers, to get the goods on, which made me a louse; and on the other hand, spending the day with her next victim, Harold Wilson, brought home what an enormous louse she was.

I was helping daughter Maggie put chairs on tables; she hadn't said a word to me yet. She had her mother's pretty green eyes and she might have been pretty herself if her scarecrow thin frame and narrow, hatchet face had a little meat on them.

The room was tidied when she said, "Nightcap?"

Surprised, I said, "Sure."

"I got a pot of coffee on, if you're sick of warm beer."

The kitchen in back was small and neat and Maggie's living quarters were back here, as well. She and her mother did not live together; in fact, they rarely spoke, other than Katie issuing commands.

I sat at a wooden table in the midst of the small cupboard-lined kitchen and sipped the coffee Maggie provided in a chipped cup. In her white waitress uniform, she looked like a wilted nurse.

"That suit you're wearing," she said.

Katie had given me clothes to wear; I was in a brown suit and a yellow-and-brown tie, nothing fancy but a step or two up from the threadbare duds "Bill O'Hara" had worn into O'Meara's.

"What about 'em?"

"Those were my father's." Maggie sipped her coffee. "You're about his size."

I'd guessed as much. "I didn't know. I don't mean to be a scavenger, Miss O'Meara, but life can do that to you. The Angles ain't high society."

"You were talking to that man all afternoon."

"Harold Wilson. Sure. Nice fella."

"Ma's signing up policies on him."

"That's right. You know about that, do you?"

"I know more than you know. If you knew what I knew, you wouldn't be so eager to sleep with that cow."

"Now, let's not be disrespectful..."

"To you or the cow?....Mr. O'Hara, you seem like a decent enough sort. Careful what you get yourself into. Remember how my papa died."

"No one ever told me," I lied.

"He got run down by a car. I think he got pushed."

"Really? Who'd do a thing like that?"

The voice behind us said, "This is cozy."

She was in the doorway, Katie, in a red Kimono with yellow flowers on it; you could've rigged out a sailboat with all that cloth.

"Mr. O'Hara helped me tidy up," Maggie said coldly. No fear in her voice. "I offered him coffee."

"Just don't offer him anything else," Katie snapped. The green eyes were hard as jade.

Maggie blushed, and rose, taking her empty cup and mine and depositing them awkwardly, clatteringly, in the sink.

In bed, Katie said, "Good job today with our investment, Bill."

"Thanks."

"Know what Harold Wilson's worth, now?"

"No."

"Ten thousand....Poor sad soul. Terrible to see him suffering like that. Like it's terrible for us to have to wait and wait, before we can leave all this behind."

"What are you sayin', love?"

"I'm sayin', were somebody to put that poor man out of his misery, they'd be doin' him a favor, is all I'm sayin'."

"You're probably right, at that. Poor bastard."

"You know how cars'll come up over the hill...25th Street, headin' for the bridge? Movin' quick through this here bad part of a town?"

"Yeah, what about 'em?"

"If someone were to shove some poor soul out in front of a car, just as it was coming up and over, there'd be no time for stoppin'."

I pretended to digest that, then said, "That'd be murder, Katie."

"Would it?"

"Still...You might be doin' the poor bastard a favor, at that."

"And make ourselves $10,000 richer."

"....You ever do this before, Katie?"

She pressed a hand to her generous bare bosom. "No! No. But I never had a man I could trust before."

Late the next morning, I met with Eliot in a back booth at Mickey's, a dimly lit hole-in-the-wall saloon a stone's throw from City Hall. He was having a late breakfast—a bloody Mary— and I had coffee.

"How'd you get away from Kathleen O'Meara?" he wondered. He looked businesslike in his usual three-piece suit; I was wearing a blue number from the Frank O'Meara Collection.

"She sleeps till noon. I told her daughter I was taking a walk."

"Long walk."

"The taxi'll be on my expense account. Eliot, I don't know how much more of this I can stand. She sent the forms in and paid the premiums on Harold Wilson, and she's talking murder all right, but if you want to catch her in the act, she's plannin' to wait at least a month before we give Harold a friendly push."

"That's a long time for you to stay undercover," Eliot admitted, stirring his bloody Mary with its celery stalk. "But it's in my budget."

I sighed. "I never knew being a city employee could be so exhausting."

"I take it you and Katie are friendly."

"She's a ride, all right. I've never been so disgusted with myself in my life."

"It's that distasteful?"

"Hell, no, I'm having a whale of time, so to speak. It's just shredding what little's left of my self-respect, and shabby little code of ethics, is all. Banging a big fat murdering bitch and liking it." I shuddered.

"This woman is an ogre, no question...and I'm not talking about her looks. Nate, if we can stop her, and expose what's she done, it'll pave the way for prosecuting the other women in the Natural Death, Inc., racket...or at the very least scaring them out of it."

That evening Katie and I were walking up the hill. No streetlights in this part of town, and no moon to light the way; lights in the frame and brick houses we passed, and the headlights of cars heading toward the bridge, threw yellow light on the cracked sidewalk we trundled up, arm in arm, Katie and me. She wore a yellow peasant blouse, always pleased to show off her treasure chest, and a full green skirt.

"Any second thoughts, handsome?"

"Just one."

She stopped; we were near the rise of the hill and the lights of cars came up and over and fell like prison searchlights seeking us out. "Which is?"

"I'm willing to do a dirty deed for a tidy dollar, don't get me wrong, love. It's just...didn't your husband die this same way?"

"He did."

"Heavily insured and pushed in front of his oncoming destiny?"

There was no shame, no denial; if anything, her expression—chin high, eyes cool and hard—spoke pride. "He did. And I pushed him."

"Did you, now? That gives a new accomplice pause."

"I guess it would. But I told you he cheated me. He salted money away. And he was seeing other women. I won't put up with disloyalty in a man."

"Obviously not."

"I'm the most loyal steadfast woman in the world...'less you cross me. Frank O'Meara's loss is your gain...if you have the stomach for the work that needs doing."

A truck came rumbling up over the rise, gears shifting into low gear, and for a detective, I'm ashamed to admit I didn't know we'd been shadowed; but we had. We'd been followed, or anticipated; to this day I'm not sure whether she came from the bushes or behind us, whether fate had helped her or careful planning and knowledge of her mother's ways. Whatever the case, Maggie O'Meara came flying out of somewhere, hurling her skinny stick-like arms forward, shoving the much bigger woman into the path of the truck.

Katie had time to scream, and to look back at the wild-eyed smiling face of her daughter washed in the yellow headlights. The big rig's big tires rolled over her, her girth presenting no problem, bones popping like twigs, blood streaming like water.

The trucker was no hit-and-skip guy. He came to a squealing stop and hopped out and trotted back and looked at the squashed shapeless shape, yellow and green clothing stained crimson, limbs, legs, turned to pulp, head cracked like a melon, oozing.

I had a twinge of sorrow for Katie O'Meara, that beautiful horror, that horrible beauty; but it passed.

"She just jumped right out in front of me!" the trucker blurted. He was a small, wiry man with a mustache, and his eyes were wild.

I glanced at Maggie; she looked blankly back at me.

"I know," I said. "We saw it, her daughter and I...poor woman's been despondent."

I told the uniform cops the same story about Katie, depressed over the loss of her dear husband, leaping in front of the truck. Before long, Eliot arrived himself, topcoat flapping in the breeze as he stepped from the sedan that bore his special EN-1 license plate.

"I'm afraid I added a statistic to your fatalities," I admitted.

"What's the real story?" he asked me, getting me to one side. "None of this suicide nonsense."

I told Eliot that Katie had been demonstrating to me how she wanted me to push Harold Wilson, lost her footing and stumbled to an ironic death. He didn't believe me, of course, and I think he figured that I'd pushed her myself.

He didn't mind, because I produced such a great witness for him. Maggie O'Meara had the goods on the Natural Death racket, knew the names of every woman in her mother's ring, and in May was the star of eighty witnesses in the Grand Jury inquiry. Harold Wilson and many other of the "unwitting pawns in the death-gambling insurance racket" (as reporter Clayton Fritchey put it) were among those witnesses. So were Dr. Alice Jeffers, investigator Gaspar Corso and me.

That night, the night of Katie O'Meara's "suicide," after the police were through with us, Maggie had wept at her kitchen table while I fixed coffee for her, though her tears were not for her mother or out of guilt, but for her murdered father. Maggie never seemed to put together that her dad had been an accomplice in the insurance scheme, or anyway never allowed herself to admit it.

Finally, she asked, "Are you...are you really going to cover for me?"

That was when I told her she was going to testify.

She came out of it, fine; she inherited a lot of money from her late mother—the various insurance companies did not contest previous pay-outs—and I understand she sold O'Meara's and moved on, with a considerable nest egg. I have no idea what became of her, after that.

Busting the Natural Death, Inc., racket was Eliot's last major triumph in Cleveland law enforcement. The following March, after a night of dining, dancing and drinking at the Vogue Room, Eliot and Ev Ness were in an automobile accident, Eliot sliding into another driver's car. With Ev minorly hurt, Eliot—after checking the other driver and finding him dazed but all right—rushed her to a hospital and became a hit-and-run driver. He made some efforts to cover up and, even when he finally fessed up in a press conference, claimed he'd not been intoxicated behind that wheel; his political enemies crucified him, and a month later Eliot resigned as Public Safety Director.

During the war, Eliot headed up the government's efforts to control venereal disease on military bases; but he never held a law enforcement position again. He and Ev divorced in 1945. He married a third time, in 1946, and ran, unsuccessfully for mayor of Cleveland in '47, spending the rest of his life trying, without luck, to make it in the world of business, often playing on his reputation as a famed gangbuster.

In May, 1957, Eliot Ness collapsed in his kitchen shortly after he had arrived home from the liquor store, where he had bought a bottle of Scotch.

He died with less than a thousand dollars to his name—I kicked in several hundred bucks on the funeral, wishing his wife had taken out some damn burial insurance on him.

AUTHOR'S NOTE

Fact, speculation, and fiction are freely mixed within this story, which is based on an actual case in the career of Eliot Ness.

SCREWBALL

Not long ago Miami Beach had been a sixteen-hundred-acre stretch of jungle sandbar thick with mangroves and scrub palmetto, inhabited by wild birds, mosquitoes and snakes. Less than thirty years later, the wilderness had given way to plush hotels, high-rent apartment houses and lavish homes, with manicured terraces and swimming pools, facing a beach littered brightly with cabanas and sun umbrellas.

That didn't mean the place wasn't still infested with snakes, birds and bugs—just that it was now the human variety.

It was May 22, 1941, and dead; winter season was mid-December through April, and the summer's onslaught of tourists was a few weeks away. At the moment, the majority of restaurants and nightclubs in Miami Beach were shuttered, and the handful of the latter still doing business were the ones with gaming rooms. Even in off-season, gambling made it pay for a club to keep its doors open.

The glitzy showroom of Chez Clifton had been patterned on (though was about a third the size of) the Chez Paree back home in Chicago, with a similarly set up backroom gambling casino called (in both instances) the Gold Key Club. But where the Chez Paree was home to bigname stars and orchestras—Edgar Bergen and Charlie McCarthy, Ted Lewis, Martha Raye—the Chez Clifton's headliner was invariably its namesake: Pete Clifton.

A near ringer for Zeppo, the "normal" Marx Brother, Clifton was tall, dark and horsily handsome, his slicked-back, parted-at-the side hair as black as his tie and tux. He was at the microphone, leaning on it like a jokester Sinatra, the orchestra behind him, accompanying him occasionally on song parodies, the drummer providing the requisite rimshots, the boys laughing heartily at gags they'd heard over and over, prompting the audience.

Not that the audience needed help: the crowd thought Clifton was a scream. And, for a Thursday night, it was a good crowd, too.

"Hear about the guy that bought his wife a bicycle?" he asked innocently. "Now she's peddling it all over town."

They howled at that.

"Hear about the sleepy bride?....She couldn't stay away awake for a second."

Laughter all around me, I was settled in at a table for two—by myself—listening to one dirty joke after another. Clifton had always worked blue, back when I knew him; he'd been the opening act at the Colony Club showroom on Rush Street—a mob joint fronted by Nicky Dean, a crony of Al Capone's successor, Frank Nitti.

But tonight, every gag was filthy.

"Hear about the girl whose boyfriend didn't have any furniture? She was floored."

People were crying at this rapier wit. But not everybody liked it. The guy Clifton was fronting for, in particular.

"Nate," Frank Nitti had said to me earlier that afternoon, "I need you to deliver a message to your old pal Pete Clifton."

In the blue shade of an umbrella at a small white metal table, buttery sun reflecting off the shimmer of cool blue water, Nitti and I were sitting by the pool at Nitti's Di Lido Island estate, his palatial digs looming around us, rambling white stucco buildings with green-tile roofs behind bougainvillea-covered walls.

Eyes a mystery behind sunglasses, Nitti wore a blue-and-red Hawaiian print shirt, white slacks and sandals, a surprisingly small figure, his handsome oval face flecked with occasional scars, his slicked back black hair touched with gray and immaculately trimmed. I was the one who looked like a gangster, in my brown suit and darker brown fedora, having just arrived from Chicago, Nitti's driver picking me up at the railroad station.

"I wouldn't call Clifton an 'old pal,' Mr. Nitti."

"How many times I gotta tell ya, call me, 'Frank'? After what we been through together?"

I didn't like the thought of having been through anything "together" with Frank Nitti. But the truth was, fate and circumstance had on several key occasions brought Chicago's most powerful gangster leader into the path of a certain lowly Loop private detective—though, I wasn't as lowly as I used to be. The A-1 Agency had a suite of offices now, and I had two experienced ops and a pretty blonde secretary under me—or anyway, the ops were under me; the secretary wasn't interested.

But when Frank Nitti asked the President of the A-1 to hop a train to Miami Beach and come visit, Nathan Heller hopped and visited—the blow softened by the three hundred dollar retainer check Nitti's man Louis Campagna had delivered to my Van Buren Street office.

"I understand you two boys used to go out with showgirls and strippers, time to time," Nitti said, lighting up a Cuban cigar smaller than a billy club.

"Clifton was a cocky, good-looking guy, and the toast of Rush Street. The girls liked him. I liked the spillover."

Nitti nodded, waving out his match. "He's still a good-looking guy. And he's still cocky. Ever wonder how he managed to open up his own club?"

"Never bothered wondering. But I guess it is a little unusual."

"Yeah. He ain't famous. He ain't on the radio."

"Not with *that* material."

Nitti blew a smoke ring; an eyebrow arched. "Oh, you remember that? How blue he works."

I shrugged. "It was kind of a gimmick, Frank—clean-cut kid, looks like a matinee idol. Kind of a funny, startling contrast with his off-color material."

"Well, that's what I want you to talk to him about."

"Afraid I don't follow, Frank...."

"He's workin' too blue. Too goddamn fuckin' filthy."

I winced. Part of it was the sun reflecting off the surface of the pool; most of it was confusion. Why the hell did Frank Nitti give a damn if some two-bit comic was telling dirty jokes?

"That foulmouth is attracting the wrong kind of attention," Nitti was saying. "The blue noses are gettin' up in arms. Ministers are givin' sermons, columnists are frownin' in print. There's this 'Citizens Committee for Clean Entertainment.' Puttin' political pressure on. Jesus Christ! The place'll get raided—shut down."

I hadn't been to Chez Clifton yet, though I assumed it was running gambling, wide-open, and was already on the cops' no-raid list. But if anti-smut reformers made an issue out of Clifton's immoral monologues, the boys in blue would *have* to raid the joint—and the gambling baby would go out the window with the dirty bathwater.

"What's your interest in this, Frank?"

Nitti's smile was mostly a sneer. "Clifton's got a club 'cause he's got a silent partner."

"You mean...*you*, Frank? I thought the Outfit kept out of the Florida rackets...."

It was understood that Nitti, Capone and other Chicago mobsters with homes in Miami Beach would not infringe on the hometown gambling syndicate. This was said to be part of the agreement with local politicos to allow the Chicago Outfit to make Miami Beach their home away from home.

"That's why I called you down here, Nate. I need somebody to talk to the kid who won't attract no attention. Who ain't directly connected to me. You're just an old friend of Clifton's from outa town."

"And what do you want me to do, exactly?"

"Tell him to clean up his fuckin' act."

So now I was in the audience, sipping my rum and Coke, the walls ringing with laughter, as Pete Clifton made such deft witticisms as the following: "Hear about the doll who found a tramp under her bed? She got so upset, her stomach was on the bum all night."

Finally, to much applause, Clifton turned the entertainment over to the orchestra, and couples filled the dancefloor to the strains of "Nice Work if You Can Get It." Soon the comic had filtered his way through the admiring crowd to join me at my table.

"You look good, you rat bastard," Clifton said, flashing his boyish smile, extending his hand, which I took and shook. "Getting any since I left Chicago?"

"I wet the wick on occasion," I said, sitting as he settled in across from me. All around us patrons were sneaking peeks at the star performer who had deigned to come down among them.

"I didn't figure you'd ever get laid again, once I moved on," he said, straightening his black tie. "How long you down here for?"

"Couple days."

He snapped his fingers, pointed at me and winked. "Tell you what, you're goin' boating with me tomorrow afternoon. These two cute skirts down the street from where I live, they're both hot for me—you can take one of 'em offa my hands."

Smiling, shaking my head, I said, "I thought maybe you'd have found a new hobby, by now, Pete."

"Not me." He fired up a Lucky Strike, sucked in smoke, exhaled it like dragon breath from his nostrils. "I never found a sweeter pasttime than doin' the dirty deed."

"Doing dames ain't the only dirty deed you been doing lately, Pete."

"Whaddya mean?"

"Your act." I gestured with my rum-and-Coke. "I've seen cleaner material on outhouse walls."

He grinned toothily. "You offended? Getting prudish in your old age, Heller? Yeah, I've upped the ante, some. Look at this crowd, weeknight, off season. They love it. See, it's my magic formula: everybody loves sex; and everybody loves a good dirty joke."

"Not everybody."

The grin eased off and his forehead tightened. "Wait a minute....This isn't a social call, is it?"

"No. It's nice seeing you again, Pete...but no. You think you know who sent me—and you're right. And he wants you to back off the smut."

"You kidding?" Clifton smirked and waved dismissively. "I found a way to mint money, here. And it's making me a star."

"You think you can do that material on the radio, or in the movies? Get serious."

"Hey, everybody needs an angle, a trademark, and I found mine."

"Pete, I'm not here to discuss it. Just to pass the word along. You can ignore it if you like." I sipped my drink, shrugged. "Take your dick out and conduct the orchestra with it, far as I'm concerned."

Clifton leaned across the table. "Nate, you heard those laughs. You see the way every dame in this audience is lookin' at me? There isn't a quiff in this room that wouldn't get on her back for me, or down on her damn knees."

"Like I said, ignore it if you like. But my guess is, if you do keep working blue—and the Chez Clifton gets shut down—your silent partner'll get noisy."

The comic thought about that, drawing nervously on the Lucky. In his tux, he looked like he fell off a wedding cake. Then he said, "What would you do, Nate?"

"Get some new material. Keep some of the risque stuff, sure—but don't be so Johnny One-note."

Some of the cockiness had drained out of him; frustration colored his voice, even self-pity. "It's what I do, Nate. Why not tell Joe E. Lewis not to do drunk jokes. Why not tell Eddie Cantor not to pop his eyes out?"

"'Cause somebody'll pop *your* eyes out, Pete. I say this as a friend, and as somebody who knows how certain parties operate. Back off."

He sighed, sat back. I didn't say anything. The orchestra was playing "I'll Never Smile Again," now.

"Tell Nitti I'll...tone it down."

I saluted him with my nearly empty rum-and-Coke glass. "Good choice."

And that was it. I had delivered my message. He had another show to do, and I didn't see him again till the next afternoon, when—as promised—he took me out on his speedboat, a sleek mahogany nineteen-foot Gar Wood runabout whose tail was emblazoned *Screwball*.

And, as promised, we were in the company of two "cute skirts," although that's not what they were wearing. Peggy Simmons, a slender pretty pugnose blonde, and Janet Windom, a cow-eyed bosomy brunette, were in white shorts that showed off their nice, nicely tanned legs. Janet, who Pete had claimed, wore a candy-striped top; Peggy, who had deposited herself next to me on the leather seat, wore a pink longsleeve angora sweater.

"Aren't you warm in that?" I asked her, sipping a bottle of Pabst. I was in a shortsleeve sportshirt and chinos, my straw fedora at my feet, away from the wind.

"Not really. I get chilled in the spray." She had a high-pitched voice that seemed younger than her twenty-two years, though the lines around her sky-blue eyes made her seem older. Peggy laughed and smiled a lot, but those eyes were sad, somehow.

I had been introduced to Peggy as a theatrical agent from Chicago. She was a model and dancer, and apparently Clifton figured this lie would help me get laid; this irritated me—being burdened with a fiction of someone else's creation, and the notion I needed help in that regard. But I hadn't corrected it.

Janet, it seemed, was also interested in show business; a former dentist's assistant, she was a couple years older than Peggy. They had roomed together in New York City and came down here a few months ago, seeking sun and fame and fortune.

The afternoon was pleasant enough. Clifton sat at the wheel with Janet cuddling next to him, and Peggy and I sat in the seat behind them. She was friendly, holding my hand, putting her head on my shoulder, though we barely knew each other. We drank in the sun-drenched, invigorating gulf-stream air, as well as our bottled beers, and enjoyed the view—royal palms waving, white-capped breakers peaking, golden sands glistening with sunlight.

The runabout had been bounding along, which—with the engine noise—had limited conversation. But pretty soon Clifton charted us up and down Indian Creek, a tranquil, seawalled lagoon lined with palm-fringed shores and occasional well-manicured golf courses, as well as frequent private piers and landing docks studded with gleaming yachts and lavish houseboats.

"Have you found any work down here?" I asked the fresh-faced, sad-eyed girl.

She nodded. "Some cheesecake modeling Pete lined up. Swimsuits and, you know...art studies."

Nudes.

"What are you hoping for?"

"Well, I am a good dancer, and I sing a little, too. Pete says he's going to do a big elaborate show, soon, with a chorus line and everything."

"And he's going to use both you and Janet?"

She nodded.

"Any thoughts beyond that, Peggy? You've got nice legs, but show business is a rough career."

Her chin crinkled as she smiled, but desperation tightened her eyes. "I'd be willing to take a Chicago booking."

Though we weren't gliding as quickly over the water now, the engine noise was still enough to keep my conversation with

Peggy private while Pete and Janet laughed and kissed and chugged their beers.

"I'm not a booking agent, Peggy."

She drew away just a little. "No?"

"Pete was...I don't know what he was doing."

She shrugged again, smirked. "Pete's a goddamn liar, sometimes."

"I know some people who book acts in Chicago, and would be glad to put a word in...but don't be friendly with me on account of that."

She studied me and her eyes didn't seem as sad, or as old, suddenly. "What do you know? The vanishing American."

"What?"

"A nice guy."

And she cuddled next to me, put a hand on my leg.

Without looking at me, she asked, "Why do *you* think I came to Florida, Nate?"

"It's warm and sunny."

"Yes."

"And..." I nodded toward either side of us, where the waterway entrances of lavish estates, trellised with bougainvillea and allamanda, seemed to beckon. "...there's more money here than you can shake a stick at."

She laughed. "Yes."

By four o'clock we were at the girls' place, in a six-apartment building on Jefferson Street, a white-trimmed-pink geometric affair among many other such streamlined structures of sunny yellow, flamingo pink and sea green, with porthole windows and racing stripes and *bas relief* zig-zags. The effect was at once elegant and insubstantial, like a movie set. Their one-bedroom apartment was on the second of two floors; the furnishings had an *art moderne* look, too, though of the low-cost Sears showroom variety.

Janet fixed us drinks and we sat in the little pink and white living room area and made meaningless conversation for maybe five minutes. Then Clifton and Janet disappeared into that one bedroom, and Peggy and I necked on the couch. The lights were low, when I got her sweater and bra off her, but I noticed the needle tracks on her arms, just the same.

"What's wrong?" she asked.

"Nothing....What are you on? H?"

"What do you mean?....Not H."

"What?"

"M."

Morphine.

She folded her arms over her bare breasts, but it was her arms she was hiding.

"I was blue," she said, defensively, shivering suddenly. "I needed something."

"Where'd you get it?"

"Pete has friends."

Pete had friends, all right. And I was one of them.

"Put your sweater on, baby."

"Why? Do I...do I make you sick?"

And she began to cry.

So I made love to her there on the couch, sweetly, tenderly, comforting her, telling her she was beautiful, which she was. She needed the attention, and I didn't mind giving it to her, though I was steaming at that louse Clifton.

Our clothes relatively straightened, Peggy having freshened in the bathroom, we were sitting, chatting, having Cokes on ice like kids on a date, when Clifton—in the pale yellow sportshirt and powder-blue slacks he'd gone boating in—emerged from the bedroom, arm around Janet, who was in a terrycloth robe.

"We better blow, Nate," he told me with a grin, and nuzzled the giggling Janet's neck. She seemed to be on something, too. "I got a nine o'clock show to do."

It was a little after seven.

We made our goodbyes and drove the couple of blocks to his place in his white Lincoln Zephyr convertible.

"Do I take care of you," he asked with a grin, as the shadows of the palms lining the streets rolled over us, "or do I take care of you?"

"You're a pal," I said.

We were slipping past more of those movie theater-like apartment houses, pastel chunks of concrete whose geometric harshness was softened by well-barbered shrubs. The three-story building on West Jefferson, in front of which Clifton drew his Lincoln, was set back a ways, a walk cutting through a golf green of a lawn to the pale yellow cube whose blue cantilevered sunshades were like eyebrows.

Clifton's apartment was on the third floor, a two bedroom affair with pale yellow walls and a parquet floor flung with occasional oriental carpets. The furnishings were in the *art moderne* manner, chrome and leather and well-varnished light woods, none of it from Sears.

I sat in a pastel green easy chair whose lines were rounded; it was as comfortable as an old shoe but considerably more stylish.

"How do those unemployed showgirls afford a place like that?" I wondered aloud.

Clifton, who was making us a couple of rum and Cokes over at the wet bar, said, "Did you have a good time?"

"I like Peggy. If I lived around here, I'd try to straighten her out."

"Oh yeah! Saint Heller. I thought you did straighten her out—on that couch."

"Are you pimping for those girls?"

"No!" He came over with a drink in either hand. "They're not pros."

"But you fix them up with friends and other people you want to impress."

He shrugged, handing me the drink. "Yeah. So what? Party girls like that are a dime a dozen."

"Where are you getting the dope?"

That stopped him for a moment, but just a moment. "It makes 'em feel good; what's the harm?"

"You got 'em hooked and whoring for you, Pete. You're one classy guy."

Clifton smirked. "I didn't see you turning down the free lay."

"You banging 'em both?"

"Never at the same time. What, you think I'm a pervert?"

"No. I think you're a prick."

He just laughed at that. "Listen, I got to take a shower. You coming down to the club tonight, or not?"

"I'll come. But Pete—where are you getting the dope you're giving those girls?"

"Why do you care?"

"Because I don't think Frank Nitti would like it. He doesn't do business with people in that racket. If he knew you were involved..."

Clifton frowned. "You going to tell him?"

"I didn't say that."

"Maybe I don't give a shit if you do. Maybe I got a possible new investor for my club, and Frank Nitti can kiss my ass."

"Would you like me to pass that along?"

A grimace drained all the boyishness from his face. "What's wrong with you, Heller? Since when did you get moral? These gangsters are like women—they exist to be used."

"Only the gangsters don't discard as easily."

"I ain't worried." He jerked a thumb at his chest. "See, Heller, I'm a public figure—they don't bump off public figures; it's bad publicity."

"Tell Mayor Cermak—he got hit in Florida."

He blew me a Bronx cheer. "I'm gonna take a shower. You want a free meal down at the club, stick around...but leave the sermons to Billy Sunday, okay?"

"Yeah. Sure."

I could hear him showering, singing in there, "All or Nothing at All." Had we really been friends, once? I had a reputation as something of a randy son of a bitch myself; but did I treat woman like Clifton did? The thought make me shudder.

On the oblong glass coffee table before me, a white phone began to ring. I answered it.

"Pete?" The voice was low-pitched, but female—a distinctive, throaty sound.

"No, it's a friend. He's in the shower, getting ready for his show tonight."

"Tell him to meet me out front in five minutes."

"Well, let me check with him and see if that's possible. Who should I say is calling?"

There was a long pause.

Then the throaty purr returned: "Just tell him the wife of a friend."

"Sure," I said, and went into the bathroom and reported this, over the shower needles, through the glass door, to Clifton, who said, "Tell her I'll be right down."

Within five minutes, Clifton—his hair still wet—moved quickly through the living room; he had thrown on the boating clothes from this afternoon.

"This won't take long." He flashed the boyish grin. "These frails can't get enough of me."

"You want me to leave?"

"Naw. I'll set somethin' up with her for later. I don't think she has a friend, though—sorry, pal."

"That's okay. I try to limit myself to one doped-up doxy a day."

Clifton smirked and waved at me dismissively as he headed out, and I sat there for maybe a minute, then decided I'd had it. I plucked my straw fedora off the coffee table and trailed out after him, hoping to catch up with him and make my goodbyes.

The night sky was cobalt and alive with stars, a sickle-slice of moon providing the appropriate deco touch. The sidewalk stretched out before me like a white ribbon, toward where palms mingled with street lights. A Buick was along the curb and Pete was leaning against the window, like a car hop taking an order.

That sultry, low female voice rumbled through the night like pretty thunder: "*For God's sake, Pete, don't do it! Please don't do it!*"

As Pete's response—laughter—filled my ears, I stopped in my tracks, not wanting to intrude. Then Pete, still chuckling, making a dismissive wave, turned toward me, and walked. He was giving me a cocky smile when the first gunshot cracked the night.

I dove and rolled and wound up against a sculpted hedge that separated Clifton's apartment house from the hunk of geometry next door. Two more shots rang out, and I could see the orange muzzle flash as the woman shot through the open car window.

For a comic, Pete was doing a hell of a dance; the first shot had caught him over the right armpit, and another plowed through his neck in a spray of red, and he twisted around to face her to accommodate another slug.

Then the car roared off, and Pete staggered off the sidewalk and pitched forward onto the grass, like a diver who missed the pool.

I ran to his sprawled figure, and turned him over. His eyes were wild with dying.

"Them fuckin' dames ain't...ain't so easy to discard, neither," he said, and laughed, a bloody froth of a laugh, to punctuate his last dirty joke.

People were rushing up, talking frantically, shouting about the need for the police to be called and such like. Me, I was noting where the woman had put her last shot.

She caught him right below the belt.

After a long wait in a receiving area, I was questioned by the cops in an interview room at the Dade County Courthouse in Miami. Actually, one of them, Earl Carstensen—Chief of Detectives of the Miami Beach Detective Bureau—was a cop; the other guy— Ray Miller—was chief investigator for the State Attorney's office.

Carstensen was a craggy guy in his fifties and Miller was a skinny balding guy with wirerim glasses. The place was air-conditioned and they brought me an iced tea, so it wasn't exactly the third degree.

We were all seated at the small table in the soundproofed cubicle. After they had established that I was a friend of the late

Pete Clifton, visiting from Chicago, the line of questioning took an interesting turn.

Carstensen asked, "Are you aware that 'Peter Clifton' was not the deceased's real name?"

"I figured it was a stage name, but it's the only name I knew him by."

"He was born Peter Tessitorio," Miller said, "in New York. He had a criminal background—two burglary raps."

"I never knew that."

Carstensen asked, "You're a former police officer?"

"Yeah. I was a detective on the Chicago P.D. pickpocket detail till '32."

Miller asked, "You spent the afternoon with Clifton, in the company of two girls?"

"Yeah."

"What are their names?"

"Peggy Simmons and Janet Windom. They live in an apartment house on Jefferson...I don't know the address, but I can point you, if you want to talk to them."

The two men exchanged glances.

"We've already picked them up," Miller said. "They've been questioned, and they're alibiing each other. They say they don't know anybody who'd want to kill Clifton."

"They're just a couple of party girls," I said.

Carstensen said, "We found a hypo and bottle of morphine in their apartment. Would you know anything about that?"

I sighed. "I noticed the tracks on the Simmons' kid's arms. I gave Pete hell, and he admitted to me he was giving them the stuff. He also indicated he had connections with some dope racketeer."

"He didn't give you a name?" Miller asked.

"No."

"You've never heard of Leo Massey?"

"No."

"Friend of Clifton's. A known dope smuggler."

I sipped my iced tea. "Well, other than those two girls, I don't really know any of Clifton's associates here in Miami."

An eyebrow arched in Carstensen's craggy puss. "You'd have trouble meeting Massey—he's dead."

"Oh?"

"He was found in Card Sound last September. Bloated and smellin' to high heavens."

"What does that have to do with Pete Clifton?"

Miller said, "Few days before Massey's body turned up, that speedboat of his—the *Screwball*—got taken out for a spin."

I shrugged. "That's what a speedboat's for, taking it out for a spin."

"At midnight? And not returning till daybreak?"

"You've got a witness to that effect?"

Miller nodded.

"So Pete was a suspect in Massey's murder?"

"Not exactly," the State Attorney's investigator said. "Clifton had an alibi—those two girls say he spent the night with 'em."

I frowned in confusion. "I thought you had a witness to Clifton takin' his boat out..."

Carstensen said, "We have a witness at the marina to the effect that the boat was taken out, and brought back—but nobody saw who the captain was."

Now I was getting it. "And Pete said somebody must've borrowed his boat without his permission."

"That's right."

"So, what? You're making this as a gangland hit? But it was a woman who shot him."

Miller asked, "Did you see that, Mr. Heller?"

"I heard the woman's voice—I didn't actually see her shoot him. Didn't actually see her at all. But it seemed like she was agitated with Pete."

Other witnesses had heard the woman yelling at Pete; so the cops knew I hadn't made up this story.

"Could the woman have been a decoy?" Carstensen asked. "Drawn Clifton to that car for some man to shoot?"

"I suppose. But my instinct is, Pete's peter got him bumped. If I were you, fellas, I'd go over that apartment of his and look for love letters and the like; see if you can find a little black book. My guess is—somebody he was banging banged him back."

They thanked me for my help, told me to stick around for the inquest on Tuesday, and turned me loose. I got in my rental Ford and drove to the Biltmore, went up to my room, ordered a room service supper, and gave Frank Nitti a call.

"So my name didn't come up?" Nitti asked me over the phone.

"No. Obviously, I didn't tell 'em you hired me to come down here; but they didn't mention you, either. And the way they were giving out information, it would've come up. They got a funny way of interrogating you in Florida—they spill and you listen."

"Did they mention a guy named McGraw?"

"No, Frank. Just this Leo Massey."

"McGraw's a rival dope smuggler," Nitti said thoughtfully. "I understand he stepped in and took over Massey's trade after Massey turned up a floater."

"What's that got to do with Clifton?"

"Nothin' much—just that my people tell me McGraw's a regular at the Chez Clifton. Kinda chummy with our comical late friend."

"Maybe McGraw's the potential investor Clifton was talking about—to take your place, Frank."

Silence. Nitti was thinking.

Finally, he returned with, "Got another job for you, Nate."

"I don't know, Frank—I probably oughta keep my nose clean, do my bit at the inquest and scram outa this flamingo trap."

"Another three C's in it for you, kid—just to deliver another message. No rush—tomorrow morning'll be fine."

Did you hear the one about the comic who thought he told killer jokes? He died laughing.

"Anything you say, Frank."

Eddie McGraw lived at the Delano, on Collins Avenue, the middle of a trio of towering hotels rising above Miami Beach like Mayan temples got out of hand. McGraw had a penthouse on the eleventh floor, and I had to bribe the elevator attendant to take me there.

It was eleven a.m. I wasn't expecting trouble. My nine millimeter Browning was back in Chicago, in a desk drawer in my office. But I wasn't unarmed—I had the name *Frank Nitti* in my arsenal.

I knocked on the door.

The woman who answered was in her late twenties—a brunette with big brown eyes and rather exaggerated features, pretty in a cartoonish way. She had a voluptuous figure, wrapped up like a present in a pink chiffon dressing gown.

"Excuse me, ma'am. Is Mr. McGraw home?"

She nodded. The big brown eyes locked onto me coldly, though her voice was a warm contralto: "Who should I say is calling?"

"I'm a friend of Pete Clifton's."

"Would you mind waiting in the hall?"

"Not at all."

She shut the door, and a few seconds later, it flew back open, revealing a short but sturdy looking guy in a red sportshirt and gray slacks. He was blond with wild thatches of overgrown eyebrow above sky-blue eyes; when you got past a bulbous nose, he kind of looked like James Cagney.

"I don't do business at my apartment," he said. His voice was high-pitched and raspy. He started to shut the door and I stopped it with my hand.

He shoved me, and I went backward, but I latched onto his wrist, and pushed his hand back, and pulled him forward, out into the hall, until he was kneeling in front of me.

"Frank Nitti sent me," I said, and released the pressure on his wrist.

He stood, ran a hand through slicked back blond hair that didn't need straightening, and said, "I don't do business with Nitti."

"I think maybe you should. You know about Pete's killing?"

"I saw the morning paper. I liked Pete. He was funny. He was an all right guy."

"Yeah, he was a card. Did he by any chance sell you an interest in the Chez Clifton?"

McGraw frowned at me; if he'd been a dog, he'd have growled. "I told you...what's your name, anyway?"

"Heller. Nate Heller."

"I don't do business at my apartment. My wife and me, we got a life separate from how I make my living. Got it?"

"Did Pete sell you an interest in the Chez Clifton?"

He straightened his collar, which also didn't need it. "As a matter of fact, he did."

"Then you were wrong about not doing business with Frank Nitti."

McGraw sneered. "What's that supposed to mean?"

"Mr. Nitti would like to discuss that with you himself." I handed him a slip of paper. "He's in town, at his estate on Di Lido Island. He'd like to invite you to join him there for lunch today."

"Why should I?"

I laughed once, a hollow thing. "Mr. McGraw, I don't care what you do, as long as you don't put your hands on me again. I'm just delivering a message. But I will tell you this—I'm from Chicago, and when Frank Nitti invites you for lunch, you go."

McGraw thought about that. Then he nodded and said, "Sorry about the rough stuff."

"I apologize for bothering you at home. But you don't keep an office, and you're unlisted."

"Yeah, well, nature of my business."

"Understood."

I held out my hand. He studied it for a moment, then shook it.

"Why don't you give Mr. Nitti a call, at that number, and confirm your luncheon engagement."

He nodded and disappeared inside the apartment.

Half an hour later, I knocked on the door again. Returning had cost me another fin to the elevator boy.

Mrs. McGraw, still in her pink chiffon robe, opened the door and said, "I'm afraid my husband has stepped out."

"I know he has," I said, brushing past her into the apartment, beautifully appointed in the usual Miami-tropical manner.

"Leave at once!" she demanded, pointing past the open door into the hall.

"No," I said, and shut the door. "I recognized your voice, Mrs. McGraw. It's very distinctive. I like it."

"What are you talking about?" But her wide eyes and the tremor in her tone told me she was afraid she already knew.

I told her, anyway. "I'm the guy who answered the phone last night, at Pete's. That's when I first heard that throaty purr of yours. I also heard you warn him—right before he turned his back on you and you shot him."

She was clutching herself, as if she were cold. "I don't know what you're talking about. Please leave!"

"I'm not going to stay long. Turn around."

"What?"

"Turn around and put your hands on that door."

"Why?"

"I'm gonna frisk you, lady. I don't figure you have a gun hidden away on you, but I'd like to make sure."

"No!"

So I took her by the wrist, sort of like I had her husband, and twisted her arm around her back and shoved her against the door. I frisked her all over. She was a little plump, but it was one of the nicer frisks I ever gave.

No gun—several concealed weapons, but no gun.

She stood facing me now, her back to the door, trembling. "Are you...are you a cop?"

"I'm just a friend of Pete's."

She raised a hand to her face, fingers curling there, like the petals of a wilting flower. "Are you here to turn me in?"

"We'll see."

Now she looked at me in a different way, something flaring in her dark eyes. "Oh. You're here to...deal."

"Maybe. Can we sit down over there?" I gestured to the living room—white walls, white carpet, glass tables, white chairs and couch, a white fireplace with a big mirror with flamingos etched in it.

I took an easy chair across from the couch, where she sat, arms folded, legs crossed—nice legs, muscular, supple, tan against the pink chiffon. She seemed to be studying me, trying to get a bead on me.

"I'd like to hear your side of it."

Her chin titled. "You really think you can make a positive identification, based just on my voice?"

"Ask Bruno Hauptmann. He went to the chair on less."

She laughed but it wasn't very convincing. "You didn't see me."

"Do you have an alibi? Is your husband in on it?"

"No! Of course not."

"Your side of it. Let's have it."

She looked at the floor. "Your...friend...was a terrible man."

"I noticed."

That surprised her. Looking right at me, she asked, "You did?"

"Pete used women like playthings. They weren't people to him. Is that what he did to you?"

She nodded; her full mouth was quivering—if this was an act, it was a good one.

Almost embarrassed, she said, "I thought he was charming. He was good-looking, clever and...sexy, I guess."

"You've been having an affair with him."

One nod.

Well, that didn't surprise me. Just because McGraw was his business partner, and a hood at that, wouldn't stop Pete Clifton from going after a good-looking doll like Mrs. McGraw.

"Can I smoke?" she asked. She indicated her purse on the coffee table. I checked inside it, found no gun, plucked out the pack of Luckies—Pete's brand—and tossed it to her. Also her lighter.

"Thanks," she said, firing up. "It was just...a fling. Stupid goddamn fling. Eddie was neglecting me, and...it's an old story. Anyway, I wanted to stop it, but...Pete wanted more. Not because...he loved me or anything. Just because...do you know what he said to me?"

"I can imagine."

"He said, 'Baby, you're one sweet piece of ass. You don't have to like me to satisfy me.'"

I frowned at her. "I don't know if I'm following this. If you wanted to break it off, how could he—"

"He blackmailed me."

"With what? He couldn't tell your husband about the affair without getting himself in a jam."

She heaved a sigh. "No...but Pete coulda turned my husband in for...for something he had on him."

And now I knew.

Clifton had loaned McGraw the *Screwball* for disposal of the body of Leo Massey, the rival dope smuggler, which put Clifton in a position to finger McGraw.

"Okay," I said, and stood.

She gazed up at me, astounded. "What do you mean...'okay'?"

"Okay, I understand why you killed him."

I walked to the door, and she followed, the sound of her slippers whispering through the thick carpet.

She stopped me at the door, a hand on my arm; she was very close to me, and smelled good, like lilacs. Those brown eyes were big enough to dive into.

Her throaty purr tickled the air between us. "You're not going to turn me in?"

"Why should I? I just wanted to know if there were any ramifications for my client or me, in this thing, and I don't see any."

"I thought Pete was your friend."

"Hell, he was your lover, and look what you thought of him."

Her eyes tightened. "What do you want from me?"

"Nothing. You had a good reason to do it. I heard you warn him."

"You're very kind...." She squeezed my arm, moved closer, to where her breasts were pressed gently against me. "My husband won't be home for a while...we could go to my bedroom and—"

I drew away. "Jesus, lady! Isn't screwin' around what got you into trouble in the first place?"

And I got the hell out of there.

I said just enough at the inquest to get it over with quick, and was back in Chicago by Wednesday night.

I don't know whether Frank Nitti and Eddie McGraw wound up doing business together. I do know the Chez Clifton closed down and re-opened under another name, the Beach Club. But Nitti put his Di Lido Island estate up for sale and sold it, shortly after that. So maybe he just got out while the getting was good.

Mrs. McGraw—whose first name I never knew—was never charged with Pete Clifton's murder, which remains unsolved on the Miami Beach P.D.'s books. The investigation into the Clifton killing, however, did lead the State Attorney's Office to nailing McGraw on the Massey slaying; McGraw got ninety-nine years, which is a little much, considering all he did was kill another dope smuggler. The two party girls, Peggy and Janet, were charged with harboring narcotics, which was dropped in exchange for their cooperation in the McGraw/Massey inquiry.

Pete Clifton really was a prick, but I always thought of him, over the ensuing years, when so many dirty-mouthed comics—from Lenny Bruce to George Carlin—made it big.

Maybe Clifton got the last laugh, after all.

THAT KIND OF NAG

When the cute high school girl, screaming bloody murder, came running down the steps from the porch of the brown-brick two-story, I was sitting in a parked Buick reading *The Racing News*.

At ten after eleven in the a.m., Chicago neighborhoods didn't get much quieter than Englewood, and South Elizabeth Street on this sunny day in May, 1945, ran to bird chirps, muffled radio programs and El rattle. A banshee teenager was enough to attract the attention of just about anybody, even a drowsy detective who was supposed to be watching the very house in question.

A guy in tee-shirt and suspenders, mowing the lawn next-door, got to her just before me.

"Sally, honey, calm down," the guy said.

"Bob, Bob, Bob," she said to her neighbor.

His name, apparently, was Bob. Like I said, I'm a detective.

"What's wrong, honey?" I asked the girl.

She was probably sixteen. Blonde hair bounced off her shoulders, and with those blue eyes and that heart-shaped face, she would have been a knockout if she hadn't been devoid of make-up and wearing a navy jumper that stopped midcalf, abetted by a white blouse buttoned to her throat.

"It's...it's *Mother*," she said, and in slow motion she turned toward the narrow front of the brick house and pointed, like the Ghost of Christmas Future indicating Scrooge's gravestone.

"Look at me," I said, and she did, mouth and eyes twitching. "I'm a policeman. Tell me what happened."

"Something...something *terrible*."

Then she pushed past me, and sat on the curb and buried her face in her hands and sobbed.

Bob, who was bald and round-faced and about forty, said, "You're a cop?"

"Actually, private. Is that kid named Vinicky?"

"Yes. Sally Vinicky—she goes to Visitation High. Probably home for lunch."

That explained the prim get-up: Visitation was a Catholic all-girl's school.

Another neighbor was wandering up, a housewife in an apron, hair in a net, eyes wide; she had flecks of soap suds on her red hands. I brought her into my little group.

"My name is Heller," I said. "I'm an investigator doing a job for that girl's father. I need one of you to look after Sally... ma'am? Would you?"

The woman nodded, then asked, "Why, what's wrong?"

"I'm going in that house and find out. Bob, call the Englewood Station and ask them to send a man over."

"What should I tell them?"

"What you saw."

As the housewife sat beside the girl on the curb and slipped an arm around her, and Bob headed toward the neighboring house, a frame bungalow, I headed up the steps to the covered porch. The girl had left the door open and I went on in.

The living room was off to the left, a dining room to the right; but the living room got my attention, because of the dead woman sprawled on the floor.

A willowy dame in her mid-thirties and blue-and-white floral dress, Rose Vinicky—I recognized her from the photos her husband had provided—lay on her side on the multi-color braided rug between an easy chair and a spinet piano, from which Bing Crosby smiled at me off a sheet music cover, "I Can't Begin to Tell You." Not smiling back, I knelt to check her wrist for a pulse, but judging by the dark pool of blood her head rested in, I was on a fool's errand.

Beyond the corpse stood a small table next to the easy chair with a couple of magazines on it, *Look, Life.* On the floor nearby was a cut-glass ashtray, which the woman presumably had knocked off when she fell forward, struck a vicious blow from behind. A lipstick-tipped cigarette had burned itself out, making a black hole in the braiding of the rug. I wasn't sure whether she'd been reaching for the smoke when the killer clubbed her, or whether she'd gone for the table to brace her fall.

With her brains showing like that, though, she was probably already unconscious or even dead on the way down.

She looked a little like her daughter, though the hair was darker, almost brunette, short, tight curls. Not pretty, but attractive, handsome; and no mid-length skirt for Rose: she had liked to show off those long, slender, shapely legs, which mimed in death the act of running away.

She'd been a looker, or enough of one, anyway, to make her husband suspect her of cheating.

I didn't spend a lot of time with Rose—she wasn't going anywhere, and it was always possible her killer was still around.

But the house—nicely appointed with older, in some cases antique furniture—was clear, including the basement. I did note that the windows were all closed and locked, and the back door was locked, too—with no signs of break-in. The killer had apparently come in the front door.

That meant the murder took place before I'd pulled up in front of the Vinicky home around ten. I'd seen no one approach the house in the little more than an hour my car and ass had been parked across the way. It would've been embarrassing finding out a murder had been committed inside a home while I was watching it.

On the other hand, I'd been surveilling the place to see with whom the woman might be cheating when here she was, already dead. Somehow that didn't seem gold-star worthy, either.

I had another, closer look at the corpse. Maybe she hadn't been dead when she fell, at that—looked like she'd suffered multiple blows. One knocked her down, the others finished her off and opened up her skull. Blood was spattered on the nearby spinet, but also on the little table and even the easy chair.

Whoever did this would had to have walked away covered in blood....

Her right hand seemed to be reaching out, and I could discern the pale circle on her fourth finger that indicated a ring, probably a wedding ring, had been there until recently. Was this a robbery, then?

Something winked at me from the pooled blood, something floating there. I leaned forward, got a better look: a brown button, the four-eyed variety common to man's suit- or sportcoat.

I did not collect it, leaving that to...

"*Stand up!* Get away from that body!"

Sighing, I got to my feet and put my hands in the air and the young patrolman—as fresh-faced as that Catholic schoolgirl—rushed up and frisked me, finding no weapon.

I let him get that all out of his system, and told him who I was, and what had happened, including what I'd seen. I left the button out, and the missing wedding ring; that could wait for the detectives.

The next hour was one cop after another. Four or five uniformed men showed, a trio of detectives from Englewood Station, a couple of dicks from the bureau downtown, a photographer, a coroner's man. I went through the story many times.

In the kitchen, a yellow-and-white affair with a door onto the alley, Captain Patrick Cullen tried to make a meal out of me. We sat at a small wooden table and began by him sharing what he knew about me.

"I don't remember ever meeting you, Captain," I said.

"I know you all too well, Heller—by reputation."

"Ah. That kind of thing plays swell in court."

"You're an ex-cop and you ratted out two of your own. You're a publicity hound, and a cooze hound, too, I hear."

"Interesting approach to detective work—everything strictly hearsay."

A half hour of repartee, at least that scintillating, followed. He wanted to know what I was doing there, and I told him "a job for Sylvester Vinicky," the husband. He wanted to know what kind of job, and I said I couldn't tell him, because attorney/client privilege pertained. He accused me of not being an attorney, and I pled guilty.

"But certain of my cases," I said, "come through lawyers. As it happens, I'm working for an attorney in this matter."

He asked the attorney's name and I gave it to him.

"I heard of that guy...divorce shyster, right?"

"Captain, I'd hate to spoil any of your assumptions with a fact."

He had a face so Irish it could turn bright red without a drop of alcohol, as it did now, while he shook a finger at me. "I'll tell you what happened, Heller. You got hired to shadow this dame, and she was a looker, and you decided to put the make on her yourself. It got out of hand, and you grabbed the nearest blunt instrument and—"

"I like that. The nearest blunt instrument. How the hell did you get to be a captain? What are you, Jake Arvey's nephew?"

He came half out of his chair and threw a punch at me.

I slipped it, staying seated, and batted his hat off his head, like I was slapping a child, and the fedora fluttered to the floor.

"You get *one*," I said.

The red in his face was fading, as he plucked the hat from the linoleum, and the embarrassment in his eyes was almost as good as punching him would've been.

"Is that a threat, Heller?"

"This reputation of mine you've heard so much about—did you hear the part about my Outfit ties? Maybe you want to wake up in a fucking ditch in Indiana, Captain....*That* was a threat, by the way."

Into this Noel Coward playlet came another cop, a guy I did know, from the Detective Bureau in the Loop: Inspector Charles Mullaney, a big fleshy guy who always wore mortician black; he had a spade-shaped face, bright dark eyes and smiled a lot. Unlike many Chicago cops who that do that, Mullaney actually had a sense of humor.

"What's this, Captain?" Mullaney had a lilting tenor, a small man's voice in the big fat frame. "My friend Nate Heller giving you a hard time?"

CHICAGO LIGHTNING

Mullaney scooted a chair out and sat between us, daddy arriving to supervise his two small children. He was grinning at Cullen, but his eyes were hard.

"When you say 'friend,' Inspector, do you mean—"

"Friend. Don't believe what you hear about Heller. He and me and Bill Drury go way back—to the Pickpocket Detail."

Captain Cullen said, defensively, "This guy found the body under suspicious circumstances."

"Oh?"

For the sixth or seventh time, I told my story. For the first time, somebody took notes—Mullaney.

"Charlie," I said to him, "I'm working through an attorney on this. I owe it to my client to talk to him before I tell you about the job I was on."

Frowning, Cullen said, "Yeah, well, *we'll* want to talk to your client, too."

I said, "Might be a good idea. You could inform him his wife is dead. Just as a, you know, courtesy to a taxpayer."

Mullaney gave me a don't-needle-this-prick-anymore look, then said, "The husband is in the clear. We've already been in touch with him."

Cullen asked, "What's his alibi?"

"Well, a Municipal Court judge, for one. He had a ten thirty at the court, which is where we found him. A former employee is suing him for back wages."

Sylvester Vinicky ran a small moving company over on nearby South Racine Avenue. He and his wife also ran a small second-hand furniture shop, adjacent.

"Any thoughts, Nate?" Mullaney asked. "Any observations you'd care to share?"

"Did you notice the button?"

"What button?"

So I filled Mullaney in on the sportcoat button, pointed out the possible missing wedding ring, and the inevitability of the killer getting blood-spattered.

"She let the bastard in," Mullaney said absently.

"Somebody she knew," I said. "And trusted."

Cullen asked, "Why do you say that? Could have been a salesman or Mormon or—"

"No," I said. "He got close enough to her to strike a blow from behind, in the living room. She was smoking—it was casual. Friendly."

Cullen sighed. "Friendly...."

Mullaney said, "We're saying 'he'—but it *could* be a woman."

"I don't think so. Rose Vinicky was tall, and all of those blows landed on the back of her head, struck with a downward swing."

Cullen frowned. "And how do you know this?"

"Well, I'm a trained detective. There are courses available."

Ignoring this twaddle, Mullaney said, "She could have been on the floor already, when those blows were struck—hell, there were half a dozen of them."

"Right. But at least one of them was struck when she was standing. And the woman was five ten, easy. Big girl. And the force of it...skull crushed like an eggshell. And you can see the impressions from multiple blows."

"A man, then," Mullaney said. "A vicious son of a bitch. Well. We'll get him. Captain...would you give Mr. Heller and me a moment?"

Cullen heaved a dramatic sigh, but then he nodded, rose, stepped out.

Mullaney said, "I don't suppose you'll stay out of this."

"Of course I'll stay out of it. This is strictly police business."

"I didn't think you would. Okay, I understand—your name is going to be in the papers, it's going to get out that the wife of a client was killed on your watch—"

"Hey, she was already dead when I pulled up!"

"That'll go over big with the newshounds, especially the part where you're twiddling your thumbs in your car while she lay dead....Nate, let's work together on this thing."

"Define 'together.'"

He leaned forward; the round face, the dark eyes, held no guile. "I'm not asking you to tag along—I couldn't ask that. You have 'friends' like Captain Cullen all over town. But I'll keep you in the know, you do the same. Agreed?"

"Agreed."

"Why don't we start with a show of good faith."

"Such as?"

"Why were you here? What job were you doing for Sylvester Vinicky?"

Thing was, I'd been lying about this coming through a lawyer, though I had a reasonable expectation the lawyer I'd named would cover for me. Really what I'd hoped for was to talk to my client before I spilled to the cops. But Mullaney wasn't just *any* cop....

So I told him.

Told him that Sylvester Vinicky had come to my office on Van Buren, and started crying, not unlike his daughter had at the curb. He loved his wife, he was crazy about her, and he felt so ashamed, suspecting her of cheating.

Vinicky had sat across from me in the client's chair, a working man with a heavy build in baggy trousers, brown jacket and cap. At five nine he was shorter than his wife, and was pudgy where she was slender. Just an average-looking joe named Sylvester.

"She's moody," he said. "When she isn't nagging, she's snapping at me. Sulks. She's distant. Sometimes when I call home, when she's supposed to be home, she ain't at home."

"Mr. Vinicky," I said, "if anything, usually a woman having an affair acts nicer than normal to her husband. She doesn't want to give him a chance to suspect anything's up."

"Not Rose. She's always been more like my sweetheart than my wife. We've never had a cross word, and, hell, we're in business together, and it's been smooth sailing at home and at work... where most couples would be at each other's throats, you know?"

In addition to the moving business, the Vinickys bought and sold furniture—Rose had an eye for antiques, and found many bargains for resale. She also kept the books, and paid off the men.

"Rose, bein' a mother and all, isn't around the office, full-time," Vinicky said. "So maybe I shouldn't be so suspicious about it."

"About what?"

"About coming home and finding Rich Miller sitting in my living room, or my kitchen."

"Who is this Miller?"

"Well, he works for me, or anyway he did till last week. I fired him. I got tired of him flitting and flirting around with Rose."

"What do you know about him?"

A big dumb shrug. "He's just this knockabout guy who moves around a lot—no wife, no family. Goes from one cheap room to another."

"Why would your wife take to some itinerant worker?"

A big dumb sigh. "The guy's handsome, looks like that asshole in the movies—Ronald Reagan? He's got a smooth way, real charmer, and he knows about antiques, which is why he and Rose had something in common."

I frowned. "If he's such a slick customer, why's he living in cheap flops?"

"He has weaknesses, Mr. Heller—liquor, for example, and women. And most of all? A real passion for the horses."

"Horses over booze and broads?"

"Oh yeah. Typical horse player—one day he's broke, next day he hits it lucky and's rolling in dough."

I took the job, but when I tried to put one of my men on it, Vinicky insisted I do the work myself.

"I heard about you, Mr. Heller. I read about you."

"That's why my day rate's twice that of my ops."

He was fine with that, and I spent Monday through Thursday dogging the heels of Rich Miller, who indeed resembled Dutch Reagan, only skinny and with a mustache. I picked him up outside the residential hotel at 63rd and Halstead, a big brick rococo structure dating back to the Columbian Exposition. The first day he was wearing a loud sportshirt and loose slacks, plus a black fedora with a pearl band and two-tone shoes; he looked like something out of Damon Runyon, not some bird doing pick-up work at a moving company.

The other days he was dressed much the same, and his destination was always the same, too: a race track, Washington Park. The IC train delivered him (and me) right outside the park—just a short walk across the tracks to the front admission gate. High trees, shimmering with spring breeze, were damn near as tall as the grandstand. Worse ways for a detective to spend a sunny day in May, and for four of them, I watched my man play the horses and I played the horses, too, coming out a hundred bucks ahead, not counting the fifty an hour.

Miller meeting up with Rose at the track, laying some bets before he laid her, was of course a possibility. But the only person Miller connected with was a tall, broad-shouldered brown-haired guy with the kind of mug janes call "ruggedly handsome" right down to the sleepy Robert Mitchum eyes. They sat in the stands together on two of the four days, going down to the ground-floor windows beneath to place similar smalltime bets—ten bucks at the most, usually to Win.

Still, Miller (and his two-day companion) would bet every race and cheer the horses on with a fist-shaking desperation that spoke of more at stake than just a fun day at the races. Smalltime bettor though he was, Miller was an every-day-at-the-track kind of sick gambler—the friend only showed twice, remember—and I came to the conclusion that his hard-on was for horses, and if anybody was riding Rose Vinicky to the finish line when her hubby wasn't home, this joker wasn't the jockey.

"That's why," Mullaney said, nodding, "you decided to stake out the Vinicky home, this morning."

"Yeah."

Mullaney's huge chest heaved a sigh. "Why don't we talk to the girl, together. Little Sally."

Little Sally had a build like Veronica Lake, but I chose not to point that out.

"Sure," I said.

We did it outside, under a shade tree. A light breeze riffled leaves, the world at peace. Of course, so is a corpse.

Sally Vinicky wasn't crying now—partly cried out, partly in shock, and as she stood with her hands figleafed before her, she answered questions as politely and completely as she no doubt did when the nuns questioned her in class.

"I went in the back way," she said. "Used my key."

Which explained why I hadn't seen the girl go in.

"I always come home for lunch at eleven, and Mom always has it ready for me—but when I didn't see anything waiting in the kitchen...sometimes soup, sometimes a sandwich, sometimes both, today, nothing...I went looking for her. I thought for a minute she'd left early."

"Left early for where?" I asked.

"She had errands to do, downtown, this afternoon."

Mullaney asked, "What sort of mood was your mother in this morning, when you left for school?"

"I didn't see her—Mom sleeps in till nine or sometimes ten. Does some household chores, fixes my lunch and...."

"How about your father?"

"He was just getting up as I was leaving—that was maybe a quarter to eight? He said he had to go to the court at ten thirty. Somebody suing us again."

I asked, "Again?"

"Well, Mom's real strict—if a guy doesn't work a full hour, he doesn't get paid. That starts arguments, and some of the men who work for Mom and Dad sometimes say they've been shorted....Oh!"

Mullaney frowned. "What is it?"

"We should check Mom's money!"

The blanketed body had already been carted out, and the crowd of neighbors milling around the house had thinned. So we walked the girl in through the front. Sally made a point of not looking into the living room where a tape outline on the floor provided a ghost of her mother.

In her parents' room, where the bed—a beautiful walnut Victorian antique as beautiful as it was wrong for this house and this neighborhood—was neatly made, a pale brown leather wallet lay on the mismatched but also antique dresser. Before anyone could tell the girl not to touch it, she grabbed the wallet and folded it open.

No moths flew out, but they might have: it was that empty.

"Mother had a lot of money in here," Sally said, eyes searching the yawning flaps, as if bills were hiding from her.

I asked, "How much is a lot, Sally?"

"Almost twelve hundred dollars. I'd say that's a lot!"

"So would I. Why would your mother have that kind of money in her wallet?"

"We were going for a trip to California, as soon as my school got out—me, Mother, and my aunt Doris. That was the errand Mother had to do downtown—buy railroad tickets."

Mullaney, eyes tight, said, "Who knew about this money?"

"My dad, of course. My aunt."

"Nobody else?"

"Not that I can think of. Not that I know of. I wish I could be of more help...."

I smiled at her. "You're doing fine, Sally."

A uniformed officer stuck his head in. "Inspector, Captain Cullen says Mr. Vinicky is here."

Sally pushed past Mullaney and me, and the uniformed man, and the girl went rattling down the stairs calling, "Daddy, Daddy!"

When we caught up with her, she was in her father's arms in the yellow-and-white kitchen. He held her close. They both cried and patted each other's backs. Cullen, seated at the kitchen table, regarded this with surprising humanity.

"I want you to stay with your aunt tonight," Vinicky said to his daughter.

"Okay. That's okay. I don't want to sleep in this house ever again."

He found a smile. "Well, not tonight, anyway, sweetheart. They let me call your aunt—she's on her way. Do you want to wait in your room?"

"No. No, I'll wait outside, if that's all right."

Vinicky, the girl still in his arms, looked past her for permission, his pudgy face streaked with tears, his eyes webbed red.

Mullaney and Cullen nodded, and a uniformed man walked her out. The father took at seat at the kitchen table. So did Mullaney. So did I.

Seeming to notice me for the first time, Vinicky looked at me, confusion finding its way past the heartbreak. "What... what're you doing here, Mr. Heller?"

"I was watching the house, Mr. Vinicky," I said, and told him the circumstances as delicately as possible.

"I take it...I take it you told these gentleman why I hired you."

"I did."

"Did you see anyone go in, Mr. Heller? Did you see that bastard Miller?"

"I didn't." I hadn't reported to him yet. "Mr. Vinicky, I spent four days watching Miller, and he always went to the track—that's why I came here. I don't believe he was seeing your wife."

But Vinicky was shaking his head, emphatically. "He did it. I know he did it. You people have to *find* him!"

Cullen said, "We're already on that, Mr. Vinicky."

I asked the captain, "Do you need his address? He's in a residential hotel over on—"

"We know. We sent a detective over there, already—next-door neighbor says this guy Miller used to hang around here a lot. Only now Miller's nowhere to be seen—his flop is empty. Ran out on a week's rent."

Vinicky slammed a fist on the table. "I told you! I told you!"

Mullaney said, "We need you to calm down, sir, and tell us about your day."

"My day! Tell you about, what...*this*? The worst day of my life! Worst goddamn day of my life. I loved Rose. She was the best wife any man ever had."

Neither cop was nasty enough to mention that the bedroom dick this weeping husband had hired was sitting at the table with them.

Vinicky's story was unremarkable: he'd got up around eight, dressed for the court appearance, stopped at the office first (where he was seen by various employees) and then took breakfast at a restaurant on Halsted. From there he'd gone to the post office, picked up a parcel, and headed downtown by car to Municipal Court. He had littered the South Side and the Loop alike with witnesses who could support his alibi.

"You're being sued, we understand," Mullaney said.

"Yeah—but that's nothing. Kind of standard with us. Rose is...was...a hardnosed businesswoman, God love her. She insisted on a full day's work for a full day's pay."

Mullaney was making notes again. "Did Miller ever complain about getting shorted?"

"Yeah. That's probably why he was...so friendly with Rose. Trying to get on her good side. Sweet-talk her into giving him the benefit of the doubt on his hours. I was a son of a bitch to ever suspect—"

Cullen asked, "Could you give us a list of employees who've made these complaints, over the last two years?"

"Sure. No problem. I can give you some off the top of my head, then check the records at the office tomorrow for any I missed."

Mullaney wrote down the names.

When that was done, I asked, "Did your wife have a wedding ring?"

"Yes. Of course. Why—wasn't it on her...*on* her?"

"No rings."

Vinicky thought about that. "She might've taken it off to do housework. Was it on her dresser? There's a tray on her dresser..."

"No. What was the ring worth?"

"It was a nice-size diamond—three hundred bucks, I paid. Did the bastard steal it?"

Mullaney said, "Apparently. The money in her wallet was missing, too."

"Hell you say! That was a small fortune—Rose was going to buy train tickets with that, and cover hotel and other expenses. She was treating her sister to a trip to California, and Sally was going along....It was robbery, then?"

"We're exploring that," Mullaney said.

Vinicky's eyes tightened to slits. "One of these S.O.B.'s who claimed they were shorted, you think?"

The inspector closed his notebook. "We're exploring that, too. This list should be very helpful, Mr. Vinicky."

I gave Mullaney the eye, nodding toward the back door, and he and stepped out there for a word away from both the husband and Captain Cullen.

"How long will you boys be here?" I asked.

"Another hour, maybe. Why, Nate?"

"I have a hunch to play."

"You want company?"

"No. But I should be back before you've wrapped up, here."

I tooled the Buick over to 63rd Street, a lively commercial district with all the charm of a junkyard. Not far from here, Englewood's big claim to fame—the multiple murderer H.H. Holmes—had set up his so-called Murder Castle in the late 1880s. The Vinicky case could never hope to compete, so maybe I could make it go away quickly.

In the four days I'd kept an eye on Rich Miller, I'd learned a handful of useful things about the guy, including that when he wasn't betting at Washington Park, he was doing so with a guy in a back booth at a bar called the Lucky Horseshoe (whose only distinction was its lack of a neon horseshoe in the window).

The joint was dim and dreary even for a South Side gin mill, and business was slow, mid-afternoon. But I still had to wait for a couple of customers to finish up with the friendly bookie in the back booth before I could slide in across from him.

"Do I know you?" he asked, not in a threatening way. He was a small sharp-eyed, sharp-nosed, sharp-chinned sharpie wearing a derby and a bow tie but no jacket—it was warm in the Horseshoe. He was smoking a cigarillo and his sleeves were rolled up, like he was preparing to deal cards. But no cards were laid out on the booth's table.

I laid mine out, anyway: "My name is Heller, Nate Heller. Maybe you've heard of me."

The mouth smiled enough to reveal a glint of gold tooth; the dark blue eyes weren't smiling, though.

"I'm gonna take a wild stab," I said, "and guess they call you Goldie."

"Some do. You the...'Frank Nitti' Heller?"

By that he meant, was I the mobbed-up private eye who had been tight with Capone's late heir, and remained tight with certain of the Outfit hierarchy.

"Yes."

"You wanna place a bet, Nate? My bet is...not."

"Your bet is right. I'm not here to muscle you. I'm here to do you a favor."

"What favor would that be?"

"There's a murder a few blocks away—Inspector Mullaney's on it."

"Oh. Shit."

And by that he meant, imagine the luck: one of the *honest* Chicago cops.

"But, Nate," he said, and I got the full benefit of a suspiciously white smile interrupted by that gold eyetooth, "why would Goldie give a damn? I have nothin' to do with murder. *Any* murder. I'm in the entertainment business."

"You help people play the horses."

The tiny shrug conveyed big self-confidence. "It's a noble sport, both the racing and the betting."

I leaned toward him. "One of your clients is shaping up as a chief suspect. The favor I'm doing you is: *I'm* talking to you, rather than just giving you over to the inspector."

Eyelids fluttered. "Ah. Well, I do appreciate that. What's the client's name?"

"Rich Miller."

The upper lipped peeled back and again showed gold, but this was no smile. "That fucking fourflusher. He's into me for five C's!"

"Really. And he's made no move to pay you off? Today, maybe?"

His laughter cut like a blade. "Are you kidding? One of my... associates...went around to his flop. Miller pulled outa there, owin' a week's back rent."

Which, of course, I already knew.

Goldie was shaking his head, his tone turning philosophical. "You never can tell about people, can you? Miller always paid up on time, before this, whereas that pal of his, who I wouldn't trust far as I could throw him, *that* crumb pays up, just when I was ready to call the legbreakers in."

"What pal of Miller's?"

He gave me a name, but it meant nothing to me. I wondered if it might be the guy Miller had met at Washington Park, two of the days, and ran a description by Goldie.

"That sounds like him. Big guy. Six four, easy. Not somebody I could talk to myself."

"Hence the legbreakers."

"Hence. Nate, if you can keep that goody-two-shoes Mullaney off my ass, it would be appreciated. He'll come around, make it an excuse to make my life miserable, and what did I ever to do to that fat slob?"

I was already out of the booth. "See what I can do, Goldie."

"And if you ever wanna place a bet, you know where my office is."

When I got back to the brown-brick house on South Elizabeth Street, the Catholic school girl was hugging a tall slender woman, who might have been her mother come to life. On closer look, this gal was younger, and a little less pretty, though that may not have been fair, considering her features were taught with grief.

Sally and the woman who I took to be her aunt were beneath the same shady tree where Mullaney and I had stood with the girl, questioning her, earlier.

I went up and introduced myself, keeping vague about the "investigative job" I'd been doing for Mr. Vinicky.

"I'm Doris Stemmer," she said, Sally easing out of the woman's embrace. The woman wore a pale yellow dress with white flowers that almost didn't show. "I'm Rose's sister."

She extended her hand and I shook it. Sally stayed close to her aunt.

"Sorry for your grief, Mrs. Stemmer," I told her. "Have you spoken to Inspector Mullaney yet?"

"Yes."

"Would you mind if I asked you a few questions?"

"But you're a *private* detective, aren't you? What were you doing for Sylvester?"

"Looking into some of the complaints from his employees."

Her eyes tightened and ice came into her voice. "Those men were a bunch of lazy good-for-nothing whiners. Doris was a good person, fair and with a great heart, wonderful heart. Why, just last year? She loaned Ray three hundred dollars, so we didn't have to wait to get married."

"Ray?"

"Yes, my husband."

"What does he do, if I might ask?"

"He started a new job just last week, at an electrical assembly plant, here on the South Side."

"New job? What was his old one?"

Her strained smile was a signal that I was pushing it. "He worked for Sylvester in the moving business. You can ask him yourself if Rose wasn't an angel. Ask him yourself if she wasn't fair about paying their people."

"But he *did* quit..."

"Working as a mover was just temporary, till Ray could get a job in his chosen field." Her expression bordered on glare. "Mr. Heller—if you want to talk to Ray, he's waiting by the car, right over there."

She pointed and I glanced over at a blue Ford coupe parked just behind a squad car. A big rugged-looking dark-haired guy, leaning against the vehicle, nodded to us. He was in a short-sleeve green sportshirt and brown pants. His tight expression said he was wondering what the hell I was bothering his wife about.

Gently as I could, I said, "I might have a couple questions for him, at that, Mrs. Stemmer. Would you and Sally wait here, just a moment? Don't go anywhere, please..."

I went inside and found Mullaney and Cullen in the living room, contemplating the tape outline. Things were obviously winding down; the crime scene boys were packing up their gear, and most of the detectives were already gone.

"Button button," I said to them. "Who's got the button?"

Cullen glared at me, but Mullaney only smiled. "The brown button, you mean? Cullen, didn't you collect that?"

The captain reached a hand into his suitcoat and came back with the brown button and held out the blood-caked item in his palm.

"You want this, Heller?"

"Yeah," I said, marveling at the evidence-collecting protocol of the Chicago Police Department, "just for a minute...."

I returned to Mrs. Stemmer, under the tree, an arm around her niece.

"Couple questions about your husband," I said.

"Why don't you just *talk* to him?" she asked, clearly exasperated.

"I will. I'm sorry. Please be patient. Does your husband have a coat that matches those pants he's wearing?"

"Well...yes. Maybe. Why?"

"Isn't wearing it today, though."

"It's warm. Why would he wear it...?"

"Could this button have come off that jacket?"

She looked at it. "I don't know...maybe. I guess. That button's filthy, though—what's that caked on there?"

Quietly, I said, "When did you say your husband started his new job?"

"Last week."

"But he didn't have to go to work today?"

"No...no. He had some things to do."

"Does he normally get Fridays off?"

"I don't know. He just started, I told you."

"So it's unlikely he'd be given a day off...."

"Why don't you ask *him*?"

"Mrs. Stemmer, forgive me, but...does your husband have a gambling problem?"

She drew in breath, but said nothing. And spoke volumes.

I ambled over to the tall, broad-shouldered man leaning against the Ford.

"Mr. Stemmer? My name's Heller."

He stood straight now, folded his arms, looked at me suspiciously through sleepy eyes. He'd been out of earshot when I spoke to his wife, but could tell I'd been asking her unpleasant questions.

"Why were you bothering my wife? Are you one of these detectives?"

"Yeah. Private detective."

He batted the air with a big paw. "You're nobody! I don't have to talk to you."

"Private detective," I picked up, "who followed Rich Miller to the track most of this week."

"...What for?"

"For Rose's husband—he thought she and Miller were playing around."

He snorted a laugh. "Only thing Richie Miller plays is the nags."

"And you'd know, right, Ray? See, I saw you and your buddy Richie hanging out together at Washington Park. You were betting pretty solid, yourself. Not big dough, but you were game, all right."

"So what?"

"Well, for one thing, your wife thinks you started a new job last week."

The sleepy eyes woke up a little. "And I guess in your business, uh...Heller, is it? In your business, you never ran across an instance of a guy lying to his wife before, huh?"

"You like the nags, too, don't you, Stemmer? Only you don't like to get nagged—and I bet Rose Vinicky nagged the hell out of you to pay back that three hundred. Did she hold back from your paycheck, too?"

He shook his head, smiled, but it was sickly. "Rose was a sweetheart."

"I don't think so. I think she was a hardass who maybe even shorted a guy when he had his hard-earned money coming. Her husband loved her, but anybody working for her? She gladly give them merry hell. She was that kind of nag."

A sneer formed on his face, like a blister. "I don't have to talk to you. Take a walk."

He shoved me.

I didn't shove back, but I stood my ground; somebody gasped behind me—maybe Doris Stemmer, or the girl.

"You knew about that money, didn't you, Stemmer? The money Rose was going to use to treat your wife to a Hollywood trip. And you could use eleven-hundred bucks, couldn't you, pal? Hell, who couldn't!"

He shoved me again. "You don't take a goddamn *hint*, do you, Heller?"

"Here's a hint for you: when a bookie like Goldie gets paid off, right before the legbreakers leave the gate? That means somebody finally had a winner."

His face turned white.

"Sure, she let her brother-in-law in the front door," I said. "She may have had you pegged for the kind of welsher who stiffs his own sister-in-law for a loan, but she probably thought she was at least safe with you, alone in her own house. That should've been a sure bet, right? Only it wasn't. What did you use? A sash weight? A crowbar?"

This time he shoved me with both hands, and he was trying to crawl in on the rider's side of the Ford, to get behind the wheel, when I dragged him out by the leg. On his ass on the grass, he tried to kick me with the other leg, and I kicked him in the balls, and it ended as it had begun, with a scream.

All kinds of people, some of them cops, came running, swarming around us with questions and accusations. But I ignored them, hauling Stemmer to his feet, and jerking an arm around his back, holding the big guy in place, and Cullen believed me when I said, "Brother-in-law did it," taking over for me, and I quickly filled Mullaney in.

They found four hundred and fifteen bucks in cash in Stemmer's wallet—what he had left after paying off the bookie.

"That's a lot of money," Mullaney said. "Where'd you get it?"

"I won it on a horse," Stemmer said.

Only it came out sounding like a question.

After he failed six lie detector tests, Raymond Stemmer confessed in full. Turned out hardnosed businesswoman Rose had quietly fired Stemmer when she found out he'd been stealing furniture from their warehouse. Rich Miller had told Rose that Ray was going to the track with him, time to time, so she figured her brother-in-law was selling the furniture on the side to play the horses. She had given him an ultimatum: pay back the three hundred dollars, and what the furniture was worth, and Rose would not tell her sister about his misdeeds.

Stemmer had stopped by the house around nine thirty and told Rose he'd brought her the money. Instead, in the living room, as she reached for her already burning cigarette, he had paid her back by striking her in the back of the head with a wrench.

Amazingly, she hadn't gone down. She'd staggered, knocked the ashtray to the floor, only to look over her shoulder at him and say, "You have the nerve to hit *me*?"

And he found the nerve to hit her again, and another ten times, where she lay on the floor.

He removed the woman's diamond wedding ring, and went upstairs and emptied the wallet. All of this he admitted in a thirty-page statement. The diamond was found in a toolbox in his basement, the wrench in the Chicago River (after three hours of diving). His guilty plea got him a life sentence.

About a week after I'd found Rose Vinicky's body, her husband called me at my office. He was sending a check for my services—the five days I'd followed Miller—and wanted to thank me for exposing his brother-in-law as the killer. He told me he was taking his daughter to California on the trip her mother had promised; the sister-in-law was too embarrassed and distraught to accept Vinicky's invitation to come along.

"What I don't understand," the pitiful voice over the phone said, "is why Rose was so distant to me, those last weeks. Why she'd acted in a way that made me think—"

"Mr. Vinicky, your wife knew her sister's husband was a lying louse, a degenerate gambler, stealing from the both of you. *That* was what was on her mind."

"...I hadn't thought of it that way. By God, I think you're right, Mr. Heller....You know something funny? Odd. Ironic, I mean?"

"What?"

"I got a long, lovely letter from Rich Miller today. Handwritten. A letter of condolence. He heard about Rose's death, and said he was sick about it. That she was a wonderful lady and had been kind to him. After all the people who've said Rose was hard-hearted to the people who worked for us? This, this...it's a kind of...testament to her."

"That's nice, Mr. Vinicky. Really is."

"Postmarked Omaha. Wonder what Miller's doing there?"

Hiding from the legbreakers, I thought.

And, knowing him, doing it at the dog tracks.

AUTHOR'S NOTE

George Hagenauer discovered the Vinicky case in an obscure true-detective magazine. I have compressed time and omitted aspects of the investigation; and some of the names in this story have been changed.

UNREASONABLE DOUBT

In March of 1947, I got caught up in the notorious Overell case, which made such headlines in Los Angeles, particularly during the trial that summer. The double murder—laced as it was with underage sex in a lurid scenario that made "Double Indemnity" seem tame—hit the front pages in Chicago, as well. But back home I never bragged about my little-publicized role, because—strictly speaking—I was the one guy who might have headed the whole thing off.

I was taking a deductible vacation, getting away from an Illinois spring that was stubbornly still winter, in trade for Southern California's constant summer. My wife, who was pregnant and grouchy, loved L.A., and had a lot of friends out there, which was one of the reasons for the getaway; but I was also checking in with the L.A. branch office of the A-1 Detective Agency, of which I was the president.

I'd recently thrown in with Fred Rubinski, a former Chicago cop I'd known since we were both on the pickpocket detail, who from before the war had been running a one-man agency out of a suite in the Bradbury Building at Third and Broadway in downtown Los Angeles.

It was Friday morning, and I was flipping through the pages of *Cue* magazine in the outer office, occasionally flirting with Fred's good-looking blonde receptionist—like they say, I was married but I wasn't dead—waiting to get together with Fred, who was in with a client. The guy had just shown up, no appointment, but I didn't blame Fred for giving him precedence over me.

I had seen the guy go in—sixtyish, a shade taller than my six feet, distinguished, graying, somewhat fleshy, in a lightweight navy suit that hadn't come off the rack; he was clearly money.

After about five minutes, Fred slipped out of the office and sat next to me, speaking sotto voce.

My partner looked like a balding, slightly less ugly Edward G. Robinson; a natty dresser—today's suit was a gray pinstripe with a gray and white striped tie—he was a hard round ball of a man.

"Listen, Nate," he said, "I could use your help."

I shrugged. "Okay."

"You're not tied up today—I know you're on vacation..."

"Skip it. We got a well-heeled client who needs something done, right away, and you don't have time to do it yourself."

The bulldog puss blinked at me. "How did you know?"

"I'm a detective. Just keep in mind, I've done a few jobs out here, but I don't really know the town."

Fred sat forward. "Listen, this guy is probably worth a cool million—Walter E. Overell, he's a financier, land developer, got a regular mansion over in Pasadena, in the Flintridge district, real exclusive digs."

"What's he want done?"

"Nothin' you can't handle. Nothin' big."

"So you'd rather let me hear it from him?"

Fred grinned; it wasn't pretty. "You are a detective."

In the inner office, Overell stood as Fred pulled up a chair for me next to the client's. As the financier and I shook hands,

Fred said, "Mr. Overell, this is Nathan Heller, the president of this agency, and my most trusted associate."

He left out that I wasn't local. Which I didn't disagree with him for doing—it was good tactically.

"Of course, Mr. Heller commands our top rate, Mr. Overell—one hundred a day."

"No problem."

"We get expenses, and require a two-hundred dollar retainer, non-refundable."

"Fine."

Fred and I made sure not to look at each other throughout my partner's highway robbery of this obviously well-off client.

Soon we got down to it. Overell slumped forward as he sat, hands locked, his brow deeply furrowed, his gray eyes pools of worry.

"It's my daughter, Mr. Heller. She wants to get married."

"A lot of young girls do, Mr. Overell."

"Not this young. Louise is only seventeen—and won't be eighteen for another nine months. She can't get married at her age without my consent—and I'm not likely to give it."

"She could run away, sir. There are states where seventeen is plenty old enough—"

"I would disinherit her." He sighed, hung his head. "Much as it would kill me...I would disown and disinherit her."

Fred put in, "This is his only child, Nate."

I nodded. "Where do things stand, currently?"

Overell swallowed thickly. "She says she's made up her mind to marry her 'Bud' on her eighteenth birthday."

"Bud?"

"George Gollum—he's called Bud. He's twenty-one. What is the male term for a golddigger, anyway?"

I shrugged. "Greedy bastard?"

"That will do fine. I believe he and she have..." Again, he swallowed and his clenched hands were trembling, his eyes moist. "...known each other, since she was fourteen."

"Pardon me, sir, but you use the term 'known' as if you mean in the...Biblical sense?"

He nodded curtly, turned his gaze away; but his words were clipped: "That's right."

An idea was hatching; I didn't care for it much, but the idea wasn't distasteful enough to override my liking of a hundred bucks a day.

Overell was saying, "I believe he met my daughter when he was on leave from the Navy."

"He's in the Navy?"

"No! He's studying at the Los Angeles campus of U.C., now—pre-med, supposedly, but I doubt he has the brains for it. They exchanged letters when he was serving overseas, as a radioman. My wife, Beulah, discovered some of these letters.... They were...filth."

His head dropped forward, and his hands covered his face.

Fred glanced at me, eyebrows raised, but I just said to Overell, "Sir, kids are wilder today than when we were young."

He had twenty, twenty-five years on me, but it seemed the thing to say.

"I've threatened to disinherit her, even if she waits till she's of legal age—but she won't listen, Louise simply won't listen."

Overell went on, at some length, to tell me of Louise's pampered childhood, her bedroom of dolls and Teddy bears in their "estate," the private lessons (tennis, riding, swimming), her French governess who had taught her a second language as well as the niceties of proper etiquette.

"Right now," the disturbed father said, "she's waging a campaign to win us over to this twenty-one-year-old 'boy friend' of hers."

"You haven't met him?"

"Oh, I've met him—chased him off my property. But she insists if we get to know Bud, we'll change our minds—I've consented to meet with them, let them make their case for marriage."

"Excuse me, but is she pregnant?"

"If she were, that would carry no weight whatsoever."

I let the absurdity of that statement stand.

Overell went on: "I've already spoken to Mr. Rubinski about making certain...arrangements...if that is what Louise and her Bud reveal to us tomorrow evening."

"Tomorrow?"

"Yes, we have a yacht—the *Mary E.*—moored at Newport Harbor." He smiled embarrassedly, the first time he'd smiled in this meeting. "Excuse my pomposity—'yacht' is rather overstating it, it's really just a little forty-seven footer."

Little?

"Louise asked me to invite her and her 'boy friend' aboard for the evening, with her mother and myself, so we can all get to know each other better, and talk, 'as adults.'"

"And you're going along with this?"

"Yes—but only to humor her, and as a...subterfuge for my own feelings, my own desires, my own designs. I want you to explore this boy's background—I don't know anything about him, except that he's local."

"And you think if I turn up something improper in this boy's past, it would matter to your daughter?"

His eyes were so tight, it must have hurt. "If he's the male equivalent of a golddigger, won't he have other girls, other women? That would show Louise the light."

"Mr. Overell, is your daughter attractive?"

"Lovely. I...I have a picture in my wallet, but I'm afraid she's only twelve in it."

"Never mind that right now—but you should know there's every possibility that these two young people...and twenty-one seems younger to me, every day...really *are* nuts about each other. Gollum may not be seeing anybody else."

"But you can find out!"

"Sure, but...aren't you overlooking something?"

"Am I?"

"Your daughter is underage. If I catch 'em in the backseat of this boy's jalopy, we can put him away—or at least threaten to."

"...Statutory rape?"

I held up two palms, pushed the air. "I know, I know, it would embarrass your daughter...but even the threat of it oughta to send this rat scurrying."

Overell looked at Fred for an opinion. Fred was nodding.

"Makes sense, Mr. Overell," he said.

Overell's eyes tensed, but his brow unfurrowed some; another sigh seemed to deflate his entire body, but I could sense relief on his part, and resignation, as he said, "All right... all right. Do what you think is best."

We got him a contract, and he gave us a check.

"Can I speak with your wife about this matter?" I asked him.

He nodded. "I'm here with Beulah's blessing. You have our address—you can catch her at home this afternoon, if you like."

I explained to him that what I could do today would be limited, because Overell understood that his son and daughter were (and he reported this with considerable distaste) spending the day "picnicking in the desert." But I could go out to the Los Angeles campus of the University of California and ask around about Bud.

"You can inquire out there about my daughter as well," he said.

"Isn't she still in high school?"

"Unfortunately, no—she's a bright girl, skipped a grade. She's already in college."

Sounded like Louise was precocious in a lot of ways.

Around ten thirty that same morning, I entered at Westwood Boulevard and Le Conte Avenue, rolling in my rental Ford through a lushly terraced campus perched on a knoll overlooking valleys, plains and hills. The buildings were terra cotta, brick and tile in a Romanesque motif.

I asked a cute coed for directions to the student union, and was sent to Kerckhoff Hall, an imposing building of Tudor design with a pinnacled tower. I was further directed to a sprawling high-ceilinged room where college kids played ping pong or played cards or sat in comfy chairs and couches and drank soda pop and smoked cigarettes. Among sweaters and casual slacks and bobby socks, I stuck out like the thirty-eight-year-old sore thumb I was in my tan summer suit; but the kids were all chatty and friendly. My cover was that Bud had applied for a job—what that job was, of course, I couldn't say—and I was checking up on him for his prospective employer.

Not everybody knew Bud Gollum or Louise Overell, of course—too big a campus for that. But a few did.

Bud, it seemed, was a freshman, going to school on Uncle Sam. Other first-year fellas—younger than Bud, probably nineteen—described him as "a good guy, friendly, and smart," even "real smart." But several didn't hide their dislike of Bud, saying he was smart-alecky, writing him off as a "wiseguy."

A mid-twenties junior with an anchor tattooed on his fore-arm knew Bud as a fellow Navy veteran, and said Bud had been a Radio Man First Class.

"Listen," the husky little dark-haired, dark-eyed ex-gob said, "if you're considering him for a job, give him a break—he's smarter than his grades make him look."

"Really?"

"Yeah, when you see his transcripts, you're going find him pulling down some low junk, so far this year...but it's that little skirt's fault. I mean, they don't let dummies into pre-med around here."

"He's got a girl friend distracting him?"

The gob nodded. "And it's pretty damn serious—she's a young piece of tail, pardon my French, built like a brick shit-house. Can hardly blame him for letting his studies slide."

"Well, I hope he wouldn't be too preoccupied to do a good job—"

"No, no! He's a right fella! Lives at home with his mom and stepdad—he's an assistant scout master, for Christ sakes!"

"Sounds clean cut."

"Sure—he loves the outdoors, always going hiking in the mountains up around Chatsworth, backpacking out into the desert."

"His girl go in for that?"

"They go everywhere together, joined at the hip...don't give me that look, buddy! I mean, haven't you ever had a female lead you around by the dick?"

"No," I said, and when he arched an eyebrow, I added, "Does my wife count?"

He grinned at me. "Does mine?"

A table of girls who were smoking and playing pitch allowed me to pull up a chair for a few questions; they weren't very cute, just enough to make me want to bust out crying.

"I don't know what a neat guy like that sees in ol' Stone Face," a blonde with blue eyes and braces said. I liked the way she was getting lipstick on her cigarette.

"Stone Face?"

"Yeah," a brunette said. She wasn't smoking, like her friends, just chewing and snapping her gum. "That gal's got this round face like a frying pan and's got about as much expression."

"Except when she giggles," a redhead said, giggling.

All the girls began to giggle, the blonde saying, "Then she really looks like a dope!"

"She laughs at everything that idiot says," the brunette said. "They hang onto each other like ivy—it's sickening."

That was all I learned at the college, and the effort took about three hours; but it was a start.

Pasadena was the richest city per capita in the nation, and the residential neighborhood where the Overells resided gave credence to that notion—mansions with sunken gardens, swimming pools and tennis courts on winding, flower-edged, palm-flung streets. The white mission-style mansion at 607 Los Robles Drive, with its well-manicured, lavishly landscaped lawn, was no exception.

Mrs. Overell was younger than her husband by perhaps ten years, an attractive dark-blonde woman whose nicely buxom shape was getting a tad matronly. We sat by the pool watching the mid-afternoon sun highlight the shimmering blue surface with gold. We drank iced tea and she hid her feelings behind dark sunglasses and features as expressionless as the Stone Face with which those coeds had tagged her daughter.

"I don't know what I can tell you, Mr. Heller," she said, her voice a bland alto, "that my husband hasn't already."

"Well, Mrs. Overell, I'm chiefly here for two reasons. First, I can use a photo of your daughter, a recent one."

"Certainly." A tiny smile etched itself on the rigid face. "I should have thought of that—Walter carries a photo of Louise when she was still a child. He'd like to keep her that way."

"You do agree with this effort to break off Louise's relationship with this Gollum character?"

"Mr. Heller, I'm not naive enough to think that we can succeed at that. But I won't stand in Walter's way. Perhaps we can postpone this marriage long enough for Louise to see through this boy."

"You think he's a male golddigger, too?"

She shrugged. "He doesn't come from money."

"You know where he lives? Have an address?"

"He's here in Pasadena."

I couldn't picture a wrong side of the tracks in this swanky burg.

"No, I don't have an address," she was saying, "but he's in North Fair Oaks...where so many coloreds have moved in."

I had been met at the door by a Negro butler, who I supposed had to live somewhere.

But I didn't press the subject. I sipped my tea and offered, gently, "If your daughter is willing to wait to marry this boy till her eighteenth birthday...which I understand is many months from now...perhaps what you ought to do is humor her, and hope this affair cools off."

The blue and gold of the sun-kissed pool shimmered in the dark lens of her sunglasses. "I would tend to agree with you, Mr. Heller. In time she might come to her senses of her own volition. But Walter is a father who has not adjusted to losing his little girl...she's our only child, you know...and I do share his concern about the Gollum boy."

"That's the other reason I wanted to speak with you, directly," I said, and—delicately—I filled her in on my notion to catch the two in flagrante delicto. I wanted to make sure she wouldn't mind putting her daughter through the public embarrassment a statutory rape accusation would bring.

Another tiny smile etched itself. "We've gotten quite used to Louise embarrassing us, Mr. Heller."

Mrs. Overell thought I might have trouble catching them, however, since they so often went hiking and camping in the West San Fernando Valley—like today. That would be tough: I was used to bagging my quarry in backseats and motel rooms.

As it turned out, Mrs. Overell was able to provide a snapshot, filched from her daughter's room, of both Louise and her beau. They were in swimsuits, at the beach on towels, leaning back on their elbows smiling up at the camera.

Louise had a nice if faintly mocking, superior smile—not exactly pretty, and indeed round-faced, but not bad; and she was, as that ex-gob had so succinctly put it, built like a brick shithouse. This girl had everything Jane Russell did except a movie contract.

As for Bud, he was blond, boyish, rather round faced himself, with wire-rimmed glasses and a grin that somehow lacked the suggestion of cunning his girl friend's smile possessed. He had the slender yet solid build so often seen in Navy men.

I spent another hour or so in Pasadena, which had a sleepy air of prosperity spawned by the many resort hotels, the formidable buildings, the pretentious homes, the bounteous foliage. The North Fair Oaks section did seem to have more than its share of colored residents, but this was still nicer than anywhere I'd ever lived. With the help of a service station attendant—the private detective's best friend in a strange city—I located the home of Dr. Joseph Stomel, married to Bud's mother, Wilhilmina. But I had no intention of talking to anyone there, as yet. This was strictly a point of reference for the eventual tailing of Gollum.

That was Friday, and between the college and the Pasadena run, I'd earned my hundred bucks. I spent all day Saturday with my wife, and friends, enjoying our premature summer vacation.

Then I went back to work Saturday night, though I looked like a tourist in my blue sportshirt and chinos. The camera I had with me was no tourist's Brownie, however, rather a divorce dick's Speed Graphic loaded with infrared film and the world's least conspicuous flash.

It was around ten o'clock when I turned right off State Highway 55, my rental Ford gliding across the low-slung spit over the mouth of an inlet of landlocked Newport Bay, dotted by sails, glistening with moonbeams, dancing with harbor lights. Seaside cottages clustered along the bay shore, but grander dwellings perched on islands in the lagoon-like bay, California-style Riviera-worthy stucco villas, a suitable backdrop for the fleet of yachts and other pleasure crafted moored here.

My behind was moored in a booth in the Beachfront Cafe, a chrome-heavy diner with a row of windows looking out on the dock and the peaceful, soothing view of lights twinkling and pleasure crafts bobbing on the moon-washed water. I ate a cheeseburger and fries and sipped coffee as I kept watch; I had a perfect view of the sleek cruiser, the *Mary E*. A few lights were on in the boat, and occasional movement could be made out, but just vague shapes. No different than any number of other boats moored here, gently rocking.

Overell had told me that he and his wife would be entertaining their daughter and her beau aboard the cruiser, having dinner, talking out their problems, perhaps even coming to some sort of understanding. What I had in mind was to follow the young lovers when they left this family powwow.

Since Bud lived at home with his mom, I figured the couple would either go to some lover's lane to park, or maybe hit a motel. Either way, my Speed Graphic would collect the evidence needed to nail Bud for statutory rape. It's not elegant, but it's a living.

Around eleven I spotted them, coming down a ladder, stepping onto the swaying dock: Bud and Louise. Hazel-haired, taller than I'd imagined her, she did have an admirable top-heavy figure, which her short-sleeved pale blue sweater and darker blue pedal pushers showed off nicely. Bud wore a yellow sportshirt and brown slacks, and they held hands as they moved rather quickly away from the boat.

I was preparing to leave the cafe and follow them up to the parking lot, and Bud's car—Mrs. Overell had given me the make and color, and I'd already spotted it, a blue Pontiac convertible, pre-war, battered but serviceable—only, they threw me a curve in addition to Louise's.

The couple were heading up the ramp toward the cafe!

Absurdly, I wondered if they'd made me—impossible, since they hadn't seen me yet—and I hunkered over my coffee as the lovebirds took a couple of stools at the counter, just about opposite my window booth.

At first they were laughing, at some private joke; it seemed rather forced—were they trying to attract attention?

Then they both ordered burgers and fries and sat there talking, very quietly. Even a trained eavesdropper like me couldn't pick up a word. Perhaps they'd had a rough evening with her folks, because periodically one would seem to be comforting the other, stroking an arm, patting a shoulder, reassuringly.

What the hell was going on? Why did they need a burger, when presumably that luxury cruiser had a well-stocked larder? And if they wanted to get away from her parents and that boat, why hang around the dock? Why not climb in Bud's convertible and seek a burger joint that wasn't in her parents' watery backyard?

Such thoughts bobbed like a buoy in my trained snoop's mind as the couple sat at the counter and nibbled at their food. It was a meal any respectable young couple could down in a matter of minutes. But forty-five minutes later, the two were still sitting on those stools, sometimes picking at barely eaten, very cold-by-now food, often staring soulfully into each other's eyes. Every other stool at that counter had seen at least three customer backsides in the same span.

I was long since used to boring stakeout duty; but it was unnerving having my subjects so near at hand, for so long a time. I finally got up and went to the men's room, partly to test whether they'd use that opportunity to slip away (again, had they made me?), and partly because after three cups of coffee, I needed to take a piss.

When I got back, Bud and Louise were still sitting on their stools, Louise ever so barely swivelling on hers, like a kid in a soda shop. Frustrated, confused, I settled back into my booth, and glanced out the window, and the world exploded.

Actually, it was just the *Mary E.* that exploded, sending a fireball of flame rising from the cruiser, providing the clear night sky with thunder, hurling burning debris everywhere, making waves out of the placid waters, rocking the pier.

Rocking the cafe patrons, too, most of them anyway. Everyone except the employees leapt to their feet, screaming, shouting, running outside into a night turned orange by flame, dabbed gray by smoke.

Almost everyone—Bud and Louise were still just sitting at the counter, albeit looking out the window, numbly.

Me, I was on my feet, but then I settled back into the booth, trying to absorb what I'd seen, what I was *seeing*. I knew my client was dead, and so was his wife—two people I'd spoken to at length, just the day before—as that cruiser was already a listing, smoking shambles, sinking stern first into the bay's eighteen feet.

Finally, the couple headed outside, to join the gathering crowd at the water's edge. I followed them. Sirens were cutting the air, getting closer, closer.

Louise was crying now, hysterical, going from one gaping spectator to another, saying, "My father was on that boat! My mother, too! Somebody save them—somebody rescue them... somebody has to rescue them!"

The boy friend remained at the side of the stricken girl as she moved through the crowd, making her presence blatantly known, Bud's boyish face painted with dismay and shock and reflected flames.

I went to my rental car and got my Speed Graphic. I wouldn't even need the flash—plenty of light.

Snagging shots of the dying boat, and the distraught daughter and her beau, I heard the speculation among the boating-wise onlookers, as to the explosion's cause.

"Butane," one would say.

"Or gasoline," another would say.

But this ex-Marine wasn't so easily fooled.

Butane, hell—I smelled dynamite.

Before long, the Coast Guard arrived, and fire trucks, and police from nearby Santa Ana and Orange County Sheriff's Department personnel. The Chief of the Newport Beach Police showed, took over the investigation, questioned the tearful, apparently anguished Louise Overell and promptly released her, and her boy friend.

Pushing through the bustle, I introduced myself to the chief, whose name was Hodgkinson, and told him I was an investigator who'd been doing a job for Walter Overell.

"A job related to what happened here tonight?" the heavyset chief asked, frowning.

"Very possibly."

"You suspect foul play?"

"Oh yeah."

"Where are you staying, Mr. Heller?"

"The Beverly Hills Hotel."

That impressed him—he didn't realize it was a perk of my security work for the hotel. "Well, obviously, Mr. Heller, I'm gonna be tied up here quite a while. Can you come by the station tomorrow sometime? Tomorrow's Sunday—make it Monday. And if I'm not there, I may be back out here."

"Sure. Why did you let those two kids go?"

"Are you kiddin'? We'll be dredging her parents' scorched corpses outa the drink before too long. It's only decent to spare that girl the sight of that."

Only decent.

Sunday I took my wife to the beach at Santa Monica—she was only a few months pregnant and still looked great in a swim suit. Peggy was an actress and recently had a small role in a Bob Hope picture, and even out here her Deanna Durbin-ish good looks attracted attention.

She ragged me, a little, because I seemed preoccupied, and wasn't terribly good company. But that was because I was thinking about the Overell "Yacht Murder" (as the papers had already starting calling it). I had sold my crime scene photos to Jim Richardson, at the *Examiner*, by the way, for three hundred bucks. I was coming out way ahead of the game, considering my client and his wife had been blown to smithereens the night before.

Call it guilt, call it conscience, call it sheer profession-alism, but I knew I hadn't finished this job. Walter Overell deserved more for that two-hundred buck retainer—just like he'd deserved better from that shrewd sexed-up daughter of his.

So on Monday, bright and early, looking like a tourist in sportshirt and chinos, I began looking. What was I looking for? A slip of paper...a slip of paper in the desert...sounds worse than a needle in a haystack, but it wasn't. I found the damn thing before noon.

Chatsworth was a mountain-ringed hamlet in the West San Fernando Valley that used a Wild West motif to attract tour-ists, offering them horseback riding and hiking trails, with the ocean and beaches and desert close at hand for lovers of the outdoors—like that Boy Scout Bud Gollum and his bosomy Campfire Girl.

The guy behind the counter in the sparse storefront at the Trojan Powder Company looked a little like Gabby Hayes—white-bearded, prospector-grizzled, in a plaid shirt and bib overalls. But he had his original teeth and a faint British accent, which took him out of the running for playing a Roy Rogers or Gene Autry sidekick.

This was the owner of the place, and he was looking at the photo I'd handed him, taking a closer look than he had at the Illinois P.I. badge I'd flashed him.

"That young woman will never drown," he said, with a faintly salacious smile.

"I'm not so much interested whether you recognize her tits as if her face is familiar—or her boyfriend's."

"I recognize the whole batch of them—both faces, both bosoms, for that matter. The girl didn't come in, though—she sat out in their convertible—a Pontiac, I believe. I could see her right through the front window."

"Did he make a purchase?"

"I should say—fifty sticks of dynamite."

Jesus, that was a lot of dinah.

"This is fresh in my memory," the proprietor said, "because it was just last Friday."

Day before the boat blew up.

"Can anybody stroll in here and buy that stuff?"

"It's a free country—but back in the early days of the war, when folks were afraid of saboteurs, city and county officials passed an ordinance, requiring purchasers to sign for what they buy."

I liked the sound of that. "Can I see the signed receipt?"

Bud had not signed his own name—"R.L. Standish" had purchased the fifty sticks of dynamite—but I had no doubt handwriting experts would confirm this as the Boy Scout's scrawl.

"Some officers from Newport Beach will be along to talk to you," I told him.

"Fine—what about reporters?"

"Good idea," I said, and used the phone.

Examiner editor Richardson paid me another C-note for the tip, and the proprietor of the Trojan Powder Company earned his own fifty bucks of Mr. Hearst's money for providing the exclusive.

I found Chief Hodgkinson at the Newport Beach dock, where the grim, charred wreckage had been surfaced from the depth of eighteen feet—about all that remained was the black blistered hull. The sun was high and golden on the waters, and the idyllic setting of stucco villas in the background and expensive pleasure craft on either side was turned bizarre by the presence of the scorched husk of the *Mary E.*

Seated in the Beachfront Cafe across from the blue-uniformed, heavyset chief, in the same booth I'd occupied Saturday night, I filled him in on what I'd discovered up Chatsworth way. He excused himself to pass the information along to a couple of D.A.'s investigators who would make the trip to the Trojan Powder Company.

When the chief returned, bearing a plate with a piece of pecan pie with whipped cream, he sat and ate and shared some information.

"Pretty clear your instincts were right about those kids," he said gruffly but good-naturedly. "It's just hard to believe—patricide *and* matricide. Only in California."

"The late Walter Overell was supposedly worth around a million. And, like I told you, he was threatening to cut his daughter off, if she married her four-eyed romeo."

"What made you think to go looking for that sales receipt, Mr. Heller?"

"I knew they'd gone 'picnicking' in the San Fernando Valley, and a college pal of Bud's said the loving couple liked to hike up around Chatsworth. Plus, I knew if Bud had been a Radio Man 1st Class in the war, he had the technical knowhow to rig a bomb. Hell, Chief, Saturday night, you could smell the dynamite in the air—and the murder."

He nodded his agreement. "It's as cold-blooded a crime as I've ever come across. We found thirty-one sticks of unexploded dynamite in the galley, crude time bomb thing, rigged with wire and tape to an alarm clock—second of two charges. Bulkhead kept the larger one from goin' off. Which was lucky."

"Not for the Overells."

"No, the smaller bundle of dynamite was enough to kill 'em plenty dead," he said, chewing a bite of pecan pie. "But it wasn't enough to cover up the rest of the evidence."

"Such as?"

"Such as what the coroner discovered in his autopsies— before the explosion, both Mom and Dad had been beaten to death with a ball-peen hammer we found aboard the ship.... That there was no water in their lungs backs that theory up."

"Jesus—that is cold."

A young uniformed officer was approaching; he had a wide-eyed, poleaxed expression.

"Chief," the young cop said, leaning in, "somebody's here and wants to talk to you—and you won't believe who it is."

Within a minute, a somber yet bright-eyed Louise Overell— in a short-sleeved, cream-colored, well-filled sweater and snug-fitting blue jeans—was standing with her hands fig-leafed before her.

"Hello, Chief Hodgkinson," she said, cheerfully. "How are you today?"

"Why, I'm just fine," he said.

"I'm doing better...thanks," the blue-eyed teenager said, answering a question Hodgkinson hadn't asked. "The reason I'm here is, I wanted to ask about the car."

"The car?"

"My parents' car. I know it was left here in the lot, and I thought maybe I could drive it back up to Flintridge...I've been staying up there, since...the tragedy."

"Excuse me," I said, getting out, and I flashed the chief a look that I hoped he would understand as meaning he should stall the girl.

"Well," the chief was saying, "I'm not sure. I think perhaps we need to talk to the District Attorney, and make sure the vehicle isn't going to be impounded for..."

And I was gone, heading for the parking lot.

Wherever Louise went, so surely too went Bud—particularly since another driver would be needed to transport the family sedan back to the Flintridge estate.

Among the cars in the gravelled lot were my own rental job, several police cars, Bud's Pontiac convertible, and a midnight blue '47 Caddy that I just knew had to have been Walter Overell's.

This opinion was formed, in part, by the fact that Bud Gollum—in a red sportshirt and denim slacks—was trying to get into the car. I approached casually—the boy had something in his left hand, and I wanted to make sure it wasn't a weapon.

Then I saw: a roll of electrical tape, and spool of wire. What the hell was he up to?

Then it came to me: while little Louise was keeping the chief busy, Bud was attempting to plant the tape and wire...which would no doubt match up with what had been used on the makeshift time bomb...in Overell's car. When the chief turned the vehicle over to Louise, the "evidence" would be discovered.

But the Caddy was locked, and apparently Louise hadn't been able to provide a key, because Bud was grunting in frustration as he tried every door.

I just stood there, hands on my hips, rocking on my heels on the gravel. "Is that your plan, Bud? To try to make this look like suicide-murder, planned by ol' Walter?"

Bud whirled, the eyes wild in the boyish face. "What... who...?"

"It won't play, kid. The dynamite didn't do its job—the fractured skulls turned up in the autopsy. You're about two seconds away from being arrested."

That was when he hurled the tape and the wire at me, and took off running, toward his parked convertible. I batted the stuff away, and ran after him, throwing a tackle that took us both roughly down onto the gravel.

"Shit!" I said, getting up off him, rubbing my scraped forearm.

Bud scrambled up, and threw a punch, which I ducked.

Then I creamed him with a right hand that damn near broke his jaw—I don't remember ever enjoying throwing a punch more, though my hand hurt like hell afterward. He dropped prayerfully to his knees, not passing out, but whimpering like a little kid.

"Maybe you aren't smart enough for pre-med, at that," I told him.

Ambling up with two uniformed officers, the chief—who had already taken Louise into custody—personally snapped the cuffs on Bud Gollum, who was crying like a little girl—unlike Louise, whose stone face worked up a sneery pout, as she was helped into the backseat of a squad car.

All in all, Bud was pretty much a disappointment as a Boy Scout.

The case was huge in the California press, the first really big crime story since the Black Dahlia. A grand jury convicted the young lovers, and the state attorney general himself took charge of the prosecution.

My wife was delighted when we spent several weeks having a real summer's vacation, at the expense of the state of California, thanks to me being a major witness for the prosecution.

I didn't stay for the whole trial, which ran well into October, spiced up by steamy love letters that Louise and Bud exchanged, which were intercepted and fed to the newspapers and even submitted to the jury, after Bud's "filth" (as the late Mrs. Overell would have put it) had been edited out.

The letters fell short of any confession, and the star-crossed couple presented themselves well in court, Louise coming off as intelligent, mature and self-composed, and Bud seeming boyishly innocent, a big, strangely likable puppy dog.

The trial took many dramatic twists and turns, including a trip to the charred hulk of the *Mary E.* in drydock, with Louise and Bud solemnly touring the wreckage in the company of watchful jurors.

Not unexpectedly, toward the end of the trial, the respective lawyers of each defendant began trying to place the blame on the other guy, ultimately requesting separate trials, which the judge denied.

After my wife and I had enjoyed our court-paid summer vacation, I kept up with the trial via the press and reports from Fred Rubinski. All along we had both agreed we had never seen such overwhelming, unquestionably incriminating evidence in a murder case—or such a lame defense, namely that Walter Overell had committed suicide, taking his wife along with him.

Confronted by the testimony of handwriting experts, Bud had even admitted buying the dynamite, claiming he had done so at Walter Overell's request! Medical testimony established that the Overells had died of fractured skulls, and a receipt turned up showing that Bud had bought the alarm clock used in the makeshift time bomb—a clock Bud had given Louise as a gift. Blood on Bud's effects was shown to match that of the late Overells.

And on, and on....I had never seen a case more open and shut.

"Are you sitting down?" Fred's voice said over the phone.

"Yeah," I said, and I was, in my office in the Loop.

"After deliberating for two days, the six men and six women of the jury found Bud and Louise not guilty."

I almost fell out of my chair. "What the hell?"

"The poor kids were 'victims of circumstance,' so says the jury—you know, like the Three Stooges? According to the jury, the Overells died due to 'the accident of suicidal tampering with dynamite by Walter Overell.'"

"You're shitting me...."

"Not at all. Those two fresh-faced kids got off scott free."

I was stunned—flabbergasted. "How could a jury face such incontestable evidence and let obvious killers go free?"

"I don't know," Fred said. "It's a fluke—I can't imagine it ever happening again...not even in California."

The trial took its toll on the lucky pair, however—perhaps because their attorneys had tried to pit Bud and Louise against each other, the girl literally turned her back on the Boy Scout, after the verdict was read, scorning his puppy-dog gaze.

"I'm giving him back his ring," she told the swarming press.

As far as anybody knows, Louise Overell and Bud Gollum never saw each other again.

Nine months after her release, Louise married one of her jailers—I wondered if he'd been the guy who passed the love letters along to the prosecution. The marriage didn't last long, though the couple did have a son. Most of Louise's half million inheritance went to pay for her defense.

Bud flunked out of pre-med, headed east, married a motor-drome rider with a travelling show. That marriage didn't last long, either, and eventually Bud got national press again when he was nabbed in Georgia driving a stolen car. He did two years in a federal pen, then worked for a radio station in the South, finally dropping out of public view.

Louise wound up in Las Vegas, married to a Bonanza Air Lines radio operator. Enjoying custody of her son, she had a comfortable home and the security of a marriage, but remained troubled. She drank heavily and was found dead by her husband in their home on August 24, 1965.

The circumstances of her death were odd—she was naked in bed, with two empty quart-sized bottles of vodka resting near her head. A loaded, cocked .22 rifle was at her feet—unfired. And her nude body was covered with bruises, as if she'd been beaten to death.

Her husband explained this by saying, "She was always falling down." And the Deputy Coroner termed her cause of death as acute alcoholism.

I guess if Walter Overell dynamited himself to death, anything is possible.

AUTHOR'S NOTE

Fact, speculation and fiction are freely mixed within this story, which is based on an actual case and uses the real names of the involved parties, with the exception of Heller and his partner Fred Rubinski (the latter a fictionalization of real-life private eye, Barney Ruditsky). I would like to acknowledge the following works, which were used as reference: *The California Crime Book* (1971), Robert Colby; *For the Life of Me* (1954), Jim Richardson; *"Reporters"* (1991), Will Fowler; and the Federal Writers' Project California guide.

SHOOT—OUT ON SUNSET

The Sunset Strip—the center of Hollywood's nightlife—lay near the heart of Los Angeles, or would have if L.A. had a heart. I'm not waxing poetic, either: postwar L.A. (circa late summer 1949) sprawled over some 452 square miles, but isolated strips of land within the city limits were nonetheless not part of the city. Sunset Boulevard itself ran from downtown to the ocean, around twenty-five miles; west on Sunset, toward Beverly Hills— roughly a mile and a half, from Crescent Heights Boulevard to Doheny Drive—the Strip threaded through an unincorporated area surrounded by (but not officially part of) the City of Angels.

Prime nightspots like the Trocadero, Ciro's, the Mocambo, and the Crescendo shared the glittering Strip with smaller, hipper clubs and hideaway restaurants like Slapsy Maxie's, the Little New Yorker and the Band Box. Seediness and glamour intermingled, grit met glitz, as screen legends, power brokers and gangsters converged in West Hollywood for a free-spirited, no-holds-barred good time.

The L.A. police couldn't even make an arrest on the Strip, which was under the jurisdiction of County Sheriff Eugene Biscailuz, who cheerfully ignored both the city's cops and its ordinances. Not that the L.A. coppers would have made any more arrests than the sheriff's deputies: the Vice Squad was well-known to operate chiefly as a shakedown racket. A mighty bookmaking operation was centered on the Sunset Strip, and juice was paid to both the county sheriff and the city vice squad. This seemed unfair to Mickey Cohen.

The diminutive, dapper, vaguely simian Cohen was a former Ben "Bugsy" Siegel associate who had built his bookie empire on the bodies of his competitors. Rivals with such colorful names as Maxie Shaman, Benny "the Meatball" Gambino, and Tony Trombino were just a few of the violently deceased gangsters who had unwillingly made way for Mickey; and the Godfather of Southern California—Jack Dragna—could only grin and bear it and put up with Cohen's bloody empire building. Cohen had the blessing of the east coast Combination—Luciano, Meyer Lanksy, the late Siegel's crowd—and oldtime Prohibition-era mob boss Dragna didn't like it. A West Coast mob war had been brewing for years.

I knew Cohen from Chicago, where in the late thirties he was strictly a smalltime gambler and general-purpose hoodlum. Our paths had crossed several times since—never in a nasty way—and I rather liked the street-smart, stupid-looking Mick. He was nothing if not colorful: owned dozens of suits, wore monogrammed silk shirts and made-to-order shoes, drove a $15,000 custom-built blue Caddy, lived with his pretty little wife in a $150,000 home in classy Brentwood, and suffered a cleanliness fetish that had him washing his hands more than Lady MacBeth.

A fixture of the Sunset Strip, Mick strutted through clubs spreading dough around like advertising leaflets. One of his primary hangouts was Sherry's, a cocktail lounge slash restaurant, a favorite film-colony rendezvous whose nondescript brick exterior was offset by an ornate interior.

My business partner Fred Rubinski was co-owner of Sherry's. Fireplug Fred—who resembled a slightly better-looking Edward G. Robinson—was an ex-Chicago cop who had moved out here before the war to open a detective agency. We'd known each other in Chicago, both veterans of the pickpocket detail, and I too had left the Windy City PD to go private, only I hadn't gone west, young man.

At least, not until after the war. The A-1 Detective Agency—of which I, Nathan Heller, was president—had (over the course of a decade-and-change) grown from a one-man hole-in-the-wall affair over a deli on Van Buren to a suite of offices in the Monadnock Building rife with operatives, secretaries and clients. Expansion seemed the thing, and I convinced my old pal Fred to throw in with me. So, starting in late '46, the Los Angeles branch operated out of the Bradbury Building at Third and Broadway, with Fred—now vice president of the A-1—in charge, while I of course kept the Chicago offices going. Only it seemed, more and more, I was spending time in California. My wife was an actress, and she had moved out here with our infant son, after the marriage went quickly south. The divorce wasn't final yet, and in my weaker moments, I still had hopes of patching things up, and was looking at finding an apartment or small house to rent, so I could divide my time between L.A. and Chicago. In July of '49, however, I was in a bungalow at the Beverly Hills Hotel, for whom the A-1 handled occasional security matters, an arrangement which included the perk of free lodgings.

Like Cohen, Fred Rubinski attempted to make up for his homeliness with natty attire, such as the blue suit with gray pinstripes and the gray-and-white silk tie he wore, as he sat behind his desk in his Bradbury Building office, a poolcue Havana shifting from corner to corner of his thick lips.

"Just do it as a favor to me, Nate," Fred said.

I was seated across from him, in the client chair, ankle on a knee. "You don't do jobs for Cohen—why should I?"

Fred patted the air with his palms; blue cigar smoke swirled around him like a wreath. "You don't have to do a job for him— just hear him out. He's a good customer at Sherry's and I don't wanna cross him."

"You also don't want to do jobs for him."

A window air conditioner was chugging; hot day. Fred and I had to speak up over it.

"I use the excuse that I'm too well-known out here," my partner said. "Also, the Mickster and me are already considered to be cronies, 'cause of Sherry's. He knows the cops would use that as an excuse to come down on me, hard, if suddenly I was on Mickey Cohen's retainer."

"But you're not asking me to do this job."

"No. Absolutely not. Hell, I don't even know what it is."

"You can guess."

"Well...I suppose you know he's been kind of a clay pigeon, lately. Several attempts on his life, probably by Dragna's people.... Mick probably wants a bodyguard."

"I don't do that kind of work anymore. Anyway, what about those Seven Dwarfs of his?"

That was how Cohen's inner circle of lieutenants/strong-arms were known—Neddie Herbert, Davy Ogul, Frank Niccoli, Johnny Stompanato, Al Snyder, Jimmy Rist, and the late Hooky Rothman, who about a year ago had got his face shot off when guys with shotguns came barging right into Cohen's clothing shop. I liked my face right where it was.

"Maybe it's not a bodyguard job," Fred said with a shrug. "Maybe he wants you for something else."

343

I shifted in the chair. "Fred, I'm trying to distance myself from these mobsters. My connections with the Outfit back home, I'm still trying to live down—it's not good for the A-1..."

"Tell him! Just don't insult the man...don't piss him off."

I got up, smoothing out my suit. "Fred, I was raised right. I hardly ever insult homicidal gangsters."

"You've killed a few, though."

"Yeah," I said from the doorway, "but I didn't insult them."

The habidashery known poshly as Michael's was a two-story brick building in the midst of boutiques and nighteries at 8804 Sunset Boulevard. I was wearing a tan tropical worsted sportcoat and brown summer slacks, with a rust-color tie and two-tone Florsheims, an ensemble that had chewed up a hundred bucks in Marshall Field's men's department, and spit out pocket change. But the going rates inside this plush shop made me look like a piker.

Within the highly polished walnut walls, a few ties lay on a central glass counter, sporting silky sheens and twenty-five buck price tags. A rack of sportshirts ran seventy-five per, a stack of dress shirts ran in the hundred range. A luxurious brown robe on a headless manikin—a memorial to Hooky Rothman?—cost a mere two-hundred bucks, and the sportcoats went for two-hundred up, the suits three to four. Labels boasted: "Tailored Exclusively for Mickey Cohen."

A mousy little clerk—a legit-looking joker with a wispy mustache, wearing around five cee's worth of this stuff—looked at me as if a hobo had wandered into the shop.

"May I help you?" he asked, stuffing more condescension into four words than I would have thought humanly possible.

"Tell your boss Nate Heller's here," I said casually, as I poked around at the merchandise.

This was not a front for a bookmaking joint: Cohen really did run a high-end clothing store; but he also supervised his other, bigger business—which was extracting protection money from bookmakers, reportedly $250 per week per phone—out of here, as well. Something in my manner told the effete clerk that I was part of the backroom business, and his patronizing manner disappeared.

His whispered-into-a-phone conversation included my name, and soon he was politely ushering me to the rear of the store, opening a steel-plated door, gesturing me into a walnut-paneled, expensively-appointed office.

Mayer Harris Cohen—impeccably attired in a double-breasted light gray suit, with a gray and green paisley silk tie—sat behind a massive mahogany desk whose glass-topped surface bore three phones, a small clock with pen-and-pencil holder, a vase with cut flowers, a notepad and no other sign of work. Looming over him was an ornately framed hand-colored photograph of FDR at his own desk, cigarette holder at a jaunty angle.

Standing on either side, like Brillcreamed bookends, were two of Cohen's dark-eyed Dwarfs: Johnny Stompanato, a matinee-idol handsome hood who I knew a little; and hook-nosed Frank Niccoli, who I knew even less. They were as well-dressed as their boss.

"Thanks for droppin' by, Nate," Cohen said, affably, not rising. His thinning black hair was combed close to his egg-shaped skull; with his broad forehead, blunt nose and pugnacious chin, the pint-sized gangster resembled a bull terrier.

"Pleasure, Mickey," I said, hat in my hands.

Cohen's dark eyes flashed from bodyguard to bodyguard. "Fellas, some privacy?"

The two nodded at their boss, but each stopped—one at a time—to acknowledge me, as they headed to a side door, to an adjacent room (not into the shop).

"Semper fi, Mac," Stompanato said, flashing his movie-star choppers. He always said this to me, since we were both ex-Marines.

"Semper fi," I said.

Niccoli stopped in front of me and smiled, but it seemed forced. "No hard feelings, Heller."

"About what?"

"You know. No hard feelings. It was over between us, anyway."

"Frank, I don't know what you're talking about."

His hard, pockmarked puss puckered into an expression that, accompanied by a dismissive wave, implied "no big deal."

When the bodyguards were gone, Cohen gestured for me to sit on the couch against the wall, opposite his desk. He rose to his full five six, and went to a console radio against the wall and switched it on—Frankie Laine was singing "Mule Train"... loud. Then Cohen trundled over and sat next to me, saying quietly, barely audible with the blaring radio going, "You can take Frankie at his word."

At first I thought he was talking about Frankie Laine, then I realized he meant Niccoli.

"Mick," I said, whispering back, not knowing why but following his lead, "I don't know what the hell he's talking about."

Cohen's eyes were wide—he almost always had a startled deer look. "You're dating Didi Davis, right?"

Didi was a starlet I was seeing, casually; I might have been trying to patch up my marriage, but I wasn't denying myself the simple pleasures.

"Yeah, I met her a couple weeks ago at Sherry's."

"Well, Nate, she used to be Frankie's girl."

Cohen smelled like a barber shop got out of hand—reeking heavily of talcum powder and cologne, which seemed a misnomer considering his perpetual five o'clock shadow.

"I didn't know that, Mick. She didn't say anything...."

A whip cracked on the radio, as "Mule Train" wound down.

Cohen shrugged. "It's over. She got tired of gettin' slapped around, I guess. Anyway, if Frankie says he don't hold no grudge, he don't hold no grudge."

"Well, that's just peachy." I hated it when girls forgot to mention their last boyfriend was a hoodlum.

Vaughn Monroe was singing "Ghost Riders in the Sky" on the radio—in full nasal throttle. And we were still whispering.

Cohen shifted his weight. "Listen, you and me, we never had no problems, right?"

"Right."

"And you know your partner, Fred and me, we're pals."

"Sure."

"So I figured I'd throw some work your way."

"Like what, Mick?"

He was sitting sideways on the couch, to look at me better; his hands were on his knees. "I'm gettin' squeezed by a pair of vice cops—Delbert Potts and Rudy Johnson, fuckers' names. They been tryin' to sell me recordings."

"Frankie Laine? Vaughn Monroe?"

"Very funny—these pricks got wire recordings of me, they say, business transactions, me and who-knows-who discussing various illegalities...I ain't heard anything yet. But they're trying to shake me down for twenty gee's—this goes well past the taste they're gettin' already, from my business."

Now I understood why he was whispering, and why the radio was blasting.

"We're not talking protection," I said, "but straight blackmail."

"On the nose. I want two things, Heller—I want my home and my office, whadyacallit, checked for bugs..."

"Swept."

"Huh?"

"Swept for bugs. That's what it's called, Mick."

"Yeah, well, that's what I want—part of what I want. I also want to put in my own wiretaps and bugs and get those two greedy bastards on my recordings of them shakin' me down."

"Good idea—create a standoff."

He twitched a smile, apparently pleased by my approval. "You up for doing that?"

"It's not my speciality, Mick—but I can recommend somebody. Guy named Vaus, Jim Vaus. Calls himself an 'electronics engineering consultant.' He's in Hollywood."

The dark eyes tightened but retained their deer-in-the-headlights quality. "You've used this guy?"

"Yeah...well, Fred has. But what's important is: the cops use him, too."

"They don't have their own guy?"

"Naw. They don't have anybody like that on staff—they're a backward bunch. Jim's strictly freelance. Hell, he may be the guy who bugged you for the cops."

"But can he be trusted?"

"If you pay him better than the LAPD—which won't be hard—you'll have a friend for life."

"How you wanna handle this, Nate? Through your office, or will this, what's-his-name, Vaus, kick back a little to you guys, or—"

"This is just a referral, Mick, just a favor...I think I got one of his cards...."

I dug the card out of my wallet and gave it to Cohen, whose big brown eyes were dancing with sugarplumbs.

"This is great, Nate!"

I felt relieved, like I'd dodged a bullet: I had helped Cohen without having to take him on as a client.

So I said, "Glad to have been of service," and began to get up, only Cohen stopped me with a small but firm hand on my forearm.

Bing Crosby was singing "Dear Hearts and Gentle People" on the radio—casual and easygoing and loud as hell.

"What's the rush, Nate? I got more business to talk."

Sitting back down, I just smiled and shrugged and waited for the pitch.

It was a fastball: "I need you should bodyguard me."

"Jesus, Mick, with guys like Stompanato and Niccoli around? What the hell would you need me for?"

He was shaking his head; he had a glazed expression. "These vice cops, they got friends in the sheriff's office. My boys been gettin' rousted regularly—me, too. Half the time when we leave this place, we get shoved up against the wall and checked for concealed weapons."

"Oh. Is that what happened to Happy Meltzer?"

"On the nose again! Trumped-up gun charge. And these vice cops are behind it—and maybe Jack Dragna, who's in bed with the sheriff's department. Dragna would like nothin' better than to get me outa of the picture, without makin' our mutual friends back east sore."

"Hell, Mick, how do you see me figuring in this?"

"You're a private detective—licensed for bodyguard work. Licensed to carry a weapon! Shit, man, I need somebody armed standin' at my side, to keep me from gettin' my ass shot off! Just a month ago, somebody took a blast at me with a shotgun, and then we found a bomb under my house, and..."

He rattled on, as I thought about his former bodyguard, Hooky Rothman, getting his face shot off, in that posh shop just beyond the metal-lined door.

"I got friends in the Attorney General's office," he was saying, "and they tell me they got an inside tip that there's a contract out on yours truly—there's supposed to be two triggers in from somewheres on the east coast, to do the job. I need somebody with a gun, next to me."

"Mickey," I said, "I have to decline. With all due respect."

"You're not makin' me happy, Nate."

"I'm sorry. I'm in no position to help out. First off, I don't live out here, not fulltime, anyway. Second, I have a reputation of mob connections that I'm trying to live down."

"You're disappointing me...."

"I'm trying to get my branch office established out here, and you and Fred being friends—you hanging out at Sherry's—that's as far as our relationship, personal or professional, can go."

He thought about that. Then he nodded and shrugged. "I ain't gonna twist your arm....Two grand a week, just for the next two weeks?"

That might have tempting, if Cohen hadn't already narrowly escaped half a dozen hit attempts.

"You say you got friends in the Attorney General's office?" I asked.

"Yeah. Fred Howser and me are like this." He held up his right hand, forefinger and middlefinger crossed.

If the attorney general himself was on Cohen's pad, then those wire recordings the vice cops had might implicate Howser....

"Mick, ask Howser to assign one of his men to you as a bodyguard."

"A cop?"

"Who better? He'll be armed, he'll be protecting a citizen, and anyway, a cop to a hoodlum is like garlic to a vampire. Those triggers'll probably steer clear, long as a state investigator is at your side."

Cohen was thinking that over; then he began to nod.

"Not a bad idea," he said. "Not a bad idea at all."

I stood. "No consulting fee, Mick. Let's stay friends—and not do business together."

He snorted a laugh, stood and went over and shut off the radio, cutting off Mel Torme singing "Careless Hands." Then he walked me to the steel-lined door and—when I extended my hand—shook with me.

As I was leaving, I heard him, in the private bathroom off his office, tap running, as he washed up—removing my germs.

I had a couple stops to make, unrelated to the Cohen appointment, so it was late afternoon when I made it back to the Beverly Hills Hotel. Entering my bungalow—nothing fancy, just a marble fireplace, private patio and furnishings no more plush than the palace at Versailles—I heard something...someone... in the bedroom. Rustling around in there.

My nine millimeter was in my suitcase, and my suitcase was in the bedroom. And I was just about to exit, to find a hotel dick or maybe call a cop, when my trained detective's nose sniffed a clue; and I walked across the living room, and pushed the door open.

Didi Davis gasped; she was wearing glittery earrings—just glittery earrings, and the Chanel Number Five I'd nosed—and was poised, pulling back the covers, apparently about to climb into bed. She looked like a French maid who forgot her costume.

"I wanted to surprise you," she said. She was a lovely brunette, rather tall—maybe five nine—with a willowy figure that would have seemed skinny if not for pert breasts and an impertinent dimpled behind. She was tanned all over. Her hair was up. It wasn't alone.

"I thought you were working at Republic today," I said, undoing my tie.

She crawled under the covers and the sheets made inviting, crinkly sounds. "Early wrap....I tipped a bellboy who let me in."

Soon I was under covers, equally naked, leaning on a pillow. "You know, I run with kind of a rough crowd—surprises like this can backfire."

"I just wanted to do something sweet for you," she said.

And she proceeded to do something sweet for me.

Half an hour later, still in the bedroom, we were getting dressed when I brought up the rough crowd she ran with.

"Why didn't you mention you used to date Frank Niccoli?"

She was fastening a nylon to her garter belt, long lovely leg stretched out as if daring me to be mad at her. "I don't know— Nate, you and I met at Sherry's, after all. You hang around with those kind of people. What's the difference?"

"The difference is, suppose he's a jealous type. Niccoli isn't your average ex-beau—he's a goddamn thug. Is it true he smacked you around?"

She was putting on her other nylon, fastening it, smoothing it; this kind of thing could get boring in an hour or two. "That's why I walked out on him. I warned him and he said he wouldn't do it again, and then a week later, he did it again."

"Has he bothered you? Confronted you in public? Called you on the phone?"

"No. It's over. He knows it, and I know it...now you know it. Okay, Nate? Do I ask you questions about your ex-wife?"

Didi didn't know my wife wasn't officially my ex, yet; nor that I was still hoping to rekindle those flames. She thought I was a great guy, unaware that I was a heel who would never marry another actress, but would gladly sleep with one.

"Let's drop it," I said.

"What a wonderful idea." She stood, easing her slip down over her nyloned legs, and was shimmying into her casual light-blue dress when the doorbell rang. Staying in a bungalow at the Beverly Hills, incidentally, was the only time I can recall a hotel room having a doorbell.

"I'm not expecting company," I told her, "but stay in here, would you? And keep mum?"

"I need to put my make-up on—"

The bell rang again—pretty damn insistent.

I got my nine millimeter out of the suitcase, stuffed it in my waistband, slipped on my sportjacket and covered it. "Just sit down—there's some magazines by the bed. We don't need to advertise."

She saw the common sense of that, and nodded. No alarm had registered in her eyes at the sight of the weapon; but then she'd been Niccoli's girl, hadn't she?

I shut her in there and went to answer the door.

I'd barely cracked the thing open when the two guys came barging in, the first one in brushing past me, the second slamming the door.

I hadn't even had a chance to say, "Hey!" when the badge in the wallet was thrust in my face.

"Lieutenant Delbert Potts," he said, putting the wallet away. He was right on top of me and his breath was terrible: it smelled like anchovies taste. "L.A. vice squad. This is my partner, Sergeant Rudy Johnson."

Potts was a heavy-set character in an off-the-rack brown suit that looked slept in; hatless, he had greasy reddish-blond hair and his drink-reddened face had a rubbery softness. His eyes were bloodshot, his nose as misshapen as a blob of putty somebody had stuck there carelessly, his lips thick and plump and vaguely obscene.

Johnson was thin and dark—both his features and his physique—and his navy suit looked tailored. He wore a black snapbrim that had set him back a few bucks.

"Fancy digs, Mr. Heller," Potts said, prowling the place, his thick-lipped smile conveying disgust. He had a slurry voice— he reminded me of a loathsome Arthur Godfrey, if that wasn't redundant.

"I do some work for the hotel," I said. "They treat me right when I'm out here."

"You goin' back to Chicago soon?" Johnson asked, right next to me. He had a reedy voice and his eyes seemed sleepy unless you noticed the sharpness under the half-lids.

"Not right away."

I'd never met this pair, yet they knew my name and knew I was from Chicago. And they hadn't taken me up on my offer to sit down.

"You might re-consider," Potts said. He was over at the wet bar, checking out the brands.

"Help yourself," I said.

"We're on duty," Johnson said.

"Fellas—what's this about?"

Potts wandered back over to me and thumped me on the chest with a thick finger. "You stopped by Mickey Cohen's today."

"That's right. He wanted me to do a job for him—I turned him down."

The bloodshot eyes tightened. "You turned him down? Are you sure?"

"I have a real good memory, Lieutenant. I remember damn near everything that happened to me, all day."

"Funny." That awful breath was warm in my face—fishy smell. "You wouldn't kid a kidder, would you?"

Backing away, I said, "Fellas—make your point."

Potts kept moving in on me, his breath in my face, like a foul furnace, his finger thumping at my chest. "You and your partner...Rubinski...you shouldn't be so thick with that little kike."

"Which little kike?"

Johnson said, "Mickey Cohen."

I looked from one to the other. "I already told you guys—I turned him down. I'm not working for him."

Potts asked, "What job did he want you for?"

"That's confidential."

He swung his fist into my belly—I did not see it coming, nor did I expect a slob like him to have such power. I dropped to my knees and thought about puking on the oriental carpet—I also thought about the gun in my waistband.

Slowly, I got to my feet. And when I did, the nine millimeter was in my hand.

"Get the fuck out of my room," I said.

Both men backed away, alarm widening their seen-it-all eyes. Potts blurted, "You can be arrested for—"

"This is licensed, and you clowns barged into my room and committed assault on me."

Potts had his hands up; he seemed nervous but he might have been faking, while he looked for an opening. "I shouldn'ta swung on ya. I apologize—now, put the piece away."

"No." I motioned toward the door with the Browning. "You're about to go, gents...but first—here's everything you need to know: I'm not working for Cohen, and neither is Fred."

The two exchanged glances, Johnson shaking his head.

"Why don't you put that away," Pott said, with a want-some-candy-little-girl smile, "and we'll just talk."

"We have talked. Leave."

I pressed forward and the two backed up—toward the door.

"You better be tellin' the truth," Potts said, anger swimming in his rheumy eyes.

I opened the door for them. "What the hell have you been eating, Potts? Your breath smells like hell."

The cop's blotchy face reddened, but his partner let out a sharp, single laugh. "Sardine sandwiches—it's all he eats on stakeouts."

That tiny moment of humanity between Johnson and me ended the interview; then they were out the door, and I shut and nightlatched it. I watched them through the window as they moved through the hotel's garden-like grounds, Potts taking the lead, clearly pissed-off, the flowering shrubs around him doing nothing to soothe him.

In the bedroom, Didi was stretched out on the bed, on her back, head to one side, fast asleep.

I sat next to her, on the edge of the bed, and this woke her with a start. "What? Oh...I must've dropped off. What was that about, anyway?"

"The Welcome Wagon," I said. "Come on, let's get an early supper."

And I took her to the Polo Lounge, where she chattered on and on about the picture she was working (with Roy Rogers and Dale Evans) and I said not much. I was thinking about those two bent cops, and how I'd pulled a gun on them.

No retaliation followed my encounter with the two vice squad boys. They had made their point, and I mine. But I did take some precautionary measures: for two days I tailed the bastards, and (with my Speed Graphic, the divorce dick's best friend) got two rolls of film on them receiving pay-offs, frequently in the parking lot of their favorite coffee shop, Googie's, on Sunset at Crescent Heights. I had no intention of using these for blackmail purposes—I just wanted some ammunition, other than the nine millimeter variety, with which to deal with these bent sons of bitches. On the other hand, I had taken to wearing my shoulder-holstered nine millimeter, in case things got interesting.

And for over a week, things weren't interesting—things were nicely dull. I had run into Cohen at Sherry's several times and he was friendly—and always in the company of a rugged-looking, ruggedly handsome investigator from the Attorney General's office, sandy-haired Harry Cooper...which rhymed with Gary Cooper, who the dick was just as tall as.

Mick had taken my advice—he now had an armed body-guard, courtesy of the state of California. His retinue of a Dwarf or two also accompanied him, of course, just minus any artillery. Once or twice, Niccoli had been with him—he'd just smiled and nodded at me (and Didi), polite, no hard feelings.

On Tuesday night, July 19, I took Didi to see *Annie Get Your Gun* at the Greek Theater; Gertrude Niesen had just opened in the show, and she and it were terrific. Then we had a late supper at Ciro's, and hit a few jazz clubs. We wound up, as we inevitably did, at Sherry's for pastries and coffee.

Fred greeted us as we came in and joined us in a booth, Didi—who looked stunning in a low-cut spangly silver gown, her brunette hair piled high—and I were on one side, Fred on the other. A piano tinkling Cole Porter fought with clanking plates and after-theater chatter.

I ordered us up a half-slice of cheesecake for Didi (who was watching her figure—she wasn't alone), a Napoleon for me, and coffee for both of us. Fred just sat there with his hands folded, prayerfully, shaking his head.

"Gettin' too old for this," he said, his pouchy puss even pouchier than usual, a condition his natty navy suit and red silk tie couldn't make up for.

"What are you doing, playing host in the middle of the night?" I asked him. "You're an owner, for Christ's sake! Seems like lately, every time I come in here, in the wee hours, you're hovering around like a mother hen."

"You're not wrong, Nate. Mickey's been comin' in almost every night, and with that contract hanging over his head, I feel like...for the protection of my customers...I gotta keep an eye on things."

"Is he here tonight?"

"Didn't you see him, holding court over there?"

Over in the far corner of the modern, brightly-lighted restaurant—where business was actually a little slow tonight—a lively Cohen was indeed seated at a large round table with Cooper, Johnny Stompanato, Frank Niccoli and another of the Dwarfs, Neddie Herbert. Also with the little gangster were several reporters from the *Times*, and Florabel Muir and her husband, Denny. Florabel, a moderately attractive redhead in her late forties, was a Hollywood columnist for the New York *Daily News*.

Our order arrived, and Fred slid out of the booth, saying, "I better circulate."

"Fred, what, you think somebody's gonna open up with a chopper in here? This isn't a New Jersey clam house."

"I know....I'm just a nervous old woman."

Fred wandered off, and Didi and I nibbled at our desserts; we were dragging a little—it was after three.

"You okay?" I asked her.

"What?"

"You seem a little edgy."

"Really? Why would I be?"

"Having Niccoli sitting over there."

"No. That's over."

"What did you see in that guy, anyway?"

She shrugged. "He was nice, at first. I heard he had friends in pictures."

"You're already under contract. What do you need—"

"Nate, are we going to argue?"

I smiled, shook my head. "No. It's just...guys like Niccoli make me nervous."

"But he's been very nice to both of us."

"That's what makes me nervous." Our mistake was using the restrooms: they were in back, and to use them, we'd had to pass near Cohen and his table. That's how we got invited to join the party—the two *Times* reporters had taken off, and chairs were available.

I sat next to Florabel, with Niccoli right next to me; and Didi was beside Cooper, the state investigator, who sneaked occasional looks down Didi's cleavage. Couldn't blame him and, anyway, detectives are always gathering information.

Florabel had also seen *Annie Get Your Gun*, and Cohen had caught a preview last week.

"That's the best musical to hit L.A. in years," the little gangster said. He was in a snappy gray suit with a blue and gray tie.

For maybe five minutes, the man who controlled bookie operations in Los Angeles extolled the virtues of Rodgers and Hammerstein's latest confection, aided and abetted by Irving Berlin.

"Can I quote you in my column?" Florabel asked. She was wearing a cream-color suit with satin lapels, a classy dame with a hard edge.

"Sure! That musical gets the Mickey Cohen seal of approval."

Everyone laughed, as if it had been witty—me, too. I like my gangsters to be in a good mood.

"Mickey," the columnist said, sitting forward, "who do you think's been trying to kill you?"

"I really haven't the slightest idea. I'm as innocent as the driven snow."

"Yeah, but like Mae West said, you drifted."

He grinned at her—tiny rodent teeth. "Florabel, I love ya like a sister, I can talk to you about things I can't even tell my own wife."

Who was not present, by the way.

"You're in a neutral corner," he was saying, "like a referee. There's nothin' I can do for you, except help you sell papers, and you ain't got no axes to grind with me."

"That's true—so why not tell me what you really think? Is Jack Dragna behind these attempts?"

"Even for you, Florabel, that's one subject on which I ain't gonna spout off. If I knew the killers were in the next room, I wouldn't go public with it."

"Why not?"

"People like me, we settle things in our own way."

She gestured. "How can you sit in an open restaurant, Mick, with people planning to kill you?"

"Nobody's gonna do nothin' as long as you people are around. Even a crazy man wouldn't take a chance shooting where a reporter might get hit...or a cop, like Cooper here."

I was just trying to stay out of it, on the sidelines, but this line of reasoning I couldn't let slide.

"Mickey," I said, "you really think a shooter's going to ask to see Florabel's press pass?" Cohen thought that was funny, and almost everybody laughed—except me and Cooper.

Several at the table were nibbling on pastries; Didi and I had some more coffee. At one point, Niccoli got up to use the men's room, and Didi and I exchanged whispered remarks about how cordial he'd been to both of us. Florabel, still looking for a story, started questioning the slender, affable Neddie Herbert, who had survived a recent attempt on his life.

Herbert, who went back twenty years with Cohen, had dark curly hair, a pleasant-looking grown-up Dead-End Kid with a Brooklyn accent. He had been waylaid in the wee hours on the sidewalk in front of his apartment house.

"Two guys with .38s emptied their guns at me from the bushes." Herbert was grinning like a college kid recalling a frat-house prank. "Twelves slugs, the cops recovered—not one hit me!"

"How is that possible?" Florabel asked.

"Ah, I got a instinct for danger—I didn't even see them two guys, but I sensed 'em right before I heard 'em, and I dropped to the sidewalk right before they started shooting. I crawled up onto the stairway, outa range, while their bullets were fallin' all around."

"Punks," Cohen said.

"If they'da had any guts," Herbert said, "they'da reloaded and moved in close, to get me—but they weaseled and ran."

Fred came over to the table, and—after some small talk—said, "It's almost four, folks—near closing time. Mind if I have one of the parking lot attendants fetch your car, Mick?"

"That'd be swell, Fred."

I said, "Fetch mine, too, would you, Fred?"

And as Rubinski headed off to do that, Cohen grabbed the check, fending off a few feeble protests, and everybody gathered their things. This seemed like a good time for Didi and me to make our exit, as well.

Sherry's was built up on a slope, so there were a couple steps down from the cashier's counter to an entryway that opened right out to the street. Cohen strutted down and out, through the glass doors, with Neddie Herbert and the six-three Cooper right behind him. Niccoli and Stompanato were lingering inside, buying chewing gum and cigarettes. Florabel and her husband were lagging, as well, talking to some woman who I gathered was the Mocambo's press agent.

Then Didi and I were standing on the sidewalk just behind Cohen and his bodyguards, under the Sherry's canopy, out in the fresh, crisp night air...actually, early morning air. The normally busy Strip was all but deserted, only the occasional car gliding by. Just down a ways, the flashing yellow lights of sawhorses marking road construction blinked lazily.

"I love this time of night," Didi said, hugging my arm, as we waited behind Cohen and his retinue for the attendants to bring our cars. "So quiet...so still...."

And it was a beautiful night, bright with starlight and neon, palm trees peeking over a low-slung mission-style building across the way, silhouetted against the sky like a decorative wallpaper pattern. Directly across from us, however, a vacant lot with a Blatz beer billboard and a smaller FOR INFORMATION CONCERNING THIS PROPERTY PLEASE CALL sign did spoil the mood, slightly.

Didi—her shoulders and back bare, her silvery gown shimmering with reflected light—was fussing in her little silver purse. "Damn—I'm out of cigarettes."

"I'll go back and get you some," I said.

"Oh, I guess I can wait..."

"Don't be silly. What is it you smoke?"

"Chesterfields."

I went back in and up the three or four steps and bought the smokes. Florabel was bending over, picking up all the just-delivered morning editions, stacked near the cashier; her husband was still yakking with that dame from the Mocambo. Stompanato was flirting with a pretty waitress; Niccoli was nowhere in sight.

I headed down the short flight of steps and was coming out the glass doors just as Cohen's blue Caddy drew up, and the young string-tied attendant got out, and the night split open.

It wasn't thunder, at least not God's variety: this was a twelve-gauge boom accompanied by the cracks of a high-power rifle blasting, a deadly duet echoing across the pavement, shotgun bellow punctuated by the sharp snaps of what might have been an M-1, the sound of which took me back to Guadalcanal. As the fusillade kicked in, I reacted first and best, diving for the sidewalk, yanking at Didi's arm as I pitched past, pulling her down, the glass doors behind me shattering in a discordant song. My sportcoat was buttoned, and it took a couple seconds to get at the nine millimeter under my shoulder, and during those slow-motion moments I saw Mickey get clipped, probably by the rifle.

Cohen dropped to one knee, clawing at his right shoulder with his left hand, blood oozing through his fingers, streaming down his expensive suit. Neddie Herbert's back had been to the street—he was turned toward his boss when the salvo began—and a bullet, courtesy of the rifle, blew through him, even as shotgun pellets riddled his legs. Herbert—the man who'd just been bragging about his instincts for danger—toppled to the sidewalk, screaming.

The Attorney General's dick, Cooper, had his gun out from under his shoulder when he caught a belly-full of buckshot and tumbled to the cement, yelling, "Shit! Fuck!" Mickey Cohen, on his knees, was saying, I swear to God, "This is a new goddamn suit!"

The rifle snapping over the shotgun blasts continued, as I stayed low and checked Didi who was shaking in fear, a crumpled moaning wreck; her bare back was red-pocked from two pellets, which seemed not to have entered her body, probably bouncing off the pavement and nicking her—but she was scared shitless.

Still, I could tell she was okay, and—staying low, using the Caddy as my shield—I fired the nine millimeter toward that vacant lot, where orange muzzle flash emanated from below that Blatz billboard. The safety glass of the Caddy's windows spiderwebbed and then burst into tiny particles as the shotgunning continued, and I ducked down, noting that the rifle fire had ceased. Had I nailed one of them?

Then the shotgun stopped, too, and the thunder storm was over, leaving a legacy of pain and terror: Neddie Herbert was shrieking, yammering about not being able to feel his legs, and Didi was weeping, her long brunette hair come undone, trailing down her face and her back like tendrils. Writhing on the sidewalk like a bug on its back, big rugged Cooper had his revolver in one hand, waving it around in a punch-drunk manner; his other hand was clutching his bloody stomach, blood bubbling through his fingers.

I moved out from behind the Caddy, stepping out into the street, gun in hand—ready to dive back if I drew any fire.

But none came.

I wanted to run across there and try to catch up with the bastards, but I knew I had to stay put, at least for a while; if those guys had a car, they might pull around and try to finish the job. And since I had a gun—and hadn't been wounded—I had to stand guard.

Now time sped up: I saw the parking lot attendant, who had apparently ducked under the car when the shooting started, scramble out from under and back inside the restaurant, glass crunching under his feet. Niccoli ran out, with Stompanato and Fred Rubinski on his tail; Niccoli got in the Caddy, and Cohen—despite his limp bloody arm—used his other arm to haul the big, bleeding Cooper up into the backseat. Stompanato helped and climbed in back with the wounded cop.

Fred yelled, "Don't worry, Mick—ambulances are on the way! We'll take care of everybody!"

And the Caddy roared off.

Neddie Herbert couldn't be moved; he was alternately whimpering and screaming, still going on about not being able to move his legs. Some waitresses wrapped checkered tablecloths around the suffering Neddie, while I helped Didi inside; she said she was cold and I gave her my sportjacket to wear.

Florabel came up to me, her left hand out of sight, behind her; she held out her right palm to show me a flattened deer slug about the size of a half dollar.

"Pretty nasty," she said.

"You get hit, Florabel?"

"Just bruised—where the sun don't shine. Hell, I thought it was fireworks, and kids throwing rocks."

"You reporters have such great instincts."

As a waitress tended to Didi, Fred took me aside and said, "Real professional job."

I nodded. "Shotgun to cause chaos, that 30.06 to pinpoint Cohen...only they missed."

"You okay, Nate?"

"Yeah—I don't think I even got nicked. Scraped my hands on the sidewalk, is all. Get me a flashlight, Fred."

"What?"

"Sheriff's deputies'll show up pretty soon—I want a look across the way before they get here."

Fred understood: the sheriff's office was in Jack Dragna's pocket, so their work might be more cover-up than investigation.

The vacant lot across the street, near the Blatz billboard, was not what I'd expected, and I immediately knew why they'd chosen this spot. Directly off the sidewalk, an embankment fell to a sunken lot, with cement stairs up the slope providing a perfect place for shooters to perch out of sight. No street or even alley back here, either: just the backyards of houses asleep for the night (lights in those houses were blazing now, however). The assassins could sit on the stairs, unseen, and fire up over the sidewalk, from ideal cover.

"Twelve-gauge," Fred commented, pointing to a scattering of spent shells in the grass near the steps.

My flashlight found something else. "What's this?"

Fred bent next to what appeared to a sandwich—a half-eaten sandwich....

"Christ!" Fred said, lifting the partial slice of white bread. "Who eats this shit?"

An ambulance was screaming; so was Neddie Herbert.

"What shit?" I asked.

Fred shuddered. "It's a fucking sardine sandwich."

The shooting victims were transferred from the emergency room of the nearest hospital to top-notch Queen of Angels, where the head doctor was Cohen's personal physician. An entire wing was roped off for the Cohen party, with a pressroom and listening posts for both the LAPD and County Sheriff's department.

I stayed away. Didi's wounds were only superficial, so she was never admitted, anyway. Cohen called me from the hospital to thank me for my "quick thinking"; all I had done was throw a few shots in the shooters' direction, but maybe that had kept the carnage to a minimum. I don't know.

Neddie Herbert got the best care, but he died anyway, a week later, of uremic poisoning: gunshot wounds in the kidney are a bitch. At that point, Cohen was still in the hospital, but rebounding fast; and the State Attorney's man, Cooper, was fighting for his life with a bullet in the liver and internal hem-orrhaging from wounds in his intestines.

Fred and I both kept our profiles as low as possible—this kind of publicity for his restaurant and our agency was not exactly what we were looking for.

The night after Neddie Herbert's death in the afternoon, I was waiting in the parking lot of Googie's, the coffee shop at Sunset and Crescent Heights. Googie's was the latest of these atomic-type cafes popping up along the Strip like futuristic mushrooms: a slab of the swooping red-painted structural steel roof rose to jut at an angle toward the street, in an off-balance exclamation point brandishing the neon *googie's*, and a massive picture window looked out on the Strip as well as the nearby Hollywood hills.

I'd arrived in a blue Ford that belonged to the A-1; but I was standing alongside a burgundy Dodge, an unmarked car used by the two vice cops who made Googie's their home away from home. Tonight I was wasn't taking pictures of their vari-ous dealings with bookmakers, madams, fellow crooked cops or politicians. This was something of a social call.

I'd been here since just before midnight; and we were into the early morning hours now—in fact, it was after two a.m. when Lieutenant Delbert Potts and Sergeant Rudy Johnson strolled out of the brightly illuminated glass-and-concrete coffee shop, into the less illuminated parking lot. Potts was in another rumpled brown suit—or maybe the same one—and, again, Johnson was better-dressed than his slob partner, his slender frame well-served by a dark gray suit worthy of Michael's habidashery.

Hell, maybe Cohen provided Johnson's wardrobe as part of the regular pay-off—at least till Delbert and Rudy got greedy and went after that twenty grand for the recordings they'd made of Mickey.

I dropped down into a crouch as they approached, pleased that no other customers had wandered into the parking lot at the same time as my friends from the vice squad. Tucked between the Dodge and the car parked next to it, I was as unseen as Potts and Johnson had been, when they'd crouched on those steps with their shotgun and rifle, waiting for Mickey.

Potts and Johnson were laughing about something—maybe Neddie Herbert's death—and the fat one was in the lead, fishing in his pants pocket for his car keys. He didn't see me as I rose from the shadows, swinging an underhand fist that sank six inches into his flabby belly.

Like a matador, I pushed past him, while shoving him to the pavement, where he began puking, and grabbed Johnson by one lapel and slammed his head into the rear rider's side window. He slid down the side of the car and sat, maybe not unconscious, but good and dazed. Neither one protested—the puking fat one, or the stunned thin one—as I disarmed them, pitching their revolvers into the darkness, where they skittered across the cement like crabs. I checked their ankles for hideout guns, but they were clean. So to speak.

Potts was still puking when I started kicking the shit out of him. I didn't go overboard: just five or six good ones, cracking two or three ribs. Pretty soon he stopped throwing up and began to cry, wallowing down there between the cars in his own vomit. Johnson was coming around, and tried to crawl away, but I yanked him back by the collar and slammed him into the hubcap of the Dodge.

Johnson had blood all over his face, and was spitting up a bloody froth, as well as a tooth or two, and he was blubbering like a baby.

Glancing over my shoulder, I saw a couple in their twenties emerging from Googie's; they walked to the car, on the other side of the lot. They were talking and laughing—presumably not about Neddie Herbert's death—and went to their Chevy convertible and rolled out of the lot.

I kicked Potts in the side and shook Johnson by the lapels, just to get their attention, and they wept and groaned and moaned while I gave them my little speech, which I'd been working on in my head while I waited for them in the parking lot.

"Listen to me, you simple fuckers—you can shoot at Mickey Cohen and his Dwarfs all you want. I really do not give a flying shit. But you shot at me and my date, and a copper too, and that pisses me off. Plus, you shot up the front of my partner's restaurant."

Potts tried to say something, but it was unintelligible; "mercy" was in there, somewhere. Johnson was whimpering, holding up his blood-smeared hands like this was a stick-up.

"Shut-up," I said, "both of you....I don't care what you or Dragna or any gangster or bent fucking cop does out here in Make-believe-ville. I live in Chicago, and I'm going back tomorrow. If you take any steps against me, or Fred Rubinski, or if you put innocent people in the path of your fucking war again, I will talk to my Chicago friends...and you will have an accident. Maybe you'll get run down by a milk truck, maybe a safe'll fall on you. Maybe you'll miss a turn off a cliff. My friends are creative."

Through his bloody bubbles, Johnson said, "Okay, Heller... okay!"

"By the way, I have photos of you boys taking pay-offs from a fine cross section of L.A.'s sleazy citizenry. Anything happens to me—if I wake up with a goddamn hangnail—those photos go to Jim Richardson at the *Examiner*, with a duplicate batch to Florabel Muir. Got it?"

Nobody said anything. I kicked Potts in the ass, and he yelped, "Got it!"

"Got it, got it, got it!" Johnson said, backing up against the hubcap, patting the air with his palms.

"We're almost done—just one question....Was Stompanato in on it, or was Niccoli your only tip-off man?"

Johnson coughed, getting blood on his chin. "Ni-Niccoli... just Niccoli."

"He wanted you to take out the Davis dame, right? That was part of the deal?"

Johnson nodded. So did Potts, who was on his belly, and to see me had to look over his shoulder, puke rolling down his cheeks like a bad complexion that had started to melt.

Just the sight of them disgusted me, and my hand drifted toward my nine millimeter in the shoulder holster. "Or fuck... maybe I should kill you bastards...."

They both shouted "no!" and Potts began to cry again.

Laughing to myself, I returned to the agency's Ford. These L.A. cops were a bunch of pansies; if this were Chicago, I'd have been dead by now.

In the aftermath of the shoot-out at Sherry's, various political heads rolled, including Attorney General Fred Howser's, and several trials took place (Cohen acquitted on various charges), as well as a Grand Jury inquiry into police and political corruption. Potts and Johnson were acquitted of corruption charges, and despite much talk in the press of damning wire recordings in the possession of both sides, no such recordings were entered as evidence in any trial, though Cohen's lawyer was murdered on the eve of a trial in which those recordings were supposed to figure.

And the unsuccessful attempts on Cohen's life continued, notably a bombing of his house, which he and his wife and his bull terrier survived without scratches. But no more civilians were put in harm's way, and no repercussions were felt by either Fred Rubinski or myself.

A few months after Mickey Cohen got out of the hospital, his longtime crony Frank Niccoli—who he'd known since Cleveland days—turned up missing. Suspicions that Niccoli may have been a stool pigeon removed by Mickey himself were offset by Cohen losing $25,000 bail money he'd put up for Niccoli on an unrelated beef.

The next summer, I ran into Cohen at Sherry's—or actually, I was just coming out of Sherry's, a date on my arm; another cool, starlit night, around two a.m., the major difference this time being the starlet was a blonde. Mickey and Johnny Stompanato and two more Dwarfs were on their way in. We paused under the canopy.

The rodent grin flashed between five-o'clock-shadowed cheeks. "Nate! Here we are at the scene of the crime—like old times."

"I hope not, Mickey."

"You look good. You look swell."

"That's a nice suit, Mickey."

"Stop by Michael's—I'll fix you up...on the house. Still owe you a favor for whispering in my ear about...you know."

"Forget it."

He leaned in, sotto voce. "New girl?"

"Pretty new."

"You hear who Didi Davis is dating these days?"

"No."

"That State's Attorney cop—Cooper!"

I smiled. "Hadn't heard that."

"Yeah, he finally got the bullet removed outa his liver, the other day. My doc came up with some new treatment, makes liver cells replace themselves or somethin'....All on my tab, of course."

My date tightened her grip on my arm; maybe she recognized Cohen and was nervous about the company I was keeping.

So I said, "Well, Mick, better let you and your boys go on in for your coffee and pastries...before somebody starts shooting at us again."

He laughed heartily and even shook hands with me—which meant he would have to go right in and wash up—but first, leaning in close enough for me to whiff his expensive cologne, he said, "Be sure to say hello to Frankie, since you're in the neighborhood."

"What do you mean?"

Actually, I knew he meant Frankie Niccoli, but wasn't getting the rest of his drift....

Cohen nodded down the Strip. "Remember that road construction they was doin', the night we got hit? There's a nice new stretch of concrete there, now. You oughta try it out."

And Mickey and his boys went inside.

As for me, my latest starlet at my side, I had the parking lot attendant fetch my wheels, and soon I was driving right over that fresh patch of pavement, with pleasure.

AUTHOR'S NOTE

Most of the characters in this fact-based story appear under their real names; several—notably, Fred Rubinski, Didi Davis, Delbert Potts and Rudy Johnson—are fictional but have real-life counterparts. Research sources included numerous true-crime magazine articles and the following books: *Death in Paradise* (1998), Tony Blanche and Brad Schreiber; *Headline Happy* (1950), Florabel Muir; *Hoodlums—Los Angeles* (1959), Ted Prager and Larry Craft; *The Last Mafioso* (1981), Ovid DeMaris; *Mickey Cohen: In My Own Words* (1975), as told to John Peer Nugent; *Mickey Cohen: Mobster* (1973); *Sins of the City* (1999), Jim Heimann; *Thicker'n Thieves* (1951), Charles Stoker; and *Why I Quit Syndicated Crime* (1951), Jim Vaus as told to D.C. Haskin.

Original publication:

"Kaddish for the Kid," *Private Eyes* (1998)

"The Blonde Tigress," *Ellery Queen Mystery Magazine* (2008)

"Private Consultation," *Justice for Hire* (1990)

"The Perfect Crime," Raymond Chandler's *Phillip Marlowe: A Centennial Celebration*, 1988 (story originally featuring Marlowe, revised to feature Heller in *Kisses of Death*, 2001)

"House Call," *Mean Streets* (1986)

"Marble Mildred," *Eye for Justice* (1988)

"The Strawberry Teardrop," *The Eyes Have It* (1984)

"Scrap," *The Black Lizard Anthology of Crime Fiction* (1987)

"Natural Death, Inc.," *Diagnosis Dead* (1999)

"Screwball," *The Shamus Game* (2000)

"That Kind of Nag," *Murder at the Racetrack* (2006)

"Unreasonable Doubt," *And the Dying is Easy* (2001)

"Shoot-out on Sunset," *Mystery Street* (2001)